PENGUIN CANADA

SEER OF EGYPT

PAULINE GEDGE is the award-winning and bestselling author of twelve previous novels, nine of which are inspired by Egyptian history. Her first, *Child of the Morning*, won the Alberta Search-for-a-New-Novelist Competition. In France, her second novel, *The Eagle and the Raven*, received the Jeanne Boujassy award from the Société des Gens de Lettres, and *The Twelfth Transforming*, the second of her Egyptian novels, won the Writers Guild of Alberta Best Novel of the Year Award. Her books have sold more than 250,000 copies in Canada alone; worldwide, they have sold more than six million copies and have been translated into eighteen languages. Gedge lives in Alberta.

Also by Pauline Gedge

Child of the Morning

The Eagle and the Raven

Stargate

The Twelfth Transforming

Scroll of Saqqara

The Covenant

House of Dreams

House of Illusions

LORDS OF THE TWO LANDS

Volume One: The Hippopotamus Marsh

Volume Two: The Oasis

Volume Three: The Horus Road

THE KING'S MAN

Volume One: The Twice Born

SEER
OF
EGYPT

PAULINE
GEDGE

PENGUIN
CANADA

PENGUIN CANADA

Published by the Penguin Group

Penguin Group (Canada), 90 Eglinton Avenue East, Suite 700, Toronto, Ontario,
Canada M4P 2Y3 (a division of Pearson Canada Inc.)

Penguin Group (USA) Inc., 375 Hudson Street, New York, New York 10014, U.S.A.
Penguin Books Ltd, 80 Strand, London WC2R 0RL, England
Penguin Ireland, 25 St Stephen's Green, Dublin 2, Ireland (a division of Penguin Books Ltd)
Penguin Group (Australia), 250 Camberwell Road, Camberwell, Victoria 3124,
Australia (a division of Pearson Australia Group Pty Ltd)
Penguin Books India Pvt Ltd, 11 Community Centre, Panchsheel Park,
New Delhi – 110 017, India
Penguin Group (NZ), 67 Apollo Drive, Rosedale, North Shore 0632, New Zealand
(a division of Pearson New Zealand Ltd)
Penguin Books (South Africa) (Pty) Ltd, 24 Sturdee Avenue, Rosebank,
Johannesburg 2196, South Africa

Penguin Books Ltd, Registered Offices: 80 Strand, London WC2R 0RL, England

First published 2008

1 2 3 4 5 6 7 8 9 10 (WEB)

Copyright © Pauline Gedge, 2008

Excerpts from *Egyptian Mysteries: New Light on Ancient Spiritual Knowledge* by Lucie Lamy, trans-
lated from the French by Deborah Lawlor, © 1981 Lucie Lamy, reprinted by kind permission of
Thames and Hudson Ltd., London.
Excerpts from *The Hermetica*, by Timothy Freke and Peter Gandy, published by Judy Piatkus Ltd.,
London, used with permission.

*Publisher's note: This book is a work of fiction. Names, characters, places and incidents either are
the product of the author's imagination or are used fictitiously, and any resemblance to actual persons
living or dead, events, or locales is entirely coincidental.*

Manufactured in Canada.

LIBRARY AND ARCHIVES CANADA CATALOGUING IN PUBLICATION

Gedge, Pauline, 1945–
Seer of Egypt : volume II of The king's man / Pauline Gedge.

Sequel to: The twice born.
ISBN 978-0-14-305293-7

I. Title.

PS8563.E33S44 2008   C813'.54   C2008-902643-8

Visit the Penguin Group (Canada) website at **www.penguin.ca**

Special and corporate bulk purchase rates available; please see
www.penguin.ca/corporatesales or call 1-800-810-3104, ext. 477 or 474

AUTHOR'S NOTE

HUY, SON OF HAPU, later known as Amunhotep, Son of Hapu, was born of a peasant family in the modest Delta town of Hut-herib, where he lived until he was middle-aged. Yet between his late forties and late fifties he had become more powerful than Egypt's Pharaoh Amunhotep the Third, and by the time he died in his eighties, he was already worshipped as a god of prescience and healing. How did such a man, a commoner, acquire so much authority so quickly? Ability alone, even genius, would not have been enough in an age full of well-educated, highly capable men. Something extraordinary must have singled him out.

In *The Twice Born*, my novel concerning Huy's early years, I attempted to delve to the roots of this puzzle, in particular to examine his remarkable relationship with the mysteries of the fabled Book of Thoth and his ultimate reputation as an infallible fortune teller and healer. I described his boyhood as a self-centred only child adored by his mother, Itu, and his father, Hapu. I related how his uncle Ker, a maker of perfumes, was able to send him away to the temple school at the city of Iunu, where he and a fellow student, the young aristocrat Thothmes, became firm friends. Also studying at the school was Sennefer, a bully who took an instant dislike to Huy and on one fateful day, when Huy was twelve, attacked him with a throwing stick, the hunting weapon of the noble, knocking him into the water of the temple's lake where he drowned. Huy's body was returned to his home town of Hut-herib. After five days he came to himself in Hut-herib's House of the Dead having believed that he had been in the Paradise of Osiris where he had been given the choice of reading and understanding the Book of Thoth, a task to which he agreed. He soon discovered that he had been given the gift of scrying, an ability he subsequently used to diagnose the illnesses of his fellow peasants and relate their futures to them. But he paid a high price for this ability. The god Atum, originator of the Book of Thoth and bestower of the gift, had rendered him sexually impotent, and every scrying resulted in a blinding headache that only responded to increasing doses of opium. Gradually Huy's fame began to spread. So did his dependence on the drug.

Huy scryed so accurately for the King that he was rewarded with gold and a small estate outside Hut-herib, which he shared with another lifelong friend Ishat, a peasant like himself, a girl who became his scribe and who had been in love with him since they were children. Having completed his reading of the forty-two scrolls comprising the Book of Thoth, Huy found himself no closer to solving their meaning, and began to realize that his future and the solution to the book's mystery were irrevocably bound together.

Other characters come and go throughout *The Twice Born*. There is Anuket, sister to Huy's friend Thothmes, who coldly manipulates Huy's boyhood passion for her. There is Methen, priest of Hut-herib's totem god Khenti-kheti, who carries Huy home from the House of the Dead, and Henenu the Rekhet, female exorcist and sorcerer, who guides Huy and protects him. There is Ramose, the High Priest of Ra at Iunu, who wants to keep Huy and his uncanny gift close by once Huy's school days are over, but fails. And always there is the King to whom Huy is beholden and the jackal god, Anubis, who conveys Atum's desires to Huy, who is often angry and resentful at the psychic responsibilities thrust upon him.

The Twice Born ends with Huy and Ishat having just moved from the poverty-stricken hovel they had occupied in Hut-herib to the estate deeded to Huy by the King. Their future seems safely predictable.

THE BOOK OF THOTH was purported to contain all knowledge regarding the creation of the cosmos, gods, and men as well as the laws relating to magic, nature, and the afterlife. It was dictated by Atum, the creator god, to Thoth, god of Writing, the Sciences, and Time, who set down the information on forty-two scrolls which were divided between the temples of Ra at Iunu and Thoth at Khmun.

It survives in fragmented form as the so-called Pyramid Texts, found on the walls of the burial chambers of pyramids of the Fifth and Sixth Dynasties, at the temples of Esna and Edfu, and in certain coffins where it is called, of course, the Coffin Texts. Pieces of it also appear in The Book of Knowing the Modes of Existence of Ra and of Overthrowing the Serpent Apophis, and The Book of Coming Forth by Day, commonly known as The Book of the Dead.

According to Egyptian legend, before the reign of King Menes of the Protodynastic Period, the country was ruled for 13,420 years by the Servitors of Horus, the Shemsu-Hor. The Book of Thoth was said to predate the Shemsu-Hor by over twenty thousand years.

The Greeks identified Thoth with their god Hermes, hence the Hermetica, a collection of modernized writings attributed to Thoth.

PART ONE

I

WHEN HUY was an old man, looking into his extraordinary past with awe and a measure of resignation, he admitted to himself that the time spent with Ishat on the small but entrancing estate Pharaoh Amunhotep the Second had deeded to him had been the happiest of his life. He knew that, in accepting the King's generosity, he had become a virtual prisoner of the Horus Throne, and it was true that he was obliged to See for any court official requesting the use of his peculiar gifts, but between their visits he continued to help whoever came to his gate. Although Ishat had pointed out that allowing an indiscriminate number of townsfolk to wander through the garden and mill about the fountain was dangerous, Huy was reluctant to put any limit on the numbers slipping past Kar, his gate guard. After all, the walk from Hut-herib itself to the privacy of his arouras was long. Those in need arrived hot, tired, and thirsty, and many were ill. Some came on behalf of relatives too sick to leave their houses, begging Huy to return to the town with them and place his hands on their loved ones.

They began to gather before dawn. Huy would wake to the murmur of their voices rising to his bedchamber upstairs. He would hurry through the fresh bread, milk, and fruit his body servant Tetiankh set beside him on the gilded couch, take a cursory wash in the bathhouse downstairs, and carry a stool outside to be faced with the eager horde of petitioners. Usually Ishat would be waiting for him in her capacity as his scribe, her palette held loosely in her arms, her sleep-swollen eyes travelling the motley crowd with disapproval. Each case was documented by her—name, malady, and whatever cure Huy's vision demanded—and the scrolls were filed in Huy's office. By late afternoon the crowd would have thinned, those still waiting would be told to return the next day, and Huy and Ishat would escape into the house, themselves hot, tired, and thirsty, Ishat to stand in the bathhouse while her own body servant, Iput, scrubbed and then oiled her, and Huy to take a draft of poppy and lie on his couch until the drug took effect against the inevitable stabbing in his head and he felt able to go down to the reception hall for the evening meal.

This went on for several months, until both Ishat and Merenra, their chief steward, protested.

"I do pity them, Huy," Ishat said one evening as they sat picking over a meal of ox stew and cold lentil salad they were too exhausted to finish. "But they will never stop coming. There will always be disease and accidents, let alone the people who just want you to tell them about their future." She took a gulp of her palm wine, then set the goblet back on her table with a click. "We talked about getting a skiff and perhaps a barge with a cabin. The litter Merenra bought for us sits idle beside the house, and the bearers sleep all day and gamble all night out of boredom. Shouldn't we be the ones at leisure?" Lifting the long black hair away from her ears, she flicked at her lobes. "You were going to order jewellery for me—and what about you? You are still wearing the same earring day after day, and you make poor Tetiankh launder and starch your one spare kilt that is falling apart. You'll soon find yourself reduced to Seeing in nothing but your loincloth unless you take a little time to at least meet your need for new linen. Besides, the townsfolk trample on Seshemnefer's flowers and vegetables. They urinate against the outer wall and defecate behind the grain silo. We can't keep doing this!"

Behind her, Merenra stepped into the soft light of the alabaster lamps. "May I speak, Master?"

Huy nodded uncomfortably. He did not think he would ever become used to the care of servants who not only kept the house clean and cooked the food, as Hapzefa, Ishat's mother, still did for his parents and his brother, Heby, but who were responsible as well for making his life as easy and free as possible.

"Your scribe speaks good sense," the steward went on. "Khnit cannot continue to provide water and juices to the multitudes, let alone the bread and honey they demand. The King sends you gold every month, but even his coffers in Mennofer could not feed the whole of Hut-herib indefinitely. Your gate guard, Kar, has been jostled and threatened. It is time to seek a solution to this problem."

Huy did not want to agree with them. Did he not have a duty to the god who had given him this onerous gift, to use it to the limit of his strength? Both Ishat and Merenra were watching him expectantly.

"The first thing we need is a contingent of soldiers stationed in front of the gate," Ishat pressed him. "The second is some sort of restriction on the days you will be available and the numbers of people you will allow to come. Huy, I have not seen my mother since we moved in here!" she burst out. "And you need to visit your family. What good are you to anyone if you are dead from all this confusion?"

Huy knew rebellion when he saw it, and indeed he was secretly relieved that this decision had been taken from him.

"Very well," he said. "Let us reorganize our life. Merenra, is there any more wine?"

He remembered Anhur, the soldier who had guarded and befriended him on his visits to the temple of Thoth at Khmun, where he had read the portions of the Book of Thoth stored there. Anhur now served in the King's army; he had become one of the elite Shock Troops. *But perhaps Pharaoh would release him into my service,* Huy reflected as the golden palm wine cascaded into his cup and Merenra stood back. *Amunhotep values my gifts. Already I have Seen for his Vizier and namesake, Amunhotep, and his chief scribe, Seti-en. We would all be safe if Anhur came here with a small detachment. I will petition High Priest Ramose for the release of Amunmose also. He came with me to Khmun carrying scrolls for Thoth's High Priest. He was cheerful and begged me to remember him if I ever needed a good cook. At the time I could not imagine the turn my fortunes have taken, not in my wildest dreams of success and vindication, yet here we are, Ishat and I, living like the aristocrats we are not.* He smiled and raised the silver cup to his mouth, knowing that the flavour of palms would bring to mind a picture of the river in spring and the faint aroma of damp foliage along its banks. He had given up hoping for inebriation a very long time before.

He dictated a respectful request to Wesersatet, the King's Commander-in-Chief, and to his old guide and overseer High Priest Ramose at Iunu, his eyes on Ishat, sitting cross-legged at his feet, her pink tongue caught between her teeth as she laboured to produce the neatest hieroglyphs she could. Then he took each scroll from her and wrote his own name, *Huy son of Hapu, Seer.* "Give them to Merenra. He can go into Hut-herib and find a herald," he told Ishat as she stoppered her ink and scrambled up. "I think that until we receive replies, we will close and chain the gates, and you and I will take the litter into town, to the finest jeweller Merenra can recommend. It's time we used some of Amunhotep's gold on ourselves. Merenra can find us a barge and a few sailors as well."

Dropping her palette on Huy's desk, she flung her arms around him, hugging him tightly. "Thank you, my dearest brother, thank you!" she breathed. "Oh, Huy, I love this house and my big bedchamber and the glorious food I don't have to cook myself and seeing our laundry come in from the tubs outside while my hands get softer every day! Am I becoming shallow, do you think?"

Enveloped in the combination of myrrh, cassia, and henna flowers Ishat had taken to wearing, reaching up to smooth the strands of her hair away from his face, Huy was filled with a familiar sadness. *I wish with all my heart that I could love you as you deserve, my Ishat,* he thought. Aloud he said, "Yes, you are becoming the most shallow, spoiled, demanding princess Egypt has ever seen. Soon you will refuse to rise from your couch until the noon meal and make Merenra serve you only wine of year one of the King, four times good."

She laughed and withdrew, her eyes shining. "I want my mother and father to come and see me here when the jeweller has finished making my hair ornaments and bracelets and anklets and rings and necklaces and ... Huy, shall you invite Thothmes to stay soon? After all, he's been your close friend since you and he were at school together. He'll rejoice at your good fortune." She had wept with shame and embarrassment when Thothmes, whose aristocratic father was a Governor, had arrived with the King but chose not to accompany Amunhotep on his way to war. Instead, he stayed moored close to Hut-herib and invited both Ishat and Huy to dine aboard his barge. Then she had possessed no jewellery or face paint, and one spare coarse sheath. She had never been a guest before, never been waited on by servants— who were in reality her equals—and she had been afraid of what they might think. But the evening had run smoothly thanks to the tact of Thothmes' steward Ptahhotep and Thothmes himself, who had fallen in love with Ishat before the week was out.

Huy understood her question perfectly. "As soon as you are ready, I will write to him myself," he promised. "Now, let us discuss the other matter, Ishat. How many people should be admitted, on how many days?"

It was some weeks before a reply to Huy's request came from Wesersatet, and during that time the flood of Hut-herib's needy was forcibly slowed to a trickle of no more than ten petitioners on four days of the week. True to his word, Huy took Ishat to the jeweller, and, leaving her inside the small workshop that smelled of hot metal and faience dust, he lowered himself to the pavement outside, his back against the warm mud-brick wall, and contentedly watched the bustle of the street. In spite of the happiness his new estate brought him, he sometimes missed the noisy life of the district where he and Ishat had lived in three dark, tiny rooms next to a beer house. Times had been hard, but he had felt a sense of accomplishment in his close connection with the suffering denizens of the town, a connection that had become more formalized and somehow less personal now that he was no longer on an equal social footing with them.

Ishat's voice drifted to him through the open door, her tone authoritative, her laugh spontaneous. She was quickly finding the self-assurance and poise that grew with the acquisition of wealth, Huy observed, yet he knew her peasant heart, sturdy and immovable in its ability to see through any posturing, critical of anything that smacked of a certain arrogant dishonesty. She would order whatever pretty baubles she wanted, but not to excess. She would order jewellery for him also, earrings, bracelets, and necklaces, all bearing the stamp of her innate good taste, simple yet beautifully harmonious.

But she would not buy him rings. Stretching out his fingers, Huy examined the amulet rings the Rekhet had made for him: the Soul Protector with its hawk body and man's head, and the Frog of Resurrection, its deep blue lapis eyes gleaming dully in the strong sunlight. He had never removed them from his hand. Thinking of the old woman and her powerful magic gave him a twinge of guilt. He had not written to her since leaving the town, yet he loved her for her wisdom. She and Ramose, High Priest of Ra, were related. Both were Huy's mentors, but the Rekhet brought to him a tolerance and understanding that had been largely lacking in Ramose's advice to Huy, who saw that the Priest was torn between his ambition for Huy and his obvious affection for his unique pupil. Huy had not written to him either. The thought gave him a moment of physical agitation. At once his litter-bearers, sprawled in the shade a polite distance from him, sat up and glanced at him expectantly, but he waved them down again, drawing up his knees and resting his chin on them.

Obligations, he thought dismally. *To the Rekhet and Ramose, to my parents, to Thothmes and his family—all of them waiting to receive an invitation from me to stay in my house, exclaim over my good fortune, when all I really want is an occasional visit from Methen. He would lay aside the formality of his position as priest to Hut-herib's totem, Khenti-kheti, and talk to me with the ease of a friendship begun when he found me naked outside the House of the Dead and carried me home. His presence ought to remind me of that miserable time, but when I am with him I remember only his warmth and kindness. I do not want the past brought to life on my estate by the people who determined it. Except for Thothmes, of course, but even he would bring a threat with him. What if he is still in love with Ishat? What if he still wants her for his wife, and her decision to remain with me becomes weakened in his presence?*

As if his thought had summoned her, Ishat came out of the doorway and stood smiling down at him. "He will send the pieces as he finishes them," she said. "All will be in our boxes two months from now. You look pensive, Huy. What were you thinking?"

Huy swung to his feet, disliking the question. "I was feeling the lack of regular exercise and wondering when Anhur might arrive," he lied.

Ishat snorted. "No, you weren't." She straightened the sa amulet hanging from its gold chain on his naked chest, then laid a hot palm against his skin. "You were remembering with nostalgia the hovel we used to inhabit, because this street reminds you of it." She waved at the bearers, who rose reluctantly and picked up the litter. "Let's go home, Huy. May we stop on the way and buy some hot date pastries? I'm hungry."

He tugged at her hair, his good humour restored, as they scrambled onto the cushions of the litter. "Of course." He called the order to the bearers, then pulled the curtains closed. "Now, tell me what adornments His Majesty's gold is paying for," he teased her. "How many circlets will be cluttering up your cosmetics table?"

She grinned across at him. "Only three. One to keep for when the aristocrats come to consult you, one for everyday wear, and one to fill our less illustrious guests with awe when we give the parties I'm sure you will allow me to plan."

Huy turned to her anxiously. "But Ishat, we have work to do. I don't intend—"

She put a finger to his mouth. She often touched him with what appeared to be unselfconsciousness. Huy could always sense the need behind her gestures and had learned to harden himself against the compassion welling up in him. They had grown up together, both of them peasant children, the long days of child-hood forming a bond between them that even Huy's years away at the temple school in Iunu had not severed. Huy loved her deeply as his lifelong friend, but Ishat desired him with all the fervour of her passionate nature. It was not in her character to dissemble the matter, to hide her feelings behind a wall of feminine guile or attempt to win him by subtle manipulation. She had openly and frankly declared herself. The knowledge of her pain was often hard for Huy to bear

"I'm not serious," she said. "Or at least, not really. I look forward to entertaining our families. I want to show off our good fortune, Huy. You have been vindicated in the face of your uncle Ker and your father, and Thothmes will be delighted to see you living without worry about the future. Invite his father as well—Nakht must have his nose rubbed in the glory of your success after refusing to help you gain a position as a scribe. A scribe! You are far above such a humble station now."

"Scribes need not be humble," Huy responded swiftly. "Their skills are vital to the efficient administration of every aspect of Egypt's life." Privately, he was thinking that his future depended on a continuation of the King's generosity, and that the King's open hand would swiftly close if his gift deserted him. He sometimes wished it would. Then perhaps he would be free to get happily drunk on hot summer nights like everyone else, and free to throw off the burden of enforced virginity the god Atum had laid upon him and experience the final intimacy he had only been able to imagine. If he was able to make love to Ishat, would that love become something rounded, more complete, turning his desire from Thothmes' sister Anuket to the young woman sitting so cheerfully beside him now, the folds of her scarlet sheath resting lightly on his thigh, her perfume filling the stuffy, enclosed space of the litter? He knew that such thoughts only led to anger and sadness, and he was glad when the litter was lowered and the aroma of hot pastries edged out the scent of Ishat's fragrance.

Huy grew to value the precious three days when his garden lay empty of strangers and the house remained quiet but for the polite comings and goings of the few servants. During that time his headaches began to ease, although he still dosed himself with the poppy against the fourth day, when they returned as he went about the business of Seeing for those lucky enough to be admitted.

For a month the new routine ran its course. Pieces of jewellery began to arrive from the craftsman, each wrapped in white linen and placed in a soft leather bag with drawstrings. Ishat withdrew them reverently. Huy shared her admiration. They were both delicate and bold, each creation seeming to Huy to reflect a combination of the facets of Ishat's personality. The man had done his work well, with intuition and skill.

"This one," Ishat said, holding up a thick gold circlet from which a single large red jasper hung to rest in the centre of her forehead, with smaller orbs of the stone set around its upper rim, "this one I shall save for meeting the King's ministers. Look, Huy! A net of golden threads is attached to its back, to hold my hair. How very elegant. But I like the silver one too. So simple. A thin band hung with tiny silver ankhs. I shall wear it every day."

"But silver is much more rare and expensive than gold," Huy told her, amused. "The King's ministers would be far more impressed by the silver band than by the gold and jasper one."

"Perhaps. Do you like the earrings he made for you, Huy? Three tiny scarabs of green turquoise hanging onto each other? And the one of Ra-Harakhti, Ra at the dawn, the hawk's feathers inlaid with blue faience, and the Disc of the sun on his head done in pale yellow chalcedony so smooth that the light flows over it? The gold talons of the bird almost brush your shoulder."

"Yes, I do like them, and the belts of gold links and the decorated sandals. The servants are more pleased than you are, have you noticed, Ishat? I suppose that now they can feel we are worthy of their ministrations. They are even more snobbish than you!"

"May the gods grant that I never develop the arrogance of riches!" she said fervently. "My rings, bracelets, and necklets are to come." She lifted the silver circlet and placed it on her head. "Let's go on the river in our new barge at sunset and drink wine and watch Ra being swallowed up by Nut. You can fish. Your head is better today, is it not? And I can lean on the railing while the sandbars glide by. Oh, Huy! What a dream I am living!"

But before they walked up the ramp and onto the cedar deck of the barge that still smelled of sweet wood and paint lacquer, Huy dictated an invitation to his family and to Ishat's; one to Thothmes, Nakht, and Nasha; one to High Priest Ramose; and one to the Rekhet. Ishat, in her role as his scribe, looked up at him from her perch on the floor as she capped her ink and flexed stiff fingers. "I hope they don't all come at once," she said.

They ate their evening meal aboard their boat while the litter-bearers, learning to double as sailors under the sharp eye of Ibi, a captain Merenra had hired permanently, rowed them clumsily upstream and back to their watersteps as the river turned from brown to gold to red and the long shafts of the sun's last rays began to shred over its rippled surface. Dust motes danced in the pink light. The evening breeze sprang up. Ishat took Huy's arm as they stood contentedly side by side, her long black hair lifting with the moving air, her eyes closed with pleasure against the glare of Ra's final burst. Neither of them spoke. Huy too allowed himself a moment of unadulterated serenity. His head was free of pain, his mind calm. The captain's peremptory commands began to echo against the riverbanks as the sun's rim disappeared, and suddenly the sky opened up above, a new presence of pale blue and weakly blinking stars.

Ishat opened her eyes and sighed. "I will not think of Ra's twelve transformings as he battles through the womb of Nut," she murmured. "I will concentrate on lamplight and a bath and then a quiet night on my couch. We are approaching the watersteps, Huy. Now who is that, standing just outside the gate with Kar beside him? Your scrolls of invitation haven't left the house yet."

Huy's heart sank. He was not expecting a visit from a court official, but doubtless many of them felt they possessed the right to demand his attention whenever they chose. The watersteps drew nearer. At Ibi's shout, the oars were shipped and the ramp lifted from its resting place against the railing. Huy peered through the gathering gloom at the tall figure now striding onto the topmost stone step, and recognition struck him in a burst of gladness.

"Anhur! It is Anhur, Ishat!" He waved and the man waved back. The boat bumped the foot of the watersteps, the ramp was run out, and Huy hurried to embrace his old friend. "We did not expect you so soon!" he breathed as they pulled apart. "There has been no word from Commander Wesersatet! He must have petitioned the One and then released you from the army very quickly."

"He did." Anhur took Huy's shoulders and stood back, surveying him critically. "It seems that whatever the Seer wants, the Seer gets, particularly now, when the Queen has presented the country with a Hawk-in-the-Nest and His Majesty is happily scattering favours to all and sundry like chaff in the wind. I barely remembered you until the King ordered Wesersatet to replace me in the Shock Troops and send me to guard you. Gods, young Huy, look at you! How old were you when I saw you last? Thirteen? You've become a handsome man, but I'd still recognize those eyes. Is there anything to eat? It's been a long march and we're starving."

"We?"

Anhur waved towards the house. "I've brought ten soldiers with me. The King didn't know how much protection you needed. Neither do I. Is ten enough? What are we supposed to be protecting you from? Demons and angry priests?"

Huy laughed. "I'll explain while Merenra finds you all some food. Anhur, this is my companion and scribe, Ishat."

Anhur turned to Ishat, waiting patiently at Huy's elbow. He bowed. Ishat extended a hand.

"Welcome to our home," she said formally. "Huy has told me all about the time you spent together at Thoth's temple in Khmun."

Anhur enfolded her fingers in his own large paw, then he bent and retrieved the spear and shield leaning against the still-open gate. Behind the three of them, the boat was being moored to its post and the ramp run in. The crew dropped into the water and, wading to the steps, bowed briefly before disappearing into the strengthening darkness. Kar had ambled back to his hut just inside the gate.

"Thank you, Lady Ishat," Anhur responded.

Ishat shook her head. "I'm no noblewoman, Anhur. Call me Mistress, or Ishat. Now I suppose I had better find Merenra and he had better drag Khnit away from her stool and back to the kitchen. How many men must she feed?" At a nod from Huy, she turned towards the house.

Anhur watched her go. "You are wedded to her, Huy?" he wanted to know as he and Huy followed more slowly. "She is your wife? Well, good for you. She's very beautiful."

"Ishat is not my wife," Huy replied swiftly. "She's my oldest friend and a partner in my work."

"And you can resist that loveliness? What's wrong with you? What work are you engaged in?"

"Later." Huy smiled across at the blunt features he remembered so well. Already he felt more secure, as though with Anhur's arrival a cloak of protection had been cast invisibly over the estate and everyone in it. This was the man who had refused to leave his side during his difficult days in Khmun, who had stepped between him and an enraged Sennefer, who as a boy had attacked him with a throwing stick, precipitating his death and miraculous resurrection, and who had been banished to the temple school at Khmun, where he had again attempted to harm Huy. "Now we must fill your belly. Has my steward found accommodation for your men?"

"Your steward," Anhur said heavily. "The gods have certainly smiled on you, haven't they? No, there aren't enough cells in your servants' quarters, but it will only take a week or two to buy mud bricks and erect another row. My soldiers can pitch their tents and sleep in their blankets until then. They'll be content as long as there's plenty of food and beer."

Together they entered the house. Tetiankh and Iput were moving quietly about, lighting the standing lamps in the reception hall. They bowed briefly to both men, curiosity in their gaze.

Anhur blew out his breath. "What do you have to do for the King to earn all this? I thought you'd end up serving the priests of Ra at his temple in Iunu when you finished school. I never imagined something like this for you, and of course when we spoke briefly to each other during Pharaoh's visit to Hut-herib, there wasn't time to exchange any news."

"I'll tell you everything while you eat," Huy repeated. "Afterwards I'll take you over the house and grounds. The estate is small and will be easy to patrol. The disposition of the soldiers will be all yours, Anhur. I see that Merenra has already set out a table and cushions for you. Sit down."

Anhur dropped his equipment on the tiled floor with a clatter. "I'll see to the feeding of my men first. May I go through to the kitchen? I presume it's outside at the rear."

"Of course. I'll come with you and meet them. I'm so glad you're here!"

Later, Huy and Ishat sat with him as he folded himself behind the low table laden with the meal Khnit had provided; Merenra stood a short distance away, holding the beer jug ready to serve him. The elegant room was quiet, full of a peaceful, soft light from the steady glow of the alabaster lamps placed around the painted walls. Anhur pulled off his crumpled linen helmet, ran a hand through greying hair, and began to eat, swiftly and methodically. While he did so, Huy related the events of his life since they had parted. Anhur listened carefully, glancing up from his emptying platters occasionally to nod or raise his thick eyebrows in surprise.

When Huy fell silent, Anhur drained his goblet and, holding it out to Merenra for more beer, said, "And what about that magic Book you were reading at Khmun, Huy? Did you finish it? Weren't you supposed to interpret it for High Priest Ramose? I remember that the Chief Librarian, Khanun, at Khmun's House of Life, was eager to hear the results when you were done."

"I finished it," Huy answered reluctantly. "I have yet to understand its secrets fully. I do not think about it much anymore, Anhur. I am stretched thin with the exercise of healing and Seeing. One day perhaps I shall have enough time to ponder it anew."

He did not add that the thought of the Book of Thoth plunged him into sadness and a sourceless guilt when its words crept unbidden into his mind, and that he deliberately turned away from any thought of it, and of the sacred Ished Tree under whose branches he had first unrolled it. It was all there in his consciousness, ready to scroll through his thoughts like some portentous spell full of power whose meaning eluded him. He had agreed to read it while his body lay cold and lifeless in

Hut-herib's House of the Dead and his ka stood before the great Imhotep, who had offered the boy Huy the choice. Huy, drenched in the sunlight of Paradise while the Judgment Hall lay dim and forbidding behind him, had agreed to the will of the creator-god Atum. At twelve years old, he had not considered the cost, had not been warned that in doing so he would become Atum's property and tool. As long as he did not think about the Book, he need not be angry. As long as he moved from day to day through the tasks set before him by the acquisition of his peculiar gift, he need not look into his own future and that one duty he had been unable to fulfill.

Anhur swallowed his last mouthful, emptied his goblet yet again, and pushed the table away. "Luckily, I don't have to worry about such mysterious things. Give me a practical task that has a practical solution and I'm happy. Well, I'd better order a guard for the house and gate tonight, see that the men are comfortable, and set up my cot somewhere." He grinned. "I won't miss being a member of His Majesty's Shock Troops, but I hope I won't be bored, trudging up and down your passages."

"You can sleep in the guest room until your men have built you a suitable home," Ishat said. They were the first words she had spoken all evening.

Anhur shook his head and rose, snatching up his wilted head-dress as he did so. "If I'm to keep discipline among my ten, I must be with them, but thank you, Mistress," he replied. "I wish you both a safe rest. If you hear footsteps in the night, don't be alarmed—it will be one of the soldiers patrolling inside the house." He bowed and quickly vanished into the shadows.

Merenra began to clear away the debris of the meal and Ishat turned to Huy. "I like him and you obviously trust him," she said. "But extra cells to have built, extra mouths to feed, means too much work for Khnit and Merenra. We must hire an under steward,

Huy, and another cook, and perhaps a couple more house servants." She sighed. "Is this the negative side of how rich people live?"

"Yes." Huy got to his feet and held a hand down to her, fighting a sudden sense of suffocation. "You're right, Ishat. Merenra can see to it as soon as he has the time. We will adapt to this as we have bent to every gust of fate that has blown at us." He kissed her lightly on the cheek and called for Tetiankh and Iput. When they came, lighted tapers in their hands, he followed them and Ishat up the stairs, bade her sleep well, and went into his own bedchamber.

Tetiankh put the taper to the lamp beside the couch, and as a glow of light began to diffuse through the large room, he bowed to Huy. "Master, if you will wait until I have drawn fresh water from the barrel downstairs to put on your table, I can then prepare you for sleep. Do you need an infusion of poppy tonight?"

Huy considered. *Well, do I? I have no pain, but the drug does give me a deep and dreamless sleep. Without it, I am afraid of the visions the god might send me. Yet I am doing his will to the best of my ability, so why would he accuse me? Nevertheless, my work is arduous. I must have a good rest.* He knew that he was edging his thoughts towards a justification for taking the poppy, knew that the desire for it existed apart from any rationalization he might conjure, and stopped trying to deceive himself.

"Bring me an infusion, Tetiankh, but make it a weak one," he said heavily. "I shall undress myself. Is there no hot water for my wash?"

"I'm sorry, Master," Tetiankh answered. "Khnit asked Iput and me to help her in the kitchen. Seshemnefer prepared the vegetables, but then he left. He was tired from digging over so much ground today. At least you will have a flourishing garden when he is done."

Huy sighed. Ishat was right, more staff were needed. "I'll go down to the bathhouse," he decided. "I must clean the kohl from my eyes. I don't need your help, Tetiankh. I took care of my own bodily needs for years. Go and mix the poppy."

Tetiankh looked distressed. "It is not right that you should perform such tasks for yourself," he retorted as he left.

Huy stripped off his kilt, laid his new belt carefully over the back of one of the cedar and ivory inlaid chairs, and, pulling a sleeping robe over his head, padded barefoot along the dusky passage and down the narrow stairs at the rear of the house to the little bathhouse below. As always, the damp interior smelled of Ishat's perfume blend—myrrh, cassia, and henna flowers. Huy inhaled it with pleasure. The water for their ablutions was often left just outside, to be heated by the sun. Huy found a jug in which some warmth remained and quickly washed his face, scrubbing it with a little natron and wiping it over with ben oil. He would have liked to clean his long hair of sweat and dust, but he needed Ishat for that. *No, not Ishat,* he corrected himself as he dragged a comb through the thick tresses. *I must be tired. My mind is playing me tricks. Ishat used to do it, but it's Tetiankh's job now. I remember the evenings in our miserable little hovel, when she would kneel before me with a basin full of the water in which we would both have to wash, and she would lift my filthy, swollen feet into it. While they soaked, she would wash my face, my neck and chest, my legs, and then with the basin on the table she washed my hair. Only then would she banish me, while she took off her one serviceable sheath and cleansed herself. She is the one who deserves this sudden change in our fortunes, not I. I will begrudge her nothing.*

Tetiankh was waiting when Huy returned to his bedchamber, the small clay pot of white liquid in his hand. Thanking him, Huy took it and drank. As always, the taste was so bitter that his throat tried to constrict against it. Tetiankh was ready with water. Huy sluiced his mouth clear and swallowed so as not to waste a drop of the precious drug. The sheet on the couch had already been turned down, the doors of the shrine beside the bed opened to reveal the little statue of Khenti-kheti, totem of the town and surrounding district. A mat lay before it.

Once more, Tetiankh bowed. "Do you need anything else, Master?"

Huy shook his head. "No. Bring my first meal at dawn tomorrow, Tetiankh. Tell Khnit I will be hiring help for her. Good night."

After the servant had gone, Huy prostrated himself on the mat before the crocodile god and began his prayers. He had vowed long ago that he would not address Atum because of the grudge he held against the Omnipotent One, but it often seemed to him that the divine ears open to his words were not those of Hut-herib's protector. Khenti-kheti had been rendered deaf by Atum's superior power, and in spite of Huy's hubris, it was Atum who heard him. Always Atum. Everything reverted to the god who had brought him back from the dead and laid such burdens upon him.

Huy was seldom able to finish his petitions, and tonight was no exception. The poppy coursing through his veins was already making him sleepy and euphoric. Rising clumsily, he rolled onto his couch and into unconsciousness almost simultaneously.

He woke in the night with a start, already listening for the sound that had disturbed him. His lamp had gone out. Faint moonlight was filtering through the reed slats of the window hanging, casting bands of blurred grey on the floor. Footsteps were passing his closed door. After a moment Huy realized that they belonged to Anhur or one of his soldiers. He lay down again and turned on his side, but he did not fall asleep at once.

Suddenly he remembered a comment Anhur had made regarding the speed with which Huy's request for a guard had been answered. The Queen had given birth to a son. Egypt had an heir. What was his name? Anhur had not said. The news had been swallowed up in the excitement of their meeting. But with a pang of anxiety it came to Huy that Pharaoh had sent no summons to him to travel to Mennofer and See for the child. There had not even been a scroll announcing the boy's arrival and warning Huy that he would be called upon at a later date. *Why not?* Huy asked himself uneasily. *Surely the future of this Prince will be of vital interest to Amunhotep. Is the King afraid to know it, and if so, why?*

As if he had posed the question aloud to someone in the room, an answer came right away. All the wealth that now surrounded him, all the generosity of a grateful King, had been bestowed because Amunhotep had stopped outside Hut-herib on his way to do battle against the rebellious chieftains of the east, and Huy, being granted the privilege of actually touching the royal hand, had Seen the most vivid and detailed visions he had ever experienced. The King had later returned to Egypt triumphant, laden with all the gifts and booty Huy had predicted, and His Majesty had shown his appreciation by deeding this pretty little estate to Huy.

But with the promise of victory had come a message for Pharaoh from Atum himself. The words rang in Huy's head with perfect clarity as he lay tensely on his couch. "Tell my son Amunhotep the things I shall show you, and give him this warning," the god had said to Huy, deep in the revelations opening out before him. "He must not depart from the balance of Ma'at I have established. Already he is tempted to do so." *How is the King tempted to disturb the balance of cosmic truth and earthly justice Atum decreed for Egypt?* Huy wondered. He sat up and, swinging his legs over the edge of the couch, gazed unseeing into the calm dimness. "He must not depart ..." It was a caution, implying that Amunhotep had not yet begun to upset Ma'at but was thinking of doing so. *With full knowledge of what he was doing? How can a King make Ma'at tremble?*

Huy rubbed his forehead and reached for the water beside him, all at once thirsty. *He can do so in a hundred different ways. By subverting the cosmic laws. By ignoring justice for his subjects. By refusing allegiance to our gods, becoming ungrateful to them, setting himself above them.* Huy drank and sat holding the cup in both hands. *Supposing the King has succumbed to the temptation Atum was implying,* his thoughts tumbled on. *Supposing he remembers very well the words the god spoke to him through me but he does not care, he has set his face towards some evil believing it to be good, believing he knows better than the gods. Now his son is born. Egypt's heir. The King does not want the child's future revealed for fear I may see more than Amunhotep wishes. Or more than he himself desires to know. What course has Pharaoh embarked upon that will bring Atum's disapproval? I can think of no other explanation for the King's silence with regard to his son, and if I am right, then I will never be invited to See for the Hawk-in-the-Nest. Is there any evidence at court, in the affairs of the administration, that Ma'at's laws are being subverted? I must ask Anhur tomorrow, but carefully; and in any case, there is nothing a Seer can do in such a situation. He must wait to prophesy until Atum provides an opportunity to do so.*

Huy lay back but could not sleep again for some time. He heard the patrol outside his door pass and repass twice more before drowsiness overcame him.

Tetiankh woke him at dawn as he had requested, tidied the room as he ate, then accompanied him to the bathhouse, where hot water steamed. Huy stood on the bathing slab to be washed and then lay on the bench just outside, hidden from the rest of the garden by a wall and many shrubs, to be shaved, plucked, and oiled. By the time he sought out Ishat on the grass at the front of the house, there was an orderly queue of petitioners waiting quietly, their eyes flicking from the two soldiers who watched them to the empty stool with Ishat cross-legged beside it.

She smiled at him as he took the stool. True to her word, she was wearing the silver circlet. Its ankhs trembled against her forehead as she picked up her burnisher and began to apply it vigorously to the sheet of papyrus on her palette. "There was a large crowd outside the gate this morning," she told Huy. "Anhur was ready for them. He counted in ten of them and sent the rest away. Kar is most relieved." Laying down the scraper, she ran a hand over the smooth surface of the papyrus, uncapped the ink, and selected a brush. "Merenra has gone into the town to send our invitations and to find more servants," she went on. "He will also go to the straw pits and order bricks for the new cells. Are you ready to work?"

Huy nodded. No plants would be trampled today. No disgruntled Seshemnefer would have to clean up human feces from behind the grain silo. Each person would be escorted back to the gate by a guard when Huy had finished caring for his or her need. Ishat whispered the scribes' prayer to Thoth as Huy beckoned the first patient forward and took her hand. The day's labour had begun.

By the middle of the afternoon, the courtyard was empty. Huy wiped the sweat from his neck with the linen Tetiankh had stood ready to offer him, and Ishat rose from the grass, flexing her shoulders and yawning. "We will have to take the litter into the town tomorrow," she remarked. "The list of those too ill to come here is growing. I must eat and then lie on my couch for a while, Huy, and there is no sign of Merenra yet. I hope he's having some success." She kissed him briefly on the cheek and hurried into the shade cast by the entrance pillars.

Huy left the stool more slowly. Any swift movement would increase the pounding in his head. He debated whether or not to order poppy from Tetiankh, who had retired a short distance and was waiting for his summons, but decided to try to see if the usual hour of sleep everyone took in the heat of the afternoon would calm the pain. He was about to follow Ishat into the house when he saw Anhur approaching through the glare of full sunlight. He waited, eyes screwed half shut and beginning to water, and when Anhur came up to him, he took the man's arm and drew him into the coolness of the portico. At once Tetiankh brought in the stool. Huy sank onto it.

"You look terrible, young Huy," Anhur said, bending to peer into Huy's face. "Are you sick? Is there a physician in your house?"

"Besides me and the god?" Huy managed with a grin. "It's just a headache, Anhur. The visions seem to leave it behind, like dross from the refining of metal. I heard you in the house last night. How are your men today? Will they be content here?"

Anhur squatted in front of him. "They will. They like being close enough to the river to swim when they are not on duty. So do I. Now that your peasants have gone home, I've relieved the two guards, placed only one at the gate and one at the rear of the house, and told the rest they are free to sleep or gamble. What about the bricks? I'm anxious to begin building something permanent for them as soon as possible, before the Inundation comes and the nights grow cool."

They talked for a while, then Huy said, "It must have been wonderful to be in the palace when the Prince was born. What has he been named?"

Anhur shrugged. "If you can call a lot of cheering and shrieking and wine-drinking wonderful. We members of the Shock Troops, being household guards as well, didn't get much sleep. Drunk courtiers kept trying to stagger into the royal apartments at all hours, and the common well-wishers kept trying to push their way onto the palace grounds with gifts. A week's holiday was declared, of course, which didn't make things any easier. Our Prince has been named Amunhotep after his father."

"Pharaoh must be pleased."

Anhur frowned. "I don't think so. The One in his divinity is the Incarnation of Amun, and the Prince will also become Amun's power on earth when he succeeds to the Horus Throne, and naturally it is Amun's priests and astrologers who have the privilege of choosing his name. I was on guard in the reception hall when Amun's High Priest arrived all the way from Weset to give the King the good news. Amunhotep was angry, I could tell. He raised his voice to the High Priest. He demanded that the stars be read again, insisted that the astrologers had made a mistake. The High Priest stood firm. It was his right to name the Hawk-in-the-Nest. He was very offended when he left."

Huy felt the anxiety that had descended on him in the night suddenly return. "How strange," he said slowly. "What name would the King have preferred? Did he say?"

"I was stationed behind the Queen, on the dais. I heard Amunhotep mutter to her that Thothmes his father was a mighty warrior and a great god and his own son should bear that name. The Queen objected that it was an honour to bear the name of Egypt's saviour god, the one who had helped Pharaoh's ancestors drive out the occupying Setiu many hentis ago. At that, the King got up and left the hall." He laughed. "I thank the gods I am not married. There is no woman to nag at me or contradict me."

"Would you rather be back among the delights of the palace, Anhur? Is serving my estate a demotion for you?"

Anhur shot him a sly glance. "Everyone at court knows your power, Huy. Everyone believes you will rise in authority and influence. Everyone wants to come here to your house to meet you, to have their fortunes told, but the King allows no one but those he chooses to come near you. The spoiled little noblemen's daughters natter together about your healthy body and your famously long hair." He opened his arms in a wide gesture. "When you rise, so shall I. I want to be a general. As a commoner among the Shock

Troops, my promotion would have been no higher than a captain of fifty. One day you will make me a general."

Huy was astounded, but he had not missed Anhur's revelation regarding Amunhotep's control. It explained why he himself was not deluged with petitioners from Mennofer. Something made him ask, "Anhur, what god does Pharaoh worship?"

"Amun, of course, in spite of his annoyance with Weset," Anhur replied promptly. "Still, he does have friends among the priests of Ra, particularly your old mentor High Priest Ramose at the temple of Ra in Iunu, and right after Amun's High Priest had left Mennofer to return to Weset, Amunhotep took Kenamun and Miny and went to make an offering at the temple to the Aten in the centre of the city."

"Ra and the Aten, the gods of the sun," Huy said. All at once he was very tired.

"I don't like Kenamun." Anhur stood up and stretched. "Miny, the King's weapons instructor, is a good man, but Kenamun sneers at everyone he considers to be below him. Amunhotep should choose his best friend more carefully. He has given Kenamun the stewardship of his Mennofer Estates. Now the idiot crows louder than ever, but the King doesn't hear it. All he sees is his Foster Brother, son of his wet nurse Amenemopet. Ah, well ... time for a swim and a sleep." He placed a gentle hand on Huy's head. "Forgive my earlier use of your name, Master. I am still seeing you as that boy for whom I developed a large affection."

"Call me whatever you like, Anhur." Huy rose also. "You are expected to dine with Ishat and me every evening. Now I must lie down and get Tetiankh to put a cool, wet cloth over my eyes."

They parted, Anhur to the gate and Huy up to his room. The window hanging was down and the air a little cooler than the furnace outside. Huy put his head on his pillow with a vast relief. He did not open his eyes when Tetiankh entered. He heard the sudden rush of water as the servant wrung out the cloth, then felt it settle over his face. The action was repeated.

Huy drowsed, but at the back of his mind was a picture of Amunhotep walking across the outer court of the temple to the Aten, the Visible Disc of the sun. Huy did not know why the image disturbed him. The worship of the Disc had gone on for many hentis. The Aten was not popular with the common people; its representations were too starkly simple. It had no face, animal or human, to receive the prayers. It enjoyed a constant but small following among well-educated aristocrats, who revered it for its rays of light that struck the earth and became lions. "The Aten makes the actual physical rays of Amun, who is also Amun-Ra." Huy could hear the voice of his teacher during the time the class had been taught the intricacies of the various forms the gods took, and their modes of worship. "Lions are the physical representations of the rays of Amun-Ra. *Representations.* Do you see the difference, boys? Aten and its rays belong to the sun. When the rays strike the earth and become lions, they are representations, without the power of the rays themselves. Every sphinx with its lion's body is, however, revered for what it *represents.*" Huy remembered being supremely bored with this nitpicking. Now he wished he had paid more attention to his teacher.

The cult of the Aten was a solar cult. The rays of the Aten were superior to Amun until they touched the earth, where they became impotent, imprisoned in lions both real and stone. It was not a concept designed to appeal to the unlettered peasant, who brought his gifts and his pleas to the local totem of his town. *Why is this important?* Huy asked himself. *Why am I puzzling over it when all I want to do is sleep away this damnable pain until the evening?* Nevertheless, the vision of Pharaoh striding towards the inner court where the Disc filled the sanctuary made him afraid, and he could not rest.

2

THE SMALL BARRACKS for Anhur and his soldiers was almost finished by the time Huy's parents and his brother, Heby, accompanied by Ishat's mother, Hapzefa, alighted from the barge Huy had sent to bring them and walked hesitantly through Huy's gate. Huy and Ishat were waiting for them under the shade of the pillars fronting the house. Both watched them come with mixed emotions. "They are bunched together like frightened sheep," Ishat hissed at Huy. "Even Heby looks apprehensive. I hope Merenra is busy pouring plenty of wine!"

Huy did not answer, his mind all at once filling with his father's refusal to approach him, even to look at him, after he had been rescued from outside the House of the Dead by Methen and carried home. The Rekhet's pronouncement that he was free of any demon possession and did not need exorcising had made no change in Hapu's desertion of his needy son. *That was eight years ago*, Huy reminded himself as he stepped out into the sun's glare and prepared to greet his relatives. *Father and I have managed to arrive at a mutual respect, yet the extent of my love for him has remained small.*

The little group was slowing. Huy held out his arms to Hapu and embraced him, inhaling the man's nervous sweat, the slightly harsh underlying odour of his skin, feeling its untreated roughness. "Welcome to my home, Father," he said lightly as they broke apart. "Life, Health, and Prosperity to you."

Hapu acknowledged the polite greeting with a half smile. "Your gate guard might indeed be called a Door Opener of Heaven," he commented wryly. "Surely no temple guard protected a more beautiful place. I've missed you, my son. It's good to see you strong and happy and blessed by our King."

"My turn, Hapu!" Huy's mother, Itu, said, throwing her arms around Huy as Hapu good-humouredly retreated. "Oh, Huy! How wonderful this is! I'm so proud of you, so happy for you! Wait until I tell Ker and Heruben that you live in greater luxury than they do! They were hoping for an invitation to visit you with us."

She pulled away and a glance of complete understanding passed between mother and son. Like Hapu, Huy's uncle Ker and his aunt Heruben had turned their backs on Huy out of a superstitious fear, but unlike Hapu, Ker had never relented and had transferred his support from Huy to Heby, who now attended the temple school at Mennofer. *They will never receive an invitation,* Huy vowed silently as he regarded his nine-year-old brother, who was hopping from one bare foot to the other in impatience.

"You're shooting up like a tare in a barley field, Heby," he said. "What are you doing home from school?"

"It's Mesore," the boy replied promptly. "The school has closed in anticipation of the Inundation next month. I've been helping Father gather flower seeds from Uncle Ker's fields, ready for sowing next year."

"Oh, of course. I'd forgotten. I'm so old now that my schooldays are a dim memory," he teased Heby. "And how are you, Hapzefa?"

The servant had her arm around her daughter's shoulders. She smiled at Huy. "As well as ever, Master Huy. You've done well for yourself, haven't you? I'm pleased." She leaned forward for Huy's kiss on her cheek. "Who'd have thought that the cheeky little boy I had to spank more than once would grow up to be a favourite of His Majesty! Does he visit you often, Huy? What is he like?"

Huy returned her smile. "He's a handsome and very vigorous man, but I have only been in his presence once. He has not graced my home, Hapzefa, and for that I am grateful. Having to entertain the One would be a terrifying chore. Come inside, out of the sun, all of you. Merenra has wine waiting, and grape juice for you, Heby."

They trooped after him, some of their hesitancy returning as their eyes travelled the cool expanse of the reception hall with its delicate inlaid cedar chairs, its black and white tiled floor, its little low tables surfaced in blue faience bordered in beaten gold leaf. "The walls are still naked," Huy was forced to remark, hating himself for the weakness of his vanity but unable to prevent the words from slipping over his tongue. "Mayor Mery-neith had them whitewashed so that Ishat and I could have them decorated as we wished."

"What will you put on them?" Itu asked Ishat as Merenra glided forward, two jugs in his hands.

Ishat shrugged. "We haven't decided yet. Birds in palms and sycamores or entwining vines or fish in the river or scenes of feasting? I'd like something of all of it! Please take the cushions and our steward will serve you."

They sank awkwardly onto the pillows, more used to sitting cross-legged on the reed mats Hapzefa wove, and Merenra approached Itu. Cups had already been placed on the individual tables.

"Mistress, would you like pomegranate or grape wine?" he asked. "The grape is of a good vintage and the pomegranate not too sweet."

"Well, Ishat, have you been behaving yourself?" Hapzefa demanded as Itu chose her wine and the steward continued with his rounds, filling the cups and followed by one of Huy's new servants, who tipped juice into Heby's goblet.

Ishat let out a hoot of laughter. "Honestly, Mother, you still think of my arrangement with Huy as improper even though we've been living under the same roof together for years. Be at peace! I have my own bedchamber. I'll show it to you shortly. I work as Huy's scribe and I've begun to oversee the household." Then she sighed. "It's becoming a bit unwieldy, what with Anhur and the soldiers and all the new servants. It's a good thing Merenra knows his job."

Huy had been watching his father. Hapu was holding his cup in both hands, taking small, obviously appreciative sips of the good wine, his eyes narrowed as he glanced slowly from one to the other grouped together under Huy's little pillars. *Every word I or Ishat speaks seems to be evidence of a superiority over him and Mother that we do not intend,* Huy thought dismally. *Ishat is simply making conversation, telling the obligatory small truths of good manners, but they sound like the unspoken arrogance of comparison. Both Ishat and I grew up in poverty, but our days were happy. Food was simple but nourishing. When we were babies, we ran about naked, and when we were older, one coarse kilt apiece was enough clothing. Even when Ishat became a woman and grudgingly left her kilt behind, her sheath was made of the thick linen of the first grade and she didn't care. Our good fortune has not made us haughty, though now we go about in filmy linen of the twelfth grade and kohl our eyes and screw gems into our earlobes.*

He met Hapu's eye and to his surprise his father smiled. "I hear great things about you when I must go into the town," he said. "You have healed many grateful citizens through the power of the gods. I know that you labour long. I'm told that you suffer from continual headaches. I do not begrudge you any of this, Huy. Our King has recognized that you deserve it all." He gestured briefly around the room.

Huy felt a surge of irritation. *Why would you begrudge it to me anyway, Father? None of it has anything to do with you. Did you defend me against my uncle, your brother? Did you take me in your arms, a terrified and confused boy of twelve, and tell me how you loved me and how everything would be all right? No. You hid like a coward, and now it is up to me to struggle, to find within myself a forgiveness that flickers in and out like a guttering candle.*

"Thank you, Father," he said. "It's true that I work hard. After all, I was not raised to be idle."

Hapu grunted. "Ker should not have turned his generosity in Heby's direction," he muttered, his voice deliberately pitched so low that only Huy could hear it above the chatter of the three women. "I blame myself for that, Huy. I did not behave as a man should. I was afraid of you, I admit it." He was staring into his cup. "I did not know that the gods had blessed you. Now they bless me with another son, Heby, but I wait for their judgment. Will it fall on Heby? A fever? An infestation of worms, or worse? I'm sorry."

Huy's anger faded. Hitching his cushion closer to Hapu, he rested a hand on his father's knee. "The gods do not punish honest fear," he said, matching his tone to his father's. "Surely it is better than presumption. They expect us to run from the Khatyu, from the malicious demons and their arrows. Not to do so would be spiritual conceit." He spread his arms. "The gods have rewarded me and I am able to forgive you, Hapu. Most of the time. I try not to look back or forward. My schooling was accomplished by the good graces of the High Priest Ramose at Ra's temple in Iunu. I work diligently for Atum, the Neb-er-djer. Be at peace, dear Father."

Hapu took Huy's hand and laid it between his two call-oused palms. "The Neb-er-djer," he repeated. "The Universal God. So it is Atum and he alone who gives you the healing visions?"

"Most of the time the voice belongs to Anubis. Rarely to Ma'at. But the source is always Atum," Huy replied unwillingly. He did not want to discuss these things, so private and so personal, with his father. Only Ishat, Methen, and the Rekhet invited the comfort of such an unburdening. Fortunately, at that moment Heby spoke up.

"Ishat said you have soldiers to guard you now," he said loudly. "I've finished my juice, Huy. May I go and talk to them?" His eyes were shining with excitement. "I've never dared to speak to the temple guards at Mennofer, it's not allowed for pupils, and I've always wanted to. Have your guards had to kill anyone trespassing in your garden yet?"

Huy reached across and pulled his ear. "Go to the rear of the compound, where you'll see some new cells. The largest one belongs to Anhur, my captain. Knock on his door lintel, tell him who you are, and he might be willing to show you his weapons. But, Heby, if he's busy, don't whine. Come back into the house. Ishat and I will be showing it to everyone."

The boy nodded solemnly, scrambled up, and hurried along the corridor leading to the back of the house.

Itu sighed. "We won't be seeing him again for a while," she commented. "He's obsessed with everything involving the army, and he wants to be a soldier."

"That will pass," Ishat said, rising. "Now, come with us. Huy, are you ready? I'm longing to show you all over this wondrous estate. Though it is small, it has absolutely everything." She linked arms with her mother. "Later on we'll dine together. The cook, Khnit, is preparing a special meal."

She led them first towards the stairs, pride and excitement evident in her straight spine under the flowing scarlet linen, her new earrings, fashioned into a likeness of Hathor's mild bovine face and curved horns, swinging against her strong neck. The exotic and very rare purple gold enhanced her vibrant beauty, and Huy thought that she had never looked more lovely.

She led them into every bedchamber on the second floor, standing proudly while they exclaimed over the ornate couches dressed in fine linen sheets, the delicately carved cedar tables holding alabaster lamps fluted like lilies, the cosmetics stands with their assortment of pretty ceramic and stone vials, their brushes and copper mirrors shaped, like Ishat's earrings, in the image of Hathor, goddess of love and beauty. Half the floor in the guest room was taken up by a huge lion's skin complete with snarling head and outflung claws. Itu bent down and stroked it in awe.

"It's a special gift from the King," Ishat explained. "His Majesty shot it himself, with one arrow from the bow no one else is strong enough to draw. Or so it's said."

A ray of the Aten became this lion, the embodiment of Amun, Huy thought uneasily, *and the King killed it. Every pharaoh delights in hunting lions. Then why do I have a sense of foreboding when I look at this one?*

"How do your house servants clean it?" the ever-practical Hapzefa wanted to know. "It can't be scrubbed with natron. I suppose all they can do is take it outside and hang it up and beat it."

Beat it. Huy suppressed an inward shiver and left the room.

A narrow stair at the end of the hall led the group directly down into the bathhouse. Here the air was humid and smelled sweet. Itu drew it into her lungs. "You have many kinds of perfumed oils here," she said to Huy, "and I can detect the odour of lilies."

"I keep ben oil spiked with essence of lilies just for you, Mother," Huy told her. "Whenever I inhale it, I think of you bending over my cot to kiss me good night when I was a child. Perhaps you will spend a night or two here with Ishat and me and enjoy the pampering our staff can give. You deserve it. Now we will step out into the garden."

Itu brightened. She was an avid gardener, growing all the vegetables her family ate in tiny terraces around the pool in her own yard. Huy, in his youth, had often flattened the lettuce and cabbages by lying on them so that he could watch the activity in the pond.

"So much land to water!" Itu said. "It's hard enough to haul buckets from the field canals just beyond the acacia bushes at home!"

"Our gardener, Seshemnefer, now has an assistant," Ishat told her. "He spends most of his time bringing water from the river. Seshemnefer has had to clear the garden of tares and wildflowers and is almost ready to order the seeds and cuttings for planting when the next Inundation recedes. Then we shall have our own produce. He will dig a short canal from the river, right past the house itself and into the rear compound here, that the flood will fill. I want date palms planted along it to hide it from the house. A naked canal looks so, well, naked, don't you think?"

They had all begun to sweat under the full glare of the summer sun. Apart from the two soldiers standing stolidly to either side of the gate that led almost immediately to the water-steps, the staff had retreated to their cots for the afternoon sleep. Huy felt the first intimations of a headache begin behind his eyes. "Let's go back to the reception hall, where it's cooler," he said. "If anyone would like to lie down, the linen on the couches is clean. Mother?"

Itu shook her head. "Ishat is going to show me her new jewels and sheaths. Huy, there's no sign of Heby. Do you think he's safe?"

"Perfectly safe."

Once inside, the group broke up, Ishat, Itu, and Hapzefa disappearing upstairs and Huy and Hapu settling themselves in Huy's office. "I can fetch you barley beer, Father," Huy offered. "Merenra and his underling are resting. For myself, I would like to drink something other than wine or water. How hot it is!"

Hapu nodded, running his hands over the gleaming surface of Huy's desk, which held little more than a large lamp, Ishat's palette, and a box of fresh papyrus scrolls. "Beer would be wonderful, Huy." He leaned back and folded his arms. "So all this wealth exists on the whim of the King," he said slowly. "Have you considered that, my son? What if you displease him? Will he take it all away?"

Huy, who had already reached the door, paused and glanced back. "Yes, I have, and it troubles me sometimes. Let me fetch the beer."

As he went out again into the white heat and walked quickly towards the kitchen, where Khnit brewed the beer and kept it in large flagons, he marvelled at his father's shrewd discernment. *But it shouldn't surprise me,* he told himself as he hefted a flagon, poured the brown liquid into a jug, and grabbed up two cups. *After all, we are peasants, he and I, and peasants always know the value of everything they own or grow or must grudgingly buy. We are good bargainers, and we make sure that we never give, or take, something for nothing. The King supports me in exchange for the service of my gifts—but is it enough? Will he demand more from me in the future? Ask something of me that I cannot grant?*

Re-entering the coolness of the office, he set his burden down, poured the beer, and, setting one cup before Hapu, went

around the desk and sank into his own chair behind it. Both
men drank greedily.

"I don't know how I might displease His Majesty," Huy said.
"He asks little of me. I welcome the courtiers he sends for healing
or scrying. I treat as many of Hut-herib's townspeople as I'm able.
So far he has not sent me a complaint."

Hapu raised his thick eyebrows. Setting his cup deliberately
back on the desk, he lifted the hem of his kilt, wiped his
mouth, and stared pensively across at Huy. "What if he
demanded some service from you that you could not fulfill? Or
did not want to fulfill? I'm not talking about breaking a law of
the country. Maybe a law of Ma'at? And because you denied
him, he snapped his fingers and all this"—he jerked a thumb
behind him in the direction of the reception hall—"all this
disappeared. Kings can be fickle, Huy. Even the Incarnation
of Amun on earth can forget about mercy and justice if it
suits him. Are we not in the end his cattle, particularly we
peasants, on whose backs rests the welfare of those who
govern us?"

*He must not depart from the balance of Ma'at ... Already he is
tempted to do so ...* Huy stirred as the words he had remembered
mere days before came drifting back into his mind, together with
the same thought his perspicacious father had just voiced.

"I cannot imagine what task the King might set me that I could
not perform," he answered huskily.

Hapu rapped the desk. "The higher they are, the farther they
can fall," he retorted, "and you are already very high in this land.
There are few who do not know your name, Great Seer!" He
straightened and placed both brown forearms on the table. "You
are really no better off than I. I depend on Ker for my livelihood.
If I am injured and cannot work his flower fields, I fall. You
depend on Amunhotep. If you antagonize him, you and Ishat

also would find yourselves back in some hovel in the slums of the town."

"Well, what do you expect me to do?" Huy's rising anxiety was making him irritable. He felt as though this man his father, with his dusty greying hair, his sun-scarred skin, his splayed, rough hands, was intruding on a matter that he could not possibly understand. Yet Huy's intellect knew the truth: he *was* vulnerable, and Hapu had put his finger on his weakness with a stark accuracy.

Hapu drained his cup and, half rising, reached for the jug and refilled it. "It's simple," he said, regaining his seat. "Take some of the King's gold and invest it. Buy good arable land as it becomes available and have it cropped. I can help you there—I know the state of every farm between Hut-herib and Mennofer. Get that steward of yours to study the trade routes in and out of Egypt, what's being moved, what's profitable. Buy into a caravan, or, better still, equip one yourself. Take advantage of your good fortune while it lasts, Huy! Don't let it make you lazy and indolent! Have you considered the oases? The rich keep summer homes by the lakes, and a lot of the arouras around them are owned by the temples, but the soil is incredibly fertile if you can get your hands on any of it."

Huy stared at him. None of his father's suggestions had occurred to him, but they all made sense. "His Majesty would know," he objected.

Hapu shrugged. "He would probably applaud your wisdom, and besides, the less gold he has to send you, the more stays in the Royal Treasury. Talk to Ishat. She's a sensible young woman, for all her frivolous fussing over baubles. You should marry her, Huy. It's obvious that you love her. What are you waiting for? She's always adored you. And for Amun's sake, get your hair cut! You look like an aristocratic courtesan."

So Mother decided to keep her counsel regarding my enforced impotence, Huy thought. *She didn't even tell her husband.*

He forced a laugh and rose. "I'm so glad you came today. I think this visit has brought us closer, Father, cleared away the cloud between us. Will you forgive me the grudge I have held against you for so long?"

Hapu also got up and, coming around the desk, pressed Huy to his chest. "If you can forgive me my cowardice," he replied, his voice suddenly shaking. "I have punished myself for it every day. Your mother was braver than I in those days."

"Then let's go and sit in the shade of the portico and play a game of Dogs and Jackals while Merenra prepares the hall for the evening meal." Huy held him away and they smiled at each other. "He's awake. I hear his tread in the passage."

Hapu nodded. Huy took the box containing the gaming pieces from a shelf, and together they went along the passage, across the reception room, and out to the front of the house, where the shadows were already beginning to lengthen.

At sunset, they all gathered to eat the feast Khnit had prepared, and there was much talk and laughter as Merenra's assistant went about lighting the lamps on their tall stands and the corners of the pleasant room sprang into sight. "All we need now are enough servants to stand behind each of us with fans waving," Ishat said. "Even the few drafts moving through the room are hot. Oh, look, Huy! Merenra has somehow managed to find white water lilies and cornflowers for our tables! We simply must find someone who can make garlands. It's polite to drape guests in necklets of fresh flowers."

At once she bit her lip and cast an anxious glance in Huy's direction. Huy knew what she was thinking. Thothmes' sister Anuket was a skilled weaver of wreaths and festive garlands. Thoughts of her still filled his heart with longing and pain, and

Ishat must be inwardly cursing herself for bringing her into his mind.

"If we keep adding to our household, we shall have to build more servants' quarters and then Seshemnefer will have no room left for a garden," Huy said lightly.

Ishat's brow cleared. At that moment Heby came running into the hall, leaving a smattering of water droplets behind him.

"Am I late for the meal?" he panted. "Anhur took me swimming and we forgot to watch the passage of Ra. I'm sorry. At least I hung my kilt on a tree so it wouldn't get muddy."

Anhur had caught up to him. "They don't seem to offer swimming lessons at Heby's school. I gave him a lesson. He's a fast learner." He crossed his legs and sank calmly behind his little table, picking up the flowers lying on it and depositing them carefully on the tiles beside him.

"The river is very low, Anhur," Huy said. "At this time of the year the shallows can be full of noxious things."

Anhur nodded. "Don't worry. I carried him out to where the current still flows, and when we had finished splashing about, I carried him back."

"Anhur threw me in," Heby exclaimed. "I lost my breath, but I didn't panic. I can swim six strokes now without sinking!"

Merenra and his assistant were approaching with laden trays.

"It's a good thing that we live far from the river. You must promise to stay out of the canals and swim only when you visit your brother," Hapu told him. "Now go to the bathhouse and wash your face and hands with natron. You have pondweed in your hair and you smell rank."

They dined on lentil soup and poppyseed bread, grilled goose in a garlic sauce, broad beans made fragrant with coriander, boiled cabbage sprinkled with cumin (a universal favourite), and sweet sycamore figs drowned in honey, all of it washed down with barley beer and date wine. By the time Merenra had cleared away the last empty dish, full night had fallen and the gusts of air reaching their flushed faces were cooler. Heby fell asleep sprawled across the cushions, his head in Itu's crumpled lap.

Hapu leaned back unsteadily on his elbows. "Do you eat like this every evening, Huy?" he asked, a note of humour in his voice. "If you do, you will both be as fat as a couple of Delta cows before long!" His speech was slurred, his eyes slightly glazed.

"My father, you are drunk." Huy smiled. "Good. Then Ishat and I have done our duty by you. Most of the time we eat simply, but if we have important guests, Khnit girds up her linen and produces a feast. I'm glad you enjoyed it."

"I look forward to more fresh fruits and vegetables when they come into season," Ishat put in. "Kuku and pomegranates and grapes and those little brown plums. Melons and juicy cucumbers." She yawned. "I thank the gods that we are not working tomorrow, Huy. I shall sleep the morning away."

Her words gave Huy an immediate vision of her, barefoot and dressed in her one thick, patched sheath, slipping out the doorway of their tiny dwelling in the poorer district of Hut-herib at dawn to beg the day before's bread and a jug of milk from the owner of the beer house next door, whose wall they shared. That was before Huy's name had begun to be whispered among the sick and needy of the town, when all they had came from Methen and the temple's kitchen.

"You can sleep for a week if you want to, dearest sister," he replied through the sudden lump in his throat. He turned to Hapu. "Father, will you stay the night?"

Owlishly, the man shook his head. "Tomorrow I must rise early. The fields are lying fallow, of course, but there are essences to be distilled and a shipment of dried myrrh flowers from Wawat to be collected from the docks." He sighed. "Well, at least I am more fortunate than the workers who chop straw for the bricks all day long. Ker looks after Heby's welfare and often gives us things we ourselves could not afford." He gave Huy a lopsided grin and, rolling onto his knees, managed to stand. "This has been a wonderful day, but we must go."

At once Merenra, who had been waiting in the shadows, stepped forward, a lamp in his hand. Hapu lifted Heby into his arms and Huy helped his mother to her feet. Hapzefa was already giving her linen brisk slaps to straighten its folds.

Huy nodded to Merenra. "Have your assistant rouse the litter-bearers. They can travel on the barge and then carry my family to their door." He embraced Hapu over Heby's limp body. "I'll remember your advice," he promised, "and when I need more of it, I'll ask. Thank you, Father."

Itu was swaying, her eyes swollen. Huy kissed her, hugged Hapzefa, and together they moved across the floor and out under a star-strewn sky, following the circle of light Huy had taken from Merenra until they came to the watersteps, where Huy's barge rested almost without motion.

"The river's level has sunk even more," Ishat remarked. "The ramp now sits on the second-to-last waterstep." She kissed her mother, and she and Huy watched as the family straggled over the ramp and onto the deck. The sailors seemed to flit like wraiths as they took their stations. After a moment the bearers appeared, bowing to Huy as they too entered the barge. The litter was kept on board.

"Thank you!" Itu called as the ramp was run in and the oars hit the turgid water. The barge swung out, the sailors soon pulling against the north-flowing current, and before long it was lost to view.

Huy took Ishat's hand and lifted the lamp so that its glow fell on her face. "It was a very pleasant day," he said quietly. "Did you enjoy yourself, Ishat?"

She smiled sleepily. "More than I thought I would. And you seem to have resolved your differences with your father. They can come again soon, can't they, Huy?"

"As often as they like. Heby might as well continue his swimming lessons with Anhur until school commences again. I suppose Anhur has gone to his cot."

"Hentis ago."

They began to wander back to the house. Presently Ishat withdrew her hand. "Huy, you called me your dearest sister tonight," she said, looking away from him into the gloom of the acacia hedge. "It is what a lover calls his beloved. How did you mean the words?"

"I remembered our early days together, and how hard you strove to care for me," he answered sadly. "My heart filled with the love for you I have always felt, Ishat."

"But not ... that kind of love."

There are times when I hate you with a terrible purity of emotion, Atum Neb-er-djer, Huy thought savagely, *and this is one of those moments. You are cruel in your commands and implacable in seeing your will fulfilled. Even if I desired Ishat as I continue to crave Anuket, any attempt to make love to her would be useless.*

"No," he replied shortly. "If I could sacrifice my soul to make this one thing different, I would. But I can't. Atum has made sure of that." He did not try to keep the bitterness out of his voice, and they re-entered the house in silence, climbing the stairs and parting. Ishat closed her door behind her without bidding him good night.

Even though the hour was late, Tetiankh stood waiting by Huy's couch, a bowl of steaming water and a dish of natron beside him on the table. At the sight of him, Huy felt all at once exhausted. Pulling off his kilt, unhooking the jewellery from his ear, he slumped into his chair and allowed his body servant to wash the cosmetics from his face, cleanse and briefly massage his feet and hands, and comb and rebraid his hair. In answer to the man's raised eyebrows, he shook his head. "I don't need any poppy tonight," he said. "My head is fine. Let me wake naturally tomorrow, Tetiankh. When I need you, I shall call."

Bidding him rest well, Tetiankh took away the scummed water and cloths, shutting the door just as the night guard was passing along the corridor. Huy heard the two exchange cheerful greetings. *The soldiers and servants are beginning to mix well,* he thought as he eased himself onto his sheets. *That's good. I wish a little air would move through my wind catcher. It's too still out there tonight. Perhaps we should be sleeping on the roof.* His eyes closed.

LATE THE FOLLOWING MORNING, after spending a longer than usual time standing on the stone slab in the bathhouse while he gradually returned to full consciousness under Tetiankh's deluge of cold water, Huy went in search of Ishat. He found her pacing impatiently in the office.

"I've been up for hours and hours," she accused him, "and here are two sealed scrolls delivered just after dawn I've been desperate to unroll. One is from Thothmes. I recognize the insignia of his father's sepat. The other is from Ra's temple at Iunu. I couldn't open them without your permission, of course. Gods, Huy, your hair hasn't been oiled yet, and you need to be shaved!"

"Don't nag me, woman!" He took the letters she was holding out to him, and to tease her he broke the temple seal first. The familiar hand of High Priest Ramose's scribe leapt up at him. "'To my dear erstwhile pupil, the Seer Huy, greetings,'" he read aloud. "'You have asked that the services of one kitchen servant, Amunmose, be transferred to you, subject to the young man's agreement. I vaguely remember that he accompanied you to Khmun on one of your journeys to Thoth's temple there. Amunmose is more than eager to join your household in whatever capacity you desire, indeed he has been dogging my steps at every turn, begging to be released, since your request arrived. Therefore, you may expect his arrival within a day or two of receiving these words. May you have joy of him! Ever your friend, Ramose, High Servant of the Majesty of Ra.'"

Ishat snatched the scroll from Huy. "Amunmose sounds like rather a nuisance," she said waspishly. "You are so mean, Huy! What does Thothmes say?"

Huy cracked the seal with its hawk imprint and unrolled it, scanning the scroll quickly. "It's very short. He simply says that he will arrive at the end of Mesore and is able to stay with us for several weeks."

Ishat clapped her hands. "That's four days away! Oh, I am so pleased! Now go and finish your morning ablutions, and then Anhur wants to go over the roster of guard watches for the coming month."

Huy handed the scrolls back to her. "Make copies as usual and file these," he ordered her. "Ishat, when I've finished with Anhur, I want to talk to you about a suggestion my father had. Meet me under the shade of the front portico." He left the office with a heart both lighter, because he longed to see his friend, and somewhat apprehensive. Was Thothmes still attracted to Ishat? Would he, Huy, find himself a jealous spectator, as before? He shook off the small cloud of unease and returned to where Tetiankh was still tidying the bathhouse.

Later, sitting on cushions within the protection of the blessed shadow cast by the portico, their backs against the house wall and eyes narrowed against the fierce glare beyond, Ishat listened while Huy told her of his father's suggestions.

"It all seems very sensible," she said when he had finished. "I don't know why we didn't think of these things before. I've been luxuriating in gems and linens and thoroughly enjoying myself, and I haven't wanted to look into the future. But I see the dangers." She turned towards Huy. One bead of sweat began to trickle down her temple and she brushed it away.

Her hands are becoming softer, Huy thought, watching the careless gesture. *The colour of her skin is paler. She is losing the dark stigma of the peasant who is forced to spend too much time under the sun. I suppose I am also.*

"Ask Hapu what land is available, Huy. Let him do this favour for you. It would be a good idea to approach Mayor Mery-neith as well. He'll know what acres around Hut-herib have gone khato."

"But khato land reverts directly to the King. He controls its disposition. Will I seem ungrateful, asking his permission and using his gold to buy it?"

"Giving back to him something that was his?" Ishat responded promptly. "Surely he will applaud such thrift! Aren't we Egyptians famous for our canny dealings as well as our piety?" She leaned closer. "You're afraid to incur his displeasure, aren't you, Huy? So am I. I imagine losing all we have, and I am terrified. But to go on relying on His Majesty's good graces is terrifying also. Your father is right. Kings can be unpredictable and none dare to oppose them. Let's take the gamble."

But if we lose, and cause the King offence, my supply of poppy will dry up, Huy thought. *That I cannot risk.*

"What of his other suggestion?" he said aloud. "Egypt trades with Keftiu and Alashia, we bring in gold from Kush and incense from Karoy to the south. Both commodities belong to the King and the temples, but what else comes into the country with the caravans?"

"I don't know, but Merenra can find out. He talks to other stewards. Are we agreed on this, Huy? Of course, I'm no more than your scribe and the final decision is yours, but it would set our hearts at ease."

Huy chuckled. "You have a much better grasp of such matters than I, and you know it, Ishat! After the sleep we'll draft a letter to Mery-neith and tell Merenra to make his inquiries."

"Should you talk to your uncle? Investing with him would entail no risk to us. Everyone who can afford them wears his perfumes, and he is one of the few suppliers of the sacred kyphi to the temples."

"No," Huy snapped. "Ker shall not benefit from any gold of mine."

AMUNMOSE ARRIVED one day before Thothmes' barge nudged the watersteps. He was expected and challenged and passed through the gate by the guards. However, most of the household was sleeping away another blazing afternoon, and Huy, coming downstairs some time later, found him dozing on the floor of the reception hall, his head uncomfortably pillowed on a bulging leather satchel. Huy stirred him gently with one foot. "You asked to enter my service seven years ago if I was ever in a position to hire you, Amunmose," he said as the young man opened his eyes. "Well, here you are. I hope it makes you happy."

Amunmose scrambled up, wincing. "Ouch! I have a crick in my neck and an ache in my back," he complained. "I sailed with a herald as far as Nag-ta-Hert and then I had to walk west through fields and over canals to find your ugly town, and then I had to ask for directions to your house, and then I got lost." He rolled his eyes. "It's a miracle I found you, Huy. I'd like to say that you haven't changed at all, but in truth you bear little resemblance to that insecure boy who stood trembling with me before the door of Thoth's temple at Khmun." He bowed. "Thank you for remembering me, and rescuing me from Ra's kitchens. What would you have me do?"

Huy laughed from sheer happiness. The memory of this cheerful face, Amunmose's tactful attempts to allay a lad's fear of a strange city, his reassurances, and his pride in being given the task of accompanying Huy came vividly back to Huy now. He stepped forward and embraced him.

"You were so good to me, and you took my mind off the task ahead of me by telling me about Khmun as we sailed past its environs," he said. "A child does not forget such kindnesses. Have you returned to see your family in Khmun lately? Is your mother still making the soup you boasted to me about?"

"What a memory! Yes, my mother is well and I am still smug regarding her skills." Amunmose looked him up and down much as Anhur had done. "You've become a man," he nodded, "and a great one at that, if the stories I hear are to be believed. I suspect that from now on it will be you, Master, who educates me." He glanced around. "A lovely house, and I'm eager to begin my duties in it. Already I feel I am basking in your reflected glory!"

"Don't be ridiculous! I need an under steward, Amunmose. My steward, Merenra, is desperate for assistance. I have acquired a few domestic servants, but Merenra needs someone who can assume an authority they cannot. You read and write?"

Amunmose's brow had begun to lift at Huy's words until it almost disappeared under his thatch of dusty, unruly black hair. "You're not putting me in your kitchen?"

"No. Khnit now has all the help she needs."

Amunmose flung out his arms and hopped from one foot to the other. "Wonderful! Unbelievable! I can read simple instructions and write numbers and lists, but that's all."

"That's enough." He called and Tetiankh came hurrying down the stairs. "This is my body servant, Tetiankh," Huy explained. "Go with him to the bathhouse. He will wash you and shave your head. Then he can take you to Merenra. Are you hungry? Tetiankh, make sure Merenra feeds him after he's been cleaned up."

Amunmose sobered. Reaching down for his satchel, he slung it over one shoulder and stared at Huy. "Those six years have dealt strangely with you, Master," he said with a new respect. "You may trust me to serve you honestly and with loyalty. I consider myself privileged to be here."

Huy watched him follow Tetiankh into the passage that ran right through the house and out to the rear. He was limping slightly, but there was still a bounce to his step. Huy knew he would not regret his decision to keep the promise he had made, although it had been spoken out of a boy's panicked desire to keep a friendly face close by. He set off in search of Ishat.

Early the following day, Thothmes arrived. Huy had set one of the servants to watch by the watersteps, and as soon as Thothmes' barge hove into view, he and Ishat hurried there. Ishat was clearly nervous. She had dressed in gold-bordered, filmy scarlet linen. Her lips had been coloured with red antimony, and her eyelids, above heavy lines of dark grey kohl, had been dusted with powdered gold. The gold circlet hung with jaspers rested on her head, the one large red stone gracing her forehead, and her hair had been gathered into the net attached to the headband. Her sandals sported tiny red jaspers nestling between each toe. She moved in a cloud of perfume, the blend of myrrh, cassia, and henna flowers that was becoming her signature, and although her throat was bare, the gold bracelets on her arms clicked against each other. Her forefingers carried thick gold bands on which green turquoise scarabs sat. *The fingers of power,* Huy thought, half amused and half sympathetic to the pulse beating rapidly in her neck. *She is learning not only to hide her insecurities but also to amplify the nimbus of influence surrounding every part of our being.*

They waited while the craft nosed the steps, Anhur (as Huy's captain) gave a formal challenge that received an equally formal answer, and the ramp was run out. Thothmes did not wait. Running along it, trailed by his attendants, he flung himself on Huy and hugged him tightly, beaming with pleasure. "I would have come to visit weeks ago, but my father is not well and I was deluged with work," he explained. "I miss you every day, old friend! And you!" He turned and took Ishat's hand, bringing it to his mouth. "I relive the time we spent together, with you showing me the rather dubious delights of Hut-herib. I remember how much we laughed together, my Lady Ishat. I hope you have not forgotten me!"

Huy did not miss the pleading behind Thothmes' light words, and a little of the joy went out of the bright morning.

"No indeed, Lord," Ishat responded stiffly, withdrawing her fingers. "You were a most agreeable companion. Come into the house. Khnit has prepared a small meal for us, but tonight we will absolutely gorge on her delicious food!"

Thothmes' expression of disappointment at her decorum faded. He glanced to where the members of Huy's staff were lined up under the portico, waiting to reverence him. He whistled. "An estate, a full complement of servants, and I'm tied up beside a rather pretty barge that must be yours," he said to Huy as they linked arms and began to stroll up the path, Thothmes' train trotting behind him. "How odd are the twists and gyrations of fate, Huy! Could you ever have imagined this wealth for yourself when we shared a cell at school together, or when you and Ishat existed in that cramped hovel beside the beer house? I want to hear everything. The King must be very pleased with you indeed. Does he summon you often?"

"Not at all. His ministers and courtiers come for consultations, but His Majesty remains silent."

"How odd. You would think that he would want the future told for our new Prince Amunhotep. Now, if our wonderful King Thothmes, the third of that illustrious name, still sat on the Horus Throne, he would have insisted that you live within the palace compound and See for his family every day! He would have truly appreciated you."

Huy smiled to himself. Thothmes had idolized the late King and had mourned deeply when he went to ride in the Sacred Barque.

They had arrived before the solemn line of Huy's servants. Huy introduced them, noting that Amunmose, now fully shaved and clothed in the ankle-length sheath of a steward, was almost unrecognizable. Thothmes greeted them cheerfully, they bowed, and Huy dismissed them. As they scattered to their duties, he led his friend into the house and up to the guest room.

Thothmes whistled. "You wrote to me about the lion skin. A little overpowering, don't you think? I'd like to give the couch to Ibi and sleep on the roof myself. Do you object?"

"Of course not."

"What a good idea." Ishat had entered and was standing behind them. "You can shout for your body servant through the wind catcher, Thothmes. Now let's find some shade and drink beer, and you can give us all your news. How does the Hawk sepat fare under your lackadaisical hand?"

They half lay on reed mats and cushions under the thick canopy of the sycamores growing against the southern wall while Thothmes' steward Ptahhotep and a self-conscious Amunmose served them beer and sweetmeats. Before long, Ishat pulled off her headdress and shook out her hair. "It's too hot for such formality," she complained. "Here in the Delta the summer is bad enough. It must be unbearable further south."

A moment of silence followed. Huy, glancing at Thothmes, saw that his friend's gaze had become fixed on the wealth of black tresses suddenly tumbling past Ishat's shoulders. Ishat had also become aware of Thothmes' scrutiny. Awkwardly, she cleared her throat. "Thothmes, what's wrong with Nakht?" she said. "You mentioned an illness in your last letter. Is it serious?"

Thothmes did not answer at once. Then he sighed. "I don't think so, but he seems listless and easily fatigued. Our physician has been unable to diagnose the problem as yet. Father and I work together in his office in the mornings, but in the afternoons I am left to see to the affairs of the sepat by myself." He grinned ruefully. "I listen to farmers complaining about the encroachment of their neighbours' fields onto their own, and persons who feel the merchants have cheated them, and in another month, when the taxes are due, there will be screams from everyone as the taxgatherers go about their business for the King. But I like our Mayor. He and I have begun more beautifying in Iunu."

"I remember the city as being already very beautiful," Huy put in. "Do you go to the temple often, Thothmes? Do you ever revisit our school?"

"Nasha and I go on feast days," he replied, "and of course I pray to my dear Osiris Thothmes Glorified. I don't bother with the school. Ramose continues to run it with his usual efficiency."

"And is Nasha well?" Huy asked carefully.

Ishat shot him a glance. *I know what you will ask next,* her eyes told him scornfully. Huy looked away, lifting his cup, but there were flies struggling in the dregs of his beer. He poured them onto the grass.

"Nasha never changes," Thothmes said. He rolled onto his back and closed his eyes. "Father despairs of her. She's rejected every suitor and now few call on her. Soon no one will want to marry her. She'll be too old." He cocked one sleepy eye at Huy. "I think she's been in love with you ever since you began coming to our house on school holidays. Her tongue is sharper, but she retains her great sense of humour."

There was a moment of silence. Huy listened to the drone of bees searching in vain for flowers that had long since died. Across from him, his path to the watersteps lay white and dazzling in the sunlight, and the stiff palms lining it cast no shade. At length he could bear it no more. Ishat was idly plying her fly whisk, turning her sandalled foot back and forth to see the jaspers glow as they caught the light now creeping over her ankles.

"And what of Anuket?" Huy blurted, his throat tight. "I know that she lives with her husband, the son of the Governor of the Uas sepat, at Weset. Do you ever see her?"

"Sometimes." Thothmes turned onto his side and propped himself up on his elbow so that he could see Huy's face. "Everyone likes to get drunk at feasts, but I suspect that Anuket takes too much wine every day. She has put on weight and her eyes have become permanently swollen and dark-circled. She carps at her husband in public and no longer has any interest in weaving wreaths and garlands." He sighed. "Father has reprimanded her, but it does no good. You're not still in love with her, are you, Huy? She seems unhappy. I wonder how different she would be if Father had allowed you to marry her."

"She would still be unhappy, for Huy cannot consummate any love, as you may remember, Thothmes," Ishat snapped. She drew her feet in under her, out of the reach of the sun, with one sharp movement.

"I had forgotten." Thothmes sat up and grasped Huy's hand. "Your life has become so ... so normal, Huy. Everything that happened to you years ago seems like a very dim memory. So the god's hand still rests heavily on you? Forgive me."

It is you who should be begging my forgiveness for your outburst, Huy thought, looking across at Ishat. *You have humiliated me and you know it.* She would not look at him. She was running her hand back and forth over the dry spikes of the grass.

Huy gave Thothmes' hand a shake and withdrew his own. "Of course," he said. "I never had any secrets from you, my dear friend, and I can forgive you anything. Truthfully, I think of Anuket less often, but when I do the pain is still there. I'm sorry she's in distress."

"It may not be the wine, though," Thothmes added. "Her husband owns many acres of poppy fields. Perhaps she indulges in the drug too much."

"Poppy fields? Around Weset?" Huy leaned forward.

Thothmes nodded. "Importing it has become too expensive, so the Governor petitioned the King for a few arouras to see if we could grow our own. The experiment was successful. Now Weset is surrounded by a sea of red and white poppies, and Anuket's husband and his father the Governor are doing very well out of the sales. The quality is quite high, or so I hear. I take it rarely myself."

Now Ishat met Huy's glance. Her eyebrows went up.

"Thothmes, would it be possible to invest in this enterprise?" Huy asked. "Would you put forward my suggestion to Anuket's husband?" Quickly he explained to Thothmes how he wanted to accrue his own security. "The poppy would be a profitable venture for me, as well as purchasing land around Hut-herib. My father is looking into that. Is Egyptian poppy exported yet?"

"Not yet, but already there have been requests from foreigners." He considered, his head on one side. "I see no reason why your gold should not be as good as anyone else's. I will send a scroll to Amunnefer. I'm sure he will be agreeable."

"Thank you."

The conversation turned to other topics until it gradually died into the stunned quiet of the approaching hour of the afternoon sleep. Merenra had come out of the house and was hovering under the pillars. Huy roused himself. "Let us rest, and talk more this evening when it's cooler." He got up and held a hand down to Ishat, but Thothmes was quicker. Ishat reached for the young man's grasp, came to her feet, and smiled at him.

"I'm so glad you're here, Thothmes," she said. "I've missed you." She walked away without a glance at Huy, who followed miserably. *I am going to lose her, and why should I be resentful? I cannot offer her what she needs.*

Once on his couch, the closed slats of his window hanging casting bands of muted light across his floor, he lay staring into the dimness of his hot room feeling utterly without volition.

At dusk, the three of them gathered in the reception hall, where they fell upon the feast Khnit and her assistants had prepared, and laughed because they were grossly outnumbered by their combined servants, and applauded the music of Thothmes' harpist, who had travelled with him. Ishat seemed to have recovered her good humour. She drank copious amounts of shedeh-wine, and after the dishes had been cleared away she drunkenly insisted on dancing for them, but Huy, watching her sway in and out of the shadows cast by the flickering lamps, thought that there was a feverish edge to her gaiety. Thothmes tapped the floor in time to the music, his expression fixed on her avidly. Huy hoped that, once she had exhausted herself, she would go straight to her bedchamber, and indeed she soon bade them a good night and disappeared unsteadily in the direction of the stairs.

Huy had been looking forward to hours of companionable gossip with his friend, beginning at once, but Thothmes excused himself soon after Ishat had gone. "Ibi has carried my bedding onto the roof and erected a sunshade over it against the morning's glare," he said, yawning, "and to the roof I shall go. Will you join me?"

"Not tonight." They embraced and Thothmes strode away.

Huy sat on in a silence that seemed to echo with the hum of their chatter, the aroma of Ishat's perfume now mingling with the not-unpleasant tang of smoke from the lamp wicks as Ankhesenpepi, the house servant, went softly from one to the other, extinguishing them. When he arrived at the last one, he turned inquiringly to Huy, who shook his head. "Put them all out, Ankhesenpepi. Thank you."

The gloom was welcome. Gradually it lifted a little as starlight blurred grey in the high clerestory windows and faintly showed the open front door. Beyond it, Huy knew, a guard was stationed, but he could neither see nor hear the man. Suddenly he yearned for the poppy. He was not in physical pain; it was his heart that ached with a new loneliness. After a long time he hauled himself to his feet and made his way quietly up the stairs. Halfway along, he saw dull lamplight spilling out of Ishat's room into the hallway and he paused. Low voices came to him, Ishat's and Thothmes', and then Ishat's soft laugh. Anger seized him. Striding to the door, he was about to push his way in, but then he paused. He had caught a glimpse of the two of them, Ishat on her couch decorously smothered in a sheet while Thothmes was sitting cross-legged on the floor looking up at her. *Jealousy is an ignoble emotion,* he thought, fighting it with eyes rammed shut and fists clenched. *You love them both, Huy. They are your most intimate friends, and you know perfectly well that they also love you. Be happy for Ishat, that she has found someone who can give her what you cannot. Be happy for Thothmes, that he has fallen in love with a fine and honest woman.* Yet at that moment he came close to hating both of them.

In the end, he forced himself to continue on along the corridor and enter his own room. The effort seemed to drag down his limbs and take all the heat from his body. Collapsing on his couch, he pulled both sheet and blanket up around his shoulders, but he did not weep. A long time before he had vowed that he would never again shed tears. He tried to pray and gave up. The greed for poppy was nagging hungrily at him, and he could not sleep.

THOTHMES STAYED WITH THEM for a week. On the days when Huy and Ishat were busy with petitioners, he ambled along the riverbank with Seneb, the captain of his barge, or had Anhur set up a target away from the eager crowds, and practised with his bow and arrows. Several times they all boarded Huy's boat and cruised leisurely in the red sunsets, drinking and leaning over the rail to watch the bare and parched banks glide by. Twice Huy left his office after the usual consultation with Merenra regarding the ongoing state of the household to find that Thothmes and Ishat were nowhere on the property. Guessing that they had sought the privacy of the cabin on Thothmes' barge, Huy made his way behind the granaries, where there always seemed to be shadow between the large mud cones and the rear wall, and lowered himself onto the packed earth.

Still he did not weep. Drawing up his knees and resting his chin on them, he gazed into his future and found it to be desolate. Months earlier, when he and Ishat still lived in the town, he had placed his hands on her and Seen her painted and gorgeously arrayed. She had smiled at him in surprise, exclaiming that "they" were not expecting him. Ishat had laughed at the idea that she might be wealthy in the future, and she and Huy had simply gone about their business and forgotten the moment, but now Huy believed that he knew who "they" were. Ishat would finally give in to Thothmes' importuning, and he, Huy, would be left alone with the servants and the wounded townspeople on this beautiful but ultimately meaningless estate. *For it will be meaningless without her*, his thoughts ran on. *My pleasure has been in seeing her so happy with her jewels and fine linens and the freedom from toil that has slowly healed her body from the depredations of hard living. Now her smiles and caresses and the occasional fits of anger that stem from her indomitable spirit will go to Thothmes. He will be the one to take her in his arms, slide the sheath from her shoulders, expose her brown breasts, bring his mouth against hers, and her lips will open for him, her eyes will close ...* The same fantasies invaded his mind each time he sought refuge where the members of his staff could not find him, and he fought with a groan to banish them.

Therefore, he was not surprised when Ishat knocked on the door of his bedchamber on Thothmes' last night with them. They had feasted as usual, and for once Thothmes had begun to talk about his and Huy's schooldays together in the cell at Iunu, how they had become friends, how he had tried to pull Huy out of the temple lake when Sennefer's throwing stick had sent him toppling into the water, how Huy had become like a second son to Nsakht and a brother to Nasha and Anuket during the times of the Inundation, when the school closed and, instead of going home to Hut-herib, Huy had taken up residence in the room in Nakht's house that he soon began to think of as his own. In spite of his sadness, Huy found himself drawn in to Thothmes' reminiscences, and was soon chuckling and adding his own memories; but he did not fail to notice that Ishat had withdrawn a little, leaning back on her cushions into the shadows, her cup of wine untouched on her low table. At the end of the evening they had retired. Huy had begun to doze when the door opened and Ishat came quietly to the side of his couch and stood looking down on him, her sleeping robe clutched tightly under her chin.

"Thothmes still wants me, and this time I have agreed to marry him," she said without preamble. "He knows that I am not in love with him. He also knows that I do love him, in the same way that you love me. He says that he does not care, that my affection for him will grow with the regular joining of our bodies."

Huy flinched. Sitting up, he held out a hand and at once Ishat passed him the kilt he had worn, which Tetiankh had left draped over the back of a chair.

"You did that without being asked," he said. "We have known each other all our lives, Ishat, for so long that our thoughts often seem to merge. Are we not closer than husband and wife in this?" He swung his legs over the edge of the couch and stood, wrapping the kilt around his waist before perching tensely on its edge.

Ishat retreated to the chair and sat with fingers interlaced and knees together, her head lowered. "In your eyes we are like brother and sister. But to me you are the man I adore, have always adored, and can never have." Now she looked up. "You fell in love with Anuket and she was given to another. Notwithstanding the proscription Atum has placed upon you, you must be aware of how I feel. You are in all my memories, Huy. Do you remember how I told you that I had lost my virginity to a young man I saw coming towards me through a field? I thought it was you, come home from school. Even up close he looked like you. My whole body, my ka, my heart, filled with joy and desire and anticipation, watching him stride thigh-deep through the flowers." Her mouth trembled. "That is how I feel every day, from the moment I see you in the morning until we say good night and you disappear into your bedchamber, and the pain of it follows me into my sleep." She unclenched her hands and turned them palms upward, a gesture of despair. "Just now you stood naked before me as you put on your kilt. You had no thought for what that sight meant to me, how I longed to fling myself to my knees and press my face against you. I cannot live like this anymore."

Tears had begun to trickle silently down her cheeks, but she seemed unaware that she was crying. Huy watched her, a thousand memories of their childhood and the months together in their hovel rushing through his mind, but beneath them was the all too familiar guilt, as well as something new when he looked at her, a rage that began to grow, pushing aside both guilt and love. He rammed his teeth shut against it. *I must not hurt her, I must not hurt her,* he shouted dumbly at himself, and gradually the fury paled to a throb of ordinary anger.

"The gods have made me a selfish man," he managed, though he wanted to grab and shake her, lock her in her room, shout for Anhur to put a guard on her so that she could not slip from his grasp. "I was a self-willed, spoiled child, an only son to Hapu for a long time. I am still selfish. And possessive, Ishat. I have known for years how you love me. I have disregarded it so that I might keep my friend and dear companion beside me forever." He swallowed, tasting saliva as acrid and bitter as gall. "Thothmes has made a wise choice. I know, better than he, that you will make him a loyal and faithful wife, and your intelligence will be a great asset to him in his work as Assistant Governor of his sepat. Will you leave with him tomorrow?" He could hardly bear to see the dawning relief in her eyes.

"No, of course not," she said. "He will consult with Ra's High Priest for an auspicious day on which the contract may be signed, and he will need time to have it drawn up and to send out scrolls of invitation to his friends."

"Your mother will be overjoyed." He could not keep the sarcasm out of his voice. "The daughter of a peasant marrying an aristocrat. You are luckier than I was."

"Huy, don't!" Her face crumpled. "Please don't. I am trying to save my life!"

"Does Nakht agree to this?"

"Yes. He trusts Thothmes' judgment."

"He did not trust mine. He would not give me his daughter. But then, I was not a son of his body, was I? I was only a friend, after all." He wanted to stand and dismiss her, but he knew his legs would not hold him up. "Please go now," he croaked. "Find Tetiankh and tell him that I need a dose of poppy."

Immediately, concern flooded her. She rose and took a step towards him, her hand reaching for his forehead, and he recoiled. Dropping her arm, she hesitated, was about to speak, but turned and left the room, her step unsteady. Huy found that he could hardly breathe. His chest was tight and his head had begun to throb behind his eyes. He saw himself flinging his lamp against the wall, slamming his shrine to the floor, ripping the window hanging from its rail—but he did none of these things. *She would have made me a better wife than Anuket ever could,* he thought wildly. *She understands me perfectly. Anuket liked to play with me, the cat with the granary rat. Atum, Atum, have you no mercy for me? Will this thing between my legs remain forever useless, a constant reminder to me that I am only half a man, a reproach to every woman who might want me? Am I to spend the rest of my days Seeing for the poor of Hut-herib and the rich of Mennofer? Is my destiny to be no more than that?*

When Tetiankh knocked and approached him, he was still sitting on the edge of the couch, his limbs so stiff that the body servant was forced to hold the drug to his mouth and then help him to lie down. He refused the offer of a massage with a shake of his head. Once the man had gone, Huy waited frantically for the poppy to begin its lulling song, but even when it started to take away the pain of his body and cocoon the distress of his mind, a residue of hopelessness remained.

3

IN SPITE OF THE POPPY, Huy did not sleep much that night, and when he did, his dreams were lurid and confused. At dawn, when he heard Ibi, Thothmes' body servant, walk along the corridor, he got up, wound the dirty kilt of the previous day once more around his waist, and reached Ibi as he was about to step over the low sill leading out onto the roof of the reception hall. Bidding him a good morning, he took the tray Ibi was carrying. "I'll take Thothmes his meal," he said. "Go and heat the water for his bath."

The first hot rays of the sun had just burst over the eastern horizon, casting a fleeting shadow across the uneven brickwork of the house's upper floor. Thothmes' travelling cot had been set up behind one of the north-facing wind catchers and was still shaded. Huy approached it and stood for a moment, staring down at his friend, who lay naked on his back, his wiry little body sprawled loosely over a wilted sheet. Love and jealousy flushed through him. Countless times in the cell they had shared at school he had seen Thothmes sleeping thus, his limbs flung out, his penis in its nest of black curls resting flaccid against his thigh. Now he imagined it stirring, filling, growing firm under Ishat's caress, but before the vision could intensify, he set the tray beside his feet and gently touched Thothmes' shoulder.

Thothmes' eyes opened at once. He smiled. "There was no breeze last night," he said, rolling over and sitting up with a yawn. "I sweat and I stink, and the stubble on my scalp is itchy. Where is Ibi? Is he ill?"

"I sent him to prepare the bathhouse for you." Huy lowered himself onto the cot. "I wanted to talk to you in peace before you left." He lifted the tray, balancing it by Thothmes' tight brown buttock. "Ishat came to me last night and told me that she had at last accepted your offer of marriage. Do you really love her, Thothmes? Will you take care of her as I do?"

Thothmes sighed. Picking up the cup of water from the tray, he drained it, reached for the milk, drained that, and lifted the small bunch of red grapes. Placing one on his palm, he pushed the dusty fruit delicately to and fro, watching the action of his finger.

"I really love her. Still love her," he answered. "Nakht tried to persuade me to look for a wife among the daughters of his friends, but I never once considered doing so." Now he glanced up at Huy, his face troubled. "I feel guilty all the time, Huy, knowing how much you depend on her, how close to her you are. I could deny my desire for her, make an advantageous union with a woman of my own station, and build an apartment for Ishat as my first concubine." He smiled, a wry twist of his mouth. "Ishat would never be content to walk behind another woman. As for myself, I want a wife with whom I can share my thoughts, not just my body."

"She doesn't love you."

"I know. Her heart belongs to you. But it does her no good, does it?" He pulled another grape off its stem, put the rest back on the tray, and closed his fist slowly around both. "Since we were children together at school, we've shared every secret with each other, laughed and played together, comforted each other. While you were trying to make sense out of the Book of Thoth, you recited its words to me. I confided everything to you regarding my family, my fears and joys, my hopes for my future. Nothing has ever come between us. I beg you, Huy, let it always be so. Let me have Ishat without rancour, and go on loving us both."

Hearing the two of them coupled together in Thothmes' words gave Huy a pang of such swift pain that his hand went to his chest, as though his heart itself was writhing. "No, it does her no good," he agreed with difficulty, "and I have closed my mind to the possibility that one day she might want the respectability of a home of her own, and children. Somehow I have never thought of Ishat as particularly domesticated, even though she once cooked and cleaned in my mother's house. It hurts me, Thothmes. I need time to accept this. I wish that you had not tried to avoid me, that you had come to me, not I to you."

Thothmes put a warm hand on his wrist. "I know. I'm truly sorry. Guilt has made me a coward. I left it to Ishat to give you her final word instead of me." He opened his fist, bounced the grapes on his palm, then flung them over the edge of the roof. "She's stronger than me, Huy. Stronger than both of us, I think. I believe that the deep affection she has for me will one day become as powerful as her love for you. I need your blessing. More than her mother and her sad peasant of a father, you are her guardian. Bless us, and go on loving us for the sake of the friendship that binds us all."

"I am not generous enough to see her pass into your arms without a morass of bitterness," Huy retorted. "I want to keep her for myself, to myself, even if it means that her womanhood withers away." He rose. "You have always known how selfish I truly am, Thothmes. Who will aid me in the god's work? Know what I am thinking, what I want, with just a glance into my eyes? Love for me gives her that gift, a gift you may find she is unable to exercise with you. No Egyptian man may own a woman. Take her, then, of her own free will, and give me time to remember how I love you both."

He could say no more. The tears that he had sworn he would never again shed prickled behind his eyelids and thickened his throat. Striding away across the roof, he hardened himself ruthlessly against them until, by the time he turned in at the door of his bedchamber, he had achieved an equilibrium. Tetiankh had made up his couch with fresh linen, set out a kilt and jewels for the day, and left a tray on his table containing the same food Huy had carried to Thothmes. Huy's gorge rose at the sight of it.

Returning to the hallway, he shouted for his body servant. "Bring me beer this morning," he ordered as Tetiankh appeared at the head of the stairs. "I feel too parched for either water or milk. And send to me at once when Thothmes has finished in the bathhouse. Put my jewellery and my sandals away. I don't want them today."

The usual crowd of townspeople was already gathering outside the closed gates. Huy did not want to deal with their problems until after Thothmes and his staff had left. Ishat was waiting for him in his office. She looked pale under her face paint, and the eyes that met his were wary. "A scroll has come from the palace," she said. "The wax bears the imprint of the sedge and bee. Shall I read it to you?"

Huy nodded. She fumbled as she broke the seal, and cried out as pieces of red wax floated to the floor, then she tossed the scroll onto the desk and covered her face with both hands. "Don't hate me, Huy," she sobbed. "I could no longer live if you hated me."

With one long step, Huy was in front of her. Grasping her wrists, he forced them apart. "Look at me!" he commanded. "I do not know this craven woman! Where is the Ishat who defied her mother, who made stealing from Khenti-kheti's kitchens a game, who called Thothmes' sister a little bitch, who was so determined to master the skills of a scribe that she used a piece of charcoal and the bulging wall of a hovel to write the symbols? That Ishat would pour scorn upon these feeble tears and take the consequences of her decision, whatever they might be." He dropped her arms. "I should give you a good shake and send you to your room. Read the scroll."

Instead, she flung herself against him, pressing him to her with a ferocity that alarmed him, her wet cheek jammed into his neck, her mouth trembling on the skin of his shoulder. "I cannot leave you and I cannot stay," she half whispered, her muffled words broken by sobs. "I have to do this or I will never know true contentment. I will be good to him, and loyal—but oh, Huy! What memories will come to torment me in the night! How do I purge myself from you?"

He held her with his eyes closed, feeling her long body hot under the thin sheath, her lips invisibly imprinting her distress onto his own body, her hair soft against his forearms.

"By becoming the wife of the future Governor of Iunu's sepat," he said, forcing his voice to remain even. "By giving birth to beautiful children, and loving them, and teaching them everything you have learned about how to live, Ishat. And one day, sooner than you might think, you will see me alight from my barge and walk towards you where you stand beside Thothmes, and you will recognize an old friend. The man you love and cannot have will be gone. Ishat, my dearest, this parting will be bitter for me also. Don't doubt that I too will suffer."

"Good." She lifted her head. Kohl had run down her cheeks and streaked across her temples. "I want you to suffer. I want you to miss me terribly. I want your new scribe to be careless and inept and rude. The gods are very cruel, Huy, as you well know." She pulled herself away from him. "Have you forgiven me?"

"Yes, but not Thothmes. Not fully yet." He snatched up the scroll and held it out to her. "I'm glad to see my Ishat restored. Now read, and then find Iput and have yourself washed and painted again. Thothmes will go away upset if he sees you in such an unseemly mess."

She was still hiccuping, but she unrolled the letter with steadier hands. Huy was glad to see that she had almost completely recovered from her loss of control.

She raised her eyebrows. "It's from Heqareshu, Overseer of Royal Nurses. I presume he is in charge of Prince Amunhotep's welfare. He wants you to See for him, and he will arrive during the third week of Thoth. That's next month." Letting the scroll roll up, she used it to tap her chin. "The Inundation will be upon us, but of course Mennofer is not far away. We may get all the palace gossip, and information about our Hawk-in-the-Nest."

"So you will still be here?"

She looked startled. "For another four months, I think. Thothmes wants a marriage sometime during Peret. The season of spring will be auspicious for us, he says."

"He says." Huy shrugged. "That will give me plenty of time to find another scribe. Go and get yourself clean, Ishat, then come back for dictation. I must reply to this Heqareshu."

The King is allowing this man, who must be on very intimate terms with the whole royal family, to consult me, Huy mused when Ishat had gone. *Will he bring me something Pharaoh wants me to know? Why does the thought of our little Prince, surely nothing more than a baby as yet, make me uneasy?*

Tetiankh had entered and was bowing just inside the door. "Assistant Governor Thothmes has left the bathhouse, and I have heated fresh water for you, Master. Will you bathe now?"

His eyes rested briefly on Huy's shoulder before he politely glanced away. Huy patted himself and his fingers came away black with kohl. He followed his servant out of the room.

Thothmes seemed reluctant to leave. When it became obvious that he was about to settle himself in the shade of the garden instead of on the deck of his barge, Huy gave the order allowing the townspeople to come in. While he and Ishat dealt with them, he was aware of his friend watching from beyond the pool, and when Anhur had ushered the last of them back through the gate and Amunmose emerged from the house with a jug of beer and two cups balanced ceremoniously on a tray, Thothmes left the grass and joined them. As usual after emptying himself before the needs of Hut-herib's citizens, Huy was exhausted, wanting nothing more than an hour or two on his couch; but today, as Thothmes approached and Amunmose bent to offer him a drink, he admitted grimly to himself that he did not want to leave Thothmes and Ishat alone together. *Please, Thothmes, just go away. You will have the rest of your life to spend with my Ishat. Can't you see that I begrudge you these fleeting moments before you take her away from me forever?*

"Amunmose, go and get another cup," he said wearily, his head beginning to pound as Thothmes lowered himself onto the stone of the little portico into whose shade Huy and Ishat had retreated. Amunmose set the tray on the ground and went back into the house. Ishat poured the beer, holding it out to Huy first with a deliberate solicitude that suddenly angered him. He drank thirstily. Amunmose returned with the cup, passed it to Thothmes, and filled it. Thothmes sat swirling the brown liquid slowly around, his eyes on its gentle motion. A constraint had fallen on all three of them that was not broken until Thothmes cleared his throat.

"I suppose I ought to get onto my barge and go home," he said, "but I wish I could stay here with both of you until the closeness that used to exist between us came back."

Neither Huy nor Ishat replied, and after a moment Thothmes drank, called for Ibi, and went into the house.

He and Huy embraced at the watersteps where Seneb, his captain, waited to draw in the ramp. They held each other tightly, both struggling to break the dam that held their affection for each other in check. Huy was the first to pull away. "I shall want to see a copy of the marriage contract before I bring Ishat to you, and of course one must go to her parents, whether they can read it or not," he said huskily. "Please keep writing to me, Thothmes, for the sake of our schooldays together."

Thothmes nodded, his eyes large with unshed tears. Turning to Ishat, he lifted her hands and kissed them lightly. "You honour me, Ishat," he told her quietly. "Be well." Running along the ramp, he disappeared into his cabin.

Seneb bowed to the pair on the steps, shouted an order, and quickly the ramp was hauled in. Sailors appeared with poles and began to push the barge away from the bank and into the centre of the sullen river. Ishat put a hand on Huy's arm. She was about to speak, but Huy shook her off.

"Not now," he said tersely. "I need poppy and an hour on my couch. Tell Merenra to begin preparations for the Royal Nurse's visit." *None of this will have any meaning once she is gone,* he thought as he felt the blessed coolness of the reception hall enfold him. *Not the estate, not my work. She has become the heart of everything in my life. How shall I fill the chasm her going will leave? Already I feel it opening all around me.*

He lay on his couch once Tetiankh had given him the drug and had withdrawn, turning onto his side and staring into the dimness of the room. *This is not anger,* he realized all at once with a shock the poppy did not dull. *This is fear. I am afraid of loneliness, afraid of missing her, afraid of decisions that must be made without her clear voice arguing us both into consensus. Fear? This is panic. Ishat is my link to the world of normality and practicality I began to leave the moment Sennefer's throwing stick sent me plunging into Ra's temple lake, a world I crave desperately but can only partially inhabit. I cannot get drunk, although I may drink. I cannot make love, although I may feel both love and desire. I must carefully discipline my mind to appreciate the beauty of Egypt, thrusting away any comparison my ka wants to make with the incomparable glories of Paradise. I am Atum's pawn, at the mercy of whatever visions he chooses to send me, without the security of knowing his will, for even though the words of the Book of Thoth are sharply embedded in my consciousness, I still have not been able to solve their final riddle.*

As if he had deliberately summoned them, the first phrases of the Book rose into his mind. "I Thoth, greatest of heka-power, giver of the sacred gift of language to man out of my own Hu, set down these mysteries at the command of Atum so that he who is possessed of the gift of wisdom may read and understand what is the will of the Holy One. Let him who desires this knowledge take care that his eyes be diligent and his reverence complete. For he without sia will read to his harm, and he without diligence will enter the Second Duat."

The opium was spreading its warmth through his blood, loosening the tension in his limbs, gently lifting memories out of the dimness on the periphery of his consciousness where they hid, and imbuing them with all the colour and immediacy of moments long gone. Once again he was stepping down from the wicker floor of the chariot after his lesson on the school's training ground and running his hand over Lazy White Star's moist flank as he prepared to unhitch the horse. He could smell his own sweat mingling with the not unpleasant odour of the animal. The sun was hot on his head. Dust clung to his calves. But he was oblivious to the physical world around him for the torment in his mind. What was the Second Duat? He had cursed the sluggishness and ignorance of his own sia, his perception, as he freed the horse from the vehicle, led it into its stall, and washed and brushed it while it drank, his movements automatic. He had then gone outside, and was struggling to wrench the chariot free of the sand when the solution had come to him, flooding his mind. The Second Duat was what every Egyptian thought of as the first and only one, a place through which the dead must pass in order to reach the Paradise of Osiris, a nightmare populated by djinns and demons. The First Duat was the place where Atum willed a metamorphosis for himself.

Huy, lying drugged on his couch, no longer saw the far wall of his room. The expanse of the training ground shimmering in the heat had given way to the cool, roofless confines of the place where the sacred Ished Tree had been planted by Atum at the beginning of time. Huy was sitting with his back against its trunk, a scroll across his thighs. Above him, the leaves of the Tree rustled and whispered. His nostrils filled with its curious scent, honey and garlic, orchard blossoms and the merest whiff of something corrupt, something rotting. The beauty of the ancient hieroglyphs contained within the Book of Thoth filled his vision as he began to read. *At that moment I understood that I equated Atum's metamorphosis with my own,* Huy remembered as his younger self sat on in that magical room, cocooned by the vast labyrinth of the temple of Ra. *I was declared dead of Sennefer's throwing stick and of drowning at Iunu.*

The walls around him dissolved, the floor lengthened and became hot beneath his sandalled feet, and he was standing in Ra's temple forecourt, Thothmes beside him, his bow in his hand. They were on their way to the training ground, Huy for archery practice and Thothmes gauntleted for the chariot. Beyond them, in the trees, Sennefer was brandishing his new throwing stick, his sycophantic follower Samentuser watching admiringly. Sennefer, seeing

them come, started towards them, a string of insults already streaming from his mouth. Bully that he was, he hated both Huy and
Thothmes, but in Huy's peasant roots he had found the perfect
target for his jibes. On this day, as Huy and Thothmes came to a
halt, the hurtful invective was all about throwing sticks, and how
only the nobles were allowed to own them, which was a pity, for
Huy's father might have used one to kill the rats in his hovel. Huy,
unaware that his body lay flaccid on his couch, once again stood
stiff with a mounting rage as Sennefer's voice echoed across the
wide stone flagging of the temple's forecourt and the verge of the
lake fronting the apron sparkled in the strong afternoon sunlight.
Thothmes put a warning hand on his arm, but Huy shook it off.
"Not this time," he said through clenched teeth, his heart
pounding, a redness before his eyes. Somewhere deep behind the
vivid re-creation of this memory Huy knew that the opium he had
taken was compelling him to relive this most terrible day, but the
knowledge was a faint whisper come and gone. He lunged towards
Sennefer, saw the boy's expression change from a sneer to one of
frightened surprise, saw Sennefer's arm come up and back, and then
the throwing stick was speeding through the air, turning over and
over, glinting as it came. It struck, and Huy the man in his dimly lit
room, Huy the twelve-year-old pupil at Iunu's temple school, cried
out together. In the grip of memory, Huy began to crawl sightless
over the hot stone, insensible to the pain in his hands and knees.
Then there was space beneath him and he was falling into the lake,
the water cool against his skin.

Such a terrible death, Huy groaned silently through the smoth-
ering mantle of the drug. *But I did not know that I had died until
much later, for while my lifeless corpse was being floated north to
Hut-herib, to the House of the Dead, I was in the Beautiful West, the
Paradise of Osiris, speaking with the Great Seer and Physician
Imhotep himself, and agreeing, in my innocence, to read the fabled*

Book of Thoth. Five days later, as a sem priest was about to cut open my abdomen with the obsidian knife and begin my Beautification, my ka was returned to me and I sat up, not knowing where I was, ill and confused. Methen found me naked and sobbing under a palm tree and took me to my parents' house.

The memory did not fade; it was snuffed out as though its bright candle flare had been doused in a shower of water, and Huy found himself staring across at the wall of his room. *That rebirth was my First Duat*, he realized dully. *Of course. I metamorphosed into the Twice Born, the one favoured by the gods, the one who had died and been restored to life. Will Ishat's going plunge me into my Second Duat, a place of demons, of dark pools and rivers, where terror lurks? Has Atum decreed that my comfort should be removed from me, taking sanity and normality with her, because I have been drawing ever closer to the world of the senses and forgetting, dismissing, the god's will for me?* The idea was insupportable. Huy could imagine the god's voice speaking words of correction: "You belong to me alone … You are my instrument … My will for you must be your only resting place …" He had heard Atum's voice once, giving a message to Pharaoh Amunhotep through Huy's own lips. Huy lay tense and miserable. The poppy had not sent its soothing magic to blanket his mind and body today. He wanted to call to Tetiankh for more, but his throat, his tongue, would not obey him.

Three weeks later, Royal Nurse Heqareshu stepped from his barge and answered Huy and Ishat's profound obeisance with a brief nod. Huy had imagined him as plump and fatherly, with a ready smile and warm eyes, but the man regarding him with calm intelligence owed nothing at all to his fantasy. Fully painted and bejewelled, clad in a linen gown that shimmered with gold thread in the breeze, he exuded power and confidence. The members of his retinue were already giving their orders to Anhur and Merenra, and out of the corner of his eye Huy saw a flustered Amunmose backing surreptitiously in the direction of the kitchens, only to be summoned back by an impatient wave from Merenra.

"This is not going to be fun," Ishat whispered to Huy under cover of their bows. "He'll drive us all into the Duat before he leaves."

Huy hid the jolt her comment had given him. Heqareshu was striding towards them. He stopped before Huy.

"So," he said smoothly, "you are the Seer Huy. I am the Noble Heqareshu. I believe that you have met my son Kenamun, Foster Brother of the Lord of the Two Lands." His expression conveyed Huy's good fortune. "My steward and the commander of my bodyguards will decide where I am to sleep, and whether or not your staff may remain in the house while I am here. I do not have time to waste. I must return to Mennofer as soon as possible to continue my care of the Prince Amunhotep. Therefore, you will See for me as soon as I have broken my fast tomorrow morning."

Huy bowed again. "You are welcome in my home, Royal Nurse Heqareshu," he responded carefully. "However, as you can see, it is small. Perhaps you would prefer to rest for the night aboard your barge."

"My steward will make that determination. For now you may escort me within and offer me water and wine. The sun is hot."

Huy, feeling Ishat's indignant struggle to keep her mouth closed, fought against his own desire to laugh. He was distinctly nervous. "I trust that both His Majesty and the Prince are in good health?" he inquired politely as he and the small crowd began to move.

Heqareshu nodded. "They are both well. His Majesty has just announced that Her Majesty Tiaa, his half-sister and Second Wife, is pregnant. I shall, of course, be appointed as Royal Nurse to the new baby."

Of course, Huy thought as they entered the reception hall, where cushions and low tables were waiting. *Amunhotep wants a prediction for this birth. He needs to know whether or not it will be a male. If so, it will be either an insurance against the death of the heir or a latent threat to him if he proves weak. But why the privacy, the need to acquire the Seeing through this man?*

He and Ishat waited while Heqareshu chose a table, lifted his linen with one graceful gesture, and sank onto the cushion behind it. At once a servant began to wave an ostrich fan over him. Huy could feel the minute but pleasant backrush of air. Heqareshu's steward took the flagons of water and wine a stone-faced Merenra was holding and began to serve his master.

Heqareshu looked about him. "You have good taste, Seer Huy," he said, sipping his water. "Your house is indeed small, but well appointed. How long have you lived at Hut-herib?"

A polite conversation began, from which Ishat was excluded. It was not a conscious slight on Heqareshu's part, Huy decided. The man simply did not see Ishat at all. To formally acknowledge the presence of another's scribe would never have occurred to him.

After some moments, the commander of his bodyguard came up to him, bowed, and spoke quickly into his ear. Heqareshu inclined his head. "Your guest room will be suitable for me," he said. "I shall not need to deprive you of your own couch, Seer Huy. However, my body servant must be near me. Therefore, he will occupy your scribe's quarters."

Ishat had taken a sharp breath, her cheeks flaming. Huy reached across and gripped her shoulder hard. "The arrangement will be acceptable," he said firmly. "But Ishat must not sleep in the servants' cells. She must be ready to take my dictation at any hour. Merenra! Have a pallet set up in my room for Ishat!" He felt the muscles loosen under his fingers and withdrew his hand.

Heqareshu looked interested. "Do the gods speak to you in the night, then?" he wanted to know. "Kenamun told me of your prediction to Pharaoh, how every detail of it was fulfilled. You are blessed, Seer Huy."

"He ate every single pastry Khnit made," Ishat remarked later to Huy as they lay slumped on reed mats under the garden's shade. "How does he stay so skinny?"

Heqareshu had gone upstairs for the afternoon sleep, and the lesser members of his retinue had flocked back onto his barge. Neither Huy nor Ishat wanted to retire to Huy's room, so close to the one where Heqareshu was doubtless snoring on the couch.

Huy smiled at a purely feminine question that did not really require an answer. "His food is surely nothing but fuel for his overweening arrogance, and does not benefit his body at all," he replied. "The King must have formed an affection for him in his younger days, before he acquired discrimination. Such early associations cannot easily be broken." He was immediately aware of the truth of his words, and glumly fell silent. Ishat said no more. Both of them drowsed uncomfortably as the implacable heat of the afternoon shrivelled the grass around them.

In the evening, after finding fault with everything in the bathhouse, from the temperature of the water to the quality of the massage oils and the grit in the natron, Heqareshu sat in the reception room and methodically demolished the sumptuous feast Khnit, Huy's cook, had laboured all day to produce. Yet between mouthfuls his conversation was light and correct, the accomplished patter of the seasoned courtier. He continued to behave as though Ishat failed to exist. Afterwards, surrounded by his guard and with his body servant holding a parasol over his head, he took a short walk along the river path in the red-drenched sunset. Once full night had fallen, he climbed the stairs to the roof, where he sat listening to the stories his scribe read to him from his box of scrolls.

Huy and Ishat retreated once more to the now dusky garden and lay looking up at the stars. "How clear the Red Horus is tonight!" Ishat commented. "Can you see the Leg of Beef? The Inundation is late. The Running Man Looking Over His Shoulder should be appearing on the horizon very soon."

She turned towards him, propping her head on her hand, her features indistinct in the weak starlight, but Huy did not need illumination to trace every line and curve of the face he had known since boyhood. Her perfume rose to his nostrils as she moved.

"I can hardly wait until he sails away tomorrow," she went on. "Even his scribe deigns to speak to me only if I ask him a deliberate question, and then very brusquely. Are all courtiers like him, do you think? Must I continually put up with them for Thothmes' sake?"

Yes, they are, Huy wanted to insist with vehemence. *I met some of them during my audience with the King. You will come to hate them all, Ishat. Stay here with me!*

"No, they are not," he admitted. "His son Kenamun is unpleasantly jealous of his closeness to Amunhotep, but the rest of the King's servants and companions I met were kind. You will only have to curb your tongue upon occasion, Ishat."

She was quiet for a moment, then she said, "Why do you think he's here, Huy? It has seemed to you that Amunhotep is reluctant to allow any noble to consult you. Is he afraid of what you may discover about him? Something about his future? Why him?"

Why indeed, Huy thought, sitting up.

"I don't think he's here on his own behalf, although I expect that he believes otherwise," he said. "In my opinion the King wants information regarding his unborn child."

"But why send the Royal Nurse? Why not send Queen Tiaa?"

"Because a Royal Nurse spends far more time with a royal child than does a Queen. He engages the wet nurse, appoints the nursery guards, oversees the daily routine. He even selects the tutors who will guide the Prince or Princess—under the King's direct approval, of course. His responsibility is heavy. Amunhotep will learn more about his child's future from Heqareshu than he would if the Queen had come for a Seeing."

"He is clever and subtle, then, our King."

Clever and subtle. And filling me with anxiety for some reason, Huy thought.

"I wish he would go to bed. I need to be on my couch instead of lurking in my own garden like a criminal," was all he said.

He spent a restless night, sleeping fitfully, unable to still his mind, his body too hot under the one thin sheet with which he had covered his nakedness for Ishat's sake. He worried, as always before a Seeing, that the god would reveal nothing and he would seem like a charlatan. Added to that, when he attended the few nobles allowed to consult him, was the fear that if he Saw nothing, Pharaoh would begin to doubt his power and remove the patronage that had so suddenly and wonderfully changed his and Ishat's lives. And this time there was a new concern: what if he Saw something that would anger or distress Amunhotep? He wanted to wake Ishat, sleeping quietly on her pallet, her sleeping robe a grey jumble on the floor between his couch and the slatted hanging of the window. He wanted to hear her reassurance that the King's generosity would continue regardless of what was Seen, that even if no vision was fed to Huy through the Royal Nurse's aristocratic fingers, Amunhotep would be satisfied. *But soon Ishat will be gone,* he told himself miserably. *I must learn to rely on my judgment alone. I can ask for her advice through letters. I can even visit her if I must. But that strong, honest, often caustic voice will answer to Thothmes' needs, not mine. How in the name of all the gods can I go on without her? Ishat!*

As though he had cried her name aloud, she stirred, muttered something unintelligible, and fell into deep unconsciousness again. Huy resigned himself to an anxious boredom.

Heqareshu took his morning meal in the privacy of the guest room. By the time he was escorted to the bathhouse by his guards, his body servant, his masseur, and his tiring woman, Huy and Ishat had been washed, painted, and dressed and were waiting tensely in Huy's office for their summons. Heqareshu, for all his protestations of haste, took his time, but at last Merenra bowed himself into their presence. "Royal Nurse Heqareshu will receive you now, Master," he said, unable to fully conceal the relief on his face. "He has already given orders for his belongings to be transferred to his barge, and his sailors wait to cast off."

"Well, thank the gods!" Ishat blurted, reaching for her palette. "Let's hope that this Seeing will be over quickly, Huy, and we can wave goodbye to a most disagreeable man. Lead on, Merenra. You can announce us."

Half a dozen pairs of eyes were fixed apprehensively on Huy and Ishat as Merenra bowed them into the guest room and withdrew. *It is as though none of them has seen me before,* Huy thought irritably as he performed his obeisance, Ishat beside him, and rose to meet Heqareshu's heavily kohled gaze. *But I suppose this morning I have become something exotic and perhaps even threatening in my guise as mouthpiece of Atum.*

Heqareshu gestured him forward. "I do not wish to hear the words of the gods in the presence of your scribe. Dismiss her."

"My scribe always transcribes the proceedings so that those who consult me may have an accurate record of what is said," Huy said mildly. "Ishat must stay."

Heqareshu frowned. There was a flutter of shocked whispers from those around him. "My scribe will perform this duty," Heqareshu answered coldly.

Huy shook his head. "Your pardon, Great Lord," he objected. "I fully trust my scribe, even as you trust yours. This is the way I work. Perhaps you wish to leave at once, and carry a complaint to Pharaoh?" For the first time Huy saw uncertainty flit across the haughty face. He pushed his advantage. "Furthermore, I would like you to order all your servants to leave the room. I do not know what Atum may say to you, but his words must be private, for you, me, and my scribe's records alone."

The frown deepened, but after a moment an imperious hand waved once, betraying the savagery of the man's acquiescence. The room emptied swiftly. Ishat went to the floor, saying the customary prayer to Thoth under her breath as she plied her papyrus scraper and uncapped and mixed her ink.

Huy approached Heqareshu and knelt. "I must hold your hand. Atum speaks through the physical connection between us. Forgive my temerity."

For answer, five heavily ringed fingers were extended. Huy took them softly, laying them between his palms, and as he did so a wave of pity swept over him. Startled, he glanced up. Heqareshu's eyes were closed and he had folded against the gilded back of the chair, the stiffness of blood and protocol going out of him. Huy closed his own eyes. *Now*, he said mutely to the god, *let your power flood through me, Neb-er-djer, Lord to the Limit. Show me why I tremble with compassion for this proud creature. Tell me what it is that you wish Amunhotep to know.*

There was no moment of transition, no vertigo. At once he found himself standing in a pleasant room facing Heqareshu across an ornate crib. Behind him, the chatter of many female voices mingled sweetly with the swish of linens. He could feel the rhythmic swirl of perfumed air as someone just beyond the range of his vision plied a large fan. He bent over the crib. A pair of alert black eyes regarded him solemnly out of a tiny face.

Suddenly the baby smiled. His arms and legs jerked in excitement. Heqareshu leaned down and picked him up, crooning
wordlessly to him, the mop of black hair settling against the
hollow of his shoulder.

A hush fell. Heqareshu turned and so did Huy. A woman was
sweeping towards them, her delicate little face dwarfed by the
ornate crown of Mut, the queens' crown, which sat firmly on her
long, ringleted wig, its vulture beak jutting over her forehead,
its golden wings wrapping behind her ears and touching her
shoulders. With a rustle and a sigh, the servants behind Huy
went to the floor. Heqareshu, the baby in his arms, bowed low.
"Give him to me," the woman said. "I wish to hold him for a
moment. Is he well? Does he feed lustily?"

"He is perfect in every way, Majesty," Heqareshu answered,
passing him carefully to his mother. She bent her head and kissed
her son's button nose. The baby gurgled blissfully. The scene
was touching: the naked child held close to the Queen's lapis-
and-gold-hung breast, her face, as she gazed down at him, soft
with love, the vulture goddess on her head seeming to lean over
the boy protectively. But Huy, caught up in the charm of the
moment, was startled by a sudden shadow that passed over him
and came to rest on the crib. He glanced up. A hawk was hovering erratically over the baby, uttering cries of distress. One of its
wings hung bedraggled and useless. It was trying unsuccessfully to
make it beat. Huy automatically put out an arm so that the bird
might have a place to rest, and right away it struggled towards
him, perching awkwardly on his wrist. Then, as he turned his
head towards it, it drove its sharp beak against his mouth and
vanished. Stunned, Huy put a finger to his lips. It came away red.

The Queen was handing the baby back to the Royal Nurse.
"The priests have chosen his name," she was saying. "He is to be
called Thothmes. Pharaoh is pleased. It is an honourable name,

full of the powers of godhead." Huy heard the words, but his attention was fixed on the baby. A circlet had appeared on his head. Attached to it, the royal uraeus, the vulture Lady of Dread and the cobra Lady of Flame, reared up together, but there was something wrong. The mighty protectors of kings were not facing forward, united in their warning and defence of a pharaoh. As Huy watched, the cobra's frill closed up and the vulture's head sank slowly to lie against the snake's skin. It was as though the two potent symbols had turned to each other for support.

A thrill of terror shot through Huy as the sight dissolved, taking with it the baby, the Queen, the crowd of whispering women, until nothing remained but the face of the Royal Nurse. Rapidly it aged. The cheeks hollowed. The blue-painted eyelids puffed and sagged. Deep lines appeared beside the widening nostrils. Distress was clouding the tired eyes. "But Majesty, it is not right, it is not just!" Heqareshu was saying. "I have raised both princes. They are both estimable, both honourable! I beg you, for the love in which you hold me as your own Foster Father and the father of your dearest friend—reconsider this decision!"

Huy's hand trembled slightly. He looked down. The fingers enclosed in his own moved. The rings bit into his palm. Opening his hand, he rose with difficulty. His knees felt weak and a pounding in his head made him wince as he groped for the stool set ready and slumped onto it.

"Well?" Heqareshu snapped, rubbing at his rings.

Ishat picked up her pen.

"Queen Tiaa will give birth to a healthy boy," Huy managed. "He will be named Thothmes. He will survive. You yourself will also survive into old age, Royal Nurse, but an event in the far future will bring you much grief. The god did not show me what it will be." In the moment of silence that followed, Huy could hear the faint pressure of Ishat's brush against the papyrus.

Heqareshu leaned forward. "That is all?" he asked sharply. "I have come all this way for that?"

Huy smiled, a mere twitch of his mouth. "Considering that the King moved his capital from Weset back to Mennofer over a year ago, you will be back at the palace in about two days. His Majesty will be very pleased at the news you will bring him. Would you like a little wine before you go, Royal Nurse? It will take my scribe a moment to make a copy of my words for you to take away with you."

"No." Heqareshu stood and shook out his linen impatiently. "If you will allow my servants back into the room, I will have them escort me to my barge." His tone was sarcastic. "Your steward can bring me the finished scroll."

Huy had had enough. "Is it my peasant origins that disturb you so much, Heqareshu, or my calling? For I had no choice in either one. If the gods had decreed otherwise, you yourself might even now be padding barefooted through the dust of the river path somewhere, sweating into your coarse and much-mended linen. I would remind you of the words of Amenemopet: 'Man is clay and straw. Atum is the potter. He tears down and he builds up every day, creating small things by the thousands through his love.' You and I, my Lord, are merely clay and straw, and in the balance of Ma'at we are small indeed."

Heqareshu had gone gradually pale as he spoke. Huy had expected an angry rebuff that would put him in his place, but he stared at him for a moment, head on one side, then nodded. "Egypt fears you, Seer, and fear often manifests itself as anger. With your permission, I will thank you for your hospitality and leave your house." He bowed to Huy, walked to the door, opened it, and was gone. Through ears ringing with pain, Huy heard his retinue scatter along the hallway and down the stairs.

"I have completed the copy, Huy," Ishat said. "The Seeing was very short." She made as if to set her palette down, but Huy forestalled her.

"Take another roll of papyrus and write what I will tell you," he ordered. "I withheld something from the Royal Nurse that I want recorded and filed with my private scrolls. It disturbs me greatly, Ishat." Quickly, he spoke of the wounded hawk and the twisted uraeus. When he had finished, he made his way unsteadily to the door. "Have Heqareshu's scroll delivered at once to the barge, and stay at the watersteps until he has gone. I want to talk to you about what I saw, but later. I have seldom suffered such an extreme physical consequence to the Seeing." He was ridiculously grateful to see Tetiankh waiting for him outside his room a short way along the passage. "Poppy," he grunted, and lurched towards his couch.

He slept the day away, waking only to gulp a cup of water before falling back into a sodden unconsciousness, and the sun was setting before he woke fully, wrapped himself in a sheet, and went in search of Ishat. He found her in the garden with a flagon of shedeh-wine and a bowl full of fruit, vegetables, and bread beside her.

"The peaches and figs are simply luscious," she said as he lowered himself beside her, "and the currants are very sweet. You should eat something, Huy. Wine?" She handed him a brimming cup, and he tossed a handful of currants into his mouth before drinking and reaching for the sticks of crisp green celery. "Seshemnefer tells me that there is a small rise in the level of the river," she went on. "He asks that we put the soldiers to work digging the canal we promised him so that he can care for the garden without hauling water. We could make it pretty by planting palms along its length beside the house." She paused, looked bewildered, then laughed without humour. "What am I saying? I won't be here to see the palms grow."

Huy did not respond. He felt calm and emptied, as though the poppy had scoured both body and mind.

Ishat spat out a melon seed. "Huy, is it your duty to give the King the rest of the Seeing? You described terrible omens over the little Prince."

"I know. But I have a strong intuition that they are for me as well as for Thothmes, that I am obliged to ponder their meaning with regard to that baby before I decide what to do. What do they mean to you?"

"I've been thinking about it. Horus hovers above the Prince. He is in pain, unable to fly properly, unable to soar. But Thothmes is not the Hawk-in-the-Nest. His older brother Amunhotep is the heir to the Horus Throne. Is Amunhotep to die, then? Is Thothmes to become the Hawk-in-the-Nest? And if so, why is Horus wounded? The holy uraeus appears on Thothmes' brow, but it too is wounded, disfigured, perhaps even impotent. Will Thothmes take the Double Crown by force from his brother, and try to rule without Ma'at?"

Without Ma'at. Her words struck an answering chord in Huy. *The visions have something to do with Ma'at, with cosmic and earthly rightness,* he thought to himself. *They speak of more than just a brother usurping the throne or a Prince dying. They shout to me of an Egypt wounded to the heart.*

"I have got no further in my guesses than you," he put in, "but I believe I must keep this knowledge secret until Atum wills its exposure. It makes me nervous, Ishat. In fact, even before Heqareshu arrived, his coming made me anxious. All I can do is wait."

4

IT WAS A GOOD FLOOD that year, a full twenty-five cubits, the water completely covering Huy's water-steps and lapping at his gate. Although it was the season for fevers, fewer townspeople bothered to negotiate the sodden path that ran past Huy's estate, and neither he nor Ishat ventured into Hut-herib. It was Amunmose, as under steward, who went to and fro, fulfilling the necessary errands for the household. Huy put Anhur's soldiers to work, first building a small dam at the flood's edge and then digging a canal beside the house and into the garden. Seshemnefer, in his capacity as gardener, had the privilege of breaking the dam when the work was finished, and everyone on the property turned out to watch the deep ditch fill swiftly and the water run out to pool on and then sink into the thirsty soil. The soldiers rebuilt the dam, this time to keep the water in, and Seshemnefer began the task of planting date palms along the verges of the canal, to both provide fruit and prevent subsidence.

Letters began to arrive, one from Thothmes, one from Hut-herib's Mayor, Mery-neith, and one from Pharaoh's Treasurer. Ishat broke the wax seal bearing the imprint of the sedge and the bee first, unrolling the slim scroll while Huy waited. Both of them had been sprawled deep under the shade of the sycamores that clustered close to the estate's outer wall, trying without much success to escape the heat and idly watching Seshemnefer's naked, bent back as he dug small irrigation hollows around his precious young palms.

Ishat scanned the papyrus quickly. "The King has agreed to allow you to buy into his incense monopoly," she said as Huy hauled himself into a sitting position and reached for the water. "According to the Treasurer, you may either pay the gold directly into the Royal Treasury or have the amount deducted from our allowance." She wrinkled her nose. "It's a huge amount, Huy. What do you want to do?"

Huy considered. "The incense trade with Karoy is very secure," he said after a while. "Either way, we won't suffer a loss. Send a letter to the Treasurer and tell him to deduct the gold from our allowance. Also whatever tax is assessed from our profits before he sends them to us each year. What does our Mayor have to say?"

Ishat laid the royal scroll aside and took up another. "Apparently there is khato land available to the west of Hut-herib, across the tributary, in the Andjet sepat," she said presently. "He will apply to the King for ownership on your behalf if you wish, and suggests offering His Majesty four deben's worth of silver for it because it is very fertile." She frowned down on the black lettering. "It is too much to pay, Huy, considering that once you have it, you must hire an overseer and labourers for it, and buy seed. And what if the crop fails or becomes diseased? Add that cost to the price of buying into the incense caravans and we will be poor again!"

"But Ishat, you won't be here after the season of Peret," he reminded her gently. "You will be living with Thothmes at Iunu. These problems will be mine alone."

She flushed and bit her lip, glancing at him and then away. "I forgot for a moment. How could I forget? It seemed that as soon as Thothmes went home, he became like a dream in my mind. It has something to do with the aura of this place, Huy, something you exude and that fills the air around you."

Huy's hand jerked in shock, and tepid liquid from the cup he held dribbled onto his naked thigh. "You have never spoken like this before," he said, privately wondering at this new avenue of perception opening in her. She had always been able to divine his moods, but, woman-like, her interest in his influence on what surrounded him, whether people or objects, had ceased at the limit of her own participation.

She grimaced. "You see into the future without effort," she replied, still looking away, as though her own words were an embarrassment to her. "You are not bound by the passage of time like the rest of us, Huy, whether you realize it or not. Every time you touch a petitioner who asks for a reading, you enter eternity. Living with you, working beside you, is to inhabit a place where the hours slide by unremarked, and sometimes I must think hard to try to remember what day it is, even what month."

"Ishat! I make you afraid? You have become afraid of me?" He was appalled.

"No!" Swiftly, she gripped his knee. "When we were almost destitute and living in that tiny house, and you had to haul water for us from the river every day and we fell onto our cots each night exhausted from tramping all over Hut-herib as you answered every plea for help, and I was trying to prepare food for us, and desperate to find some way of easing the terrible pain in your head—then, in spite of your gift, we were just two peasants struggling to survive. There was no time for an awareness of anything but the needs of the next moment." Her nails were digging into him, the tendons of her wrist standing out under the brown skin. She was bending forward, the scrolls in her lap forgotten. "But it's different now. There is poppy for your pain, oil for our bodies, good food set out by others on our pretty tables, fine linen for our couches, and *time*, Huy, so much time, in spite of the people you still treat. Time for me to wake in the night and know myself held in a place of such stillness, such otherness, that I can imagine neither birth nor death. Time to taste the air around us in idleness and find it ... foreign." She swallowed. "I see myself snared in it so that I will not age, the power of my love for you will not diminish but go on tormenting me, and in the end any reality outside your presence will not exist. That is what I fear."

"Oh, my dearest sister." Huy pulled her hand from his knee and held it loosely. The tension in her fingers did not relax. "These are nothing but foolish fantasies! Our whole life changed when the King moved to lift us out of the mud, and since then we have been faced with so many new faces, new challenges that have taken away the soil on which we used to plant our feet and put a very different ground under us. In spite of the luxuries we enjoy, there is still a strangeness to it all. We are still adjusting."

She shook her head vigorously. "It's more than that. I have the oddest feeling that you will not show your age, that the god will keep your body suspended in the aura of which I spoke until he has no further use for you." She withdrew her hand. "I've told you before that I want to be loved, to enjoy a husband and children, to have a life where change is possible. To be chained to you by my unanswered desire is to be chained to your changelessness forever."

Huy studied her face. Her words were insane, surely a wild justification for leaving him, a goad she had fabricated to use on herself so that she would be forced to tear herself away from him. *I am tired of this guilt, my Ishat, and tired of my own selfishness in this matter.*

For a long time neither of them spoke. Seshemnefer's labours had taken him farther away. Huy could no longer see him. One of the soldiers appeared, walking briskly along the path leading from the servants' quarters to the rear entrance of the house. He bowed to Huy as he passed. A *change of shift*, Huy thought. A sudden gust of burning air brought the fleeting aroma of roasting goose to his nostrils from the unseen kitchen. He gestured, and heard Amunmose scramble to his feet somewhere behind him. The young man approached, yawning, his sandals dangling from one hand.

"Bring beer, and a cup for yourself as well," Huy ordered. He turned to Ishat, who had clasped her hands around her calves and was gazing into the blinding dazzle of the afternoon. "I can see that you believe what you say. I do understand, Ishat. Shall we hear what Thothmes has dictated?"

She sighed, nodded, and reached for the third scroll. "More good news," she said after a moment. "Thothmes has talked to his sister's husband, and he would be glad of your gold. He will plant more poppy fields this Tybi and so must hire many labourers and soldiers."

"I presume that you are referring to Anuket's husband, Amunnefer," Huy broke in. "Why would he need to put soldiers in the fields, I wonder?"

"That's obvious," Ishat said tartly, and Huy was relieved to see that her disturbingly reflective mood had fled. "To prevent the peasants from stealing the young plants for their own gardens, and the city dwellers of Weset from planting them on their roofs. At least, I presume so. We don't know anything about poppy cultivation, do we, Huy?"

"Only that the sale of the drug will bring me a good return. I must discuss the matter with Amunnefer when we go south for your wedding. Does Thothmes say anything else?"

"Not really. Amunnefer will take as much gold as you can offer him as soon as possible, and he will have papyrus for you to read

and sign when he sees you. Thothmes sends both of us his love."
She looked up. "Gold for the poppy, for the khato land, and for
the incense caravans," she said, tapping Thothmes' scroll against
her palm. "How will you manage it all, Huy? We don't know
anything about how such agreements are concluded. Perhaps you
should ask your uncle?"

"No. I want no favours from Ker," Huy snapped. "He abandoned me when Methen brought me home from the House of the
Dead. He was too cowardly to come near me when he thought I
was possessed by a demon, and even after an exorcism was proved
unnecessary he shunned me and removed his support at the
school! Surely you remember how it was, Ishat."

"Of course I remember. Only your mother and I would come
close to you. I used to climb in your bedroom window at night."
She grinned across at Huy. "I was fascinated by the gruesome
wound on your skull, and I did think I might see your eyes turn
red with evil." She sobered. "But seriously, Huy, can you rely on
Merenra to help you?"

"He's a good steward, and if he doesn't know how to conduct
this business, I can always go to the Mayor."

"Thothmes would help you."

"Thothmes has done enough. Here comes Amunmose with
beer. Let's hurry up and drink it in case I can't afford to have
Khnit make any more!"

Later, in the relative cool of the evening, Huy dictated letters
of acceptance to the Royal Treasurer, to Mayor Mery-neith, and
to Amunnefer, through Thothmes. Merenra had told Huy tact-
fully that the offer of a deposit of gold would be considered
appropriate for all but the khato land, and Huy had instructed
him to send an adequate amount south in the company of a
couple of Anhur's soldiers. Lying sleepless on his couch that
night, staring up at the stars painted on his ceiling, he felt a rush

of pride mingled with apprehension. *I shall be far richer in the end than my uncle the perfume grower. In the end. After I have paid for my land. If the poppy harvest is good. If the incense caravans come through unscathed. I must go over the household accounts very carefully with Merenra.*

Then another realization brought him upright, his breath coming fast in the stultifying air. Ishat would be gone as soon as the flood receded. He would need a new scribe. The idea was horrifying. Even a steward was not as close to his master as a scribe. Scribes became so intimate with their employers that no secrets existed between them. *How can I make someone new understand my dealings with the god, the sometimes urgent necessities of my work for Atum, the often illogical, even frightening pronouncements that move through me to the petitioner and must be not only recorded but discussed with me afterwards in private, as Ishat helps me to dissect them to their meanings, their roots? How can I possibly trust these things, let alone my own needs, the cries of my own ka, to anyone other than Ishat? And I must choose a new scribe soon. He must be fully trained before Ishat and I go south for her marriage. He. Ishat is the only female scribe I have ever seen, and she became one because I taught her to read and write myself. This house will be full of men. Ishat's body servant Iput will go with her to Iunu. No coloured linens floating half glimpsed along the passages, no smell of sweet perfume heated by a woman's gleaming skin, no bursts of female laughter, no wealth of rich black hair falling into the small of a naked back as I am preceded into the dining hall. Ishat, have you considered these things yourself? Are you fully aware of what you will be taking away from me?*

He left the couch and, wrapping a sheet around his waist, opened his shrine to Ra, god of the temple where he had spent so many years as a student, and taking up his censer, he lit the charcoal from the lamp beside his bed. When it was ashy, he sprinkled frankincense on it, and the light yet pungent smoke immediately began to fill the room. Kneeling, holding the censer carefully, he suddenly knew that he had no prayer for the god. He could not ask to keep Ishat. To do so would be so utterly self-serving that the god's feathered ears would close. Yet there was nothing else he wished to say; not even a request for a good replacement. *If I cannot keep Ishat*, he vowed as he capped the incense holder and closed the doors of the shrine, *then I don't want anyone. I shall write every letter, keep every account, myself.*

Making his way quietly along the dim passage, he stepped over the low sill at its end and went to stand in the middle of the flat roof. The moon was at the half. The Sopdet star hung like a chip of white fire above the dusky line of drowned growth dotting the flood, reflected in a marching succession of wind-stirred wavelets. *Atum*, Huy said silently, *I know that I am your tool, yet I am more than that. If you love Egypt, if you love me at all, then help me.* At that, his thoughts dried up. Folding his arms about himself in a gesture of self-protection, he sank onto the gritty surface of the roof, leaned his back against the sturdy arc of the wind catcher, and fell into a doze.

IT TOOK HUY ANOTHER MONTH to decide to at least go into Hut-herib's marketplace and talk to the scribes who congregated there, waiting for business from the citizens who needed to send letters they were unable to write themselves. Such men were usually less well educated than their fellows who had obtained good positions in various households, and eked out a precarious living. Huy, watching how often Ishat sent for her palette to take down lists of supplies, inventory tallies for the coming planting season, weekly shift changes for Anhur, as well as his own directions or predictions for the people shepherded through his gate, came to the conclusion that, if he was not to drown in ink and papyrus himself, he must replace Ishat. He did not discuss the matter with her. It did occur to him that she might be more capable than himself of choosing someone suitable for the task, but, perversely, he did not wish to involve her. It was petty of him, he knew, but he told himself that the necessity of a replacement for her services ought to have crossed her mind. If it had, she had kept quiet about it. Watching her bent head as she worked over her palette at his knee, as she smiled at him before she raised her wine cup to her mouth at dinner, encountering her, tousled and sleepy-eyed, as she wandered along the upstairs passage on her way to the bathhouse in the mornings, he forced himself to imagine the house, the garden, without her.

As soon as the flood had receded at the beginning of Peret, they had spent every evening on the river, leaning side by side on the deck rail of Huy's little barge to watch the view along the shore turn rosy and then scarlet before dusk had them turning around to glide to the watersteps, where Merenra with a lit torch would be waiting for them. *Who will stand at my elbow exuding the scent of myrrh and cassia and henna flowers, and chatter about herons' nests glimpsed in the reeds or the water dripping from the muzzles of tired oxen, their daily work in the fields now over? Who will take my arm as we walk from the watersteps to the welcoming aroma of hot food waiting for us in our own dining hall? Not a scribe or a servant,* Huy thought repeatedly in a despair close to panic. *Only a wife or a friend, Ishat. I can have no wife, and what friend exists as close to me as you? Thothmes, perhaps, but his life as Assistant Governor under his father at Iunu keeps him far away from me, and soon you will be joining him, my two dearest companions loving each other while I am left here alone.*

He waited, irresolute, until the beginning of the month of Paophi, a time when the heat always became a burden so familiar that he almost ceased to be aware of the constant discomfort. In two weeks the Amun-feast of Hapi, god of the river, would lift Egyptians from their lassitude. The orgy of thanksgiving to Hapi for his promised gift of fecundity would continue until the twelfth day of the following month, Athyr. Few letters would be dictated, and Huy decided that he did not want to wait until the festival ended. A new scribe would need to be trained. Between Athyr and Tybi there was only the month of Khoiak, and then Ishat would be gone.

Grimly, Huy ordered out his litter, four sturdy soldiers to bear both him and the heat, and Anhur to guard him. He had instructed Merenra to tell Ishat when she emerged from her massage that he had gone into the town on a personal matter. Merenra had raised his carefully plucked eyebrows but had not questioned Huy. The early morning was already stale. Dawn had brought its usual brief whisper of wind without coolness that had died almost at once, and Huy felt his clean, starched kilt beginning to wilt as he strode towards his waiting men. Anhur greeted him with a nod.

"We are going into the central marketplace," Huy told him as he bent and pushed the curtains aside. "Your men can walk on the edge of the flood if they like. It's a long way, and the water will be cool on their ankles." As he felt himself lifted at Anhur's command, his hand went to the sa amulet on its gold chain around his neck. The metal was oddly cool, feeding the reassurance of its protection into his fingers, and all at once the Rekhet's face came clearly into his mind, the leathery skin wrinkled, the eyes sharply alert and friendly. The old exorcist had made the sa for him herself, as she had made the rings he wore: the Soul Amulet intended to prevent any unnatural separation of body from ka until the time of his Beautification, the frog amulet, symbol of resurrection. He had not written to her in a long time, yet she was one of the few people who understood and accepted his uniqueness as Twice Born without question.

What would she say to me now? he wondered as he heard the feet of his bearers begin to splash in the water. *Would she tell me that it is necessary for Ishat to go so that I may be more open to the demands of Atum? I wish that she was beside me, the cowrie shells that festoon her clacking as she talked to me. She would make the choice for me, pick someone who will not bring the Khatyu into my house.* At the thought of Ra's legion of demons, he sighed. "They cannot touch you," she had said. "You are immune by Atum's will, and Ra himself honours you because you have bowed before the sacred Ished Tree."

Anhur had begun a conversation with one of his soldiers. Behind the drapery of the litter, Huy could not make out the words, but the timbre of Anhur's deep voice was comforting. *The Ished Tree,* Huy thought, his thumb running absently over the surfaces of his rings. *I stumbled upon it first when I was still a child, fleeing from discovery in the temple because I had sneaked into forbidden places, and I was caught. The High Priest had me purified, then took me back into its presence. In answer to my childish question, he told me that the Ished was the Tree of Life, holding within itself the full knowledge of the mysteries of good and evil. I read half the Book of Thoth under those fragrant branches.*

Suddenly a desire to be back there in the temple school seized Huy—to be sitting cross-legged on the floor of the cell he shared with Thothmes, in the evening lamplight, a sennet board between them, the sound of the stragglers returning to their cells after a game of stickball in the dusky compound; lessons prepared for the following day, a faint whiff of incense reaching him from the temple's inner court, where Ra was enjoying the nightly ablutions and offerings; and, best of all, the promise of a few days' holiday spent in the luxury and security of Nakht's house. *Henenu, I need your guidance now,* he said silently to the Rekhet, using the secret name known only to those she trusted so that the demons could not appropriate it to her harm. *And yours also, Ramose, kindest and most ruthless taskmaster of my fate. I wrenched it from you, yet you still care for me. Would I indeed have been happier if I had stayed in the temple instead of running back to Hut-herib and ending up in that hovel with Ishat? Ishat!* Sweat had begun to trickle down his face. Impatiently, he pulled the curtains open, but the air held only an illusion of coolness.

The marketplace was crowded and noisy. Huy ordered the bearers to set him down on the edge of the dusty expanse, told them to go to the nearest beer house and refresh themselves, and he and a watchful Anhur walked into the confusion of shouting stall keepers, haggling buyers, and naked, dusty children. Huy looked about. The scribes for hire usually gathered together under the few scraggly acacia bushes, talking idly to one another or playing knucklebones while they waited for customers, and today was no exception. Huy saw them beyond the cheerful melee around him. A few of them were already employed, their customers squatting beside them as they wrote, but most of them sat staring impassively at the scene before them. Huy scanned them swiftly, wondering which of them had been hired by his father to take down the infrequent scrolls Hapu had been able to afford to send to his son, away at school. Those letters had been delicately inscribed. *But the matter of a permanent scribe, someone to be trusted, is another question entirely,* he thought anxiously. *Will I be able to make a judgment simply by looking into a man's face, his eyes? Anubis, it is your voice I hear most often when the god speaks to me. I hear his directions in your harsh animal tones. Guide me now, I beg you, for I am soon to be lost, without rudder to steer me or anchor to hold me firm.*

"They're a scruffy-looking lot, Huy," Anhur commented. "You didn't say so, but I presume you're trying to find a replacement for the Lady Ishat. Why don't you ask the Mayor for help? Or even the Governor?"

Huy turned to him. "Because I must have a scribe who owes his allegiance to me alone," he said heavily. "Most of my staff were hired for me by Mery-neith. Are any of them spies for him or for the Governor? Or for Pharaoh himself?"

Anhur cocked an eye at him. "One or two of them, perhaps. What else would you expect? Pharaoh is your patron. His gold supports you, me, all of us on your estate. It's only natural that he should want to make sure he's not wasting the Royal Treasury." He waved dismissively at the quiet group ahead. "Choose from them? Well, how? Take hold of them one at a time and expect the god to show you what to do?" He shook his leather-clad head vigorously to forestall Huy's furious response. "I do not disrespect the god or your gift! I point out that you mustn't be tempted to make a decision in that way and risk the god's displeasure."

"I was not so tempted!" Huy hissed. "And don't tell me what I must or must not do! I know more of the god's mind than you!"

Anhur was not upset. He merely shrugged and hefted his sword belt. "I speak my mind, Huy. You know my affection for you. I warmed to you when we were both stranded at Thoth's temple while you pored over that Book, and I had to protect you when your old classmate wanted to give you a punch on the jaw. Now, can we at least get out of the sun?"

Huy was laughing. "Sennefer, the boy who sent me plunging into Ra's public lake with his throwing stick. Well, let us approach these scribes and see what we can find."

Several pairs of expectant eyes swivelled towards them as they approached the group. There was a stir. Palettes were lifted. The men would not cry their proficiency as common stall keepers shouted their wares, Huy knew. Their status forbade it. But the anxious straightening of their spines, the tense, almost imperceptible inclination of their bodies to meet him, was a silent plea. Only one of them seemed indifferent. He was sitting apart from the others, his palette still on the ground beside his hip. He had glanced at Huy and Anhur and then away, his face unreadable within a large piece of coarse linen that shaded his features and neck. The hem of his long, thick shirt had been lifted and laid across his knees, held in place by his folded arms, and he was slumped forward, hands loosely drooping. Huy was intrigued by the very impassiveness of his attitude.

Ignoring the group, he made his way to the thin sliver of shadow in which the man sat, glancing at the palette as he came to a halt. It was resting on a rectangle of linen much cleaner than the man's stained and smudged clothes. A clay bowl in which another small scrap of linen floated sat beside it, and at once Huy knew that the water was both for wiping the constantly accumulating dust from the surface of the palette and for mixing ink, should it be required. *A good scribe takes care of the tools of his trade*, he thought approvingly. *This man may be poor, but he values the dignity of his calling.* He waited, but the head did not move. At last, annoyed, he said, "Scribe, are you for hire, or have you written so many letters today that you are too tired to even acknowledge yet another customer?"

The man stirred but still did not look up. "I am sure that you will be better served by one of my fellows, over there," the scribe said, gesturing slightly in the direction of the others. "Few patrons trust their words to a woman." The voice was cool, polite, and definitely female.

Huy stepped backward in surprise. Anhur grunted.

"On the contrary, my present scribe is a woman," Huy said. "May I speak with you?"

Now the chin rose, and Huy found himself staring down at a small brown face and two dark, alert eyes without a trace of kohl. The short nose was slightly uptilted, giving the girl—for this was no mature woman—an air of arrogance Huy doubted. Arrogance would not have caused the long fingers to clench suddenly in what was surely apprehension before being deliberately uncurled. He waited while the eyes flicked over him and then moved on to briefly scan Anhur.

"If you already have a scribe in your household, then you are not here to dictate, unless she is ill," the self-possessed voice pointed out. "And even so, a man of your station does not come into the market in person." Both hands rose, pulling the linen more firmly around her cheeks so that her face was hidden. "I am occasionally mistaken for a whore," she went on, and now Huy heard hesitancy in the low tones. Her accent held none of the harshness of a peasant's cadence, nor did it hold the cultured softness of the nobility and their servants. It was as anonymous, Huy decided, as the faceless thousands who inhabited the region in between. "If you have come looking for such a service, I must disappoint you. If you have no work for me, please let me alone so that I might be available to someone else."

Huy was tempted to laugh. Only the most desperate man could possibly lust after this ragged creature with her thick, voluminous linens and unpainted features. But as he looked down on her, the impulse died. There was a certain rather touching vulnerability beneath the defiant words that made him warm to her.

"Perhaps I do require a dictation taken," he said, squatting beside her. "Perhaps I want to see just how good a scribe you are."

For answer, she lifted her palette and, setting it across her knees, laid a hand protectively over it. From what Huy could see, it was very plain but for two long grooves intended to hold her brushes, one in use and one spare, and the hollow for an ink pot.

But the wood was highly polished and the palette well made, the edges sharp and true, the small drawers under the writing surface fitting perfectly into the whole.

"Forgive me, but I would like a small payment first as evidence of your good faith," she replied. "Otherwise I may not be able to fill my belly tonight." She glanced at him sideways, then froze. Huy saw her eyes narrow. "I think I know who you are." She swallowed, and the fingers lying on her palette trembled. "You are the Seer Huy son of Hapu, aren't you? What do you want of me?" There was real fear in her voice. Her gaze went from Huy to Anhur's intimidating bulk beside him.

"I want you to take a dictation before I and my captain fry in this heat." Opening the pouch on his belt, Huy drew out a piece of gold. "Now, will you prepare your papyrus or not?"

The girl shook her head and the loose linen hood fell back, revealing a short cap of dusty, dark brown hair swept behind two tiny ears. "Master, unless you intend to dictate to me for the rest of the day, you are paying too much," she pointed out warily. "And if you are simply dispensing charity, I do not need it."

Anhur, who had begun to shuffle his feet and breathe increasingly heavily, burst out, "Oh, for Thoth's sake take the gold and do what the Master demands, you stupid girl! Unless, of course, you have chests full of it in whatever slum you inhabit and you simply sit here because you enjoy burning with thirst. As I am," he finished irritably.

The girl gave him a level stare, then she nodded, took the gold, and, opening one of the drawers in her palette, removed a sheet of papyrus and a well-worn burnisher before putting the piece of glinting metal inside. Huy sank off his heels onto the ground and watched her deft movements as she briskly scraped the papyrus smooth, got out her ink and expertly added water, mixed the black powder, set the pot in its cavity on the palette, and, pulling open another long drawer, retrieved two brushes. Both had seen better days. Her lips moved in the traditional prayer to Thoth, god of the written word—dry lips, Huy noted, as dry and rough as the skin of the fingers that had touched his as she took the gold.

"I am ready," she said.

"Begin. 'The tribute of the chiefs of Rethennu: the daughter of a chief with ornaments of purple gold, lapis lazuli of this country, 30 slaves belonging to her; 65 male and female slaves of his tribute; 103 horses; 5 chariots wrought with gold, with axles of gold, 5 chariots wrought with electrum, total 10; 45 bullocks and calves; 749 bulls; 5,703 small cattle; flat dishes of gold, which could not be weighed; flat dishes of silver and fragments making 104 deben, 5 kidet; a gold horn inlaid with lapis lazuli; a bronze corselet inlaid with gold; 823 jars of incense; 1,718 jars of honeyed wine; much two-coloured ivory, carob wood, mery wood, many bundles of firewood, all the luxuries of this country gathered to every place of His Majesty's circuit, where the tent was pitched.'" He had deliberately recited quickly, watching the girl, alert for any hesitation, but she wrote steadily, pausing only to dip her brush swiftly into the ink before continuing. "Now take another sheet of papyrus and copy in formal hieroglyphs what you have written in hieratic," he ordered.

Calmly she did so, her nervousness gone, her attention fully absorbed by the work. Only once did she stop, and then it was to wipe the sweat from her palms onto her shirt. When she had finished, Huy held out a hand and she passed the sheets to him. He scanned them carefully. Her writing was a trifle cramped and untidy, in order to conserve papyrus, Huy surmised, but her spelling was faultless and she had not dropped one word or figure. "Do you know what you have just inscribed?" he asked, testing her.

She grimaced. "No, Master," she said hesitantly. "You did not tell me to be aware of the meaning. A scribe does not consider the meaning unless asked to do so."

"Very good. Read now and then tell me what I said."

Her head went down over the paper, one finger straying to a strand of hair that had crept across her temple. Absently she pushed it back behind her ear and her palm remained pressed there, an unconscious and well-worn habit, Huy supposed. When she had finished and he had removed the work, she clasped her hands together and closed her eyes, reciting haltingly the list he had quoted. Halfway through it, she stopped. Her shoulders rose towards her ears and stayed there.

"I am sorry, but I can remember no more," she told him. "No one has requested such a thing since I was at school. The townspeople who come to me only want their letters written or other letters read to them." Slowly her shoulders relaxed. "I know that memorizing is a skill a master or mistress would require. I have neither."

Huy looked up at a resigned Anhur. "Tell her what I quoted."

"It's a list of tribute Osiris Thothmes the Third collected in year twenty-four of his reign during his second campaign in Rethennu and beyond," he replied promptly. "It's incised into one of his great monuments. Your friend Assistant Governor Thothmes would have been able to recite it all, Master, and more besides. He is a fervent admirer of our present pharaoh's father."

Huy smiled. "So he is. We are almost ready to leave, Anhur, and I'm sure I am quite safe here. Go and find my litter-bearers."

Anhur bowed. "Good!" he said, and strode away.

Huy turned back to the girl. "What is your name?"

"Thothhotep." She said it loudly.

"Thothhotep? But that's a man's name. Did the priests choose it for you?"

"No. Only the rich can afford to pay for a name that is chosen by the totem of one's town." She flushed, the colour creeping faintly under the sun-darkened skin of her neck. "My father had wanted a son. I am his fourth daughter. He named me."

"And did he send you to school? Where did you study? Where are you from?"

"My father is a sailor and shipbuilder in Nekheb, far to the south, beyond Weset. Nekheb has always been known for its fine ships," she said defensively, and Huy made a brusque gesture.

"I know much about the history of your town, and its totem the goddess Nekhbet, the Lady of Dread who sits above Pharaoh's forehead with the Lady of Flame. I am hot and dry and uncomfortable, perched here in the dirt. Please be brief." It was another test, but she was not aware that he was trying to force an equally irritable and certainly unprofessional outburst from her.

"One of my cousins does duty in Nekhbet's temple, as a scribe," she explained diffidently. "His father, my mother's brother, being Assistant Overseer of His Majesty's Docks, was able to send him to the temple school. He is literate. He insisted that I take lessons from him. He said that because I am the fourth daughter, my chances of making a good marriage will be slim and I needed a trade." She gave Huy an apologetic smile. "I did not want to study with him, but he pressed my father for permission to teach me, and Father did not object. I don't think he cared very much, seeing that my sex at my birth had disappointed him." She began to tidy away her utensils, swirling her brushes in the basin of water beside her, tipping the remaining ink into the sandy grass and wiping out the pot, putting everything away in the drawers as she spoke. "My cousin wanted a marriage contract with me when I turned fifteen, last Khoiak. My father agreed to it, but I did not. I ran away to Weset and sat in one of the marketplaces there, but too many scribes much more proficient than I were plying their brushes, and besides, my father found me and tried to make me go home. He is a good man, and did not beat me for running away." Setting her palette back on its square of cloth, she draped her shirt over her knees once more, her eyes straying past Huy to the noisy crowds milling about the stalls. "When he saw that I was making an attempt to earn my own living, he gave me his blessing, with some relief, I think, and left me. Since then I have worked in every town between here and Weset. I earn enough for papyrus and food," she finished almost harshly, *as though,* Huy mused, *I might accuse her of something.* "Now, if I have acquitted myself to your satisfaction, Master, do you require anything else from me?"

Huy stood up. It seemed to him that he had made his decision before he had heard her voice or known her sex. Out of the corner of his eye he saw Anhur and his soldiers approaching, carrying the litter.

"I want you to serve in my household as my personal scribe," he said. "My own scribe is leaving me in two months. That will be enough time for her to train you, and for me to confirm your suitability. No other tasks will be required of you," he added, seeing the question forming on her mouth as she swung towards him, startled. "Your needs will be met, and I promise not to turn you into a toad or a lizard if you displease me."

His lame attempt at humour did not amuse her. She stared up at him, her features still. "You are not making sport with me, are you," she said. It was a statement, not a question.

Huy shook his head.

"Then why are you not seeking recommendations for a more accomplished person from among your friends? Why me? I am in many ways an ignorant girl."

The litter had been lowered behind him and the men stood waiting with obvious impatience. *There is no point in beginning this partnership with a lie,* Huy told himself. *I must presume that she knows how vulnerable an employer can be, how important it is to earn his trust.*

"My scribe is also my oldest friend," he said. "I have only two friends, Thothhotep, she and the son of the Governor of the Heq-at sepat. The two of them are to marry. They are the only people I trust completely. My household mostly consists of servants chosen for me by our Mayor." Deliberately, he waited to see whether or not her perception was as acute as her writing skill.

"And it is the King who provides for Egypt's Great Seer," she said slowly. "I believe I understand. Shall I be able to trust you, Master, as you hope you may trust me?"

"Yes. Anhur, captain of my guards, will come for you with a litter tomorrow morning."

"If I am not happy in your house, you will let me go?"

"Of course." Huy felt suddenly exhausted. "This is Egypt, not some barbarous country. If you agree to serve me, be ready here, in this spot, with whatever possessions you wish to bring." He turned on his heel and, taking the few steps to the litter, got into it and drew the curtains closed. *It's done,* he thought dully. *I had no choice, Ishat. I did not intend to hire a woman, much less a girl, but somehow it has happened. You will surely see my necessity, but will you accept it?* He was too thirsty to doze on the long walk home.

Ishat was waiting for him, pacing the reception hall. He could hear the slap of her sandals as he paused in the passage to draw water from the large urn kept freshly filled each day by Seshemnefer. Drinking deeply, he went through into the relative coolness of the room. At once she ran to him, taking his arms and searching his face. "Where have you been?" she demanded sharply. "I've been so worried, Huy. Merenra wouldn't tell me anything. Look at you, covered in sweat and your feet filthy with dust! You gave a reading to someone without me!"

"No." He pulled himself out of her grasp and, going to a chair, he sat, unlacing his sandals and placing the soles of his feet on the tiles of the floor with great relief. "I'm sweaty and dusty because I had Anhur take me into the marketplace. The heat there was unbearable."

"You had to go in person to buy something?"

"No. For Set's sake, come and sit down, Ishat."

"You swear by the god of chaos. Now I know that something is wrong." Tugging one of the pretty cedar and ivory chairs close to him, she perched on its edge and leaned towards him. "The King has withdrawn his support, hasn't he? I knew it! Buying into the incense caravans was a dangerous idea. Who told you? What did Mery-neith have to say?"

She had voiced her greatest fear, and Huy, looking into her contorted face, felt a rush of love for her. Reaching across, he ran a hand down her cheek. "It's nothing like that, my Ishat. If I had received word from Mennofer, you would have known about it. I went into the town to hire a new scribe."

For a moment she stared at him, blinking, obviously puzzled. "A new scribe? Whatever for? Do you think you need two of us?" Then her expression changed and, sitting back, she covered her face with both hands. "Oh gods, Huy, of course you need a new scribe. *Will* need one. I'll be gone. I should have thought about it myself, talked to you about it, offered to select someone suitable myself. I'm so sorry." Her hands fell into her scarlet lap. "But why the marketplace? Why not apply to Mery-neith? As Mayor he would know of many suitable men."

"You know why. I had to choose someone entirely uncon-nected to any noble household."

"Oh, of course," she said again. "How stupid of me. But it makes me sad to think of someone else sitting on the floor at your knee, sharing your thoughts and decisions." She laughed self-consciously.

"I'm a little jealous. How hard you worked to teach me the mystery and beauty of the written word, and how hard I worked to learn! Now it is all wasted. I suppose you want me to train him."

With alarm, Huy saw that the full import of his need was at last overtaking her. Her fingers had wound around each other and she was smiling, grimacing, in an effort to control an impulse to cry.

"Train *her*, Ishat. I have hired a woman."

There was a moment of shocked silence, then her eyes narrowed. The action forced two tears to dribble down her cheeks. Slowly she wiped them away with her knuckles like a wounded child. "A woman," she said with difficulty. "Why a woman, Huy? How is it that in a profession made up almost entirely of men you managed to go out and in a few hours find yourself a woman? Are you trying to replace me in every way?" Her mouth twisted. "Or perhaps the god sent you a vision in the night, a message of absolution from your impotence, and you went seeking a bedmate." She sprang from the chair and, hands on hips, began to stride back and forth across the floor in front of him.

He was relieved. He was used to handling an angry Ishat. Her fire was familiar. Her tears were another matter entirely. "Don't be ridiculous!" he said curtly. "If such a wonder had come to me, I should have rushed straight into your bedchamber and shaken you awake and poured it into your ears! We've known each other all our lives, Ishat. No one is closer to me than you. Even Thothmes doesn't know things about me that you do!" *Please don't use your own pain to hurt me*, he begged her silently. *My impotence is a raw, constant wound, and you know it.* "I went into the market intending to hire the best independent scribe I could find. I was drawn almost at once to this girl."

"Girl? First it was a woman. Now it's a girl." She threw up her hands. "And what exactly drew you to this ... girl?"

"I don't know. Her indifference, I think." He was trying to remain calm, to keep her calm.

"How old is she?"

"About fifteen, I think."

"You think! You *think!* Gods, Huy, you intend to place your whole life, all the complexities of your gift, your business dealings, your very character, into the hands of a fifteen-year-old stranger?"

"No. By the time I take you south for your marriage, you will have completed her training and you will tell me honestly, Ishat, *honestly*, whether or not she will be adequate. I cannot hope to replace you, my dearest one." He got up and, pulling her tight, he held her rigid, furious body. "But you know I cannot function without a scribe, and there is too much work for me to do myself."

"I hate her already." Her voice came muffled against the hollow of his shoulder, and above her head, unseen, Huy began to smile. It was going to be all right. "She will be some silly, wide-eyed child who will fall in love with you at once," Ishat went on waspishly, "and she will end up worshipping you and your gift so utterly that she will be of no use whatsoever. How will she ever learn to give you advice as I do, let alone take a faultless dictation!" She lifted her head and looked up into his face. "How did she do at that, anyway?"

"Passably well." Huy let her go. "I don't expect you to like her, Ishat. Just try to prepare her for her work. I'm not trying to make a new friend. I shall still have Anhur to talk to when I get lonely."

She stood back, smoothing down her ribboned braids and canting her head so that she could begin to unscrew her earrings. "I'm going to my couch for the afternoon. When may I expect this pupil?"

"I'll send Anhur for her in the morning. I'm sorry, Ishat. I should have taken you with me today."

"But you were afraid that I might make a scene." She was already in the doorway. "We are both sorry, Huy. Every decision we have made lately has been a compromise. I hate Atum for what he has done to you. I have hated him for a long time, almost as much as I have hated the bitch who broke your heart. Rest well."

Her last words came floating from the passage. Before following her towards the stairs and his own bedchamber, Huy stood for a moment, listening to the silence of the house. *Anuket*, he thought. *In two months I shall see you again, for surely you will come to Thothmes' wedding feast.* Her tiny, delicate face swam into focus in his mind. Brutally he dismissed it, mounting the stairs and greeting a drowsy Tetiankh, who was waiting to wash him before seeking his own pallet. *I must decide on a wedding gift for Ishat,* Huy thought as he pulled the sheet up over his shoulder and closed his eyes. *Better if I ask her what she would like. Perhaps this evening, in the garden. I sometimes hate Atum also, my Ishat, and that is permissible as long as I am obedient to him. Soon the petitioners will line up again at my gate. This respite won't last. Thothhotep—Ishat will laugh at the name. I hope that Thothhotep has a great deal of courage. She is going to need it all.*

5

BY THE TIME the litter bearing Thothhotep approached the house, Ishat and Huy were standing together in the shadows cast by the entrance pillars to welcome the girl. *Or perhaps to let her know her place immediately,* Huy thought to himself, enveloped in a miasma of Ishat's perfume. Ishat was wearing the scarlet, gold-trimmed sheath and the thick gold circlet with its large jasper resting on her forehead. The smaller ones around the rim nestled in her hair. She had removed from the circlet the net of golden threads meant to imprison her tresses. Her earlobes were heavy with electrum earrings fashioned in the likeness of Hathor's face. Rings sat on every one of her capable fingers, and silver bracelets tinkled on her wrists at her slightest movement. Huy had not been able to repress a smile when he had seen her sweep down the stairs to greet him before they took up their station, and her chin had risen. "I have not arrayed myself like this because your new scribe is a person of importance," she had said. "But if I am to train her, she must understand my superior position from the start. Besides," she had finished in true Ishat fashion, "if I feel in any way inferior to her, I shall be tempted to treat her sternly." She had grinned back at him, her carefully hennaed mouth curving upward, her kohled eyes sparkling.

"You have always somehow managed to make your honesty either a stick to beat me with or an unguent to soothe me," Huy had retorted. "You look wonderful. You would awe even Pharaoh himself this morning."

She had nodded. "Thank you, Huy. But perhaps the gold circlet is a little too overpowering just to impress the daughter of a sailor."

So that was it, Huy thought again. *The daughter of a sailor is less lower-class than the daughter of a peasant who labours in the fields. I understand. I share your roots, Ishat, but my gift has compensated me for them. Thothmes has not yet been able to lift you above your own lingering sense of inferiority.* For answer he had pulled a strand of her hair free of her earring and watched it settle against her cheek. "Your ability alone is enough to impress anyone," he had said.

Now the litter was approaching, and at a word from Anhur it was set down. The curtains had obviously remained tied back. The form inside seemed smaller, slighter than Huy remembered, hidden as it had been by loose linens. A foot appeared, shod in a worn reed sandal, then a head capped by short, gleaming black hair. Thothhotep stepped forward and bowed. With a shock Huy saw that she was taller than the delicate hands and narrow shoulders of the day before had indicated, as tall as Ishat, and slender to the point of emaciation under a stained sheath with a tattered hem.

"Gods, Huy, is she going to collapse and die on our doorstep?" Ishat murmured as the girl straightened, her eyes flicking nervously between them. She was clutching a small linen bag to her chest. In the moment before Huy spoke, he heard Ishat sigh, a sound of both compassion and exasperation. *Good,* he thought. *Ishat's pity always takes a practical form.*

"Welcome to our home, Thothhotep," he said. "There is beer and food for you in the reception hall. Amunmose! Take her bag up to the guest room."

The young man emerged from behind him, smiled at the girl, and held out his hand. After some hesitation Thothhotep thrust her possessions at him. "My palette is in there," she said breathlessly.

"My name is Amunmose. I am the under steward here, and whatever is in your bag will be perfectly safe," Amunmose replied. "Incidentally, the leek soup waiting for you in the house was made especially for this occasion by Khnit, our cook, from my mother's famous recipe. It may be eaten hot or cold, and today it is cold. I accompanied the Master to Khmun some years ago when he had business in Thoth's temple. My family lives at Khmun, where my mother is well known for her kitchen skills. I—"

"Amunmose!" Ishat said sharply.

He wheeled about. "I was trying to put her at ease," he muttered as he passed between Huy and Ishat, bag in hand. "I swear, if Anhur coughed behind her, she'd faint with fright."

Huy indicated the doorway. "Come inside, out of the heat. Thank you, Anhur, I'll see you at dinner. This is my scribe and my dear friend Ishat," he went on as Thothhotep came forward. "She will be your mentor for the next two months."

Again Thothhotep bowed. "I know that I am very privileged to be here, Lady Ishat. I promise to work hard and learn from you as quickly as I can. My name is Thothhotep."

"You will indeed work hard," Ishat replied as she preceded Huy into the house. "This appears to be a most informal household, Thothhotep, but that is only because the Master's needs are varied and change from day to day. We all serve him, and he serves Atum and the King."

They had reached the reception hall. Huy, turning to show the girl to the small, low table that would become her place at meals, saw her eyes widen as she quickly scanned the large room with its costly furnishings, its tall, gracious lampstands, the dull gleam of the black and white tiled floor, before she sank onto her cushion. *Good*, he thought again. *She is awed, perhaps even overwhelmed, but she keeps it to herself.* Ishat was watching her critically as she picked up a spoon and stared down at the bowl of soup. Huy could read Ishat's mind. *She is wondering if she will have to teach Thothhotep social graces as well as a scribe's skills. As long as she is busy organizing the girl's life, she will forget that she is training her usurper.* But Thothhotep ate and drank politely, thanking Merenra when he refilled her bowl and cup and answering Ishat's abrupt questions when her mouth had emptied.

Later, she was shown the guest room, where the shrine stood open, ready for the totems of visitors. "I presume that you worship Thoth and Nekhbet," Ishat said.

Thothhotep nodded. "I do, but I have no effigies to stand guard over me," she replied. She did not add that she could not afford them, and again Huy was pleased.

"Show me your palette," Ishat demanded, and the girl opened the bag Amunmose had placed on the couch and passed the palette to her. Ishat examined it respectfully. "You have managed to care for it well," she commented.

Thothhotep flushed. "My cousin gave it to me when he thought I would agree to be betrothed to him," she told them. "I tried to return it before I left Nekheb, but he was kind enough to let me keep it."

"Otherwise you would have starved or ended up selling your body," Ishat said tartly, passing it back to her. "Doubtless he knew that. Put it on Huy's desk in the office beside mine. I'll show you where, and then you can go to the bathhouse and be bathed and oiled. Iput?" Her body servant, who had been hovering with interest by the door, came forward. "Will you mind caring for this girl until I or the Master can find a replacement for you? Thothhotep, have you any more linens in that bag of yours?"

Huy was outside talking to Seshemnefer when Ishat pulled him away. "She and Iput are in the bathhouse, getting rid of that indefinable smell of poverty we ourselves used to carry about with us when we couldn't afford enough natron to wash ourselves every day," she told him. "She owns nothing apart from her palette and the sheath she's wearing but a huge old man's shirt and an equally big kilt. She needs literally every-thing, Huy, even new brushes and a better quality of ink. Couldn't you have found a less drastic drain on Pharaoh's Treasury? Iput is a good girl and can sew well, but I wouldn't trust her to barter for sheath linen. Merenra and I will have to go to the flax merchants and then the weavers. What a bother! And she must have kohl for her eyes and at least one pair of earrings and two pairs of sandals and a belt and a lot of time-consuming care on Iput's part for her hands. After all, the servants here must represent you properly, particularly a scribe." She threw out her arms. "And I don't even know yet whether or not she can spell!"

"Do your best with her," Huy said. "I think that she will prove to be a ready pupil and will adapt to our ways. Take whatever gold you think you may need and go into the town with Merenra tomorrow. Perhaps you could lend her some of your sheaths in the meantime."

"No! No, Huy. For one thing, she's skinnier than a dry reed and nothing I have will fit her. For another ..." She pulled him to a halt and stepped to face him, lifting defiant eyes to meet his own. "For another, I am doing my best not to resent her being here. I know how necessary she will be to you, but I don't want anyone to be necessary to you but me! It is not logical, but I do not apologize. Let Iput alter her ugly shirt and kilt. I am giving her my life with you. I will not have my sheaths rubbing against her miserably dry flesh!"

So Ishat was indeed fully aware of what she was being called upon to do. Huy kissed her. Together they began to walk towards the house.

"You're right and I'm sorry," he said. "I should not have made that suggestion. Forgive my insensitivity." They had almost reached the house when all at once Huy remembered the ivory monkey toy his uncle Ker had given him on his fourth Naming Day. He had hated it from first sight, hated its mindless grin, its grasping paws that would clap together if one pulled the cord in its back, and he had grown to fear it also, for reasons he did not understand. It had seemed to him to have a malevolent sentience, to hate him in return and wish him harm. One night some years later, he had taken it into his mother's garden and, setting it on one of the rocks surrounding the pond, he had picked up a stone and pounded it into little pieces, not realizing that he was weeping as he did so, crying with the grief of his father's betrayal and his uncle's desertion after the priest Methen had carried him home from the House of the Dead and everyone but his mother and Ishat had disowned him out of fear. Ishat had come up behind him in the darkness as he was trying to scrape the remains of the monkey together. "I will dispose of the pieces, Huy. Don't worry about it. Go and wash your face and then sleep," she had said. "Your hand is bleeding." He had held her tightly then, his loyal friend, full of the pain of nostalgia for a time of simplicity that would never come again.

"The times only *seem* easier now," he said thickly aloud as the memory bloomed, bringing with it the old familiar ache of loss. "Underneath all this luxury there is still a well of uncertainty. I love you so much, Ishat." *Please don't leave me*, the words ran on silently. She took his arm, briefly laying her head against it as they entered the passage, and did not answer.

Dinner that evening was a quiet affair. Thothhotep's appetite seemed to have deserted her. She looked tired and vulnerable, hunched over her table in one of Iput's worn sheaths, and after the meal she begged to be allowed to retire to her room. Ishat, wine cup in hand, watched her go. "Iput tells me that she has been shaved and plucked, and oiled all over twice, but looking at her, there's no way to tell," she commented. "Let her sleep long and soundly, and then perhaps tomorrow she'll be ready to begin her training. I do know how she feels, Huy. I had to hide my panic when I met Thothmes officially for the first time. I broke down and cried in front of you, though, didn't I?"

Huy looked across at her affectionately. "Yes, you did, but you conquered your fear and went on to conquer him. Ishat, I would like to give you something special as a marriage gift. What would you like? A piece of jewellery? A goodly supply of your perfume? I cannot think of anything Thothmes will not be able to supply."

"I suppose I ought to ask for gold," she replied. "The gods know that my father is far too poor to offer Thothmes a dowry. Let me think." Her nose disappeared into the cup and she drank, afterwards running her tongue over her upper lip to savour the last droplets of wine clinging to her mouth, her eyes dark as she stared past him into the pleasant dimness of the room. Then she set the cup slowly back onto her table. Her hands remained clasped to its stem. "There is one thing, but you may not want to part with it."

"Just name it," Huy protested. "Everything I own apart from my protecting amulets is yours, Ishat."

"The scarab, then." She lifted her face to meet his gaze. "The scarab I found and gave to you all those years ago. It has always comforted me to know that you cherished it. I thought of it as something that bound us together. I still regard it in that way. No matter how contented I may become as Thothmes' wife, no matter how much we both may change in the future, the scarab is a symbol of the link that joins us and may never be broken. You still have it?"

"Of course! You presented it to me on a lettuce leaf while the remains of my fourth Naming Day feast lay scattered on the plates and the grass and on your tiny kilt, Ishat." *On that same day Ker and Aunt Heruben gave me the compartmented cedar box with an image of Heh, god of eternity, etched in silver into the lid,* he remembered. *Above the kneeling god with his arms outstretched and holding the notched palm ribs was my own silver name, Huy, also sunk into the fragrant wood. Hapzefa found me a piece of fresh linen and I laid the scarab on it in one of the compartments. The other boys at school envied me such a precious and unusual gift.*

"Merenra," he called, and the steward slid out of the shadows. "Go up to my room and bring me my little cedar box. It is somewhere at the bottom of one of my tiring chests." He turned back to Ishat. "You may have it gladly, dearest sister. It has delighted me, reassured me, and comforted me also through the years. You want nothing more?"

"No." She had relaxed. Her fingers left the stem of the wine cup and at once Amunmose appeared beside her, proffering the jug. She shook her head. "No more wine for me, Amunmose." He retired.

Huy and Ishat waited in silence for Merenra to return. A kind of formality had fallen between them, Huy realized—why he did not know. It seemed to carry with it an aura of solemnity, as though a ritual was about to be performed. *And so it is. In giving the scarab back to Ishat, I am closing the door on a smooth continuity of closeness and love that began almost before I could stagger naked about my mother's tiny garden and Ishat, one year younger than I, would try to crawl after me.*

Merenra returned, placing the box on Huy's table, and for a moment Huy ran his fingers over the lovely figure of the god and over the notches on the palm ribs that represented millions of years. *The future*, he said to himself. *No longer a mystery to me whenever I wish to explore it. Did Ker experience a flash of presentiment when he ordered Heh incised here?*

"The Anniversary of my Naming Day takes place this week," he said, lifting the lid and carefully extracting the scarab. "I was born on a very lucky day, the ninth of Paophi. It seems fitting that this should go to you now, Ishat. Be gentle with it." He passed it to her on its bed of linen and she took it cautiously.

"Even in the lamplight its carapace still gleams golden!" she marvelled. "Two of its legs have come off and are loose on the linen, Huy. Thank you, thank you. No matter what other gifts I may receive on the day of my marriage feast, this will always be the most prized." She struggled to her feet, holding the beetle reverently before her. "I have an empty alabaster ointment pot Iput can scour out. The scarab will be quite safe in it." She smiled at Huy and then yawned. "Good night, my Seer. I suppose we must invite your family and my parents to a feast for your Naming Day. I had completely forgotten about it. I wonder when Thothhotep was born."

"On the twenty-eighth day of Khoiak."

Ishat shot him a keen look and then laughed. "The Feast of the Procession of the Obelisk. Truly a neutral day, neither lucky nor unlucky. Well, I shall see if I may discover something about her that you don't know." Her shadow snaked through the doorway as she approached the torch set in the wall of the passage beyond, and then she was gone.

Huy shivered. The hour was late, but he did not think that weariness was sapping his khu-spirit. He felt the loss of the scarab as a minute hole in the wall of his defence against the Khatyu, the demons waiting to thwart the will of Atum and destroy him, Huy; and he wondered if the opening was large enough to allow the Sheseru, the arrows of the evil host, to get through and pierce him. *I wonder if I should find a spell of protection and write it on papyrus and soak it in beer to drink in the morning,* his thoughts ran on anxiously. Then he laughed at himself and, rising, signalled to Merenra that he could now extinguish the lamps. *I wear on my body the most powerful symbols of protection, made for me by the most powerful Rekhet in Egypt,* he told himself as he mounted the stairs. *I never take them off. May the scarab bring you safety, my Ishat, and good memories of the years that have slipped beyond the ability of even the most powerful of Seers to restore.*

The following two months, Athyr and Khoiak, passed peacefully while the flood water stood at its highest. A trickle of towns-people came to Huy for diagnosis and treatment, and on those occasions Ishat herself took down the instructions of the god as they issued from Huy's mouth, but she made sure that Thothhotep recorded them also, and meticulously scanned and criticized the girl's work. Thothhotep herself seemed to be settling well into the routines of the house. Her increasing confidence was evident in a straighter carriage and a more ready smile, but she remained quiet and self-contained, a foil for Ishat's volubility. She met Huy's parents and Heby, his brother, with correct deference when they came for Huy's Naming Day feast together with Ishat's parents and Methen, priest to Khenti-kheti, the town's totem, and Huy's good friend. She and Ishat spent every afternoon in Huy's office, Ishat dictating difficult passages from pieces of old correspondence and making the girl write hieroglyphs over and over on shards of discardable pottery until her neatness approached the standards Ishat had set for herself years before, when Huy in his turn had been teaching her.

Thothhotep was obedient and patient. Her progress was swift, but Huy had not yet wanted to ask her for her opinions of the letters that arrived from the King's Treasurer regarding Huy's request, or the confirmation of his share in the cultivation and sale of the poppy drug that came from Amunnefer, Anuket's enthusiastic husband. Occasionally Huy, passing his office door after the daytime sleep, heard Ishat's sharp voice berating the girl, but he did not interfere. Inspecting her work, he could see the improvements she was making. She had asked his permission to write to her father, to let him know what shape her new life was taking, and of course he had agreed, privately unrolling the unsealed scroll and reading it before giving it to Merenra to send south to Nekheb. Its contents were touching. "To my esteemed father, greetings," it began in Thothhotep's pretty and increasingly neat hand. "I bring you the good news that I have been hired by the Great Seer Huy son of Hapu as his apprenticed scribe. His own scribe will soon leave his employ, at which time, if blessed Nekhbet wills it, I shall take her place. I am treated with much kindness. The Seer is a man of honour, with a mild and forgiving disposition. You need no longer worry for my welfare. Embrace my sisters and mother, and greet cousin Ahmose on my behalf. Your obedient daughter Thothhotep. Signed by my own hand this thirtieth day of Athyr in year seven of the King."

Huy let it roll up and passed it to Merenra with a smile. *Mild and forgiving, am I?* he thought, amused. *It is a good thing, little Thothhotep, that you cannot yet see into the depths of my ka as Ishat does.* He had given Thothhotep a pair of gold earrings on her Naming Day, plainly fashioned in the likeness of her totem, the goddess Nekhbet, and Ishat, with perhaps more glee than was appropriate, had heated a sliver of metal and pierced the girl's lobes. Thothhotep now wore them every day with obvious pride. The sheaths Ishat had grudgingly commissioned arrived during Athyr, together with two pairs of leather sandals and a simple white leather belt. Huy, passing the open door of the guest room one early morning soon after the clothing arrived, had glanced in to see Thothhotep holding the soft linen of the new sheaths bunched against her mouth, her eyes closed, a look of sheer joy on her face.

His own treasury was dangerously depleted after the expenditures to the King, the Mayor, as the King's representative for the khato land, and Amunnefer, for the poppy fields, and Merenra had warned him that no more gold would be forthcoming from the Royal Treasury until the beginning of the season of Shemu. But Huy, temporarily content, had not cared. There was enough remaining from the last payment to take him, Ishat, and the household to Iunu for her marriage celebrations, and he had no desire to look beyond that day. Ishat had grudgingly assessed Thothhotep's ability as adequate, which meant, of course, that—barring any great professional or personal lapse—she was almost ready to be confirmed in her position. Yet Huy waited. Ishat might still change her mind, decide to stay with him; Thothmes might even now be meeting some woman by chance who would drive Ishat utterly from his mind. In his more reasonable moments Huy knew that such impulsiveness was not in his friend's nature, that Thothmes genuinely loved Ishat; but in the hot afternoons when he lay on his couch in agony following the Seeings, when the blessed drug Tetiankh brought him had not yet begun to spread its balm through his body and numb his mind, when all he wanted was Ishat's comforting hand in his, he allowed himself to believe otherwise.

Then it was the beginning of the month of Tybi and the Feast of the Coronation of Horus. Neither Huy nor Ishat had bothered much about marking the various gods' days throughout the year. For them, the feasts meant a welcome respite from Huy's work of healing and scrying. But Thothhotep asked Huy's permission to go to Horus's small shrine near the centre of the town and pray. Surprised, Huy gave her leave and ordered out the litter for her. So she was a religious girl, he mused as he stood with an annoyed

Ishat and watched the conveyance sway out of sight. "I wonder how she really regards me, then," he voiced his thought aloud. "Am I a figure of great veneration to her, a man singularly blessed by Atum, or a potential enemy of all other gods because of the power Atum has given to me?"

"It's difficult to tell," Ishat retorted waspishly. "She does her work as diligently as I could wish, but ventures no opinions on the members of the household and does not gossip. I suppose that such attributes are valuable in a scribe, but I find her boring." She turned back towards the coolness of the house. "Two scrolls came from Thothmes yesterday, Huy. I did not want to unseal them in her presence. They are obviously private. One is addressed to my father."

"It will be the marriage contract, then, and a copy for me as your guardian. The time has come to make your final decision, Ishat, before they are signed. Are you sure of what you want?"

He was following her, and as she reached the shadow of the rear doorway, she said over her shoulder, "I am not staying with you, Huy, and don't ask me again. You have Thothhotep now. You will find her entirely unobjectionable. You no longer need my services." Her voice was shaking.

Huy did not argue. Together they entered his office. Ishat picked up one of the thin scrolls lying on the desk. "Sign it quickly and I will take my father's copy to him as soon as the litter returns," she went on. "Then they can both be sent back to Thothmes. Shall I unroll this?"

He nodded. Crisply she broke the wax. "Peasants do not bother with marriage contracts," she said as she scanned the document. "A man merely promises to provide for his new wife and any children he may have, and a woman promises to be faithful and keep her house in order. Is this a standard contract for the nobility?"

The question was careless, but Huy noted the anxious curiosity behind it as she passed the scroll to him. Quickly, he read. "I have no way of knowing," he replied after a moment, "but I expect that the clauses are usual. Thothmes promises to support the household, and in the event of his death you are entitled to one-third of all his property, of every kind. The remaining two-thirds will be divided between any children you may have. You retain sole possession of everything you bring with you to the marriage—all land, trading contracts and profits, and personal belongings—and if later you decide to divorce him, you may take it all away with you." He glanced up. "I think that this must be a common sort of contract, Ishat. However, if you commit adultery and thus bring the paternity of your children into doubt, you will be disinherited. I suppose all that is necessary to protect the inheritance. Nakht is rich, and so is Thothmes."

She had lowered herself into his chair and was sitting staring at her hands, which rested limply on the surface of the desk. She had gone pale beneath her face paint. "What if I can't live up to the image of a Governor's wife, Huy?" she asked in a low voice. "What if I can't learn, and Thothmes becomes so irritated with me that he has to send me back to Hut-herib?"

Then I would be a happy man, Huy thought immediately, and was at once ashamed.

"Look at all you have learned since we left my father's house," he pointed out. "I also, Ishat. Your fears are ungrounded." His gaze returned to the scroll. "There is little more, apart from the traditional gift to your parents." His eyebrows rose. "Thothmes is being very generous. Did you notice?"

"No," she said dully.

"He has negotiated the sale of two arouras of land from my uncle's perfume fields so that your father might farm them for himself. He offers a cow in calf, two oxen, a plough, three pigs, flax and barley seed, and a servant to work at your father's bidding. For your mother there are six ells of linen of the eighth grade, olive and ben oil, new pots and knives, and one deben's weight of gold dust for trading in exchange for anything else she might need for her household. A gift to a bride's family is expected, but this ... this is extraordinary! He loves you very much indeed."

He watched her in sudden pain as she fought whatever bleak emotion had taken hold of her at his words. Slowly, her spine straightened. Her hands disappeared into her lap. Pursing her lips against a visible trembling, she came to her feet.

"I will do my best to be worthy of him," she said steadily. "I hope that little paragon of holiness will not spend all morning praying at Horus's shrine, but in the meantime I'll write to Thothmes. Sign your copy of the contract, Huy, and I will seal it and have it ready to be returned to Iunu with my father's. I'll have to read it to him and then watch him as he makes his mark on the papyrus. No doubt he and Mother will be pleased. They seemed to like Thothmes when they met." Going to a shelf, she took down her palette, sank cross-legged to the floor, and busied herself in preparing her utensils. After a moment Huy left her.

Thothhotep returned in time for the afternoon sleep, and at once Ishat had Anhur provide fresh bearers and set out for her father's house. Huy retired to his room and fell into a troubled sleep. Ishat had still not reappeared by the time he woke, had Tetiankh bathe him, and changed his loincloth and kilt. It seemed to him that the early evening was a little cooler than usual, and his impression was confirmed when Seshemnefer hurried up to him in the garden.

"Master, the flood is receding," the gardener said. "Very soon it will be time to sow your new fields. Have you thought about what you want to grow? Flax would be profitable, but flax quickly depletes the soil. Better to seed the arouras to barley and emmer for the first year. In what state is the soil? Will it need manuring? Has it been neglected? You must hire a boy to keep the geese away from the strewn seeds, and someone to weed out the dock leaves and wild poppies and clover as the crop appears."

Huy, looking into his polite but eager face, laughed in spite of the gloom that had dogged him ever since Thothmes had made his desires regarding Ishat known. "If you can find a suitable replacement to tend my flowers and vegetables on the estate, I'll be happy to appoint you Overseer of the Crops of the House of Huy son of Hapu," he chuckled. "You're a good gardener, Seshemnefer. The Mayor chose you well for me. Go and assess my holding as soon as the river regains its banks. Hire whatever help you need. I cannot be concerned with this matter, but bring me a report every month. Your payment will of course be a percentage of the crop to store or trade as you wish. I hope Khnit won't mind!"

Seshemnefer bowed several times. "Thank you, thank you, Master," he said fervently. "Khnit will be so happy to see me advance in your service that she will be full of advice. Now, with your permission, I must ask Anhur for a couple of soldiers to strengthen the dike. The water feeding the new palms must not be allowed to seep back into the river."

Huy waved him away and took a deep breath. *Another step has been taken towards a defence against the possibility of the King's capriciousness if I anger him in the future. Why does he not send more of his ministers and advisers to me for Seeing? Perhaps he relies on his court magicians for predictions as well as entertainment, but somehow I doubt it. Atum's words to him through me have troubled him, I sense it. He watches me and he waits, but for what?*

Ishat emerged from the litter, hot and tired, as Merenra was unsealing the wine for their last meal of the day. Amunmose stood waiting with obvious impatience, the steam of boiled cabbage and onions rising from the tray he held. Thothhotep and Huy were already on their cushions in the dining hall. The house was full of the odours of fried fish, garlic, and coriander. Ishat flung herself down behind her table. "I need beer before wine, please, Merenra," she sighed. "I'm very thirsty. Well, Huy, it is done. I've put the scroll on your desk. Did you sign your copy?" Huy nodded. "Good. Tomorrow it can all go south to Iunu. Serve us, Amunmose."

"Your parents are well?" Huy asked as the under steward came forward and set the vegetables before him.

"Yes. And relieved to see me go, I think. Mother said that no matter how much the gifts improved their circumstances, she would go on caring for your family. I had no time to walk to your father's house, but I saw Heby playing in the orchard. He needs a friend." She paused to take a long draft of the beer Merenra had quickly brought, and in that moment Huy was assailed by a torrent of memories of the two of them, himself and Ishat, half naked and dusty, crouched together under the trees while they argued over the toy soldiers his uncle Ker's chief gardener had made for him. Ishat always wanted to be the King but usually ended up as Commander of the Braves of the King, Egypt's elite fighting force. Huy's fingers tingled as he remembered how often he had pinched her into submission.

"Next year he can come and stay with me while the school is closed during the flood," he responded. "Father can no longer object, seeing that you will be gone and no question of immorality in this household will exist."

"Oh, no?" Ishat jerked her spoon at Thothhotep, who was quietly chewing, her glance moving from one of them to the other. "Your father will use any excuse to keep Heby away from the knowledge of your eccentric past. It's bad enough that his son has become a Seer. Tell me, Thothhotep, has anyone spoken to you of your master's terrible accident during his schooldays at Iunu?"

Thothhotep looked startled. "No. The people of the town call him the Twice Born because it was at his school that he became a favourite of Atum, and thus a Seer. That is all I know."

Her inflection had risen at her last words, but neither Huy nor Ishat responded to the implied question. Ishat, her beer cup empty, was sniffing the cabbage appreciatively and ignored the girl. Huy gave her a smile but gestured to Merenra. "Pour the wine now," was all he said.

The scrolls went south, and a mere week later a letter arrived from Thothmes addressed to both Huy and Ishat, warning them that he would be arriving in the middle of the month to gather up Ishat and her belongings and escort them both to Iunu.

"I have already asked Iput if she wishes to continue to serve as my body servant in Thothmes' house," Ishat told Huy as they stood staring at the scroll quivering in the breeze from the window where Huy had laid it on the desk.

It looks so innocuous, so harmless, he thought, *but it holds within it the spell that will change my life forever.*

"I dare say she agreed at once," he replied wryly. "What is this household compared to the luxuries and excitement of an Assistant Governor's home? I suppose I must find a replacement for her, someone to serve Thothhotep."

"Thothhotep is quite used to seeing to her own personal needs," Ishat said darkly. "A body servant will only embarrass her."

Huy laughed aloud. "How long did it take you to become used to having your hair dressed every day by other hands than your own, and your laundry done, and your face painted?" he mocked her. "How quickly we forget the days when you hauled our linen to the river to wash it yourself, and kohl was something you could only dream of! Thothhotep must be cared for, Ishat, otherwise she will not have the time to attend to my needs."

Ishat made a face. "All the same, Huy, she's a simple girl who wants nothing more than a few plain dresses and a pot of unscented oil to keep her happy. Anything more will corrupt her."

Huy cupped her face. "Your jealousy is flattering," he began, and at that she jerked her head out of his hands.

"And your insensitivity is wounding!" she flashed back. "Gods, Huy, why can you not see my pain? Find her some town waif of her own class she can gossip and giggle with if you like! Why should her welfare outside her duties as scribe matter to you anyway?" She stalked away, her four gold-hung braids swinging.

I do see your pain, Huy replied to the empty air still redolent with her perfume. *I have seen it every day for years, my darling Ishat, and I cannot bear it anymore.*

He instructed Merenra to hire a suitable body servant for Thothhotep, his only stipulation being that the woman must not come from the household of any of the King's local officials; and within hours of the directive Huy was accosted by Amunmose as he was walking along the passage to the rear door. The under steward was half buried under a load of what Huy recognized as Ishat's freshly laundered sheaths. "A word, Master, if you please," he called as Huy brushed by him with a smile. "Merenra tells me that you're looking for a body servant for Thothhotep?"

"Yes. Iput will be going south with her mistress."

Amunmose's chin descended onto the precarious pile he held as the gossamer linen slid this way and that. "Then I'd like you to consider my sister Iny." The young man's voice was muffled. "She's only fourteen, but she's been helping my father in his capacity as cosmetician to the wife of one of Khmun's administrators. She knows how to work hard and she's a quiet little thing."

Huy grinned. "If she's at all like you, she's anything but quiet," he retorted. "Would she want to leave the incomparable delights of Khmun to come to this miserable estate?"

Amunmose grinned back at his master's sarcasm. "I do rattle on about how wonderful Khmun is, don't I? But I'm certain that Iny would rather serve your scribe than mix henna and apply kohl to the aging eyes of an exacting woman. You may trust that she is a virgin and reveres the laws of Ma'at and the King," he went on more soberly. "Thothhotep will not know how to train her, but it will not matter. She already knows the rudiments of face paint and the dressing of the hair."

"You will need Merenra's permission," Huy said. "He rules the servants. If he agrees to talk to her and assess her suitability, you can send a message to Khmun."

"Thank you, Master! Now I must get these sheaths upstairs. Iput is packing the Mistress's things."

I was not at ease in Khmun, Huy remembered as he emerged into the glare of the morning, where the ten townspeople allowed entrance waited for his hands to touch them and where Ishat sat with her palette across her knees, Thothhotep beside her. *I felt Thoth's heka, his powerful magic, weighing on me as I went about the business of reading the scroll in his temple. It was not like the happy turbulence of Ra's presence at Iunu. Thoth was watching me, weighing my worth to read the Book Atum had dictated to him before the Nun was created. Was he, the giver of writing to Egypt, the mighty Remembrancer of Time and Eternity, jealous of me?* The idea had not occurred to him before. He assumed that his earlier conversation with Ishat had prompted thoughts of resentment, but now they seemed logical, for was not he, with his gift of divining the future, not in some small way himself like a god, abrogating Thoth's prerogatives even if it was by the command of Atum? Uneasily, he pushed such sacrilege away and, taking his stool, nodded to Anhur, who stood guard at the head of the line.

"Who's first, and what is his request?" he said reluctantly.

The flood continued to recede with its usual speed, and every farmer followed the ebbing water, strewing seeds onto the glistening rich silt and trampling them deep beneath the replenished soil. Seshemnefer disappeared for days at a time, to be replaced by a strange man named Anab, who limped about the estate dragging a club foot. Huy watched him doubtfully until it became obvious that the palms loved him, rapidly shooting out soft new green fronds that seemed to uncurl into full glory as the man passed them, and the young vegetables and flowers in the garden forced themselves into the sunlight long before those on the neighbouring estates.

Then, at noon on the fifteenth day of the month, three barges glittering with gold-woven ribbons tied to their masts and fluttering from their deck rails tacked to Huy's watersteps. Sailors jumped into the water to moor them. One ramp was run out to rest on the watersteps; the other two sat on the dense foliage of the riverbank. Soldiers in full armour, brass-studded leather breastplates, and leather helmets, with gazelle-hide shields and tall spears, swords at their belts, filed onto the watersteps. Huy, standing on the path with a nervous Ishat, saw a host of servants, led by Thothmes' chief steward, Ptahhotep, emerge from one of the other barges and approach him. The servants fanned out between Huy and the soldiers, but Ptahhotep came on, his long steward's gown swirling white against his trim ankles, his oiled, shaved skull gleaming in the sun. As he neared Ishat, the butt of his gold-tipped ceremonial Staff of Office hit the ground with a soft thud and he bowed low, his painted features solemn. "I, Ptahhotep, Chief Steward of the household of Thothmes, Lord of Iunu, greet you, Lady Ishat, and pledge to you my loyal service. I and the household of my Master are yours to command. Your servants offer you their obedience."

He snapped his fingers, and one by one the servants came and knelt before Ishat, putting their foreheads to the gravel and holding out their arms to touch her feet in the age-old gesture of supreme homage. Ishat watched them impassively, but Huy saw her rapid breathing out of the corner of his eye. Her fingers brushed his own and he knew that, although she longed to grasp his hand, she was aware that she must show no weakness to these people. Her dignity, her superiority, must be established. It did not matter that Ptahhotep had seen her fallibility on other occasions. He would become her adviser and confidant, her buffer between herself and Thothmes' staff whenever necessary, but his task would be easier if Ishat was seen to be at ease in her position.

When the last servant had regained his feet, she inclined her head to Ptahhotep. "Thank you, Steward," she said, her voice only a trifle unsteady. "I will do my best to be a good mistress, firm but fair. As for you," and here she smiled, "I'm happy to see you again. Dismiss the servants to their duties."

Once more Ptahhotep clicked his ringed fingers, and the servants relaxed and dispersed, some back to the barge and some to the house. Huy saw Ibi, Thothmes' body servant, hurry between the motionless soldiers and along the ramp to the closed door of the cabin. At his knock, it opened and Thothmes himself stood there, resplendent in gold-tissued kilt, a white and gold striped helmet brushing brown shoulders covered in gold chains that disappeared under an enormous armful of flowers. Extricating an arm, he waved at Ishat and Huy, his face breaking into lines of sheer glee.

"A glorious day!" he called as he strode along the ramp and through the lines of motionless soldiers, his scribe Paroi trotting behind, clutching his palette. Huy noticed that Thothmes' sandals also glistened with gold, their thongs studded with pieces of red jasper. "Ishat, my dearest sister, you are lovelier than the blooms I bring you! Huy, you look very well!" He came up to them smiling, his black-kohled eyes crinkling, his hennaed mouth wide with delight. Bowing shortly, he presented the flowers to Ishat. "Isn't it wonderful that every ceremony is accompanied by flowers?" he went on. "Especially at this time of the year. Paroi, the scroll."

His scribe opened the pouch at his belt. Ishat was burying her face in the huge bouquet.

"White acacia, cornflowers from the fields, pink oleander, Hathor's blue water lilies," she said. "But what is this?" There were two long, thick green stems each holding one stiff, trumpet-like white petal.

"They are lilies Egypt cannot grow," Thothmes told her. "I sent for them in pots from Keftiu on the swiftest ship Pharaoh would lend me. See, Ishat! Every flower I have chosen has meaning: white acacia for your honesty, wild cornflowers for your untamed and forthright nature, pink oleander for the poison that lies in every woman's tongue and can both cow and titillate the man who loves her, Hathor's lilies for your great beauty, and of course these exotic blooms from Keftiu, because you yourself are so rare."

She looked up at him, almost in tears. "Thothmes, I don't know what to say! Thank you for this … this …"

"Homage?" he finished for her gently. "I love you, Ishat. Now, here is the scroll Huy signed as your guardian. I must take one to your father also, in person. This is your last chance to refuse marriage with me. Will you be my wife or remain here with Huy?" He held the papyrus close in both hands, ready to tear it across, both kohled eyebrows raised, sunlight glinting on the many gold bracelets he wore.

Carefully, Ishat passed the bouquet to Iput behind her and shook her head. "I do not change my mind," she replied, and at the words Huy felt her fingers jerk spasmodically against his own, hanging limply by his side. "I am honoured to live with you as your wife, Lord."

"Good." Thothmes returned the scroll to Paroi. "There are copies for you and Ishat's father to sign and keep," he said to Huy. "Now let's get out of the sun and seal our reunion with a cup of wine and all the news." Huy expected him to walk to the house with Ishat, but he slid his arm through Huy's. "I miss you so much," he went on as they turned towards the shade of the pillars together. "Each evening I want to gossip with you about the happenings of the day, the way we used to in our cell at the school. I want to play sennet with you, swim with you, share jokes. I have been discovering that an Assistant Governor can have few friends, Huy. They come to me for judgments, for favours, they try to bribe me, or they belong to the nobility as I do but my authority puts a barrier between us. My father warned me of these things when I began to work with him. I'm lonely for your trust. I don't suppose you would consider moving back to Iunu?" he finished hopefully.

Huy glanced into the thin, handsome face as the shadow of the house fell across them both. *You will never change, my dear friend,* he thought with a lump in his throat. *You and I knew instinctively from the moment we met that our kas fitted together like a child's puzzle. In spite of the blow from Sennefer's throwing stick that catapulted me into the lake and thus into the strange creature I became, in spite of Nakht's rejection of me, in spite of your passion for my own Ishat that has threatened to end our closeness, the gulf between your blood and mine that could have severed us from each other, we are still more than brothers.*

"I have thought about it from time to time," he answered slowly. "I shall be lonely here in my turn, without you or Ishat. But Thothmes, there are memories waiting for me in Iunu that I cannot face. Not just of Anuket, although that is painful enough. The Ished Tree in the temple, High Priest Ramose and his benign attempt to keep me close to him, the judgments of the Rekhet, though I love and respect her …" He spread out his hands. "These things would thrust me back into a boyhood I have struggled to escape. Besides, I don't want to appear ungrateful to the King by seeming unsatisfied with his generosity."

Thothmes nodded. "Even when you become more independent, when your land and the incense caravans and the poppy fields bring you your own gold, Amunhotep would perhaps still see a move on your part as a gesture of discontentment. Well, my favourite Seer, I am having a new house built for Ishat and me, right on the river, and there is a large guest room just for you. Come to us as often as you can."

They had entered the reception hall, where Huy's and most of Thothmes' staff stood ranged about the walls. Thothhotep hovered a little apart, her palette hugged to her breast and her eyes wary. "Who is that?" Thothmes whispered.

Huy waved her forward. "This is my new scribe, Thothhotep. Thothhotep, do reverence to the Assistant Governor of the Heq-at sepat."

Thothmes smiled at the girl's obeisance and lowered himself behind his table with a groan. Ishat and Huy followed suit and the servants sprang to life. Merenra came bearing wine with a little more than his usual dignity, and Amunmose, flushed with excitement, followed him, a tray of sweetmeats balanced tensely across his arms. Thothmes' steward watched them critically.

"You are very fortunate to be welcomed into this household, Thothhotep," Thothmes remarked as Merenra filled his cup with shedeh-wine. "A Seer's life is filled with many secrets, his own and others'. You will ultimately know more about the citizens of this country than Pharaoh himself."

"They are all safe with me, noble one," Thothhotep answered easily but with a swift glance in Ishat's direction. "My Mistress has been a very efficient teacher."

"Will you hire your own scribe when we are settled, Ishat?" Thothmes had turned to her as she sat staring into her wine.

She sighed. "I don't think so. Training one has been quite annoying enough. With your permission, Thothmes, I'll use Paroi." She smiled wickedly across at him. "If I need to write a really private letter, I'll do it myself!"

That evening, after a long and riotous feast during which Thothmes, obviously jubilant, kept Huy, Ishat, and the senior servants laughing with his tales of adventure and misadventure as his father's assistant, Ishat retired to her room and Huy and Thothmes wandered out into the moonlit garden. The air was cool, and full of the odours of wet earth and new growth. Tetiankh and Thothmes' body servant Ibi set mats and a lamp on the damp grass. Huy waved away Merenra and more wine but indicated that the jug of water should be left. The servants retired. A moving shadow on the edge of the garden told Huy that Anhur and probably Thothmes' captain had mounted guard. Thothmes sank down, then lay with one cheek propped in his palm facing Huy, who still sat upright.

"I'm a trifle drunk," Thothmes remarked, enunciating with care. "Your shedeh is better than mine at home. Where are the pomegranates grown?"

"On my uncle's estate, beside his other perfume flowers. Ishat insists on acquiring the wine even though I want nothing to do with Ker. Perhaps the fruit imbibes some blossom aroma that is translated into taste when it begins to mature on the vine." Huy gazed down affectionately at the pale oval of his friend's face. "You conducted the ceremony of attainment with great pomp and much thought today, Thothmes. Your preparations must have been long and thorough."

"They were, but I wanted Ishat to know how desperately I love her and in what esteem I hold her. Do you think she was impressed?" The anxious question might have come from the lips of a young man on the verge of his first love affair.

"Definitely," Huy replied at once. "She has instructed Iput to set the flowers on the table by her couch. She's packed and ready to leave, Thothmes."

There was a moment of silence. Thothmes struggled up just long enough to pour and drink a cup of water before lying back again. Huy sat still, his eyes on his shrouded acres. Above them, the sky was slightly hazed, the stars blurred, the moonlight diffused with the brief humidity of a Delta spring. Presently Thothmes said, "Have you forgiven me, Huy?"

Huy turned to him. In the uncertain light of the one feeble lamp, Huy could see his distress. "I've had no choice," he said harshly. "It was either forgive you or lose both of you. I've been tempted to browbeat Ishat into guilt, force her to stay with me, but such selfishness is not in the way of Ma'at, and Ma'at, as you well know, is as much my jailer as Atum."

"And what of Atum, Huy? What of the Book? I remember its words pouring from you in our cell after each reading. I remember how distressed you often became when it made no sense to you. And I can never forget the sight of your dead body when the priests pulled you out of the lake, your skin grey, your eyes open and lifeless, the water dribbling from between your teeth. Has it all been for nothing, the maiming of your sexuality, your inability to lose yourself in wine as the rest of us do, the headaches that threaten your reason? For the healing of a few citizens each week, and scrying for the one or two nobles the One sends to you? Do you know?"

"No." A knot had formed with horrifying suddenness in Huy's chest and he resisted the urge to press his fist against it. *Having someone who can rip aside the defences I have created for myself is terrifying. Thothmes, you see into my soul.*

"The final meaning of the Book of Thoth still eludes me, although its words are scored into my mind," he said thickly. "All I can do is wait here in the backwater of Hut-herib, wait for the god to show me the destiny he prepares for me, wait for the King to dispose of my gifts as he sees fit. I can see into your future with a touch of my hand on your arm, but my own fate is hidden." He could not go on.

"How do you bear it, Huy? The loneliness of it? And I am taking away your only true companion."

The stone in Huy's chest had swelled to include his throat. He said nothing.

There was another long silence. Thothmes' eyes had closed. Huy fought the overwhelming need to put his forehead against his knees, knowing that if he did so the tears would come. He was about to summon Ibi with a pillow and blanket for his master when Thothmes stirred, sighed, and struggled up.

"I have to ask you a question that you may not wish to answer," he said, crossing his legs and leaning over his knees to place both palms flat on the ground in front of him. "Before I ask it, I must assure you that whatever you have to say will make no difference to my feeling for Ishat or my decision to sign a contract of marriage with her. I need to know whether there has ever been a rival for her affections besides yourself." He glanced across at Huy and then away again. "Is she still a virgin, Huy?"

"Gods, Thothmes!" The words blurted from Huy almost before he had the time to fully comprehend his friend's inquiry. "You should be asking Ishat directly, not me. Not me! That's a private matter between the two of you! Do you understand that you want me to betray her confidence?"

"No, I don't want that." Thothmes shook his head emphatically. "But I'm painfully aware that Ishat's heart belongs to you, not to me. I shall do my best to seduce her love away from you.

I'm asking whether or not she has ever tried to tear herself away from you in the past with anyone else, anyone I might need to regard as a rival once her regard for you begins to fade, a mirage who could gain solidity if I fail."

I was crossing a field last Pakhons, taking a shortcut to the river road. Ishat's voice came whispering into Huy's mind, the echo of a confession she had made to him years before, a statement of agony as they sat together in the darkness of his parents' garden. *"... I saw a young man coming towards me. I thought it was you ... I closed my eyes and pretended it was you ..."*

"No, she is not a virgin," Huy said harshly. "And no, there will be no ghost rising from her past to tempt her away. Forgive me, Thothmes, I am very tired." He struggled to his feet. "If you wish to know more, you must speak to Ishat herself, but I assure you that in acquiring her you become the most fortunate man in Egypt. There is no capacity for deception in her." He stood looking down at Thothmes' curved spine. Thothmes did not move, and after a moment Huy bowed and left him.

Apart from the quiet voices coming from the reception hall, where the servants were clearing away the debris of the feast, the house was silent. As Huy began to mount the stairs, Tetiankh materialized out of the dimness above, waiting for him. On his way along the passage to his own room, Huy paused at Ishat's door. It was closed, but a sliver of light showed under it. He listened, but no sound reached him through the thick cedar. *I want to go in, to hold her, to start babbling about something, anything to make her eyes brighten with interest and her voice cut across my words with agreement or argument. I want to hear her laugh.* Sighing, he turned and went on along the passage to where his own door stood wide open and a lamp burned beside the clean white linen of his couch. *There's no point in it,* he told himself miserably as Tetiankh moved to unfasten his kilt and steam rose from the scented water in the bowl on the floor. *We have said it all, she and I.* He stood motionless while the body servant removed his jewellery, washed him, unbraided and combed his long hair, briefly massaged honey and ben oil into his hands and face. Once on his couch, he stopped Tetiankh from putting out the light and bade the man sleep well. The door closed.

He woke with a shock at some point in the night and realized that he was not alone. The lamp was guttering, its fuel almost exhausted, but by its frail flame Huy, turning his head cautiously, saw Ishat's tousled head resting on the pillow beside him. She was breathing lightly, her eyelids with their black lashes fluttering, one arm flung across his chest, her long body warm against him. Gently, he eased his own arm under her head. Murmuring in her sleep, she curled towards him, settling her cheek in the hollow of his shoulder. Huy, inhaling the faint odour of perfume that still clung to her hair, felt his eyes fill with tears. He lay awake and held her while the hours crawled by towards the dawn.

6

THE FLOTILLA left Huy's watersteps at mid-morning the following day, Thothmes' capacious barge in the lead, followed by one holding Ishat, Iput, and a few other female servants. Behind her the remaining craft, crammed with the rest of both households' staffs, were strung out. The day was fresh and cool with a stiff breeze off the river, and it was a noisy, happy crowd that lined the various decks to watch first the town of Hut-herib itself and then the palm-dotted countryside glide by. Huy, standing beside Thothmes, the warm deck rail under his fingers and his braids whipping against his neck, glanced back to catch a glimpse of Ishat among the wind-tossed linens of the women congregated along the barge's side, but he could not see her. He had the strong feeling that she would be inside the cabin alone, perhaps even with her eyes shut tight, not wanting to see the only district she had ever known vanish out of sight.

He had been alone on his couch when he had awakened that dawn. Only the slight ache in his shoulder and a hint of her perfume on his pillow told him that she had slept beside him. When he met her downstairs, dressed and painted simply for travel, her smile had been unnaturally bright and she had given him no more than a greeting before they made their way into the reception hall for the morning meal. Yet if he tried, he could still feel her hip against his, her regular breath spreading warmth on the skin of his chest. *What is she thinking now?* he wondered. *It had not occurred to me before that Hut-herib's dusty streets, my father's house, Ker's fields and the orchard, our little estate, have delineated her world since she was born. The city of Iunu is more familiar to me than my natal town, but to her it must loom vague and threatening in her imagination.*

"I wonder what Ishat will think of Iunu?" Thothmes said, as though he had read Huy's thought. "I hope she'll adjust well to it. You came to it as a child and grew to love it, and of course I'm proud to be one of its citizens. Will she see its beauty?"

"She'll quickly adapt to its size and complexity," Huy replied. "Ishat has courage, and besides, she is determined to make you happy, Thothmes."

"I know." Thothmes grinned across at Huy, kohled eyes narrowed against the harsh sunlight. Then he sobered. "May I ask you if you ventured a glimpse into her future, Huy?" At once he shook his head. "No, no! I don't want to know. Today I'm full of joy, and the future is a delightful prospect. Let's not spoil it."

"As you wish." Huy put an arm lightly across his friend's warm, naked shoulders. "But it's all right. I Saw for her a long time ago, when we were still living in the hovel beside the beer house. I almost doubted the vision, she was so beautiful, so richly clad and bejewelled. She was greeting me with a surprised smile. 'We were not expecting you,' she said. Now I know that the 'we' meant you and she."

"Oh, good! Were there any children in the Seeing?" Thothmes kept his gaze fixed on the far bank, where a pair of white ibises were standing in the water, almost hidden by an exuberant tangle of reeds, their yellow crests ruffling in the stiff breeze.

Huy squeezed one brown shoulder and withdrew his fingers. "No, but it was clear that she had just opened some inner door and was about to emerge into a passage. I saw nothing but her face and upper body. There's no reason to suppose that she won't give you many children. She does want children, Thothmes. She told me so during one of our more serious conversations."

"Good," Thothmes repeated slowly. "And I in my turn want her to have everything she desires. Do you think she and Nasha might become friends?"

Huy laughed. "She and Nasha are very alike. Both are stubborn, wilful, and far too frank in their speech. They'll either hate each other on sight or join forces to control your household. I don't suppose Nasha has found a husband yet?"

Thothmes groaned. "Not at all. Poor Father is glad to have a woman to manage his domestic affairs one day and anxious to see her married and gone the next. As I told you, he's not well. Perhaps you can do something for him."

"I'll try, if he'll allow me to See for him." Like a shabby cloak, the memory of his last meeting with Nakht settled over Huy, and for one moment it was night, and the feast that had heralded his Naming Day was over, and he was facing the Governor and begging for Anuket, begging for work, desperate to deny the pity in Nakht's eyes. "What's wrong with him?" he forced himself to ask now.

"The physicians aren't sure. He has become very thin and tires easily." Thothmes turned to Huy, brow furrowed. "I'm afraid that he's dying, Huy, and I'm not ready to lose him. I love him. Nor am I able to fully assume the governorship of the sepat yet. He's looking forward to greeting you, by the way. He and Nasha both miss you."

Huy, holding back that hot weight of shame and resentment, did not respond. Instead he said, "Have you had any dealings with the King lately, Thothmes? Does he ever come to Iunu?"

"No. His Vizier of the North visits every year as part of his progress through the Delta sepats, and of course we, Father and I, entertain him and Father gives him a report on such things as crop estimates, and whether the staff of the various temples are content, and the maintenance of the canals. But since Amunhotep went to war in his third year as King—an occasion you must remember very well, old friend, having told His Majesty exactly how his campaign would go—he has barely stirred from the palace at Weset. His Second Wife, Queen Tiaa, is pregnant. But of course, you knew that."

"Yes, Royal Nurse Heqareshu told me when he came for a Seeing." Huy turned a troubled face to Thothmes. "Amunhotep's Treasurer continues to send me gold with great punctuality, but I have Seen for only three or four nobles from Weset since Ishat and I settled on the estate the King gave us." He hesitated, filled with a sudden foreboding. "I had imagined that His Majesty would make full use of my gift, send for me often or even come to Hut-herib, but his silence sometimes seems like a condemnation to me, as though I have offended him in some way. Why does he ignore me?"

Thothmes shot him a shrewd look. "Because you might tell him things he doesn't want to know. The power of his magicians and astrologers is as nothing compared to the authority Atum has put into your hands. He is perfectly aware that you could make him your gaming piece whenever you wished, so he resists his desire to know the course of his reign. Amunhotep rules with the force of his body, Huy. He fights, he hunts, he eats, he makes love, he is a doer with pride in his physical prowess and a secret contempt for all who live by their wits. I think that his contempt hides fear, especially a fear of you. He will not allow you to control his policies."

"I don't want to do any such thing!" Huy began, but as he spoke, the voice of Ramose, High Priest of Ra's temple at Iunu, sounded clearly in his mind … *a man who has returned from the dead with the power Atum has given you may become an invaluable adviser to the god even now preparing to sit on the Horus Throne … through you the wishes of the gods can be conveyed to Pharaoh directly …* "You still have the face of an innocent boy, Thothmes," he finished lamely. "How long did it take the administrators under you to realize that those big dark eyes hide an accurate perception and a sharp intellect?"

"About as long as it took our teachers." Thothmes jerked his head. "Come on, Huy, let's sit in the shelter of the cabin wall. This wind is beginning to annoy me."

They made themselves comfortable on cushions under the awning and talked desultorily of inconsequential matters, but speaking of Queen Tiaa's pregnancy had set up a nagging unease in Huy that would not go away, and he found it difficult to concentrate on his friend's words. He remembered all too well the details of the vision for Royal Nurse Heqareshu into which he had been thrust, and he was glad when the noon meal offered a diversion.

That evening, the little fleet tied up in a shallow bay where for some reason the marsh plants that often clogged the edges of the river had been unable to take root. Ramps were run out, cooking fires lit, and a capacious linen tent hung with golden tassels was erected for Ishat and her servants. "I'd be perfectly happy just rolling myself in a blanket and sleeping beside the two of you on the ground," she protested, watching the parade of travelling couch, table, chair, carpet, linens, and two lamps go by and disappear between the gently billowing flaps.

"An Assistant Governor's wife does not sleep on the ground," Thothmes said grandly. "Besides, dearest sister, you are not to feel the slightest cold or discomfort on this little journey."

"If you keep spoiling me, I'll soon grow fat and soft," she retorted. Then, seeing his expression, she relented. "Oh,

Thothmes, I do thank you. You've thought of everything. But please let me sit here beside the fire with you and Huy and drink beer for as long as I like. Tell me about Iunu. What shall I see first as we draw near the city? I should like to visit the school where you became friends. Will you take me there later?"

Huy lay back on his elbow and watched the orange firelight play on their faces as Thothmes answered her, one hand on her linen-clad knee, the other gesticulating with the innate grace Huy loved in him so much. Ishat was leaning forward to catch his words over the constant comings and goings of sailors and staff. She was smiling. *It will be all right between them,* Huy thought. *Already they are in tune with one another, Ishat the lute and Thothmes the drum that sets the rhythm. I shall miss them even on the occasions when we are able to be together. They are swiftly becoming two halves of one whole, a unit from which I am excluded, although they love me. They will share experiences that will serve to gradually widen the space between us, but let it not grow so vast that we suffer the dislocation of so many first meetings! That I could not bear.*

He came to himself and realized that they were both looking at him inquiringly. "I'm sorry," he said. "Did you ask me something?"

"You've forgotten all about Thothhotep," Ishat replied. "Look at her, Huy, crouched behind you like an obedient dog. Do you want her to join us?"

Huy glanced over his shoulder. His new scribe was sitting some distance away with her back against the bole of a palm tree, one hand curled protectively around the palette in her lap and the other supporting her chin as she gazed calmly about her. Huy was struck yet again by the girl's air of self-sufficiency. Feeling his eyes on her, she turned her head. Huy beckoned her forward.

"I did forget about her," he admitted as she rose and hurried towards them. "Did she travel with the servants?" He waved her down, and after bowing to Thothmes she sank cross-legged and slid her palette open.

"You wish to dictate, Master?" she inquired.

Guiltily, Huy shook his head. "No, Thothhotep. Take some wine and sit here with us. When we embark in the morning, you had better bring your mattress onto Thothmes' barge in case I decide to pass the time answering correspondence. Tell us, did you ever pass through Iunu on your travels? Do you know Ra's temple?"

She responded politely and easily, and the conversation flowed once more.

Huy was surprised to see Ishat coming aboard Thothmes' barge in the morning, followed closely by an Iput loaded down with cosmetics boxes, a fly whisk, a linen cloak, a stool, and a spare pair of her mistress's sandals. While the body servant unburdened herself under the awning's shade, Ishat approached the two men, who had been watching the last of the evening's chaos disappear into the other boats. She kissed Huy briefly on the cheek and smiled at Thothmes with what Huy recognized as a most uncharacteristic awkwardness. "I know I'm breaking some sort of betrothment rule," she confessed to Huy, "but I asked Thothmes last night if I could travel the rest of the way with you and him. To tell you the truth, I'm a little reluctant to see Iunu for the first time in the company of strangers from whom I must keep my reactions hidden. I need both of you to describe for me what I'm seeing, and I need both your hands to hold. I'm not afraid!" she finished with a reassuring spurt of indignation as she saw Huy's expression. "I'm just slightly anxious." Iput had come up behind her and was hovering with the stool. Ishat waved it down and sat.

"It will be some time before we reach the city, beloved," Thothmes said. "You shouldn't expose yourself to the sun. There are cushions under the awning. I will call you when the city is visible."

Ishat's mouth opened at once, and Huy knew exactly what words of derisive argument were forming in her mind. She would have used them on Huy without a doubt. But their eyes met, and that full mouth formed a brilliant smile for Thothmes instead.

"I do not fear the sun," she said, "but I must not allow it to tire me today. I will do as you suggest. Iput! See if Ptahhotep has any fruit juice on board. Then come and sit with me." She cast a sidelong look at the awning, where Thothhotep was already enjoying the shade, raised one yellow-clad shoulder, and left them, kicking off her sandals as she crossed the deck.

Thothmes sighed. "If I lift up my kilt, will I see my manhood beginning to shrivel?" he said wryly. "We are embarking on a tumultuous adventure, she and I, but oh, Huy! I love the fire in her!"

Just before noon, the three of them gathered at the rail and Thothmes pointed downstream. "The three obelisks. You can just see the tips of them above the forest of palms. Two of them are fairly new. The Osiris-one Thothmes the Third, the King after whom I was named and who will always have my reverence, erected two of them. The pink granite one of such great power and beauty was ordered by the Osiris-King Senwosret the First of that name, many, many hentis ago. The tombs of Ra's High Priests lie to the southeast of the obelisks. See, Ishat! Now the walls are coming into view. The palms hide much of them, but there are two, built of mud bricks. They encircle the oldest part of Iunu, the centre, but of course the city has grown vast and now spills all along the riverbank and back to the western tributary."

For a long moment the barge continued to move quietly against the north-flowing current and nothing more was said. Ishat's eyes remained fixed on the three fingers to the heavens as they seemed to creep closer and the double wall grew larger. Huy could feel her tension. Then Thothmes' captain shouted an order, the sailors hurried to man the oars, and all at once the noise of the city reached out towards them. Now the roofs and upper pylons of several temples could be glimpsed, all partially hidden by the profusion of trees. Between the walls and the long sweep of the watersteps was an ungainly sprawl of buildings of every description.

"They are warehouses and merchants' stalls and the shacks of the poor," Thothmes went on, "and see how the steps are crowded with citizens resting and gossiping and visiting with each other. Well, you would be able to see them better if so many different kinds of craft were not moored at the foot of the steps," he amended himself. "Iunu is not only an important religious centre; much trade goes on here, because Iunu is the largest city before the Great Green. Goods come in from Keftiu and Alashia and our dependencies in Rethennu and beyond, and they are unloaded here and shipped south, to cities along the river and in the end to Weset and beyond."

"Are we going to disembark at these watersteps?" Ishat asked. Huy felt her hand creep into his and was sure that Thothmes was holding her other fingers.

"No, no," Thothmes assured her, "although I would love to take a litter with you and show you the centre of the city, where the streets are wide and lined with palms and the markets are full of everything one could desire and the air is full of the scent of flowering shrubs in the spring and hazed with the incense that rises from the temples. But for now we are moving past the happy confusion of these watersteps in order to come to my father's estate, a little further south, where the nobles and administrators also have their holdings. The house I am building for us is beside my father's. It isn't quite finished, so we will live with my family for a while."

Sensing Ishat's unspoken fear, Huy tightened his grip on her fingers, his own mind full of the first time he had seen Iunu.

He had been four years old, frightened and rebellious, on his way with his uncle Ker to a school he had no wish to attend. The future had loomed before him as a dark threat, and he had been sick with longing for the safety and familiarity of his home. But gradually he had adapted to and then grown to love the school, his fellow pupils, and especially Thothmes and his family, and for several years life had been very good. Then he had fallen in love with Anuket and been knocked into the lake that fronted Ra's temple with a death-dealing wound, two disasters that often seemed linked in his mind, for the invisible injury Anuket had inflicted on him was no less painful than the stunning blow from Sennefer's throwing stick. Both attacks had changed the pleasant course of his life forever, and with his nostrils full of the various odours of Iunu, his ears assaulted by its busy cacophony, his eyes lighting on a rapid succession of well-known silhouettes as the sailors laboured to jockey the barge through the choking mass of other boats of every size and description, he found himself overwhelmed with emotion. *Today I am a ghost haunting my own past. My broken heart lies here, invisible on the floor of Nakht's office. The drowned body of a twelve-year-old boy still rocks just beneath the surface of Ra's water, although the worshippers walking past, the boats beating slowly up the sacred canal towards the entrance lake and the vast stone concourse before the outer court, the schoolboys practising their swimming strokes, cannot see it. And within the temple walls, guarded and mysterious, the Ished Tree fills the space around it with the peculiar scent of both beauty and corruption. I've hardly thought about it since I turned my back on the High Priest and the Rekhet and began the long walk back to Hut-herib, but now I fancy I can smell its strange aroma, and the feel of the Book of Thoth is smooth in my fingers.*

"So, Huy, does this feel like a homecoming?" Thothmes asked. He was craning out past Ishat, his face alight with excitement.

Huy tore himself loose from his reverie. "Yes, it does," he

answered slowly. "There are many good memories here." Ishat had begun to lean against him and, relinquishing her hand, he put his arm around her.

The sounds of the city had receded to a not unpleasant background against which the songs of nesting birds along the riverbank were clear and sweet. The barge was passing tangles of tall reeds and, beyond them, the shrubs and sparse grass that ran between the river and the clusters of palms. Now and then a set of watersteps appeared, usually with a couple of brightly painted barges and a skiff tied to the posts at their feet and a guard standing above them where paved paths ran away to be lost in the exuberant spring growth. Sometimes the flash of a white wall could be seen beyond, and once they passed a raft hung with garlands and crowded with people holding dishes and cups in their hands. Lute music drifted on the air. At the sight of Thothmes' barge many bowed, and someone called out, "Congratulations on your marriage, Assistant Governor Thothmes! Long life and health to you and your blessed wife!" The words echoed across the water.

Thothmes waved back in response. "The Noble Khawi," he said. "He and his family will be at our party tomorrow evening, Ishat. He's a very nice man, but his wife is overfull of her own importance. She spends all her time trying to prove that her family is older than mine, not that any of us care. Nasha told her once that she certainly looked as though her ancestors predated ours. I don't think she understood the insult."

Suddenly, abruptly, Ishat's laugh pealed out, and Huy felt her muscles relax before she pulled away from the comfort of his embrace.

"I think I'm going to enjoy your sister, Thothmes," she said. "I see all this"—she gesticulated at yet another guarded entrance as it glided past—"and I am struck with a terror of displaying my peasant blood before the aristocrats of Iunu. Yet you, Thothmes my dear, and your sister remind me that this is Egypt, where the laws of Ma'at fill everything with an awareness of justice and mercy and right-thinking, and a man is not judged solely on the purity of his heritage. Huy has told me how frightened he was to come here as a child, and how he learned to belong. Then so will I."

For answer, Thothmes took her face between his palms and kissed her gently on the lips. "We have arrived," he said.

With much shouting and jostling, the other barges slid to the watersteps to either side of Thothmes' and all the ramps were run out, disgorging a mass of servants who disappeared in the direction of the house and of guards who ranged themselves at the beginning of the path. Thothmes' steward Ptahhotep was the first to disembark, vanishing quickly between the palms and spring-heavy green growth of Nakht's carefully cultivated shrubs, now riotous with the fragrant white and pink blossoms of the season. Huy's tension was so great that he started when a laden Iput, coming up behind her mistress, dropped a fly whisk to the deck with a clatter. *I don't want to see him*, he thought. *I don't want to have to look into his eyes for fear that I might see regret. Then I would be forced to forgive him.*

But his first sight of Nakht, with Nasha beside him, coming slowly along the path towards the watersteps, drove all gloomy speculation from his mind. Nakht's once broad chest had hollowed under the wealth of gold and electrum chains. His shoulders curved inward. Although a sturdy belt had been cinched tightly around the top of his impeccably clean, starched kilt, Huy could see the upper curves of both the man's hip bones. The skin of Nakht's face seemed stretched like thin papyrus between his ears, but on his neck it hung in loose folds. Huy was appalled. Quickly he turned his gaze to Nasha, who was already grinning at him, her red-hennaed lips wide, her large eyes, so like her brother's, half closed against the strength of the sun. Resplendent in flowing silver-tissued linen, her luxuriant black hair imprisoned in a net of silver thread, her arms, now spreading in welcome as she and her father came to the edge of the ramp, heavy with thick silver bracelets, she sparked and glinted with every movement.

"Nasha!" he called impulsively. "You look wonderful!"

"And you look absolutely edible, my handsome Seer!" she shouted back gleefully. "I can't wait to drag you around by that indecently long mane of yours!" Wrinkling her nose at him, she halted and stood aside.

Nakht stepped up onto the ramp and approached the little group, and Huy did not fail to notice that his beringed fingers slid with him along the protecting rope as though he might need to grasp it suddenly. With a swift glance at his son, he stopped before Ishat. "I welcome you to my family and to this house, Ishat. Life, Health, and Prosperity to you. May you find safety and peace here, and a long and happy life with my son." Ishat began to bow, but Nakht caught her into an embrace. Kissing her cheek, he set her gently away and turned to Huy. "Yes, dear Huy, I am dying," he murmured. "I must speak with you soon alone, but first there will be feasting and laughter and a great celebration to mark this occasion. Come into the house. Thothmes, give me your arm."

As they left the barge, Huy expected Nasha to throw herself on him exuberantly as she used to do when he came to stay as a pupil of the temple school, but she fell into step with Ishat, behind him. "Thothmes has talked of nothing but you for months and months," Huy heard her say as she slid her arm through Ishat's. "He's become as boring as a wilted leek. I thank all the gods most fervently that you're here at last and, now that he's got you, that he'll go back to being an efficient Assistant

Governor and fill his dinner conversation with equally boring but different information. There's a small meal set out for us all, but then we'll go into my quarters and have a good gossip. I'm excited to get to know you, my new sister-in-law."

Huy sensed rather than saw Ishat begin to relax. He wanted to interrupt Nasha, to ask her if Anuket had arrived with her husband, but his eyes were on the Governor's bent spine ahead of him, and pity and anxiety quickly edged out any thought of Nakht's younger daughter.

Huy entered the house on a tide of vivid memories. The painted grapevines twining about the white pillars of the entrance hall, the ebony chairs with their intricate ivory inlays scattered about, the strong shafts of sunlight pouring down from the clerestory windows cut just beneath the blue ceiling and pooling on the green tiling underfoot, all spoke to him of his boyhood on this gracious yet comfortable estate. The voice of Nakht's wife, long dead of an accident, whispered a greeting to him from the stair leading up to the women's quarters, and he glanced up as he crossed the expanse, half expecting to see her face smiling down at him, but the sound was only the conversation of two servants, heads together, as they mounted out of his sight. He heard the clatter of Thothmes' bow and arrows as the boy flung them onto the nearest chair before heading for the bathhouse. As they moved towards the dining hall, a strong whiff of drying herbs mingled with the aroma of freshly cut flowers came funnelling at him from a side passage, bringing with it Anuket's tiny, solemn face as she sat cross-legged on the floor of the herb room, a half-woven wreath in her decorously clad lap, and looked up as he knelt beside her. He wanted to reach out and touch Thothmes between his shoulder blades, ground himself with the warmth of his friend's living flesh, and as though Thothmes had divined the thought, he looked back and raised his eyebrows.

"Is it good to be back here, Huy, or are you overwhelmed?" he asked.

Before Huy could answer, the dining hall opened out and Nakht indicated a chair set down beside the cushions and flower-laden tables. "I can't lower myself to the floor anymore," he explained to Huy as Thothmes helped him to sit. "Nasha, tell Ptahhotep he may begin to serve. Ishat my dear, take this table by my knee so that we can talk."

Nasha had already pulled Huy down beside her. Thothhotep settled herself at his rear, the ever-present palette to hand. Huy wished uncomfortably that she was not close enough to hear whatever Nasha was going to say. He still did not know her well enough to feel at ease as she began to fill Ishat's position as his scribe. Nasha clapped her hands sharply and nodded across the room at Ptahhotep. Then she plunged a hand into Huy's hair and, dragging his head towards her, planted a kiss on his forehead.

"You may be Egypt's mighty Seer and all that," she said as food-laden servants began to glide towards them, "but to me you're just a brother I've missed. So tell me everything, Huy. Your letters have been a poor substitute for the sound of your voice." Picking the flowers off the surface of her table, she tumbled them against his chest. "Ishat is as beautiful as Thothmes said," she went on. "As soon as I saw her, I remembered seeing her when Father and Thothmes and I visited you in your parents' house many years ago. She was all arms and legs then. She doesn't say much, though, does she? Will I like her, Huy?"

"She talks a great deal and always to the point," Huy broke in, amused, "but how can she open her mouth when you natter on, Nasha? You'd better decide to win her over. As an enemy, she'd be as strong as you."

"Oh, good! I mean, someone as strong as me, not as an enemy. Anuket was never much of a friend even though she's my sister, and of course Meri-Hathor got married and left home long ago. She'll be back tomorrow with her husband for the feast. Absolutely everyone will fill this hall in honour of Thothmes and his new wife. Anuket and her husband, Amunnefer, arrive tomorrow as well. High Priest Ramose has been invited, and the Rekhet, and even Harmose, your school Overseer, will be here, not to mention every aristocrat in the sepat. Father is intensely proud of Thothmes and he obviously approves of Ishat. Look at them." She waved a spoon to where Ishat and Nakht were deep in conversation, she kneeling up so that he need not bend down, while three servants with steaming trays waited patiently to fill their plates. "Oh, Huy, Thothmes is holding one of Ishat's hands while she talks to Father! How sweet!" She sighed with pleasure and indicated that she was ready to eat.

Huy sank willingly into his old, well-remembered habit of a teasing closeness with Nasha, speaking to her of his life under the King's generosity with the ease of a returning familiarity once she had exhausted her own excitement and was ready to listen. Around them the servants of Nakht's well-trained staff wove their quiet pattern, refilling plates and pouring wine. Huy found his attention divided between Nasha's happy conversation and the interaction between Nakht, Ishat, and Thothmes. Ishat looked suddenly tired, although she smiled and continued to talk to both men. Huy could not hear what was being said. *She needs an hour or two on a couch all by herself,* he thought worriedly. *Thothmes, you surely must see how much of a strain all this has been for her!*

"She's not your responsibility anymore," Nasha said. "Yes, I can still interpret your expressions, Huy, whether sour or pleased or just bewildered. You used to be bewildered a lot in the old days, didn't you? Father has asked me to take charge of her until after the contract is finally ratified tomorrow night. Look—he's already signalling me. Spend the rest of the afternoon with Thothmes. He wants to show you the house he's building for the two of them. I'll look after your Ishat." She patted his knee and rose.

Ptahhotep bent reverentially towards Huy. "Your pardon, Master. The Governor must rest now, but he wishes your presence in his office at sundown, if that is acceptable to you."

Huy nodded. Thothmes was waving at him as Ishat, with Iput behind, followed Nasha out of the room.

"I'm too excited to rest," Thothmes said as Huy reached him. "Tetiankh is unpacking your gear in your old room. Thothhotep, I'm afraid you'll have to sleep aboard my barge. This is a large house, but for the next few days it will be overflowing with guests."

Huy answered his scribe's raised eyebrows with a gesture. "I may need you in a while," he said, and as he spoke, it came to him that Thothhotep had a quality that was rare but prized among scribes: in spite of a personality that was far from lacklustre, she had the unconscious ability to fade into any background so that very quickly one forgot that she was in the room. "Will you be comfortable on the barge?"

She acquiesced coolly. "I shall go at once and set myself up in the cabin, and then return."

"Thank you, Thothhotep," he replied formally, with a rush of new respect for this determined little waif, her palette clutched to her skinny bosom and her eyes watchful. She bowed once, swiftly, and walked towards the entrance hall.

Thothmes took Huy's arm. "Through the garden, a short walk by the river, and you'll be very pleased with the home I am preparing for Ishat. Then we can go up to my room and talk. It's so good to have you here with me, Huy. We'll arrange with Harmose to revisit the school before you go back to Hut-herib. Perhaps, when you and I have finished tramping all over Iunu together, you'll change your mind about moving back here."

Huy did not reply. He followed his friend out into the white glare of the spring afternoon.

In spite of the tumbled piles of grey mud bricks everywhere, the churned sand littered with broken pots and discarded white-wash brushes baking in the sun, the architect's table laden with scrolls and the man's tools of his trade under the thin shade of a canopy, Huy easily filled in what was yet to come as he gazed at the roofless building and through the doorless aperture to an inner court where four pillars had already been erected and an empty pool waited for water. "My architect has gone for his afternoon sleep," Thothmes said, "but you can look at the plans later if you like. I wanted a house designed around a central court, with an upper storey also open to the air in the centre. This"—he waved over the dusty muddle—"this will be a garden eventually, with date palms and sycamores and acacia hedges and plenty of flowers. I thought a trellis covered with grapevines leading from the front entrance to the watersteps might be shady and beautiful. What do you think? I'm still waiting for the stonemasons to come and set the watersteps in place. Will she like it, Huy? I've ordered a door of cedar inlaid with silver."

"I think that Ishat is the luckiest woman in Egypt," Huy replied slowly. "You're building her a shrine, you know that, don't you?"

Thothmes looked away. "I never expected to be in love. I expected Father to find me a suitable mate from among our acquaintances. I expected to settle down in peace." A fly had landed on his jasper-studded belt and was sucking up the salt of his sweat where his taut belly was exposed. He made no move to brush it away; he merely stared at it reflectively. "Love is uncomfortable," he went on. "It's like a disease. She fills my mind so that I cannot concentrate on anything else. I don't notice what I eat or drink. I'm hot somewhere inside myself, but I can't find the site of the fire. And then, when I am with her, free to touch her, kiss her, I am still in pain because I'm jealous of the sheath that clings so closely to her body, the rings on her fingers. If she smiles at someone else, I want to sulk like a little boy." Now he turned to look directly into Huy's face. "Was it like that for you?"

"For me with Anuket? Yes, it was. The burden was heavy, Thothmes, because I could take no freedoms with her as you can with Ishat. None at all. I envy you. For a long time I was very bitter, especially knowing that even if your father had given her to me, the gods would have prevented me from enjoying a full intimacy with her."

"And now? You're afraid to see her tomorrow, aren't you?"

"Yes. I'm afraid that my own flame will leap into life. Time has healed much of me, but not all." He swung abruptly away. "Let's not talk about it anymore. Ishat will be more than pleased with her new house. Now, may I go to my room? I want to sleep."

"Forgive me, Huy." Thothmes flicked one gold-gripped finger at the fly then batted at it as it rose towards his neck. "I seem to be apologizing to you a great deal, don't I? But I wanted you to know exactly how I feel towards Ishat, how I shall cherish her and take care of her always, how in giving her up to me you are placing me in your debt for the rest of my life."

Huy glanced at him curiously. "But Ishat has never been a slave. She was free to choose her future, and she chose to become your wife."

Thothmes bit his lip. "If you had pressed her to stay with you, she would have denied me. You love her. Yet instead of influencing her decision, you let her go. I'm not stupid. I know what that has cost you."

"I can bed no woman. I have told you this!" Huy replied harshly. "Only Anuket ate at my vitals. My love for Ishat is different! She deserves something better than the aridity of my company,

Thothmes. Now, for the last time, I am content to see her contracted to you and I bear you no ill will. For Set's sake, let it go!"

Thothmes grimaced. "You're right. Well, let's go back now and sleep. I'm glad you think that Ishat will like her house." They linked arms and, picking their way through the debris, regained Nakht's green, well-ordered garden.

The meal that evening was a subdued affair. Ptahhotep and the servants were clearly preoccupied with their tasks for the following day. There was no music. Nakht did not appear. Thothmes, Huy, Nasha, and Ishat pushed their low tables close to one another, but their conversation was sporadic. Huy thought that Ishat still looked tired. She told him that she had managed to rest and even sleep a little but the unfamiliar room had disturbed her. Huy himself, after standing for a long time in the middle of the room where he had spent a multitude of nights, had flung himself onto the couch with the same feeling of relief and safety that had always filled him there as a boy. Nakht's house had been a sanctuary, a place where nothing could reach out to harm him, and where he had slept even more deeply than on his cot in the school cell he had shared with Thothmes. Closing his eyes, he had tumbled into a profound slumber, waking only when Tetiankh leaned over him, a goblet of diluted date syrup and a couple of honey cakes on a tray balanced in his hand.

Now Huy had barely finished his fare when Ptahhotep bent over his shoulder. "Your pardon, Master Huy, but the Governor wishes to see you as soon as possible," the steward said. Huy nodded, pushed his table away, and rose. Turning, he saw that Thothhotep had also risen from her place behind him, picking up her palette from the tiles as she did so. He did not remember seeing her enter the hall.

Nasha had overheard Ptahhotep. "We want to go on the river in the twilight," she said, indicating Ishat and Thothmes. "Shall we wait for you, Huy? Unfortunately, Father cannot talk to anyone for very long these days, and I know that he plans to stay on his couch all day tomorrow so that he'll be strong enough to receive the guests in the evening."

Ishat looked up sharply then signalled to Iput, hovering by the wall. "You have an interview with Nakht?" she said. "You'll need me, then. Iput, go and fetch my palette."

Huy forestalled her. "You are no longer my scribe, Ishat. You have trained Thothhotep well. She can begin her service now."

Ishat's expression became mutinous. Half rising, she glared at Huy. *I know exactly what you are thinking,* he said to her silently. *You want to be present to hear the Governor's words. You want to discuss them with me afterwards as you always did—but, Ishat, everything has changed. It's time to say farewell to those days.* She must have read something of his thoughts in his eyes, for after a moment she gave one sharp nod and the anger left her face. "So be it," she whispered, sitting back on her cushion.

Huy smiled at Nasha. "No, don't wait. Go and enjoy the evening. Thothhotep, come with me." He was aware of Ishat's stare as he left the room with Thothhotep at his heels. Truthfully, he would have preferred to have Ishat taking down the words of the coming meeting, but this was as good a moment as any to sever the link of master and scribe between them.

Of course, he did not need to be led to Nakht's office; he could have walked the interior of this house blindfolded. Yet as he approached Nakht's door, he faltered, the memory of his last visit springing fresh and terrible into his mind. He had begged to be given Anuket then, begged without dignity, begged like the penniless, desperate peasant that he was, and Nakht had turned him down. Nor would he agree to give Huy a scribe's position anywhere within his governmental jurisdiction. His refusal to help Huy in any way was entirely unexpected. If Nakht had

stepped up to Huy and struck him with his fist, Huy could not
have been more shocked. Nakht had been more than a father to
Huy, generous and kindly, and Huy had loved him. Thothmes
told Huy later he believed that Nakht had not dared to invite the
anger of the gods by doing anything that might thwart their plan
for Huy's destiny as their Seer, but the excuse did nothing to ease
Huy's sense of betrayal. As the tall door inlaid with the copper
symbols of the Heq-at sepat, Nakht's responsibility, loomed
ahead, Huy saw again the insulting pity in the Governor's eyes.
He took a deep breath and knocked on the smooth cedar.
Nakht's voice bade him enter and he did so, Thothhotep
following and softly closing the door behind her.

Huy expected to see the Governor rising from behind the
desk that dominated the room, but Nakht was half sitting, half
lying on a travelling cot placed between the desk and one of
the niche-hollowed walls, propped up with many cushions and
draped in a crumpled sheet. A dish containing a half-eaten
salad and a full cup of wine sat on a low table beside him.
He made no move to rise, but he smiled as Huy bowed and
waved him forward. "This way I am able to both conduct the
business of the sepat and husband my strength," he explained
as Huy approached him. "It is very good indeed to see you
again, Huy. You've filled out. You look well." His voice was
thin. Reaching out, he picked up the cup and took a sip of
wine. His hand shook.

"It's a great pleasure to see you again also, noble one," Huy
responded. "I don't think that you have met my new scribe."
He indicated the girl, who was standing motionless a polite
distance away. "This is Thothhotep."

Nakht's smile grew wider. He raised his eyebrows as
Thothhotep bent respectfully, and in that moment, in spite of
the fleshless cheeks, the taut skin stretched over the painfully

prominent bones of the Governor's face, the yellowed eyes, Huy saw the benign features he remembered so well.

"Did you deliberately select another woman to keep your secrets, Huy, or do you simply enjoy mystifying and perhaps even shocking your unsophisticated neighbours? Greetings, Thothhotep." His glance swept over her and returned to Huy. "I have the AA disease," he said frankly. "The physicians are helpless against its onslaught, as you must know. I need you to See for me, Huy, and tell me how long I have left. Thothmes will wish to devote himself entirely to his new wife for a while, and besides, he is not quite ready to take my place. His Majesty has agreed to confirm him as Governor of the Heq-at upon my death." He paused to take a mouthful of wine. "My tomb was finished before my dearest Nefer-Mut died. I look forward to a favourable weighing in the Judgment Hall and a reunion with her. Yet I am not entirely at peace." He let out a long breath that hollowed the pitiful concavity of his chest even further. "My mind keeps reliving that last time you stood before me here, in my office. It was night then too. I have been wondering if I did you a grave disservice."

Oh, Nakht, not now! I have been fighting that memory ever since I walked through your door yesterday. Let silence cover it! Let it sink into the mud of the past so that you may die with dignity and I may once again cover it with the blessed little routines of my daily life!

"You did what you believed to be right," Huy managed huskily. "I could not have been a proper husband to Anuket, although I deceived myself into seeing myself in that position because I had fallen in love with her."

"Anuket is a poison to any man," Nakht broke in harshly. "No, I mean that I should have found a place for you within my administration as a scribe, kept you close to us and to Ra's temple. I am so sorry, Huy. I condemned you to poverty, and if the King had not consulted you on his way into Rethennu, you would be in poverty still. I raised you as a young noble. You were more my son than the son of Hapu. Yet I abandoned you in the end. Forgive me, I beg you." He had begun to gasp for air.

Huy had listened to him with a mounting distress. Swiftly he went to the cot and, kneeling, took Nakht's hands in his. They were very cold. "Thothhotep, run and find Nasha and have her send for the physician," he ordered. "Are you in pain, Governor? What has been prescribed for you?"

The door opened then closed as Thothhotep hurried away.

Nakht grunted. "Anuket's husband Amunnefer has been sending me poppy. The physician has been mixing it with ground kesso root to heighten its effects. It dulls my thoughts, though, so I try not to take it until I can bear the pain no longer. I am determined to walk among my guests tomorrow. I will take the medicine at the hour of the afternoon sleep and trust it to carry me through until the festivities are over." Closing his eyes, he lay back on the cushions.

"Nakht, the gods order our lives as they see fit," Huy said carefully. "If I had not spent many months in this house, I would not have known how to address the titled persons who come to me for healing or scrying, let alone how to engage them in conversation. If you had offered me a position as a scribe here in Iunu, it's unlikely that I would have come to the attention of the One. You did as the gods wished when you refused my appeals." The capitulation had cost him a great deal. He had forced the words past the fume of resentment that dried his throat and tightened his jaw. Yet, as they left him, they seemed to take with them some of the agony of that encounter, and he was able to kiss Nakht's hand with genuine love. "You gave me far more than you ever denied me. I love you so much, my second father."

Nakht did not open his eyes, but a brief smile flitted across his ravaged face. "And I you, my talented second son," he murmured.

At that moment the door opened, and Nasha and a stranger came hurrying across the shadowed floor, Thothhotep behind them. "Huy, this is our physician," Nasha explained. She bent over Nakht. "Talking to Huy is not resting, Father," she chided him, then stepped back.

Quietly, the physician began to examine Nakht. Huy remained kneeling on the tiles, Nakht's hand in his. Presently the physician straightened. "You already know that the AA cannot be cured, noble one," he sighed, "but you will live longer if you remain calm. Do not allow yourself to become agitated. I shall prepare more poppy and kesso for you to drink tonight, and I shall return before dinner tomorrow and give you a weaker dose so that you may enjoy your son's good fortune." He spread out his hands. "I wish I could do more." Bowing, he left.

"I thought you were going boating in the twilight," Huy said to Nasha.

She nodded. "I decided to let Thothmes and Ishat go alone. Ishat needs to be with someone she's known for longer than a day. She's tired. Come and play Dogs and Jackals with me before I go to bed, Huy, and let Father drink his medicine and sleep."

But Nakht's grip tightened. "I need Huy for a little longer," he told her. "Please wait outside the door, Nasha, and take the vial when the physician returns. We must not be disturbed."

For answer, she leaned down and kissed his forehead.

"See for me now, Huy," Nakht asked when she had gone.

Huy heard Thothhotep go to the floor just behind him without being told. Her pens rattled, and presently the tiny sound of her papyrus scraper came and went. Huy sank back to sit cross-legged on the floor, and taking Nakht's hand in both of his, he closed his eyes. *Now, Anubis,* he prayed, *tell me that this man may be well.*

"Well?" The familiar gravelled voice came at once. "Not well as you mortals count the state of your bodies. Governor Nakht will die on the second day of Pakhons, three months from now. The King will send his Vizier and namesake, Amunhotep, to attend the funeral. He is sitting under his sunshade by that rock. He is uncomfortable and sweating. He is not praying for Nakht's ka. He is thinking about a drink of cool beer."

There had been no dizziness, no sense of dislocation. Huy found himself standing with a crowd of solemn people on sand under a hot sun. Before him, Nakht's embalmed and bandaged corpse stood propped beside the entrance to the tomb Huy remembered well, having mourned as Nakht's wife Nefer-Mut was carried down into its darkness. The Kher-heb, the chief funeral priest, was chanting words from the unrolled scroll in his hands. The sem priest had approached the body and was in the act of touching Nakht's mouth and eyes with a linen bag that contained pieces of red carnelian, as Huy knew, to restore the colour of health to Nakht's lips and eyelids. Thothmes, as the Son-Who-Loves, waited behind the man to perform the next ritual. He was weeping silently. Huy turned his head. Nasha had slid her arm through his. She too was crying and clutching a square of damp linen to her face. There was no sign of Anuket.

"Oh yes, she is here." The harsh tones of the god filled Huy's mind. "She sits in the shadow cast by her husband's tent. She is not praying for Nakht's ka either. She is eyeing the broad shoulders and muscled belly of the sem priest, forbidden fruit indeed, and her own ka is screaming for wine. Has your ka begun to scream yet, Son of Hapu? See to your house!"

The last words were shouted so loudly that Huy started and swung away from Nasha's grip. They ended on a deep animal wail that set his heart pounding, and as he turned, he saw the hyena. It was perching on a small hillock and staring at him, its yellow eyes slitted against the bright light. As he watched, its mouth opened and its black tongue passed slowly across sharp white teeth. There was something so greedy, so anticipatory, about the motion that a shiver trickled down Huy's spine. He tensed, fully expecting the beast to rise and come shambling towards him, fuelled by some malevolent purpose. *But how can its intention be malicious? Does it not belong in Paradise, in the Beautiful West, where evil does not exist?* The hyena hauled itself up and shook, the stiff beige hairs down its back quivering with the movement. Its gaze did not leave Huy's face. *Anubis!* Huy cried out silently. *Tell me what this means!*

"See to your house, Great Seer," the whispered reply came on the jackal god's warm breath. "See to your house." Huy felt something cold placed in his hand. Glancing down, he saw Anubis's black hand retreating, leaving a sinuous shape behind. Huy's fingers closed around it. It was an Ur-hekau, an instrument used to open the eyes of a corpse so that it could see again, the mouth so that it could speak and eat. This one was of ebony, thick and heavy, the ram's head with its uraeus perfectly executed.

"Ur-hekau, Mighty One of Enchantment," Huy muttered stupidly—but it was not an Ur-hekau, it was a hand, a human hand, wrinkled and cold. It was Nakht's hand, and as the Governor's office solidified around him, Huy's head began to pound with a suddenness and ferocity that had him pressing both palms to his temples. He had inadvertently carried Nakht's hand to his face.

"The coolness is good," he blurted, then gathered up his wits, let go of Nakht, and crawled up to sit on the cot beside Nakht's knees. "Thothhotep, I see water on the desk. Bring me some," he managed. Wordlessly, the girl obeyed, sinking back to the floor and settling her palette across her thighs as Huy drank. Relinquishing the cup, Huy faced the Governor. "I can answer your request," he said thickly. "You will die on the second day of Pakhons, Master. I have witnessed your funeral. You will be greatly mourned."

"Entombed on the twelfth day of Epophi, in the season of harvest, providing the seventy days of Beautification are observed, and I have no reason to suppose that they won't be," Nakht replied. "I have already set aside a generous payment for the workers in the House of the Dead. Thank you, dear Huy. The Seeing has made you ill, and I am tired. It's time we both sought our couches." He spoke calmly, but Huy saw that his eyes had filled with tears.

"Thothhotep, open the door and ask Nasha to please send for the Governor's body servant and for Tetiankh," Huy ordered. He was almost spent. The three of them waited in silence until Nasha and the servants hurried in, then Huy rose, bowed to Nakht, and, leaning against Tetiankh, left the room. The passage beyond seemed to stretch away into an infinite distance of dull orange torch flames and repeating pools of dimness.

Suddenly he felt an arm go around his waist. It was Thothhotep, her palette tucked under her elbow, her bony little shoulder thrust into his armpit. Surrendering to them, Huy was helped through the house, up the stairs, and into his own room.

"Tetiankh, find the poppy you packed and prepare a strong draft for me," Huy begged as they lowered him onto the couch. "Thothhotep, open your palette again and take a fresh piece of papyrus. I have something private to add to the Seeing I gave the Governor. You will of course make a copy of that and hand it to his scribe tomorrow."

"Of course, Master." Calmly she slid to the floor and prepared her utensils.

Huy dictated the words of Anubis that were meant for him alone, and described the hyena's actions. He did not ask for a comment and Thothhotep did not venture one. *I want Ishat,* Huy thought, the agony of his body rendering him defenceless against his longing for her. *I want her to give me her opinion of the god's injunction and help me to untangle the matter of the hyena. I want her to hold the vial of poppy to my mouth and send Tetiankh away so that she can bathe my forehead in cool water herself.*

"Thank you for helping me up the stairs, Thothhotep," he said. "Sometimes the visions are less painful."

"It was my privilege, Master," she replied. "I hear Tetiankh coming along the corridor. I shall seek my own cot on the barge and be ready to be of service to you at the first meal tomorrow. May you dream of visiting Aabtu." She smiled, bowed, and left, one of her thin new sheaths flowing back from that skinny yet strong little body. In spite of his pain, Huy felt his heart lighten. The head of Osiris was buried at Aabtu, and according to the priests who interpreted dreams, if one travelled there while asleep, one could be assured of a long life.

Tetiankh passed Huy the poppy and began the task of undressing and washing him. Huy drank, then submitted passively to his servant's ministrations. By the time Tetiankh set fresh drinking water by the couch and doused the lamp, the thudding in Huy's head had begun to abate under the influence of the drug. Curling up on his side, Huy set both hands under his cheek and closed his eyes. *"See to your house." What do you mean, you mysterious jackal? My house is in order. I fulfill my obligations. I have given up Ishat. I shall continue to heal and scry as always. What more is required of me?* At once the hyena filled his mind's eye, its teeth bared, its tongue glistening in the sunlight as it moved over those predatory fangs. *You gave me a tremor of unease even as I stood before Imhotep in the Beautiful West with the Judgment Hall behind me,* his thoughts ran on anxiously. *You appeared tame, but when the mighty architect and healer put his hand on you, stroked you, I felt afraid, or as fearful as it was possible to be in that glorious place. Why? How is the command of Anubis to see to my house connected with an unclean animal, a scavenger? Does it have something to do with the*

Book of Thoth? Perhaps so, for it has been many months since I allowed the words of those forty-two mysterious scrolls to stream through my mind. And tonight is not the time.

He stirred, but the poppy was singing its seductive song in his veins and slowly the pain was ebbing. *Nakht called her a poison to any man,* Huy suddenly remembered, *and in my vision Anubis described her thoughts as both lustful and self-indulgent. Anuket, lovely and delicate weaver of garlands, I shall see you tomorrow. Are you still quiet and graceful? Am I doomed to fall in love with you all over again? A poison to any man ... And what was it Thothmes said about her ...?* Huy slipped into unconsciousness.

7

THE FOLLOWING DAY passed uneventfully for all but the servants. Huy slept late and heavily, waking long after sunrise to make his way unsteadily to the bathhouse, where he submitted to Tetiankh's ministrations in a mental fog caused, he knew, by the aftermath of the poppy. Washed, shaved, plucked, and oiled, he returned to his room to eat a light meal, then he lingered in the quiet space, reluctant to begin a time that he suspected would be fraught with tumultuous emotions. Tetiankh was hovering just outside the door, waiting for his master to leave so that he could make up the couch and clear away the dishes, and in the end Huy sighed, picked up his courage, and went in search of Thothmes.

But it was Nasha who accosted him as he was crossing the reception hall, her hair coming loose from the combs holding it carelessly back, her face unpainted, her arms and the arms of the accompanying servants full of spring blooms. More servants were setting out the low tables behind which the guests would sit, laying linen squares, spoons, and knives on their pretty inlaid surfaces. One man was placing musical instruments—a harp, two drums, and a lute—at the far end of the pillared floor. Another was moving from one lampstand to another, gingerly cleaning the delicate alabaster lamps before filling them with oil and new wicks. Their voices and laughter echoed against the high, starred ceiling.

"You look ghastly this morning, Huy," Nasha greeted him. "You should go back to your couch. None of us will be sleeping tonight."

"You look utterly unpresentable yourself," Huy said.

She grimaced. "I sent Ptahhotep and his assistant to the storage hut behind the granaries to fetch more vases for the flowers an hour ago. I have no idea what has become of them. The gardeners haven't finished making the welcome garlands for the necks of the guests, and there's no sign of the dozens of perfumed cones I ordered. I'll be lucky to get to the bathhouse before the festivities are due to begin."

"So Anuket is not weaving the garlands?" Huy felt strange saying her name aloud, as though he had asked permission to go into the herb room and sit with her as he used to do.

Nasha blew a stray lock of hair away from her mouth. "She doesn't do that anymore," she said tersely. "Really, Huy, I get so few letters from her that I don't know what she *does* do. Help me sort these out. Who has the pink lotuses?" She dropped her armful on the floor and Huy bent over them with her, gently pulling the tangled stems apart and unwillingly inhaling the mingled scents of the waxy orange lilies and the little yellow acacia, the powerful aroma of narcissus, mignonette, and jasmine threatening for a moment to unseat his reason.

"How is your father this morning? And where are Thothmes and Ishat?" he forced himself to ask, and at once the present reasserted itself.

Nasha tore a withered leaf from one of the lily stems and dropped it on the tiling. "Father is resting. I visited him earlier. He seems a little stronger than yesterday, but perhaps I only wish that to be true." With a sharp gesture to the servants to continue the task, she straightened. "Thothmes waited for you, but then he took a skiff and went into the marshes. I believe that Ishat is being massaged in her room. If you want your new scribe, she's sitting under a tree in the garden, talking to Paroi. You might as well stay with me, Huy. There'll be nothing but chaos here until dusk." She frowned down at the riot of quivering colours. "Should I remove the oleander flowers? They're so poisonous, and I don't want some drunken guest to drop one in his wine thinking it's a lotus."

Huy took her hand. "You have a capable steward in Ptahhotep. Let him see to these things. Order a couple of cups of beer and let's find a quiet corner. There's been no time to talk to one another, Nasha. I've missed you."

"I've missed you, too, and I've enjoyed every word of your letters." The tress of black hair had crept over her mouth again. Giving up, she pulled out the combs. "All right. We can go into Father's office and shut the door. Beer sounds good."

They hid themselves away, drank their beer, and talked easily of the past they had shared. There was no melancholy for Huy in these reminiscences. His memories of the times he had spent with Nasha and Thothmes were mostly happy. Neither of them mentioned Anuket. Finally Nasha yawned. "I must look in on Father, have a word with Ptahhotep, and then sleep. I suggest that you spend the afternoon in your room, Huy. The contingent from Weset will be arriving soon. Unless you want to be caught, you'd better keep out of the way until you're summoned to the feast."

Huy was grateful for her tact in avoiding saying their names. Kissing her, he left the office and slipped along the passage and up the stairs. As he turned in at his own door, he heard Thothmes' voice come floating faintly up from below, but he had no urge to meet his friend. There was still no sign or sound of Ishat. Pushing the pillows off the couch, Huy reached for the ebony neck rest on the table and, lying down, relaxed against it. Comfort spread slowly down his spine, and he slept.

He was woken with Tetiankh's hand on his shoulder, and, dragging himself up from some dark dream, the details of which he immediately forgot, he sat up. Apart from the lamp on the table, the room was dim. A low rumble of voices rose from the direction of the reception hall, together with a faint drift of myrrh. "I've brought you water and dried figs, Master," Tetiankh told him as he struggled to return to full consciousness. "The guests are beginning to arrive. The Noble Amunnefer and his wife the Lady Anuket have already been asking for you. Also Ishat begs you to visit her in her room as soon as you're dressed. Hot water is ready, and if you will tell me what you wish to wear, I shall open your tiring chest."

Anuket. How does she look? How does she sound? Huy wanted to ask his servant, but he quelled the urge, emptying the water down his throat and coming to his feet. "Wash me, then, and oil and braid my hair," he said hoarsely. "The kilt shot through with gold thread, I think, Tetiankh. The belt of gold links. The sandals decorated in green turquoise, and the earrings in the likeness of Ra-Harakhti, the ones of blue faience with the sun-disc of yellow chalcedony on the god's head. They're heavy, and the god's talons brush my shoulders, but they're opulent enough for this occasion. Kohl for my eyes, and brush my mouth with a little grease so that gold dust will adhere to my lips. Sprinkle some on my hair also."

"You will be as handsome and glorious as a god yourself," Tetiankh remarked, his hands already in the fragrant water.

Huy laughed shortly. "Thank you, but I simply want to make sure that I do not shame my Ishat. I can wash myself. Go and tell her that I shall be with her as soon as possible." *I do want to be a credit to Ishat,* Huy thought, wringing out the cloth in the water and beginning to absently cleanse himself, *but I also want Anuket to see me as I am now, rich, famous, blessed by the King, as far from the poverty-stricken boy who adored her with such desperation as Weset is from my estate at Hut-herib. Atum, grant me this petty revenge and do not be angry with me,* he prayed briefly. *I have suffered much because of this love. Take it from me even as she looks at me with awe and desire.*

Tetiankh clothed him carefully, then took a soft brush and, opening the small pot of gold dust he had packed with Huy's jewellery, gently touched Huy's mouth and shook it over his head. Glittering specks drifted down through the lamplight. "There is no point in perfuming you, Master," Tetiankh concluded. "A wax cone full of myrrh will be tied onto your head as you enter the reception hall. I think you're ready. Shall I announce you to Ishat?"

"No." Huy strode to the door. "Bring your pallet in here and sleep by the couch please, Tetiankh. I may need you later."

"As you wish." Tetiankh lifted the water bowl and followed Huy through the door. "Enjoy the evening, Master. This is your hour as well as Ishat's."

Startled, Huy turned back, but his servant was already descending the narrow stairs leading directly to the bathhouse. Huy took the few steps to Ishat's room and knocked. Her quiet voice bade him enter and he did so, closing the door behind him.

There was no sign of Iput. Ishat stood in the centre of the room, her arms at her sides, her sandalled feet together. Her perfume of myrrh, cassia, and henna flowers blew to meet Huy as he stepped forward. She did not move. She was wearing her favourite scarlet sheath, its graceful folds caught to her waist by a sumptuous belt of linked golden scarabs that gleamed with a purple sheen in the light of the two large lamps. Her hair fell loose and glistening to her shoulders, and Huy wondered for the first time why she had never considered shaving her head and wearing wigs now that he could have afforded to buy them for her. Still, no wig could match the smooth thickness of that living headdress, he thought, his gaze travelling her slowly. The one large jasper attached to the gold circlet she reserved for special occasions rested against her forehead. Its smaller companions nestled around her brow, all of them complementing the red of the sheath. Golden ankhs hung trembling from her earlobes, both with the same purple glow of her belt. Iput had painted her face faultlessly, the black kohl with its admixture of gold dust lifting her beauty into the realm of the exotic, her mouth tinted with red galena and slightly parted in anxiety as his eyes rested on her face. "Oh, Huy, please say something!" she begged as the silence lengthened. "I'm frightened!"

"I'm sorry. Your incredible loveliness gave me pause. You've never looked more queenly, dear Ishat, or more desirable. No woman tonight will be able to eclipse your flame."

"I must make my new husband very proud of me, and I must eclipse his sister at any cost." Her chin rose. "No, I don't mean Nasha. I want to stand beside the one you love and have you silently acknowledge that I am the more beautiful. I'll see it in your face. No one knows you as well as I do. I shouldn't be afraid to walk into the reception hall, not after the titled men and women we've had visiting our house, but I am. Everyone down there will be judging me, the Noble Thothmes' choice. 'She looks good, but her blood is common, you know,' they will be saying. 'She's a peasant. Her parents sent their apologies for the feast tonight. You can guess why.'"

"Yes, some of them will whisper those things," Huy answered carefully, "but most of them will gossip about your beauty, your ability as a scribe, your previous position as the confidante of the Great Seer. Don't forget that many of the women who will share a bow with you are illiterate, just like your parents and mine. It's far more likely that you will make them jealous because their husbands will enjoy talking to an intelligent and educated woman. Pick up your balls, Ishat!" The coarse expression was familiar to every cattle farmer, and at that Ishat laughed.

"Gods, Huy, I'm going to miss you terribly. Please don't wander too far from me tonight. I'll have Thothmes' arm, but I shall need the support of all the years behind us, you and me. You'll sense when I'm about to panic or fall over my own tongue. You'll save me." She bit her red lip and held out her hands, palms up.

Huy stared at her for some moments. Then he said, "Ishat, it's not too late to call off the marriage, even though the contract has been signed. You bring no property or goods to the arrangement. All you have to do is tell Thothmes that you've changed your mind, and then come home with me. Have you more doubts?"

"Not more. Only the same ones. But I know I'm doing what is best for me. Thothmes knows it too. Yet it is a very hard thing, saying goodbye to you and going to my husband's bed tonight. He's so good to me." She gestured at the earrings, the belt, the thick carnelian-encrusted bracelets on her wrists. "These are made of purple gold. Nakht ordered them from the Kingdom of Mitanni, very far to the northeast, where the manufacture of such a thing is a secret. Only the gods know what this jewellery has cost the Governor. Also this." She looked down at her hands, still held out in the ancient indication of pleading or submission. "The soles of my feet are hennaed also. Because legally I am already Thothmes' wife with the signing of the papyrus. I am now the Lady Ishat, a noblewoman."

"I did notice, my Ishat. I'm overjoyed at your good fortune, but only if it's what you really want."

"It's what I need." Coming to him, she let her forehead droop onto his chest. "Hold me, Huy. Put your arms around me and let

me draw your smell, your warmth, your vitality into myself one
last time. After tonight I shall repudiate the thoughts of you that
constitute adultery."

He did as she had asked, encircling her, feeling the taut
muscles of her back, the jaspers around her circlet pressing into
his neck as he tightened his hold. For six long breaths she grasped
him as though the floor of the room had become mud into which
she was sinking, then she stood away. "Iput will trail after me all
evening carrying my cosmetics box, just in case I might need
refurbishing," she said, then laughed. This time the sound had a
hint of hysteria in it. "Well, old friend, let us go down."

They walked to the door. Huy opened it and together they
stepped into the passage. Iput left the floor where she had been
waiting, fly whisk in one hand and the cosmetics box tucked
under the other arm. Huy drew Ishat's gold-laden arm through
his. "Lady Ishat," he said.

The noise grew steadily louder as they descended the stairs,
until at the entrance to the reception hall it became a deafening
cacophony of hundreds of voices chattering and laughing. Here
they paused, and at once Ptahhotep glided up, resplendent in
gold-bordered linen, his naked scalp wound with a yellow ribbon,
his own face paint immaculate, his white Staff of Office in one
hand. "Lady Ishat, Seer Huy, my Masters await your presence,"
he said loudly above the cheerful din. "Follow me." He strode
away, calling, "Step aside for a moment, honoured guests. Step
aside." The crowd parted and Huy and Ishat went through
behind the steward's stately form. Ishat stared straight ahead, but
Huy looked curiously to right and left, both hoping and dreading
to see people he knew. Cups were raised to them. Faces broke
into smiles as they went.

A dais had been erected against one wall, and as they
approached it, Huy whispered to Ishat, "Bow to Nakht but not to

the others. You are their equal now." She nodded as Thothmes jumped the small distance from the dais onto the tiles and came beaming towards them. Ishat's arm slid out from under Huy's elbow.

Thothmes embraced her. "Ishat, you have never looked more goddess-like! Come and meet the rest of your family. Huy, there's a table and cushions for you on the dais also."

Huy glanced ahead. Nakht was sitting in a large chair, a high table before him. Huy wondered what it had cost him to be arrayed as he was, in a starched linen helmet whose lappets touched his gold-hung shoulders. The symbols of his charge, the Heq-at sepat—the crook and the fishing net—rose in delicate miniature from the golden band across his forehead to which the helmet was attached. The thick arm band of his office, which had once gripped an upper arm, now lay loosely about one of the Governor's wasted wrists. Both his hands, heavy with rings, lay in his white lap. Amethysts glittered on the thongs of his sandals. Huy, coming up to him and bowing then looking into his kohled eyes, saw the glaze of a deep poppy infusion that was walling him off from both his pain and the swirling throng that filled the hall. He smiled at Huy.

Nasha was sitting close beside him, her head level with the arm of his chair. She nodded to Huy, then jerked a thumb to her right. No words were needed. Unwillingly, with an inner shrinking, Huy turned.

But Thothmes and Ishat were blocking his view. It was obvious that Thothmes was introducing Ishat to Anuket and her husband, Amunnefer. Stepping up onto the dais, Huy moved to stand behind Ishat, his fingers hooking lightly into her belt, and he did not know whether he did so to reassure Ishat that he was there or to take courage from her. *In a moment I shall see you*, he thought wildly, *my fragile little garland weaver with the big brown*

*eyes, the aristocratic oval of a face with its flawless skin—I shall hear
your voice, always so soft, often hesitant. O gods, it is as though the
years since our last meeting have disappeared, meant nothing!* It was
only as Ishat shifted slightly and Huy moved on shaking legs to
stand beside her that he remembered the last time he had seen
Anuket. She had listened secretly to the anguish of his interview
with Nakht from outside the office window, and as he had
stumbled through the garden, half mad with grief, she had come
sliding out of the darkness to subtly reinforce her hold over him.

Now she was before him, smiling a greeting, those eyes in which
he wanted to drown limned enticingly with kohl, both graceful,
tiny hands pressed against his cheeks, and for one despairing
moment she was as she used to be and he was alone with her in the
herb room, weak with desire, inhaling the blend of flower and
drying herb scents, his gaze riveted on the motions of her long
fingers and the curtain of dark hair hiding her exquisite face.
"Anuket," he blurted hoarsely, and her arms dropped.

"Huy. Or should I say Great Seer Huy." She was appraising him,
her eyes moving rapidly and impudently up and down his body.
"By Amun, you're even more handsome than the last time I saw
you, how many years ago? Three? Four?" Leaning closer to him, she
lowered her voice. "If my father had known that you were about to
catch the eye of the One, my fate might have been very different."

Puzzled, Huy took a step back and regarded her. The voice
held an echo of the melody he had been both longing and
dreading to hear, but it had somehow thickened, become
rougher. Her body too seemed to have thickened under the white
and silver sheath she was wearing. A hint of loose flesh lay under
her chin. There were patches of greyness under eyes whose lids
were more heavy than he remembered. The eyes themselves were
slightly bloodshot. The hair on her head was clearly an elaborate
wig fashioned in dozens of long, stiff braids.

She saw him staring at it and said rather defensively, "Weset is a very hot place. The desert is close. I keep my skull shaved for coolness. This is my husband, Amunnefer." She glanced briefly to the side, where the man was waiting.

Still in the grip of bewilderment, momentarily unable to tear his eyes away from Anuket's tainted beauty, Huy's body turned to Amunnefer before he turned his head. *Where is she?* he thought incoherently even as he answered the man's smile. *Where is that delicate child? I should see a small maturing in her, of course, but not this coarse caricature!* Ishat had moved to stand beside him. Looking at her quickly, he saw a naked triumph stamped clearly on her features. A sudden distaste for all women, a flash of purely masculine bafflement at the mysterious actions of their kas, took hold of him and was gone.

He bowed to Amunnefer. "I'm glad to meet you at last, noble one," he said. "We have exchanged letters, and you were good enough to trust to my gold without knowing very much about me. I am grateful."

"The word of Governor Nakht and my wife put my mind entirely at ease, Seer Huy," Amunnefer replied. He was a tall, thin man with a wigged head that seemed too large for his body, straight and healthy though it clearly was, and with a pleasant, open expression that spoke of a cheerful honesty. "I'm sure you have many questions for me regarding the crop in which you have invested. Anuket and I will not be returning to Weset for several days, during which time I will be available to you."

"Thank you," Huy said politely. "I do indeed wish to speak with you, but tonight is of course not convenient. Tomorrow afternoon?" He was answering Amunnefer automatically, hardly aware of what he was saying, his glance continually straying to the woman who still bore a strong resemblance to Anuket but must surely be some family relation, a cousin, perhaps, whom he had not yet met. Her mouth had been painted silver to match the wealth of silver jewellery clasping her arms, her neck, and woven into the strands of her wig, and her smile held a hint of intimacy that was making him uncomfortable. *Wake up!* he told himself sternly. *This is indeed Anuket whom you loved, Anuket the sister of your friend, the girl you have known for years. But you do not know this Anuket, something* whispered inside him. *The Anuket you remember has been changed somehow.*

"We had better take our tables," Thothmes said. "Ptahhotep is about to announce the feast."

Even as he spoke, the steward's Staff of Office thudded on the floor with a measured authority that rapidly silenced the crowd. "Seek your cushions, honoured guests, and wear the garlands of celebration prepared for you. The feast begins."

There was a long confusion while men and women chose places, sank onto the cushions, and placed around their necks the flowers waiting to be lifted from the surfaces of the tables in front of them. Huy found himself between Nasha and Ishat, with Thothmes wriggling down beside his new wife and Anuket and Amunnefer beyond him. Thothmes' eldest sister, Meri-Hathor, and her husband were also on the dais, on the other side of Nakht. She waved at Huy, who waved back, pleased to see her. He had not known her well. She had married and left Nakht's house at about the same time Huy had begun to visit there, but he remembered her as being willing to take the younger children into the marshes or light fires for them on the verge of the river. *She looks well and happy,* Huy thought. *Unlike Anuket.*

Snatching up Ishat's garland, Thothmes set it gently over her head and kissed her. Nasha had stood to do the same for Nakht. Young girls Huy had never seen before had begun to move through the glittering throng, tying perfume cones onto every head.

"Father hired them specially," Nasha remarked, lowering herself beside Huy. "They look lovely, don't they, in those little yellow kilts and ribbons. You're pale, Huy. I can guess why."

Nakht touched her shoulder, wanting something, and as Nasha leaned up to hear him, Ishat put her mouth against Huy's ear. *Don't say it!* Huy begged her silently. *Please leave it alone!*

But Ishat knew better than to gloat over her victory. She stroked the back of his hand once. "I'm sorry, my dearest brother," she murmured before lifting her chin for the tying of the cone that had been settled in her hair. Huy, feeling a polite hand on his shoulder, did the same. At once the pungent, compelling aroma of myrrh began to insinuate itself into his nostrils with the slowly melting beeswax.

A servant bent. "Ox liver with fennel, Great Seer? Inet fish grilled with coriander? A stew of fava beans, parsley, and pepper? The Governor imported that black and powerful spice just for this occasion. Do try it. Fresh lettuce and mint with cucumber, celery, and sesame bread? The wine is coming."

Nakht had spared no trouble or expense for the marriage feast of his only son. Course followed course: beef, gazelle, fish, waterfowl, and pigeons; lentils and many different kinds of beans prepared with every herb and spice available; an abundance of fresh young vegetables, desserts of honeyed tigernut cakes, date and fig confections, and wines. Pomegranate, red and white grape, palm and fig and date wines filled and refilled the cups of the revellers. One wine in particular had been reserved for the company on the dais. "Year two of the Osiris-King Thothmes the Third, he whom I loved and after whom I was named, high-quality wine six times good, of the Vineyard Food-of-Egypt, made under the supervision of the Chief Overseer of the Vineyard Duauf," Thothmes told them proudly as Ptahhotep unsealed the four precious clay flagons and the red liquid was poured out in a shining stream.

"This vintage is better than the one Father served at *my* wedding feast." Anuket's voice came faintly to Huy over the growing din in the hall. "You are very honoured, Lady Ishat." The words were slightly slurred, but the tones stirred echoes in Huy's heart. He sipped his wine, noted its undoubted excellence, and fixed his attention on the melee below the dais.

The music of Nakht's players could be heard intermittently through the happy noise. A few women, already drunk, were dancing to the tap-tapping of the drum, loose bodies bending and swaying between the tables, the melted wax from their cones gleaming on brown necks and half-covered breasts. The heat had become oppressive, compounded by hundreds of bodies and dozens of lamps on their tall stands ranged about the walls. Huy could see the linens of the feasters closest to the wide-open doors stirring in the night breeze. Ptahhotep would have made sure that the rear door to the garden remained open and guarded also. But no coolness came to those on the dais. Thothmes said something to Ishat that made her laugh, the familiar sound returning Huy to his own small reception room at Hut-herib, its gleaming tiles, its pretty pillars, its shadowed quiet. He closed his eyes. He was sitting there and she was laughing as she came hurrying to him along the passage, full of something to tell him. He would see her in a moment. Hair and necklaces flying, she would rush up to him, perhaps with a scroll in her hand. "Huy ...," she would say. "Huy ..."

"Huy?" The voice was Nasha's. "Father has had enough. He asks that you and Ptahhotep put him to bed. Your touch comforts him, he says."

At once Huy rose, aware that Anuket's drunken gaze had swivelled to him immediately. Gently, he and the steward helped Nakht out of the chair. He had eaten and drunk little. Food remained on his platter and his gold cup was still half full of wine. Together, the three of them moved slowly down the two steps from the dais and started across the littered floor. Silence fell around them as they made their way to the passage. The crowd bowed deeply and fell back. When they reached the relative peace of the hallway, they paused. Deeply moved, Huy felt the Governor's head fall against his shoulder.

"It's all right, Ptahhotep," Huy said. "He weighs no more than a few feathers. Go back to your duties. I'll deliver him to his body servant." Ptahhotep bowed quickly and went away. Huy picked Nakht up, climbed the stairs under the eyes of the guards stationed along the hall and at the foot, and came at last to Nakht's large bedchamber. The body servant came forward at once. "Governor, do you need more poppy?" Huy asked as the two of them lowered Nakht's emaciated body onto the couch.

Wearily, Nakht shook his head. "No," he muttered. "I took enough of the drug before the feast to kill one of my horses. I think I can sleep. Thank you, Huy, for your strong arm. Thank you for loving my son. Thank you for trying to save my wife from her fate. I have always loved you …" The words trailed away.

"He sleeps," the servant whispered. "I stay with him all night, Great Seer."

Huy nodded and left, closing the door quietly behind him and starting along the dim corridor. He was reluctant to rejoin the carousing going on below, but he knew that somewhere in the throng Ramose would be looking for him, although he had been unable to spot the High Priest among the densely packed bodies.

The noise hit him as he plunged into the reception hall. Servants were removing the tables. Many more people were dancing now, wine cups in their hands. Huy saw Anuket among them, one shoulder strap of her sheath hanging down her back, her wig slightly askew, her cheek smeared with kohl. She spotted him as he came forward and began to hurry towards him, but a familiar form blocked his view of her and Huy found himself enfolded in a crushing embrace. The High Priest's smile filled his carefully painted face.

"Huy! I've been watching you up there with Nakht's family. How well, how lordly, you look, my erstwhile pupil! I hear wonderful things about you. Do you remember how I caught you by the sacred Ished Tree? You were, what—five? You received a beating, and no one knew then how intertwined your fate would be with the Tree and the Book. Will you come to the temple before you go back to your estate so that we can catch up on all the news? It's rather difficult to do tonight."

Huy laughed. He felt genuinely glad to see Ramose, although when he left the priest's care he had been desperate to escape the awe and near-veneration of the denizens of Ra's domain. "Thothmes is eager to walk down that particular lane of memory with me," Huy responded. "If I can tear him away from Ishat, we'll certainly visit you, and the school."

"Good." Ramose looked about. "Henenu is here somewhere and is eager for a word or two with you. I think I shall summon my litter, pay my respects to the Noble Thothmes and his beautiful new wife, and return to my cell before the proceedings here become truly wild." Embracing Huy again, he strode towards the dais, bowed, then bent forward to hear something Thothmes was saying to him.

Huy edged away from where Anuket was swaying. He wanted to find Henenu the Rekhet. He did not expect her to be drunk and dancing, but he threaded his way through the unruly mass of bodies anyway, his nostrils assailed by a myriad of different perfumes blending with human sweat and the rank odour of crushed blooms. Several young men loomed in his way, faces he recognized as fellow students, who embraced him and exchanged a few careless words before melting back into the press. There was no sign of the Rekhet, but just beyond the gyrating celebrants he came across Thothhotep and Paroi, Thothmes' scribe, deep in conversation, their backs against the wall, forgotten wine cups beside them. At the sight of him they began to scramble up. Huy waved them back down.

"You look lovely tonight, Thothhotep," he told her, and it was true. Wine and heat had brought a flush of colour to her thin cheeks. Lamplight glinted on the gold earrings he had bought for her. She had rather inexpertly attempted to tie up her hair with a white ribbon. Most of it had sprung free and was trailing about her ears. She had also limned her eyes crudely with kohl, from Ishat, Huy surmised. Even though her touch had been clumsy, the effect was pleasing. With a smile and the first hint of a genuine fondness for her, he saw her palette resting on the floor under the edge of her sheath.

"Thank you, Master."

"Are you enjoying the evening?"

She returned his smile. "Yes indeed! I am privileged to be here, among so many noble people."

Leaving them to whatever it was they had been discussing so seriously, Huy made his way to the open door, breathing in the sweet night air that came gusting to meet him. He was about to step past the guards and out into the darkness when a hand fell on his shoulder.

"Where do you think you're going without me, Master?" Anhur said. "It's a grand night for cutting a Seer's throat, with all these wine-addled aristocrats staggering about. They've begun to take over the rear garden, you know, but I think there'll be more falling down and sleeping than copulating."

Huy laughed. "Anhur. I've hardly seen you since we arrived."

"Maybe not, but I've been watching you. So has that sister of the Noble Thothmes. I presume you know her well. She's very beautiful, but the marks of dissipation are on her already. A pity. Now, the other one!" He shook his head in admiration. "The Lady Nasha. So much life bubbling up in her!"

"What have you been doing with yourself apart from watching me?" Huy asked, deliberately steering his soldier's thoughts away from Nakht's family. He loved this blunt man, had loved him ever since Anhur had been sent from Ra's temple here in Iunu to guard him as he read and pondered the scrolls of the Book of Thoth that were kept at Thoth's temple in Khmun. Amiable yet frank, Anhur had treated Huy like a son to be respected, protected, and occasionally comforted. Huy allowed him more freedom of speech than any of his other servants. The two of them had begun to walk slowly along the vine-hung path to the watersteps.

"Keeping an eye on the Mistress as well," Anhur replied. "Sharing the news with Seneb and the Governor's other captains. If you go to the temple while you're here, please take me with you. The temple guards were my friends when I worked there. I'd like to see them again, if you allow it."

"Of course." Huy's ears had caught a familiar sound, the faint clicking of shells against one another. Peering ahead to where torches flared and guttered to either side of the watersteps, he saw a patch of greyness a short way in under the trees by the path. He pointed. "There's the Rekhet. I want to talk to her. You can go back into the hall if you like, Anhur. I'm really in no danger here."

Anhur grunted. "Only from wine-soaked women, I suppose. I won't mind sitting in the grass for a while, Master. The air's cool."

Huy nodded and left him, cutting across the path and into the trees. The Rekhet was on a reed mat, her back against the trunk of a palm, her knees drawn up under her white sheath and both shell-hung arms folded across them. Seeing him come forward, her lined face broke into a smile. The cowries pinned into her grey hair clicked softly.

"Huy! I knew you'd find me tonight. This is a true pleasure. Let me look at you."

Huy sank onto the sandy grass beside her. "Henenu," he said after making sure there was no one within earshot. Few people were given the privilege of knowing her name. She was an exorcist and diviner of spirits and demons, who must on no account discover what she was called. A name held great power, and in the mind of a demon that knowledge could be used to destroy her.

She scrutinized him slowly in the faint orange light of the torches filtering through the trees. "You are sad," she said at last, taking his hand in her warm fingers. "Setting your oldest friend free was an effort of the will that has left you empty. Yet the sacrifice is pleasing to Atum. It has given you a new strength, though you are not yet aware of it. How has it been to see Anuket again?"

The question was put very gently. Huy looked away to where the shadows deepened beyond the reach of the guttering torch flames. *How has it been?* he thought dismally. *It has been as though for years I have drunk directly from the tears of Isis, only to find that they have always been bitter to the taste. It has been like waiting every day for the arrival of a beloved friend who comes at last and drives a dagger into my heart and walks away. It has been a dying.*

"You know," he answered hoarsely, "I hardly recognized her. Nakht called her a poison to any man, but his words did not penetrate my consciousness at the time."

"She was named under unlucky auspices. Do you remember? Many years ago Anuket used to be a chaste and innocent water goddess. In these days she has become a creature of wild licence, worshipped by those who seek satisfaction in the excesses of the flesh. She and the goddess Bastet have much in common. We cannot escape the twist of destiny our name bestows on us."

"Nakht was furious," Huy remembered. "Who told me that? Did she? Did Thothmes? No, it was Ramose. He read the stars and named her. Nakht made him do it over again—the time of her birth, the weight of luck carried by the day, the astrological chart. Ramose did so, but the name did not change. Oh, Henenu! Anuket told me once that she would rather be named Satis, after the goddess who stands at the entrance of the Duat to pour purifying water over each King as he enters the place of the dead. She told me that no totem of the goddess Anuket will ever stand in her bedchamber. And Ramose himself said that he cast her horoscope three times and conjured against the seven Hathors, and tied seven red ribbons about her limbs for seven days to bind any evil bau that might be hovering, but the name had to stand. He and Nakht almost lost their friendship over it. My Anuket was the water goddess, pure and good! What has she to do with the whore goddess of today!" He pulled his hand from Henenu's grasp and covered his face with both palms, and the gesture served to break the dam behind which his disillusionment had been hiding all evening.

"Store her away in some deep niche of your mind and forget her," the Rekhet said. "She is a source of great pain to her family, and particularly to her poor long-suffering husband, who is often on the point of divorcing her. But he loves her, I think. She dons coarse linen and spends many evenings in the beer houses of Weset. At home she drinks wine in which lotus petals have been steeped. She is addicted to the elation the brew gives her. So far I do not think that she has dared to stoop to adultery. She is fortunate to be married to a man of patience, but she is becoming an embarrassment to him. After all, he is the son of the Governor of the Uas sepat, of which Weset is the capital."

"Stop!" Huy came close to jamming a hand across her mouth. "Every one of your words hurts me! My love for her is dead as of tonight, but I desire her again in every memory of my days in Nakht's house! Can nothing save her?"

Henenu leaned close. "Not you, Huy. Not you. If Nakht had given her to you in marriage as you begged him to do, she would have annihilated your gift and reduced your soul to the level of a grovelling beggar seeking any show of affection from her, no matter how slight. When will you accept your celibacy as a necessary portion of Atum's gift?"

"Never! I chose to read the Book of Thoth. That was all. I did not choose celibacy, or my inability to get drunk like everyone else. Those things were secretly added to the result of my choosing."

"True. But see what compensations Atum has provided! The King now takes care of you as Egypt's most valuable living person, and you will continue to gather fame and riches about you as you heal and predict the future and guide those in authority." She turned away. "Go home to Hut-herib. Keep examining the Book that resides whole and bright in your mind, until understanding comes to you. Pray. Order your life as simply as you are able. I love you, Huy. Continue to write to me."

He was dismissed. He kissed her soft, lined cheek and rose. "I love you also, Henenu. Keep the demons away from me." He thought of asking her for one of her cowrie shells. They were an excellent protection against the malevolence of the unseen world, even those made of clay. Henenu's were genuine, and fiercely expensive. Instead, he bowed to her in homage to her prescience and retraced his steps to where Anhur was sitting cross-legged in the dimness.

He yawned as Huy came up to him. "I took a look into the hall a while ago," he said as he hauled himself to his feet. "The Noble Thothmes and Lady Ishat have gone. The Lady Nasha also. The crowd is thinning out, but so far no one is seeking the barges. Will you sleep now, Huy? You seem very tired."

"I am. Let's see if we can cross the hall without being accosted."

At the foot of the stairs, they parted. There had been no sign of Anuket or her husband, to Huy's relief. He said good night to his captain, mounted the stairs, and entered his own room. Tetiankh was asleep on his pallet by the couch and Huy did not wake him to be washed. Quickly, he threw off his clothes, removed his jewellery, and crawled onto his couch, blowing out the lamp as he did so. Darkness and silence descended. *They are making love, Thothmes and Ishat*, he thought as he turned on his side and closed his eyes. *I must not imagine it. He will make her happy, and that is all that matters. My dearest Ishat, playmate of my childhood, friend of my youth, your destiny is a pleasant one. Unlike Anuket's.* He groaned. *What shall I say to her tomorrow?* he wondered. *She will hunt for me, I know it.* The image of Anuket hunting him was somehow sinister, and Huy was aware of being glad that sleep was claiming him at last.

He woke, feeling grimy and enervated, when Tetiankh began to raise the reed window hangings. Cool morning air flowed into the room. Sitting up, Huy reached for the fresh water his body servant had placed beside the couch and drank rapidly. "No food, Tetiankh?" he wanted to know.

The man began to gather up Huy's soiled clothes. "A meal has been set out in the garden for those who were unable to get to their litters or barges last night," Tetiankh told him. "It's mostly a selection from the feast, with today's bread and milk added. If you will go down to the bathhouse, Master, and secure a place, I shall take these to the washerman, put your jewellery away, and join you at once."

"There's a queue in the bathhouse?"

"Unfortunately, yes." He grinned across at Huy. "Sore heads and grass-stained kilts are the least of it. Ptahhotep has had to send for more natron and oil. He miscalculated the number of guests who would be unable to go to their homes. Dismiss me, Master."

Huy did so, wrapped himself in a sheet from the couch, and cautiously let himself out into the passage. It was empty. Padding barefooted along it, he descended the rear stairs and entered the bathhouse. It was crowded with naked bodies and harried servants but curiously quiet. The bathing slabs were all occupied. The room was pleasantly humid and redolent with the scents of perfumed oils, jasmine, and lilies, Huy decided, inhaling deeply. Ptahhotep and his assistant steward stood in the doorway leading to the interior of the house, ready to answer any demand. Huy glanced towards the garden. Under the shade of the huge sycamores, the benches were all occupied by recumbent figures being shaved or oiled. Huy wondered whether he should grab up some natron and go to the river to wash himself. He was about to approach the salt dishes when someone touched his arm. Turning, he found Anuket's husband, Amunnefer, smiling at him.

"Good morning, Huy," Amunnefer greeted him loudly and cheerfully. Several people standing close by winced and moved away. "I see by your eyes that you are suffering no ill effects from Nakht's excellent wine. Neither am I. I drink very little."

Unlike your wife, Huy thought, smiling back.

"I am never drunk," he replied. "But I am in need of hot water." He was suddenly conscious of the braid that had worked loose in the night to spread strands of unruly hair down his back and curling onto his collarbones. He had slept fully painted and knew that his cheeks must be streaked with black kohl. He rubbed at them ineffectually. "Forgive my appearance, noble one. I did not wake my servant to wash me last night."

"You are a considerate man." Amunnefer indicated the stone shelf that ran around the bathhouse walls, where the jars of oil and natron were kept. "Let's sit down and talk while we wait for a turn on the slabs. 'Considerate' was a word my wife often used to describe you," he went on as they settled rather uncomfortably on the damp ledge. "She spoke often of the times when you stayed in this house and kept her company in the herb room while she wove her garlands. It's a pity that she no longer follows that blessed pursuit. I believe that she was very adept."

Those fingers moving so surely among the green stems scattered in her lap and all around her on the floor will haunt me forever if I let them, Huy thought.

"Yes, she was," he agreed aloud. "I was in love with her, helplessly and hopelessly, for years, you know." He had not meant to say that, but Amunnefer had an air of guileless warmth about him that quickly melted any barrier between himself and another. Too late, Huy recognized it as an admirable attribute for a future Governor.

Amunnefer laughed. "Yes, I do know. She told me. What agonies we suffer in the throes of young love, don't we, Huy? It's a good thing that we grow up and away from such dangers. The sober affection that grows slowly in a marital union lasts much longer and is far less uncomfortable."

Ruthlessly, Huy quashed the urge to ask him how much he loved Anuket, how he could tolerate the shame of her behaviour day after day, how and when such behaviour had come about. Instead he nodded. "So I am told, not having a wife myself. But tell me about your venture into poppy growing, noble one. My interest is larger than my investment of gold."

"I, or now I should say 'we,' have ten arouras of land south of Weset—on the east bank, of course, just out of reach of the Inundation—and another ten arouras on the verge of the lake at the oasis of Ta-she, in the desert west of Mennofer. His Majesty was anxious that Egypt should begin to produce her own drug. Every physician wants a constant supply of it, of course, and importing it from Keftiu and the Bend of Naharin, far to the northeast, was becoming very expensive for His Majesty. That's why he has allowed me to attempt cultivation." He grimaced ruefully. "His Majesty deeded the arouras to me. They were khato, and had reverted to the Horus Throne. But I had to buy the seeds and the knowledge of two foreign overseers myself. No one is as rich as Pharaoh! The sowing was done two years ago, after the land had been thoroughly cleared. The overseers send me reports every week. I am learning that the handling of the mature plants and the extraction of the drug is a delicate business. The quality is not as potent as the imported poppy—not yet, anyway. But you've made a very wise investment that should result in much gold for you, me, and the Horus Throne."

"When is the harvest?"

"Flowers appear during Epophi, eight months from the sowing, but the crop at Ta-she was sown first. The sowings are staggered so that we do not have to wait for our reward! If you are ever in Weset, come and see the arouras for yourself. I spend too much time there at the moment. I'm anxious that no calamity takes our profit away from us."

"In the meantime, the King will continue to supply me with the drug."

Amunnefer shot him a sympathetic glance. "Everyone knows how much pain you suffer after a Seeing. The King told me how concerned for you he was when you almost collapsed in his presence after the marvellous predictions you made for him."

"He did?" Huy was astonished. He and Ishat had been living hand to mouth on a noisy street in Hut-herib when the King, on his way to make war on the recalcitrant tribes of Rethennu, had summoned Huy to See for him. Every prediction Atum had given Huy for the King had come to pass, but no thanks had arrived from His Majesty Amunhotep the Second for months. Huy had resigned himself to the King's ingratitude and had believed himself forgotten until his and Ishat's fortunes had been changed overnight by His Majesty's decree.

"He did. Would you like me to send you copies of the letters I receive from the overseers of the poppy fields?"

"Yes, indeed! I'll be anxious to follow the progress of our venture." Huy stood and bowed. "There are bathing slabs available now and my servant is waiting to wash me. I thank you for allowing me to entrust you with my gold, noble one, and I wish us both great success. Greet Anuket for me. I may not have an opportunity to speak with her before I leave Iunu."

"Oh, we'll be here for a few days yet," Amunnefer replied, "and Thothmes tells me that you and he will be visiting your old school tomorrow. Anuket will doubtless be available to you this afternoon."

Huy's heart sank. Bowing again, this time in agreement, he took the few steps to the nearest slab, dropped the sheet, and beckoned Tetiankh. *So I will not be able to avoid her after all,* he thought as Tetiankh untied what was left of his braid and warm water began to cascade over him. *What am I to say to her? Will she see the disenchantment in my eyes and be distressed? I need Ishat's sharp tongue to remind me how shabbily I was treated. Surely she would tell me not to waste any sympathy on the bitch because sympathy would weaken me when facing her.* Huy smiled ruefully as Ishat's voice echoed scornfully in his mind.

Later, shaved, oiled, and clothed in fresh linen, he made his way to the rear garden, where a long table had been set up and its contents covered with a cloth. Servants waited behind it to serve the guests. Huy had his plate filled with cold duck, bread, and a few dried figs, picked up a cup of beer, and, looking about for a shady spot, saw Nasha sitting by the acacia hedge with cushions piled around her and her body servant kneeling at her side, wringing water from a piece of linen. Huy approached her cautiously, and seeing him come, she raised a languid hand. "Sit by me if you like, Huy, but don't speak above a whisper and try to eat quietly. I'm so ill this morning that I couldn't even bear to have my hair combed. I should have stayed in my room, but it stinks of wine fumes and my own body. Gods, how stupid I am! Still, it was a marvellous marriage feast, wasn't it?"

Huy lowered himself onto one of the cushions. Nasha was peering at him through swollen, slitted eyes. The servant pressed the damp linen to her forehead and she sighed. "It doesn't help much. I took a dose of castor oil when I crawled off my couch, and I've been drinking the infusion of fenugreek our physician gave me to cleanse my stomach and calm my liver, but I still feel like a week-old corpse. The physician is very busy this morning. Father is a little stronger. Having Thothmes married at last has been a relief to him, seeing that I am almost certainly condemned to remain a virgin for the rest of my life. Give me a sip of your beer. I'm still thirsty even though I've drunk the river dry. And keep that plate away from me—the smell of the duck is nauseating."

"I love you, Nasha," Huy chuckled, passing her his cup and watching her nose disappear into it. "And you love wine. Don't deny it."

"I won't." She licked her pale lips and passed the cup back to him. "I do love it, but I thank Ra, my totem, that I do not love it the way my sister does. And speaking of Ra, before you ask, Thothmes and Ishat ate their early meal in their bedchamber and now they are in the temple, carrying offerings of thanks to Ra for their joining. They'll be back on their couch like the rest of us this afternoon. Isn't that the captain of your guard?"

Huy turned to see Anhur scanning the grounds. When he saw Huy, he nodded, obviously satisfied, and went away again.

"He watches you very closely, doesn't he?" Nasha observed, holding out her arms so that her body servant could soak her wrists. "If you've finished eating, why don't we play sennet for a while? I refuse to move until the last of the guests have left."

She sent her woman for the game, and Nasha and Huy settled down with the cones and spools. Huy was glad to be occupied. If Anuket appeared, she would see that he was busy and not alone. He knew that he was being cowardly, but for the moment he did not care. He wished fervently that he could scoop up Ishat, get onto their modest barge, and go home.

By noon, all the guests but the members of the family had gone. An exhausted silence seemed to settle over Nakht's estate. Food had been set out in the hall, but no one appeared to eat it. Huy, like everyone else, took to his couch early for the afternoon sleep, and did not wake until the sky outside his window had begun to fade to pink. He had Tetiankh dress him in clean linen and paint his face before he went downstairs, hoping to find Thothmes or Ishat, but only the servants preparing the hall for the evening meal greeted him. In the end, feeling lost, he wandered out into the garden, walking slowly along the narrow paths that wound between flower beds and shrubbery and brought him back at last to the rear entrance of the house. Reluctant to go inside, he decided to find Anhur, who was surely not far away, and leave the estate to watch the river craft float by.

His own barge was tethered close to the watersteps. Perhaps Thothhotep would be on board. *I have never felt so rootless,* he thought as his feet found the path running straight to the steps, and he did not dare substitute the word *lonely* for *rootless.* The vine leaves clinging to the tall trellis that provided shade to either side of the path smelled sweet, patting against each other with a quiet susurration as the early evening breeze strengthened.

"Anhur, are you close by?" he called, turning towards the entrance to the house, and as he did so, he saw a woman emerge from between the pillars and come gliding towards him. Behind her, Huy saw Anhur pause and then stand still. In spite of the sudden need to run away, Huy felt his heartbeat quicken. He waited, unsmiling. Anuket did not smile either. Halting in front of him, she scanned his face, then her hands lifted to trail down his cheeks, across his eyelids, flutter gently against his mouth.

"I have dreamed of touching you again, Huy. Do you remember when I did so here in this garden, in the darkness, when you kissed me and begged me to leave my family and go with you? I was a fool to say no, but I was very young and unsure. Can you forgive me?"

Unsure of what, Anuket? Huy thought as those seductive little hands came to rest on his naked shoulders. *Unsure of your hold over me? I do not think so. You were so cold that night, unresponsive, even cruel. You knew that it did not matter how you behaved towards me, that I would carry my love for you wherever I went, whatever you did.* The slowly bronzing light was gentle on the features she was lifting to his gaze, softening the premature lines traced there by her indulgences, giving the sallow skin a youthful flush, but it could not erase the slight pouches under those huge eyes or the fold under the determined chin. *How dare you demolish such a long-held and familiar fantasy with this gross distortion, Anuket!* he demanded silently, full of a sudden and wholly irrational anger. *How dare you render the pain of the years behind me worthless!*

He stepped back so that she was forced to drop her arms. "There is nothing to forgive," he answered her smoothly. "I also was young and unsure. You were a part of the security I was leaving behind. I wanted to take that part with me, for solace. Since then I have been very happy with Ishat and my growing good fortune, and you have made a most advantageous marriage. Think nothing of it. Do not berate yourself for the foolishness of youth."

Her expression had been changing as he spoke, the eagerness replaced by a growing sullenness that she was clearly struggling to control. "Ah yes, Ishat," she said. "Your old peasant friend. Your scribe, so I've heard. Will you miss her in more ways than one, my handsome Huy? And is there a hidden reason for replacing her with yet another woman? Perhaps they have both been substitutes for someone else, someone you could not have?" She was unable to conquer the spite in her voice, the voice that had lost its clarity and become overlaid with a thickening of tone. Yet beneath what Huy saw as a crust, he could also see that the Anuket he remembered and loved still existed, as though he might take a hammer and tap that crust and it would fall away to reveal Anuket the water lady, slim and graceful, shy and beautiful. The image saddened him.

"What happened to you?" he said, tenderness welling up in him from the reservoir of the past. "You told me that you would never resemble the besmirched goddess Anuket of today, that you would remain pure and chaste and good. Why are you trying to destroy yourself?"

Her body jerked as though he had prodded her with a stick, and then her eyes filled with tears. "I used to envy you the powerful emotion you felt when you were near me," she blurted. "I remember telling you that I would never allow the fire to consume me. I remember everything, Huy. But secretly, I longed to feel the fire. Sometimes I pretended that I did, and then Nasha called me a manipulator and a flirt." Now the tears spilled over and began to trickle down her cheeks. "I believed that with marriage would come the flames, that one day I would look at my husband and all at once be filled with so much desire that I could not eat or sleep for wanting him, for needing to be in his presence, but it did not happen. Amunnefer does not understand. Only the wine understands." Lifting the hem of her sheath, she swiped clumsily at her face, leaving a smear of black kohl on the thin white linen.

Huy did not know what to say. *Is this an act to ensnare me once more? A kind of insanity? An excuse she tells herself? What?*

"They say you're still a virgin," she went on more calmly. "They say it's because of the gift of Seeing. But I don't believe in your virginity, not when I look at Ishat, or even her skinny replacement. Did you fall in love with Ishat after I rejected you, Huy?"

"No. I love her dearly, but not that way."

"Do you still love me?"

How can I tell her the truth? Huy thought, torn between pity and horror. *How can I describe how the years of fighting against that love came down to one moment when I saw her yesterday in the reception hall, and the flame she craves for herself went out in me? The ashes smoulder with compassion and memory, that is all.*

"I still have a great affection for you as a companion of my youth and the sister of my friend," he replied. "It grieves me to see you living up to your name. Amunnefer seems full of kindness and love for you. You live in luxury at Weset. Why can't you be happy?"

"My thirst for wine has grown," she said in a low voice. "I cannot get through a day without it now. And Huy, I am surrounded by beautiful young men—the servants, my husband's assistants, his friends among the nobility of Weset—and I watch them and wait for the fire, and when it doesn't strike, I drink and drink. It is as though the goddess Anuket has indeed possessed me!"

The last words were shouted. Huy saw Anhur start forward out of the shadows by the house entrance and raised a hand to stop him.

"If you think that, then you must seek an exorcist," Huy said urgently. "Go to Ramose while you are here and request an audience with the Rekhet, his friend. You need help, Anuket!"

She smiled, an unlovely twist of the mouth. "I need you to See for me, Huy. I need to know my future."

"But in knowing it, you will be tempted to do nothing, to allow fate to rule you," he objected, appalled at the thought of taking her hand and being precipitated into the maelstrom of her disordered life. "Decide to rule yourself, Anuket. It's not too late to find again the girl I adored!"

"Hypocrite," she whispered. "Fate rules your life entirely. Is it not so? In what manner do you rule yourself?" She held out her hands. "You See for the peasants of Hut-herib. You have Seen for my brother and Nasha. See for me. I am not afraid."

But I am, he told himself glumly. *I did not intend to See for Nasha. The moment came upon me years ago when the gift was new and untamed. What terrors would Atum show me if I granted this?*

To his unutterable relief, he heard a warning shout from the direction of the watersteps behind him and, turning, he saw a servant step into the water and catch the tether for Nakht's barge. At once the ramp was run out and Thothmes and Ishat came hurrying towards him. When he turned back, it was to see Anuket disappearing in the direction of the garden.

"We went to the temple and then we slept on the barge and then we took a little sail in the sunset," Ishat told him as the three of them linked arms and started for the house. "Now we are starving. Was that Anuket I saw walking away? I'm getting to know Nasha a little, but there hasn't been time to talk to Anuket. Perhaps this evening."

Huy glanced at Ishat curiously, his mind presenting uncalled-for images of her and Thothmes locked together naked in the close confines of the barge's cabin. She smiled up at him. "I'm really happy, Huy. I have the most wonderful, attentive husband. I'm not afraid anymore."

Huy looked across at Thothmes.

"I'm really happy also," Thothmes said. "I want to sit with Father for a moment before I eat, so I'll leave you together." He kissed Ishat and hurried inside. The others followed more slowly, trailed by Anhur.

The reception hall seemed empty and gloomy in the gathering dusk, in spite of the lamps being lit one after another by Ptahhotep's under steward. He bowed to Ishat as he went by. Eight tables had been placed close together in the centre. The dais had been dismantled. As Huy and Ishat moved forward, Meri-Hathor, Thothmes' eldest sister, and her husband emerged from the interior passage and greeted them cheerfully. "We are having cabbage and broad beans and perch fish tonight," Meri-Hathor told them as all four settled on the cushions behind the tables. "Then we are going home. Do you like the house Thothmes is building for you, Ishat?"

"More than anything!" Ishat replied fervently.

Nasha came striding into the hall looking a good deal better, Huy thought, than she had that afternoon, and behind her Amunnefer was peering about. "Have you seen Anuket?" he asked no one in particular, and no one answered him. She did not appear until the meal was half over, when she slid down beside her husband and called sharply for her food.

"Tomorrow we go back to school," Thothmes said to Huy. "We'll share a litter right after the morning meal. I wonder what sad little scraps are inhabiting our old cell." He lifted his wine cup. "Here's to the past! May it—"

But Ishat tugged at his arm. "Not to the past, dearest brother," she objected. "To the future, and all the magic it will hold."

The small company drank the toast and the conversation became general once more, but Huy fell silent. *She called him dearest brother, the most loving expression of affection there is. She used to call me that. Truly the times are changing.* Anuket was drinking steadily and bleakly. She was ignored.

Soon after the meal, the group scattered and Huy, anxious that an inebriated Anuket should not waylay him, went to Nakht's room, but the Governor's body servant turned him away.

"My Master is sleeping," Huy was told. "The physician attended him an hour ago." In answer to Huy's next query, the man shook his head. "He drinks much water and goat's milk, but will eat only a little, and only if I mash the food. Attending the feast was too strenuous an undertaking. Now he must recover some strength."

Huy thanked him and retreated to his room, feeling emotionally drained. He had set up the statue of Hut-herib's totem, Khenti-kheti, in the empty shrine. Now he made his prostrations and tried to pray—for Nakht, for Thothmes and Ishat's happiness—but the vision of Anuket's tears kept intruding, and in the end he closed the shrine and sat moodily on his couch.

Tetiankh's knock startled him. "The Lady Nasha is here," he said. "She wishes to play Dogs and Jackals with you, Master."

Huy greeted the young woman with relief, and for the rest of the evening the two of them sat over the game board, talking easily of nothing in particular. By the time he bade her a good night and Tetiankh had brought the hot water for his wash, Huy had recovered his equilibrium.

Tetiankh woke him early the following morning with warm bread, butter, a plate of dates, and a cup of water. Huy ate cheerfully. Today he would be spending at Ra's temple with Thothmes. Before long, bathed, painted, and dressed, he went downstairs and summoned Anhur. The litter was already waiting by the entrance pillars, the bearers slumped in the shade. Huy just had time to greet them and sniff the morning air before both Thothmes and Anhur appeared. "The temple school has never educated a pupil who became as famous as you," Thothmes said as he and Huy slid onto the litter's cushions and the bearers sprang into position. "Everyone will want to catch a glimpse of the Great Seer. I shouldn't be surprised if the High Priest hasn't granted them a free day in honour of your visit."

"Don't be absurd!" Huy looked across affectionately at his friend. "I'm only slightly famous. Besides, no one knows we're coming today. We'll be able to wander about and indulge ourselves in memories all we want."

Thothmes looked sheepish. "Actually, I sent a message to the High Priest yesterday, warning him that we would see him today. We are expected. Don't poke me. I thought it was polite."

Huy did not answer. He studied the familiar features of the boy who had shared a cell with him, listened to him recite the Book of Thoth, nursed him through a dangerous fever, and stoutly defended him in the swift antagonisms of childhood. Those features had changed little. The eyes had always held a thoughtfulness that had become an acute perception in the adult. The chin was perhaps less pointed, the sensitive mouth a little fuller, the body, always thin and wiry, had acquired more flesh. *Thothmes has retained the good manners and dignity that marked him for both teasing and admiration at school,* Huy mused. *His kindness and honesty will not be corrupted over the years.*

"Is my kohl running?" Thothmes asked.

Huy shook his head. "No. I was just feeling grateful for everything you have meant to me, and remembering your loyalty to the Osiris-one, King Thothmes the Third. You deserve to be happy, Thothmes."

"I am. I shall continue to be, providing Father rallies to hold his grandchildren on his knees. Did you See for him, Huy?"

"Yes. He asked me to. I can't tell you what I Saw, Thothmes. You must go to him if you want to know."

There was a silence, broken only by the quiet conversation of the bearers. Huy looked out to where Anhur was striding easily beside him.

"Perhaps I shall," Thothmes said finally. "But I can see what's written on your face and in the tension of your body, dearest Huy. I think I must prepare to become the next Governor of the Heq-at sepat."

Huy did not reply.

8

AS THOTHMES HAD PREDICTED, a large crowd of boys and priests had gathered on the vast stone expanse of the temple forecourt, and as Huy stepped out of the litter, a hush fell. He had no time to stare into the depths of the small lake where the canal from the river ended, where visitors to Ra's domain moored their boats, where he had learned to swim, and where Sennefer's throwing stick had plunged him to his death. He saw it out of the corner of his eye, though, as Ramose approached him and Thothmes, and Anhur moved to stand beside him. The water glittered innocuously in the bright sunlight, cool and inviting. *I drowned there*, Huy thought with an inward shudder. *For five days I lay dead while my body was taken to the House of the Dead at Hut-herib and my parents mourned. Since Ishat and I left our tiny home next to the beer house on that noisy street and moved onto the estate Pharaoh provided for us, I have seldom pondered the matter, but standing here with Thothmes in the place where I spent most of my childhood, I can imagine him and me walking across the forecourt on our way to the practice ground; imagine Sennefer shouting his usual insults at me, a peasant, son of a worker of the soil; feel my shame and anger suddenly turning to a blind rage that makes me launch myself at him. I feel Thothmes reaching to pull me back. I hear his cry, "No, Huy! No!" And I feel the stunning blow of the throwing stick as it struck my head and knocked me into this water. This water.*

He blinked. Ramose, clad in his priestly robes, the leopard skin draped over one shoulder as though it was one of Ra's feast days, bowed and then embraced him. "Welcome back to your second home," he said. "The students have been given a free day in your honour. They would like to sing for you the Hymn of Praise to Ra, just as you sang it every evening at dusk in your compound. Let it serve to remind you of the benevolence of the god and your own maturing here, under his roof." He bowed to Thothmes. "I do not forget you either, Assistant Governor. You are always welcome here."

He turned and held up a hand. There was a general shuffling among the gathering. Then the first notes of the Hymn rose clear and true into the limpid air, bringing a lump to Huy's throat. After a moment he and then Thothmes joined in, the words and melody slipping from their tongues easily and without reflection, the music rising and falling in its solemn cadences until the last note was held. It had always been followed by a sung prayer for Ra's safety as he travelled through the twelve houses in the belly of Nut the sky goddess, but today Ra was nearing his zenith. The boys fell silent.

Huy stepped forward. "Thank you all for this sacred greeting," he called. "The honour of this visit is more mine than yours. Enjoy your day of freedom."

Ramose gestured sharply at them and they bowed and scattered, a horde of white-kilted brown bodies with the ribbons of different colours that denoted their seniority tied into neatly braided youth locks.

Thothmes watched them go. "Gods, Huy," he breathed. "Were we ever so incredibly neat and well behaved?"

The High Priest laughed. "You were always very fastidious, Thothmes, but the lessons of cleanliness and tidiness came hard for you, Huy. You were a very spoiled, capricious child when your uncle Ker left you in our care. Well." He hoisted the leopard skin higher on his shoulder. "I'll leave you to explore your old home at your leisure. Feel free to eat the noon meal with the boys if you like. Come and see me before you return to Nakht's house." He strode away, his white sheath swirling against his ankles.

Huy turned to Anhur. "Go and visit the guards. I'll send a servant for you when it's time to go."

Anhur looked doubtful. "Remember how the boys in the temple school at Khmun pestered you. This lot is just waiting to dog your heels with all sorts of questions. Perhaps I should stay with the two of you."

"No. We can see to ourselves." It was Thothmes who spoke. "And Anhur, tell the bearers to leave if they want to, and come back before the afternoon sleep. Come on, Huy! Let's see if our old cell still smells of rinsing vinegar and lamp oil!"

Together they took the path that led them left from the concourse, beside the temple's wall, and on into the grassy compound lined with the cells of the pupils. It was crowded with expectant faces. At once a boy of about eight ran up to them and executed a breathless bow. "Honoured Lords!" he gasped. "I am Maani, son of the Governor of the Theb-ka sepat on the shores of the Great Green! I and my companion inhabit the cell where your blessed bodies used to lie! We are very proud to live there. Often I have dreams of you, Great Seer. Be pleased to grace our home with your presence."

Huy stifled an impulse to laugh. He thanked Maani gravely, and as he and Thothmes moved towards the open door of their old cell, Thothmes murmured, "They're like a flock of eager little sparrows waiting for crumbs, Huy. They make me feel rather old and terribly important."

The cell was pleasantly dim and cool. Huy, looking about, thought that it was really much smaller than he remembered it, and it did indeed hold the odours of vinegar and lamp oil. The furnishings had not changed. He recognized the dark swirl of a knot in one of the wooden legs of the couch where he had spent so many nights. Each couch had a little table beside it on which stood a statue of the inmate's totem and a clay lamp. Crammed between them were two tiring chests. The room and the linen on the couches were spotlessly clean, and there was no untidiness.

Maani was hovering behind Huy. "You slept to the left of the door, Master? Yes? That is where I sleep now."

Huy turned to him. "Does the servant Pabast still take care of your needs? Is he still here?"

"Oh yes! He is very grumpy and refuses to tell us about your time in our cell, but he did say that you were a brave boy."

"Did he?" Huy was taken aback. He and Pabast had not liked each other, but Huy remembered that when he left the temple to walk to Hut-herib under the High Priest's orders to take nothing but his own belongings and some food, Pabast had given him a bag of salt and one of his old razors. "Why brave?" he wondered aloud. "Because I left here with so little? Because I took my whippings without yelling or squirming?"

Maani's eyes grew round. "You were whipped, Master? You? What for?"

"When I was your age, I disobeyed many rules. So did the other boys. We would sometimes venture into the kitchens or the animal pens at the rear. One day I was caught and punished." *Well, that is the truth as far as it goes. There's no point in speaking of how I blundered into the presence of the Ished Tree and had to be purified in Ra's sacred lake and then do homage to the Tree before taking a nasty beating from Harmose, our Overseer.* "I was lucky not to be expelled." Maani looked horrified, then pained. "I was no different from you," Huy said gently. "The gift of Seeing conveyed on me after my accident, when I was twelve, did not grant me godhood, Maani."

"I can vouch for that!" Thothmes added with a grin. "Shall we find Pabast and tease him a bit, Huy, or shall we visit the schoolroom?" Looking about him, he shook his head. "We spent many happy hours in here, but there were many anxious ones too. Remember how sick you became and how I was given permission to nurse you through the fever? And how you used to come tired and frustrated from reading the Book of Thoth and recite the passages to me?"

The Book, Huy thought. *The Book. I am close to it here. It lies within the temple, a few steps away.* As though the mere idea of it could give it life, the words of the scrolls began to flow unbidden through his mind. He forced them away. He knew the contents of all forty-two portions. The words had been indelibly inscribed onto his consciousness at the moment he had read them, never to be forgotten. Yet the ultimate meaning of the mighty work dictated to Thoth by the creator-god Atum still escaped him, and he had set the exercise of interpretation firmly aside.

"Let's go to the schoolroom," he decided. "If I stood before Pabast, I'm sure I'd be reduced to the level of a guilty child all over again. Thank you for allowing us this indulgence, Maani."

They stepped out into the sunshine. Immediately the boys jostled one another to be close to him, and more than once he felt swift fingers brush his naked flesh, as though to touch him would confer luck or healing or simple confidence. A brief fear that their contact with him might precipitate an unwelcome vision came and went. The questions began as the pupils lost their shyness.

"Twice Born, may we see the scar on your head?"

"Twice Born, is it true that the gods come to you when you summon them? What do they say?"

"Master, what did you like learning best when you studied here?"

"How many people have you healed?"

"You have seen the King. What does he look like?"

"We take our swimming lessons in the water where you drowned. Is the water cursed or blessed by that event? And should we continue to call down anathema upon your attacker Sennefer when we say our prayers?" This was from an older boy who stood slightly apart from the others and stared at Huy with solemnity.

Huy was appalled. He pulled himself free from the questing, admiring hands. "The water is neither cursed nor blessed," he answered urgently. "It is no more to blame or to praise than the air you draw into your lungs. As for my attacker, you must know that the King removed from him the noble's right to wield the throwing stick, and he was sent away to another school, where he was very unhappy. I know, because I spoke to him there. He acted in his own defence. I had thrown myself towards him in a fit of furious rage. You must stop calling down the wrath of the Sheseru against him!" There was a sudden hush at the mention of the Sheseru, the host of demons divided into the ranks of the Khatyu and controlled by the gods. They could be used to bring harm or be transformed into the Habyu, the emissaries. "Remember that there is great power in ritual words," he finished. "Make those words creative, not destructive, or you may find your own totems unleashing the Sheseru-arrows against you! Now the Noble Thothmes and I would like to continue our visit by ourselves. May Ra shine his benevolence upon your day of leisure." Suitably cowed, the children made their obeisances and drew away.

Thothmes whistled as he and Huy walked out of the compound and started towards the schoolroom. "Phew! I keep forgetting that you're already a legend, at least among schoolboys, and you're certainly the subject of idle gossip amongst the King's huge entourage. We're almost there. Can you smell food?"

The dining room was directly accessible from the schoolroom, and Huy remembered how often he had lost his concentration towards the end of the morning's work as delicious odours began to waft over him and the other students. He and Thothmes stepped into the schoolroom.

"Same old smells: clay dust and charcoal with a whiff of papyrus," Thothmes commented. "How we loved it when Sennefer got punished, didn't we?"

"The more he was punished, the more angry he became with us, insulting my base birth and mocking your devotion to our Osiris-one King Thothmes the Third," Huy replied. "I can see now how miserable he was with himself."

"You're too generous," Thothmes said sourly. "Let's brave the throng of your admirers once more and have something to eat. Unfortunately, there'll be no beer."

The Overseer Harmose, who always presided over the meal, waved them to his table as the boys stood to reverence Huy and Thothmes again before sitting back down on the long forms to either side of their huge tables. Huy greeted him happily. "I'm glad to see you still ruling this little kingdom, Master," he said as he and Thothmes settled down, and at once a servant came bustling forward to serve them.

"I love my work." Harmose smiled. "There are few boys I'm unable to help turn into good Egyptian citizens by the time they leave here. You were a challenge, I do admit. Thothmes, I enjoyed your marriage feast very much and I wish you the blessings of every god upon your union. Now we will eat!"

He and Thothmes chatted as the meal progressed, but Huy found little to say. A familiar sense was stealing over him, a mixture compounded of the safety these walls had always provided to him, the mild anxiety he used to feel when faced with the constant need to achieve, and the complex spell of both fascination and dread the Book of Thoth had woven around him. It was as though some perspective he had lost was regaining its focus, some path from which he had inadvertently wandered was appearing again beneath his feet. There was sanity in it and there was Ma'at, right-thinking, a re-establishment of himself within the mighty confluence of cosmic and earthly order that met and flowed together to fashion the laws under which every Egyptian, commoner as well as king, must live. *Harmony,* he thought as he ate and drank and listened to the cheerful uproar around him. *When was the last time I experienced such concord? Not in Nakht's house, tormented by my love for Anuket, though I was happy there. Not with the pressure of the Book of Thoth a constant concern underlying my contentment in this place. Not in my parents' home at Hut-herib, a place I began to outgrow the moment I stepped from Ker's barge onto Ra's sacred concourse as a frightened little boy. When did all the components of my life, both positive and negative, achieve a perfect balance?* "When you stood in Paradise, in the Beautiful West, with Imhotep and the hyena before you and the Judgment Hall behind," a voice he instantly recognized whispered in his head. "For what is eternity but the perfect resolution of light with darkness? The exact plummet of the scales? The centre of the fulcrum of creation? Atum waits for your understanding in the place of no-time, Great Seer Huy. Go home. Heal the sick. Make the future your servant. Your destiny is not yet seasoned. The meat needs more salt." Huy, a vision of wet fangs and pointed black ears flashing across his inner vision, drew in his breath. "Anubis," he said.

At once he felt Thothmes' hand on his arm. "What is it, Huy? Anubis? What's wrong?"

"Nothing," Huy managed. "My thoughts were wandering, that's all." Both Thothmes and Harmose peered at him, then Thothmes' touch became commanding, urging Huy to his feet, and Huy saw to his surprise that his plate was scoured, his cup empty, and half the boys had gone.

"We must take a look at the training ground and pet the chariot horses before we leave," Thothmes said to Harmose. "Thank you for your hospitality, Overseer Harmose. It has been a joy to be here again."

Harmose stood and returned Thothmes' bow. "You two were favourites of mine. Be well. Come back and visit us any time you wish."

Outside, in the passage leading back to the front of the temple, Thothmes released Huy. "Perhaps this was not such a good idea," he said heavily. "The memories are not all benign, are they, Huy? What did Anubis say to you?"

"He told me to go home and become more seasoned."

"You hear his voice because you are so close to the Book here in the temple," Thothmes said soberly. "Its magic emanations are reaching out to you. Why don't I go to the training ground by myself while you talk to Ramose? He's expecting you to call on him before the sleep. I'll have Anhur summoned. The bearers will be waiting for us soon. Then we can leave."

Huy nodded and at once Thothmes left him, walking briskly away. Huy turned towards the priests' quarters, where Ramose's large and pleasant office lay.

The High Priest opened the door himself to Huy's knock and ushered him inside. "The boys will be in your debt for a long time." He smiled. "Only gods' feast days and visits from members of the high nobility merit a day off for them. Come and sit. Tell me how you really are. Your letters are full of what you do, but not what you think or feel. The Rekhet and I speak of you frequently, and I know that she continues to conjure on your behalf even though you are protected by the amulets she made for you, the sa on your breast and the two rings on your fingers. Has the King severely limited your freedom to work among the citizens of Hut-herib? Your letters did not say."

You are a shrewd and perceptive man, Huy thought as he took the stool he knew so well, in front of the desk. *But I discovered that long ago. I am still wary of your desire to control my gift, but seeing that I live well away from your influence, I may honour your past great kindnesses to me with the truth.*

"I am a prisoner of the King's generosity, but he is a benevolent jailer. I am permitted to do such work as is presented to me, providing I am always available to See for anyone the King himself sends to me. So far the requests from Mennofer have been very few."

Ramose had regained his customary chair behind the desk. He leaned back and folded his arms. "Ah yes, Mennofer," he said heavily. "I was alarmed when the King moved the capital back to Mennofer from Weset. His predecessor Thothmes the Third, his father, spent many years campaigning in the east, consolidating Egypt's hold on her vassal states and increasing their number. The Queen Hatshepsu, his aunt-stepmother, forbade any wars of conquest so that Egypt's treasury might increase through peaceful trade. Many believe that Thothmes got rid of her when he became powerful enough, so that he could expand our territories."

"Got rid of her?" Huy echoed, shocked. "He murdered her?" *Thothmes would be horrified to hear such a thing about his hero,* Huy thought.

Ramose nodded. "It's believed so. However, my point is that Thothmes poured wealth and care into Weset and into Amun's arms. It was right. It was Ma'at. Amun saved Egypt from the occupation of the Setiu hentis ago. Our present Incarnation does not seem to give Amun the loyalty he ought. Moving the court north to Mennofer returns him to the influence of the great centres of Ra-worship. Of itself, this would not matter. But Amunhotep spent his formative years here in the north, at Mennofer. I think that his primary allegiance is shifting away from Amun. If the balance of Ma'at is maintained, it will not matter, but I am disturbed. He comes here to pay his vows to Ra, but he goes more often to the shrine of the Aten."

"The Aten?"

"Our King is young, healthy, and vigorous," Ramose said wryly. "He cares more for the energies of the god than for his essence. Aten is all energy, the rays of light that become lions when they strike the earth."

"Between Ra and the lion is the Aten," Huy said. "I understand. But—"

"As I say, if the King gives due honour to Amun, we are safe," Ramose cut in. "But the rumours from Weset say that he is beginning to neglect the god. Nothing very overt, nothing openly alarming, but I am concerned. Especially seeing that the King ignores you, although he provides well for you."

The words of Atum's warning to the King came back to Huy. "I can do nothing unless he wills it, unless he sends for me. All I can do is go home and continue the work Atum has set for me. What do you advise, Master?"

Ramose shrugged. "I have no advice. I can pass on to you whatever news from the court at Mennofer my fellow High Priests around the country send to me, and that is all so far. Now, Huy, tell me how you fare. It must be hard for you to lose Ishat. But your poppy investment and the arouras you have been deeded—you are happy with all this? And you continue to heal?"

Huy answered the High Priest's questions easily and honestly. At last, obviously satisfied, Ramose stood. "You are making a good life for yourself at Hut-herib. I'm relieved. Please continue to write to me so that I can make the correct petitions to Ra on your behalf. Now." He came around the desk and Huy left the stool. "Would you like to do reverence to the Ished Tree before you leave? I think that such an act is appropriate."

Huy hesitated. The Ished sat at the centre of the mystery of the Book. Its branches had overshadowed his schooldays after he had inadvertently stumbled into its presence, even before Sennefer's throwing stick had sent him plunging into a unique and tumultuous existence. He had managed to forget it, as he was able to dismiss the words of the Book from the far more reassuring day-to-day details of life on his estate, and he did not relish confronting the Tree's insistent reality. Ramose was waiting, a mild stubbornness clear beneath his patience. Finally, Huy nodded.

At once the High Priest ushered him to the door. Together they paced the passages lined with priests' cells Huy remembered vividly. This area of the temple was forbidden to the schoolboys unless they had been summoned. Its atmosphere reminded Huy uncomfortably of both well-deserved punishment and unwanted responsibility. Soon they slowed before a small, guarded door set into the inner wall. After absently greeting the soldier, Ramose swiftly untied the knots holding the two closed metal hooks set into wall and door, handed the rope to the guard, and pushed the door open, waving Huy through.

The Tree was in its full late spring blossom, its thick leaves glossy, its branches laden with red and white blooms stirring gently in the breeze that funnelled down into the roofless space. As Huy took the few steps that brought him close to the rim of the hollow in which it sat and in which water was regularly poured, a momentary gust of air lifted the braid lying between his shoulder blades and sent a shower of petals floating to the ground. *Welcome, Huy,* the leaves seemed to rustle as he dropped to his knees and then performed a full prostration. *Welcome, Great Seer. Have you come to read the Book of Thoth again?*

Three times Huy and Ramose extended themselves in worship, then they stood side by side, regarding the Tree in silence. *It still gives off a combined aroma of honey and garlic and orchard flowers together with the stench of ukhedu when a wound begins to suppurate,* Huy thought. *Sweet and pungent and otherworldly. Heka is strong in here, it is always present. I was surrounded with it, the magic of the Tree, every time I sat in its dappled shade to read one of the Book's scrolls.*

"The Tree of Life," he said aloud, "holding within it the full mysteries of good and evil, planted here when Atum created the All out of the Nun, and tended by every High Priest of Ra since the beginning. So you told me, Ramose, when you dragged me here after I'd been discovered on this very spot, lost and covered with animal dung and trying to get back to my cell. I was sure that you were going to hang me from one of those branches for my desecration."

Ramose laughed. "I remember how terrified you were, but not so terrified that you couldn't ask me why the Tree was holy. I knew even then that you and the Tree shared a kinship. Now it's clear that your power to see into the future parallels the mystery inherent in the Tree. Both have to do with the ponderous inevitability of consequence."

Huy glanced at him curiously. "The fruit of the Tree holds within itself the knowledge of both good and evil. For us humans, such knowledge means that we must choose one path or the other, and take the consequences. In seeing the future, do I share the same purity of comprehension inherent in the Ished's fruit?"

Ramose nodded. "I believe so, for surely your gift enables you to see the consequences of actions not yet performed." He bowed to the Tree and turned to the door. "My thoughts often become clearer in here. It's the magic surrounding the Tree. The heka."

The heka. Huy cast a last look at the huge, gnarled branches heavy with foliage and followed Ramose out into the passage.

By the time Huy emerged onto the concourse, it was the middle of the afternoon. The bearers were yawning. Anhur was leaning resignedly on his spear, and Thothmes, already lying back on cushions inside the litter, seemed asleep. Huy slid in beside him, Anhur straightened and barked at the bearers, and the temple was left behind.

"Are you all right, Huy?" Thothmes wanted to know. "I had time to let off a few arrows and talk to Mesta and take a nap."

"Mesta? So he's still the Master Charioteer?"

"Of course. What kept you so long?"

"The Ished Tree."

"Oh. Was it difficult?"

"A little. The sight and scent of it certainly took me back to my childhood. I think I'll go home tomorrow morning, Thothmes. It's time for both of us to settle down to our customary routines."

Thothmes grunted. "Unfortunately. Having you here has been wonderful, and I'm sorry we haven't been able to spend more time with each other. Perhaps you will come back during the next Inundation. Even a Governor has little to do when the land turns into a lake."

Huy himself had fallen into a doze by the time the bearers turned from the river road onto the vine-hung path leading to Nakht's entrance. Once beyond the pillars, the two friends parted, Thothmes to inquire after his father's health before joining Ishat in their room and Huy to seek his couch. He was halfway up the stairs when Amunnefer hailed him, and looking up, he saw the man waiting for him. Taking the last few steps, Huy greeted him.

"I wanted to speak to you while the household was asleep," Amunnefer explained. His eyes slid away from Huy's and Huy realized that something was embarrassing him. He seemed reluctant to go on.

"What is it, noble one?" Huy prompted. "Is there bad news from our poppy fields?"

Amunnefer's kohled eyebrows rose. "Oh, no, Huy, nothing like that. It's … my wife … Anuket greatly desires that you should See for her. She says that she had begun to ask you yesterday but you and she were interrupted. Will you do her this favour?" His anxious gaze returned to Huy.

You have no idea what you are asking of me, Huy thought, his stomach shrinking. *Has love completely blinded you to what your wife is becoming? I strongly suspect it is what the god will show me if I take those tiny fingers between my own, and I don't want to. I don't want to!*

"I had hoped to enjoy this reprieve from the violence of the headaches that accompany every Seeing," he responded cautiously. "If the Lady Anuket was ill, it would be a different matter. Or if some event in her life was looming over which she was fretting. As it is …" He spread out his arms and did not finish the sentence.

Amunnefer sighed. "She is not ill and no difficult decision waits for her at home in Weset," he admitted. "She seems upset because you have Seen for her brother and for Nasha and have neglected her."

It was on the tip of Huy's tongue to explain to this good man that the Seeing for Nasha had been entirely accidental, and that for Thothmes it had been an act of love. He repressed an urge that he knew was merely the desire to please Amunnefer, even placate him, whether because of their future business dealings or

Amunnefer's superior blood Huy did not know. *Once again she is trying to exert her influence over me,* he thought angrily. *I thank the gods I am purged of the disease of loving her!*

"I'm sorry, noble one, but I hear no reason why I should accede to her request."

Amunnefer passed a distracted hand over his shaven scalp. "She is most upset. I can't ... I don't know what ... I am unable to appease her!" he finished, desperation in his voice. "If you will not See at her request, will you do so at mine? Please?"

Love has made you weak, Amunnefer, Huy wanted to say. *Anuket will never bind up the wound in you that she herself has caused. She will watch it bleed until all your virility has been leached away.* Everything in him shouted a refusal, but even as his ka recoiled, he found himself nodding reluctantly.

"Very well," he said tonelessly. "For you, Amunnefer. Do you understand that what I See, if anything, will be shared with Anuket alone unless she gives me permission to share it with you?" Anger welled up in him, at Anuket, at Amunnefer's inability to control his wife, at his own lack of courage. "I am going home in the morning," he added brusquely. "When do you wish me to do this thing?"

Relief flooded Amunnefer's pleasant features. "At once, Master, if you will. She has woken from her sleep but is still on her couch."

Huy caught his arm. "Whatever comes of this in the future, you must swear to me now that you will not hold me responsible!" he said roughly. "I am a tool of the god and nothing more! I See only what Atum wishes me to See, not what I will the future to be!"

"Of course!" Amunnefer looked bewildered. "I have the utmost respect for you, Great Seer, and that will not change."

Huy let him go. Amunnefer turned into the passage and Huy followed, every nerve screaming at him to retreat, to run to the safety of his own room, but that damnable surge of compassion for the man whose slender legs strode ahead of him kept him moving forward. At the last door on the left, Amunnefer paused, smiled at Huy briefly, and pushed it open. Woodenly, Huy followed.

Anuket was on the couch, leaning back against a pile of cushions. A sheet covered her nakedness. Only her slightly swollen eyes told Huy that she had been asleep, for she was fully painted and a black wig lay sleekly shining to her shoulders. Seeing Huy, she held out both hands. "Huy, I am so grateful!" she said as he approached her. "I was not sure that you would agree to See for me, but here you are!" She cast a fond glance at her husband. "Thank you, my dearest!"

Huy did not take the eager fingers. "Lord, would you please send a servant to Thothmes' barge and summon my scribe? I need her to transcribe my words," he said deliberately to Amunnefer. The man left at once.

Anuket pouted. "Is it really necessary to have her here, Huy? I don't want that chit knowing the secrets of my future." The instant jealousy Huy had seen before fumed with the edge of spite in her tones and the sudden narrowing of her heavily kohled eyes.

"I make no exceptions to this rule," Huy snapped. "My scribe is no different from any other, even though she is female. Scribes keep their mouths closed and thus hold to their positions."

Anuket did not answer. They waited in silence for Thothhotep.

She entered barefoot with her usual quiet poise, her old, scored palette under her arm, her brown skin damp, wet hair curling haphazardly behind her ears. Bowing deeply to Anuket, she turned to Huy. "Forgive my unkempt appearance, Master. I was just leaving the river after a swim when the noble Amunnefer approached me. I came as swiftly as I could." Her free hand was pulling her linen sheath away from her body as she spoke.

Huy nodded. "It's of no consequence. Sit here beside me and prepare for the dictation." She went to him quickly, hitching up her linen and folding onto the tiles. *I am not angry with you, Thothhotep,* Huy wanted to say as she fumbled open the palette and began to retrieve her tools. *I am angry at my own spinelessness.*

For a few moments the soft sound of the papyrus burnisher filled the room, and then Thothhotep laid it by her hip, lifted up a brush, and glanced at him. He smiled. Her face cleared. She began the short prayer to Thoth, and Huy's attention returned reluctantly to the couch as he took the stool already resting beside it. *You knew that I would bend to this, didn't you?* he thought bitterly as he put out a hand. *You made sure that your face paint had been renewed and your wig was in place before you ordered Amunnefer to speak to me, and while he was doing so, you had this stool placed just so.*

"Put your hand in mine," he said, fighting to create an inner calmness. "Be still and say nothing." As her fingers came to rest on his, he repressed the desire to ask Thothhotep if she was ready, to look about for a drink of water, to allow the chirping of the birds outside to capture his attention. Sighing, he closed his eyes.

At once the noise of the birds began to grow louder, filling the space around him discordantly, and he frowned, trying irritatedly to focus his mind beyond the sounds. After a moment he felt that he had succeeded. The jumble slowly grew more quiet, fell to a confused murmur, and suddenly Huy recognized it as a blend of human voices and bursts of laughter coming from a beer shop not far away. He was standing in a narrow, rutted street. Low buildings jostled against one another to either side. Some were spilling lamplight out onto the uneven dirt in front of them, but most of Huy's surroundings were dim, the street running on into darkness, the roofs limned faintly against weak starlight. Huy had no idea where he was.

"Not yet," a familiar voice rasped in his ear, "but one day you will know every cubit of this place. You are in the holy city of Weset, and even holy cities have their drunkards and whores, don't they, Mighty Seer? This street is some distance from the districts of privilege where the aristocrats can lie on their couches and hear the low conversations of the fishermen echo against the farther bank of the river as their skiffs float past in the night. Oh, Huy—blessed of the god or cursed, who can yet say which?—why do you choose to be here? What do you expect to See?" A black arm hung with golden bracelets came into Huy's view over his right shoulder, and one long ebony fingernail pointed along the street. "In the shadows there is a flutter of greyness. What can it be?" Uneasily, Huy heard a note of mockery colour the harsh tones as his gaze found the object. It looked like a discarded piece of linen stirring in the intermittent breeze being funnelled towards him. Anubis grunted, and to his horror Huy felt a cold touch upon his back. "Where are your bones, Son of Hapu?" the grating voice went on. "Will you go forward or will you remove your hand from the pressure of a female thumb?" Huy glanced down. Anuket's hand lay lightly on his palm, and as he watched, he saw another set of fingers, black and heavily ringed with gold, come to rest on Anuket's. "Choose!" Anubis barked. "Shall I lift her arm and fling it back into her lap? Her eyes are wide open, Seer. She is eating you up. You can always lie, create a vision for her while your spine ladders itself within you again. The linen lifts and falls as Shu gives life to a wind that will not blow along this filthy street for many years. Will you step into its embrace or not?"

"I do not want to lie." Huy felt as though he was uttering a foreign language. "I do this for Amunnefer, as a f—"

Anubis laughed. There was no mirth in the sound. "So be it. I wish you the satisfaction you secretly crave, proud Huy. As you step into the street, are you walking towards a future truth? Will it satisfy your thirst for revenge? Why are you waiting?" The icy fingers now bit into his shoulder, propelling him forward, then all at once Huy felt the god's presence leave him. He heard the faint slap of his sandals against the beaten earth of the street. His hair lifted as the breeze gusted into his face, and the huddle of linen lifted also, collapsing back into the dust.

There was something lying beside the linen, a darker smudge against the barely seen roughness of a wall, and even before Huy recognized it as a naked female body, his ka knew, and it dried his mouth and cut off his breath. Coming up to it, he squatted, pulling the pile of filthy linen away and reaching out with the other trembling hand to turn the face towards him. The figure groaned, the eyes opened lazily, and Huy found himself staring into Anuket's ravaged features. She licked her cracked lips and smiled faintly up at him. "I hope you've brought a big litter, Amunnefer," she slurred, her words only half formed and seeming to slide with impossible slowness into his ears. "I don't think I can even sit up, let alone walk. Help me." He wanted to pound his fist against that swollen mouth, press his palms to either side of that shaven skull and bash her head against the hard ground beneath her, yet under the terrible urge to violence was an even more horrifying maelstrom of love, pity, and impotence. Huy, imprisoned in Amunnefer's body, powerless against the other man's painfully racing heartbeat and the wild tumult of his emotions, could only watch and listen with numb shock.

"You are a disgrace to my house and an embarrassment to the Horus Throne, Anuket," Amunnefer said hoarsely while his arm went around her shoulders and lifted her to a sitting position. "Here, put on your sheath. The bearers—"

"The bearers have seen me naked countless times," she croaked as he pushed the sheath over her head and lifted one loose arm, trying to force it under a shoulder strap. "Why do you bother to come looking for me night after night, Amunnefer? Don't you know that our destinies are written in the symbols that make up our names? Amun is Beautiful." She laughed, a throaty, painful sound. "Well, aren't you lucky, my husband, to carry such a pretty sentiment with you every moment of every day. I am only fulfilling the worship of my namesake when I get drunk and spread myself naked on the beer house tables for the pleasure of any man who wants to take me." The bearers behind Amunnefer murmured.

"Be quiet!" he begged her on a note of hysteria. He drew her other arm through the linen and tugged the sheath down over her breasts. "Look at you! A bite mark by your nipple and bruises on your thighs. Why, Anuket? I have given you everything any wife could want. I have loved you, been faithful to you, made excuses for you, and defended you before Pharaoh himself. He tells me to divorce you and send you home to your brother, but I cannot! I still love you and pray to Amun for you. I—"

"Oh, be quiet yourself," she said perfectly clearly, then bent to the side and vomited a stream of beer and sour wine onto the dust beside him. "We've been over all this before," she went on, wiping her mouth on the sheath now bunched around her waist. "If you were a real man, you'd have me whipped and confined to my quarters and guarded all the time. You would hunt down my lovers and flay them too. Why don't you?" Ridding herself of the contents of her stomach seemed to have revived her a little. Her speech had become more intelligible and her eyes beneath their inflamed lids were losing some of their vagueness. "Even now you cannot strike me!"

Wearily, Amunnefer came to his feet, lifting her with him. Huy could smell the sourness of her and something else, something of which he did not think her husband was aware. The odour of tears clung to her skin, a scent both acrid and full of desolation, as if anguish could be inhaled like a fragrance. *Save me,* her ka was screaming soundlessly, *rescue me from this pit into which I have so willingly crawled.* But Huy knew, as he felt himself lifting her and carrying her to the waiting litter, that Amunnefer had neither the level of empathy nor the strength of purpose to stand against the complex power of her character. He was a good and honest man, but his love for Anuket was as diffused as the miasma of incense that hung about a temple's inner court. Only a man who was able to see the fissures in her soul and understand them could control her and thus keep her respect. *Thothmes can!* Huy cried out to Amunnefer as Anuket was lowered clumsily onto the cushions of the litter. *Send her back to her brother, noble one! End her pain, and yours!* Amunnefer was bending to draw a sheet up over his wife's polluted body, and Huy bent with him. To his surprise he smelled fresh perfume and a faint tang of vinegar.

Opening his eyes, he found himself on his feet, clutching Anuket's fingers in both hands while his cheek rested by her hip on the white cleanliness of the couch. He straightened carefully and sank onto the stool, letting go of her fingers. Already the hammer inside his head was thudding rhythmically against his skull. He reached for the water on the table, but Anuket forestalled him, lifting the ewer and pouring before passing him the cup. He drank all of it, feeling her eyes on him inquiringly, but he would not meet her gaze. He gestured to Thothhotep. "Write," he said huskily. "A vision of the future for the Lady Anuket …" And he began to recount everything he had heard, seen, and felt, omitting only the words Anubis had meant for him alone. *Revenge?* he thought as he narrated and Thothhotep's brush worked busily on the papyrus. *Yes, revenge. But it will not be sweet, Anubis.* He sensed Anuket's increasing agitation, but not until he had finished and Thothhotep had bowed herself out to make the copy that would be filed at home in Hut-herib did he swivel on the stool and look at her.

She had gone very pale, but there was a glint of rebellion in her eyes. "I drink much wine, it is true, and it makes me happy. But Huy, I shall never descend to the whorish depths you have described! Never! Your vision is … is …" It was obvious that she did not want to accuse either him or, worse, the god of lying.

Huy resisted the need to touch his paining head. "You wanted me to See for you," he said roughly. "I have done so. What you make of what I have Seen is up to you, but beware, Anuket! The god does not lie. I pray that what I saw is not fixed, that you can alter your future if you want to …" He closed his mouth abruptly. *Nasha*, he thought. *Nasha and her mother. Stay away from the Street of the Basket Sellers, I told Nasha after the Seeing had come upon me without my volition, and she obeyed me, but it was her mother who died in the Street of the Basket Sellers, and I still do not know why. If Anuket decides to become the perfect wife, will Amunnefer lie drunk and besmirched in the arms of some whore?* His mind shied away from the question as though he had been stung. *I have pondered this before to no avail. All I can do is tell what I See.*

Another silence fell between them. Huy sat very still, vainly willing the beating of his heart to stop reverberating behind his eyes. Anuket was staring at him expressionlessly. He was gathering himself up to stand and take his leave, desperate for the dose of poppy Tetiankh would bring him, when she spoke. "Sometimes I dream that I am copulating with a pig. According to the Purified, it is an omen of foreboding. What do you think, Huy?"

"I am not an interpreter of dreams," he answered her stiffly, "but if I were one of the Purified and if I had been told the vision of your future, I would warn you to go to the nearest temple, fast and pray, and then go home and amend your life."

"How cold you are," she protested softly. "How formal and faraway, as though you are a stranger and not a man I have

known since we were both little more than children! How have
I angered you?"

By treating my love for you as a plaything, he answered her
dumbly. *By making a game out of teasing a defenceless boy and then
pushing him away.*

"I'm not angry with you anymore, Anuket," he said aloud.
"All my school years were coloured by my love for you, and when
you refused to run away with me, I was almost destroyed. Until
now I have kept an image of you entirely separate from all else in
my mind, but I thank the gods you came to Thothmes' wedding.
Seeing you again has cured me of that youthful malady." He did
not know whether or not he had intended to offend her, but at his
words her eyes narrowed briefly and her full mouth turned down.

"It's true that I toyed with you. I tried out my new power as a
woman on you, as though I was a baby cutting its teeth on a sliver
of reed. That was wicked of me, especially seeing that I loved you
as though you were blood kin to me." She cleared her throat, a
sound that could have signalled embarrassment or genuine
shame, Huy thought. He doubted if it meant either. "I often look
at Amunnefer and wonder what my life would have been like if
I had crept out of the garden with you on the night my father
refused your request. I think I really was half in love with you
then, but I was already becoming very adept at the game of
manipulation."

Huy had had enough. Rising, he bowed to her. "Stop playing it,
Anuket, or it will lead you to the degradation I saw," he managed
hoarsely. "Amunnefer deserves better. So does the memory of your
illustrious mother. Find some respect for yourself."

She waved one languid hand as if to dismiss him and his
words, but Huy could see the rage beneath the whitening of her
face. "Say what you like, but my name is a curse that must be
fulfilled. No one can fight the destiny of his name."

He had been turning to the door, but now he paused and looked back at her. "Then change it," he forced out through a blur of pain. "Go to Amun's temple at Ipet-isut and beg one of his priest-astrologers to make a new chart for you based on the name you have chosen. It is sometimes permitted. You know this! Bring back the chaste and fragile maker of garlands who so captured my heart!"

She began to cry, the tears welling up and overflowing down her painted cheeks. "And will you love me again then, Huy?" she choked. "Will you?"

He shook his head. She had spared no thought for her husband at all, and her tears were for herself alone. Walking to the door, he bowed once more to her superior station and went out into the passage. It was not far to his own room. Thankfully, Tetiankh was there, folding kilts that had obviously just been starched. The servant took one look at Huy and then went to the window, lowered the slatted hanging, and came to him, gently removing his jewellery and his clothing.

"I packed plenty of poppy, Master. I'll prepare a draft at once and bring cool water for your forehead." Huy let Tetiankh's arm lower him onto the couch.

"Keep everyone away but Ishat if she wants to see me," he murmured. "Find Merenra and tell him to prepare for our return to Hut-herib tomorrow. I want to go home, Tetiankh."

The man made soothing noises and left. Now Huy was free to put both palms against his temples and close his eyes. Every muscle in his body had tensed against the knife point jabbing inside his skull, but woven into the pain, like some harsh, discordant harmony for which his heart was providing the rhythm, the images Atum had fed to him of a naked, befouled Anuket paraded through his mind. Unable to banish them, he groaned. "The ponderous inevitability of consequence," the High Priest's voice cut in suddenly. "The ponderous ... inevitability ... of ... consequence. The ... ponderous ... inevitability ..." Huy, his arms, Amunnefer's arms, going around Anuket once more, inhaling that odd, terrible odour of her inner hopelessness, knew the futility of his words to her. *She may change her life, busy herself on their estate, give up her adulteries, but her doom will fall anyway,* he told himself, hugging his knees under the sheet, trying to cradle the pain. *The goddess Anuket herself was not able to remain the pure water creature of the past. Did she become the licentious whore some now worship from choice or by decree? Whose decree? Atum's? Does she exist at all, or is High Priest Ramose right and every god, every goddess, is only an expression of the eternal energies of the mighty Neb-er-djer, Lord to the Limit, the Great He-She? Oh Tetiankh, hurry or I must scream out this agony!*

As if in answer, the servant came in. Huy struggled up and, taking the cup, drained the contents eagerly. "Find my oil of lemon grass," he asked. "This mixture is very strong and bitter, Tetiankh, and I need the oil on my tongue." He opened his mouth for the drop then lay down thankfully. The opium was already doing its blessed work, warming his blood, numbing his limbs, flowing around the loud visions and voices in his mind and encapsulating them, making them fade. "I can sleep now," he whispered, and fell into the drug's embrace.

He woke to full darkness. A lamp was burning on the table beside his couch, and as he struggled to sit up, its light wavered. Ishat rose from the chair by the window and came quietly to sit on the couch by Huy's knees. Rubbing his cheeks, he accepted the goblet of water she was holding out and drank quickly. "Tetiankh knew you would need me," she said, taking the cup when he had finished and setting it back beside the jug. "He asked me to watch over you while he ate with the other servants. Who did this to you, Huy?"

"You make it sound as if I was attacked in some way," he responded. His lips still felt numb and his limbs only loosely coordinated. Tetiankh's dose of the poppy had been unusually powerful. "Amunnefer asked me to See for Anuket. Actually, he begged me."

"And of course you couldn't refuse." Her tone was waspish, and Huy was able to smile to himself. Even though she was now married to Thothmes, her long jealousy of Anuket could still prick her. "Well, because of it you've missed your last chance to feast with me and Thothmes and the rest of the family. Tetiankh told me that you'll be leaving in the morning. We had lotus seeds in purple juniper oil, and sedge roots and cumin, and roast goose and leeks and celery. Fig cakes. Beer flavoured with mint. Nasha made sure that there was plenty left for you. Are you hungry?"

"A little. If Tetiankh is outside in the passage, send him to the kitchen." *Put your hand on my forehead the way you used to do,* he beseeched her silently. *Massage my head.* She was watching him doubtfully. She looked truly beautiful in her scarlet sheath. Gold dusted her eyelids and cheeks. Her mouth was hennaed, her hair caught up in the gold mesh that could be attached to the circlet she had ordered from the jeweller in Hut-herib and that he, or more properly the King, had paid for. She could have passed for any aristocrat. Reaching out and taking her hand, he turned it over. The orange henna felt slightly rough to his questing fingers. Absurdly, he wanted to cry.

"When you've eaten, will you join Thothmes and me on the raft?" she wanted to know as she rose. "We're just going to sit on it and be rocked by the river in the torchlight and drink wine and talk. Nasha may come too. Please, Huy?"

"Perhaps. I feel dirty and slightly nauseous. How is Nakht?"

"He ate in his own quarters." She opened the door and spoke a few words to Tetiankh, then regained the couch and bent towards him. "I'm glad he asked you to See for him. Perhaps the god will be pleased to heal him?"

Huy shook his head. "He doesn't want it. He misses his wife. He has nothing left to look forward to but grandchildren, and that's no great lure for him. The AA disease is merciless, Ishat. Let him go."

"Still, I hope there will be time to get to know him better," Ishat sighed. "I could easily learn to love him."

They both became quiet, but it was a close, companionable thing. Huy's mind sharpened as he pulled himself free of the last effects of the opium, and by the time Tetiankh entered with a loaded tray, his appetite had fully returned. Ishat left the couch and went to the chair, and while Huy ate, they talked easily of innocuous matters. Huy knew that Ishat was more than curious about the Seeing he had done for Anuket, and he waited for her inquisitiveness to get the better of her. At last she said, "I suppose Thothhotep took the dictation for the Seeing, Huy? Did she perform well? Do you need me to check her work?"

Huy began to smile and then to laugh, engulfed in a wave of love for her. "Her deportment was exemplary, Ishat, and as for the scrolls, I'll check them myself before giving Anuket her copy. You know perfectly well I can say nothing about what I Saw."

Ishat made a face that took Huy back to their time together in Hut-herib. "If I was still your scribe, I'd know. We'd discuss the Seeing."

"But you are no longer my scribe. Now I think I'll go to the bathhouse with Tetiankh and then meet you and Thothmes on the river. I'm almost fully recovered."

Getting up, she came and planted a swift kiss on his cheek before admitting the servant, tossed back a smile, and disappeared. Huy wrapped a sheet around himself and took the stairs to the bathhouse, now dimly lit by one lamp. The water was barely warm.

Huy refused Tetiankh's offer to heat it, standing on the bathing block while Tetiankh scrubbed him down and thinking of all the occasions when he and Thothmes had come here together, covered in river mud or sweat or simply getting ready to begin their day, when every moment had been full of the pleasure of holiday, and Nakht had been strong and vigorous, and Anuket had been in the herb room every morning, weaving her wreaths and bouquets amid the mingled aromas of flowers and drying herbs, and the future stretched ahead in all its promise. Nostalgia began to wind about him, but before it could tighten its hold on his heart, he bade Tetiankh dress him and tie back his long hair.

Walking through the house, he met no one. The garden too was empty and peaceful, but beyond the watersteps there was a glow of welcoming yellow light and Nasha's loud laughter. Huy ran to join his friends. There was no sign of either Amunnefer or Anuket, and he was glad. Settling on a pile of cushions, he accepted a cup of palm wine, returned Nasha's impudent kiss, and gave himself up to the warm night.

There was no serious conversation. Old jokes were aired and rather lamely explained to Ishat, who had no history with the family. Nasha regaled them with all the latest local gossip. Huy joined in but often fell silent, content to watch the play of wind-tugged light and shadow pass across these faces that were so very dear to him. Thothmes kept Ishat's fingers woven with his. Nasha half lay with her head inches from Huy's thigh, gesticulating widely with her cup. The river was a dark, slowly heaving presence, moving the huge raft sluggishly and soporifically beneath them. On the watersteps, the two guards carried on their own intermittent exchange, a pair of dark shapes against the tangle of black foliage hiding the house. *I will never forget this,* Huy thought. *Only the Paradise of Osiris can surpass the peace and sweetness of these hours, and I will not think of the*

Beautiful West now, not with Nakht's slow dying, not with the Book of Thoth lying deep beneath everything I do or think or say. Now I will exist, just exist and nothing more, caught willingly in this moment where time has ceased to flow, where we do not grow old or ill, where change and decay are impossible. In the end the talk faltered and then ceased altogether, and they fell deeply asleep on the cushions, limbs entwined, Thothmes enfolding Ishat, Nasha's cheek against Huy's calf. His dreams were gentle.

They woke as one, roused by the brief chill that heralded the imminent birth of Ra, and scattered quickly to their different quarters. Huy made his way through a house already full of the bustle of servants sweeping, dusting, and setting out the tables for the first meal of the day. They reverenced him and he greeted them absently, intent on finding Tetiankh and seeing that his chests were packed. On his way upstairs he met Amunnefer coming down. It was too late to retreat. His heart sank as he bowed and Amunnefer came to a halt.

"Huy," the man said heavily, "I looked for you last night, but your body servant told me that you were ill and had retired early. So it is true that the Seeings you perform make you sick?"

Huy nodded, inwardly blessing Tetiankh.

"I'm sorry," Amunnefer continued. "Anuket is much distressed by what you told her. She did not fall asleep until an hour ago. She will not talk to me about it. Are you permitted to give me some hint regarding what you Saw?"

"No," Huy answered to the homely, worried face. "All I can suggest to you is that you keep her close to you at all times, particularly at night."

"There is danger for her while Ra is in the womb of Nut?" Amunnefer's expression cleared. "She knows what kind?"

"It is not quite that simple," Huy replied. "I wish I could say more."

Amunnefer regarded him closely, his eyes moving from Huy's own to Huy's mouth and back to his eyes. Huy could almost hear the man's rapid thoughts. Finally, Amunnefer lifted his shoulders and held out his hands, hennaed palms up. "She is an Egyptian wife, and a noblewoman at that," he said slowly. "No law allows me to forcibly keep her in her quarters, or on the estate for that matter."

"But you can amuse her, play board games, take her on the river, perhaps even share the problems of your governorship with her."

Amunnefer's mouth twisted. "I try. If you would confide the Seeing to me, I might understand." He paused. Huy said nothing, and after a moment Amunnefer swung away. "I do not hold this against you, Great Seer," he called back as he reached the foot of the stairs. "You acceded to my request reluctantly and I apologize for compelling you. Expect regular letters from me regarding your investment."

Grimly, Huy took the few remaining steps to his room. Merenra, Tetiankh, and Thothhotep turned as he entered.

"The chests are ready to be taken on board and Thothhotep has checked that nothing will be left behind," Merenra said. "Shall I alert your captain, Master?"

"Yes. Put Anhur in charge of the servants' barge. I'll eat with the family, pay my respects to Nakht, and then we can go. Thothhotep, have you delivered the scroll to the Lady Anuket?"

"I have, and the original will not leave my pouch until I file it in your office."

"Good. Tetiankh, I'll bathe now."

On their way to the bathhouse, Huy thanked him for his protection from Amunnefer. "You need not thank me, Master," Tetiankh replied crisply. "I was merely doing my duty."

And so was I this morning, Huy thought. *Then why do I feel as though I have betrayed a friend?*

The meal was a sober affair. Nasha, obviously suffering from an overindulgence of wine the evening before, yawned often and answered Huy's attempts at conversation in monosyllables. Ishat picked at her food, her eyes on Huy, but when he looked at her directly, her gaze slid away from his.

Even Thothmes' customary cheerfulness had deserted him. "I wish you would stay in Iunu permanently," he begged Huy yet again. "Soon I'll be Governor. I'll make sure you get a good piece of land right on the river where you can build." He leaned across and touched Huy's shoulder. "A Governor must choose his friends very carefully or he risks being accused of partiality in his dealings with the citizens of his sepat. Our affection for each other exists far above such corruption—except in deeding land to you, of course!" He grinned but only succeeded in looking ghoulish. "You are my only friend in a sea of acquaintances, Huy. I need you."

Huy pushed away the plate of delicacies before him. "I need you also, Thothmes, but you know why I must remain in Hut-herib. I will come when your beautiful house is finished."

"I do know, but I'll keep trying to seduce you here," Thothmes sighed.

They sat on while a pall of silence fell over the dusky room.

Nakht was lying propped up on pillows when Huy was admitted by the body servant, and for one anxious moment Huy believed that he was approaching a corpse. The Governor's skeletal arms lay limply on the sheet. His yellowed, sunken features were turned slightly towards the door. His thin mouth hung open. But when Huy bent over him, lifting the cold collection of bones that made up his hand, he stirred and opened his eyes. "Huy," he whispered. "My physician has gone to mix me more poppy. I can eat only pap, but I drink milk and fruit juices. Thothmes and Nasha will begin to take turns sitting with me through the nights. Shall I tell them I have three more months of life? I'm so glad Thothmes has Ishat. I wish Nasha had someone to love her. I wish Anuket—"

"Hush, Lord," Huy said quickly. "Have no fears for Anuket. Her husband adores her."

Nakht gasped, and it took Huy a moment to recognize the sound as the man's effort to chuckle. "I have more fears for Amunnefer," Nakht managed. "I have done my best for all of them. I have memorized every answer to the questions the gods of the underworld will put to me so that I may pass in safety to my wife. Every answer, Huy. It has taken me ten years." The fingers resting in Huy's own, lighter than feathers, twitched suddenly in agitation. "I did not do right by you, my second son …"

Huy placed his other palm gently against Nakht's forehead. "You did do right by me," he murmured, his mouth close to Nakht's ear. "Your decisions that night were correct, for my life since has followed a privileged path. We have said all this before, my father. Be at peace."

There was a movement behind him and Huy looked back to see Nakht's physician step forward holding a cup.

"Ramose will come soon and pray for me." Nakht's voice was now less than a wisp of sound. "Go back to Hut-herib, Huy. Keep loving Thothmes. Make offerings at my tomb when the Beautiful Feast of the Valley comes around each year." He fell silent and his eyes closed.

Huy straightened. At once the servant and the physician hurried to the couch and Huy left, closing the door quietly behind him and taking deep breaths of the warm draft of air flowing along the passage. It was time to go home.

At the foot of the ramp, he hugged Thothmes fiercely, kissed a sleepy, solemn Nasha, and pressed his lips against Ishat's warm temple, deliberately drawing into his body the blend of myrrh, cassia, and henna flowers that made up her distinctive perfume.

She clung to him briefly, her grief expressed in every taut muscle pressed against him, then she let him go. "Write to us," she said thickly, and as he met her eyes, the message was clear: Do not send me personal letters, for I could not bear it. Let me force a gap between us so that I may learn contentment.

"Thank you, old friend, for your hospitality," he said to Thothmes, "Make my apologies to Anuket and her husband."

"They've gone," Nasha told him. "They didn't even bother with food. I shan't miss her, my own sister, and I don't think you will either, will you, Huy?"

Huy did not reply. Walking up the ramp of his barge to where Thothhotep stood waiting, he glanced along to the servants' boat. Anhur had already slipped its mooring. Huy signalled to his captain. The oars were run out and slowly the barge left Nakht's watersteps, seeking the north-flowing current. The trio left on the steps raised their arms in farewell. Soon, too soon, they shrank, and then the river caught the barge and bore it ponderously around a bend.

Nothing was said until Iunu itself had been left behind. Then Thothhotep stirred. "Two scrolls were delivered for you late last night, Master. Shall I read them to you?"

Startled, Huy glanced at her. He had been thinking of the empty house awaiting him, the rooms devoid of Ishat's voice, the passages empty of her quick footsteps and the swirl of her linen, the loneliness of waking from the afternoon sleep and remembering that she would not be there to take his arm and walk in the garden.

"They were sent on from Hut-herib?"

"Yes. Amunmose has inked his name on them to let me know that they did come to the house."

Amunmose, Huy thought, bewildered for a moment. *Oh, of course. My new under steward. Gods, I feel as though I've been away for hentis!*

He left the rail. "Let's sit under the awning," he suggested. "You read them and tell me what they say, Thothhotep. I'm in no mood to deal with correspondence."

She shot him a sympathetic glance, opened the drawstring of her leather pouch, and withdrew the scrolls as she lowered herself cross-legged beside him on the cushions. He watched her as she broke the seals and scanned first one letter and then the other, a tiny frown of concentration between her dark brows, her bottom lip caught in white teeth. *Shall we become friends, Thothhotep*, he wondered, *or shall we remain master and scribe?*

She looked up. "This one"—she tapped it on her knee—"is from Seshemnefer, your gardener. It is dictated, and he wants you to know that, seeing his pay is ample, you need not reimburse him for the cost of hiring a scribe." Huy smiled and the melancholy that had dogged him began to lift a little. "He says that the barley and emmer on your khato land has sprouted vigorously and that your fellahin weed it continually. He has arranged for deliveries of donkey dung during the next Inundation to mix with the silt when the flood recedes. He needs your permission to have silos built to hold the crops after the harvest."

"You can deal with all that. Of course there must be storage for the grain. Seshemnefer is simply reminding me that he is important, and so he is. What of the other?"

"It is from Amunmose, written by himself. I didn't know he could read and write."

"Many of the servants working in the temples learn from all the literate priests around them. What does he want?"

Thothhotep was all at once uncomfortable. "His sister Iny has arrived from the south. He has set her to work preparing for me to take over the Lady Ishat's quarters. Master—"

Huy held up a hand. His gloom had returned. "You are my scribe. Ishat's quarters are now yours. I asked her to talk to

Merenra some time ago about providing you with a cosmetics table and mirror and pots of kohl and whatever else you might require—oils, bolts of linen, combs, feminine things, but also the things that will make my scribe acceptable to the nobles who come to my house for Seeings. You need not bridle about it, Thothhotep, and do not thank me. It is all to my advantage."

She nodded and returned the scrolls to her pouch. They sat without speaking for a long time, but Huy did not notice. His mind, his heart, was buried in the past he and Ishat had forged together, and the loss of her was already more than he could bear.

PART TWO

9

HUY SAT CONTENTEDLY with his back against a sycamore, Thothhotep beside him, a cup of date wine cradled absently in both his hands. The afternoon was hot but not unpleasantly so, although it seemed warmer for the press of noisy people crowded into Heby's small garden. Heby himself, with his new wife, Iupia, had retreated to the lengthening shade of the house with its two sturdy entrance pillars. Iupia's hand rested on Heby's white-kilted thigh and their heads were together, Iupia saying something into Heby's ear that brought a smile to his lips. *Nineteen years ago you were my little brother, running wide-eyed with excitement through the house the King had deeded to Ishat and me outside Hut-herib on the occasion of your first visit,* Huy thought as he watched them. *You had to lift your chin to look into my face while you told me how you had been into the flower fields with Father to gather seeds. Now we stand eye to eye, you at twenty-seven and me at thirty-eight, and those who do not know us take us for twins. Not because you age poorly. There is almost no evidence of all your Naming Days apart from a few almost invisible smile lines at your temples and around your mouth, and your body has achieved a fully masculine beauty. No, we resemble each other so closely because the god prevents the passing years from entering me. Now there you sit, a handsome man in the full glory of a healthy maturity, and where has the time gone?*

"No one wants to go home," Thothhotep remarked. "The wedding feast last night was such a success, even though half the guests had to celebrate outside because your brother's house is so small, and the nights are so sweetly mild that everyone slept on the grass or on the roof. It's a pity Governor Thothmes and Ishat had to leave."

"Particularly as Thothmes kept Assistant Treasurer Merira occupied," Huy added. "No doubt he's an honest man and an efficient keeper of the King's finances, but he's the most pedantic, boring man I've ever been trapped by. I pity Heby, with a father-in-law he must visit regularly. Although the match is an advantageous one for Heby. Even though he's Chief Scribe to the High Priest of Ptah here in Mennofer, he's not a noble. Iupia is. If Heby's ambitious as well as incredibly patient, he might secure a position at court through Merira. In time."

"In time." Thothhotep sipped thoughtfully at her own wine. "He's a happy man, Master. He has the ability to remain cheerful and optimistic no matter what the gods send him from day to day. The only time I've seen him weep was when you were summoned to See for Sapet."

Sapet. Huy did not answer his scribe. Heby's first wife had been the daughter of his employer, the High Priest of Ptah's temple here in the royal city, a seventeen-year-old girl of breathtaking loveliness whose name, Sapet, meant "bud of the water lily." Heby, at eighteen, had fallen desperately in love with her, and a delighted Hapu had hastily signed the marriage contract. *Heby deserved to achieve his desires, once with Sapet and now with an even more illustrious joining, Huy's thoughts ran on. He loves freely, and those he cannot love he does his best to like. He is generous with his laughter, reliable in his work, and was an exemplary husband to Sapet. I wish that Atum had chosen to save her. Kneeling beside her couch and watching the fever eat her up was worse than having to face Nefer-Mut's bloody and painful dying. Nefer-Mut, though I loved her, was only the mother of Thothmes, my friend. Sapet was my brother's cherished wife. I dare not allow myself to consider all the many strangers, commoners as well as nobles, who have been healed by Atum through me when the god withdrew his hand from two such beloved women. Not to mention those who have been given a vision of a bright future. If I begin to tread that path, I am in danger of losing the peace and equanimity I have struggled to attain since Ishat left me to marry Thothmes. I am thirty-eight years old, eleven years older than Heby, yet already he is embarking on a second marriage while I remain alone. And only six months ago, Sapet was entombed. This marriage is for his son's sake, he tells me, but also because Sapet and Iupia were good friends and Iupia knows him well. There is comfort in such closeness, I suppose.*

As if in response to his musing, there was a screech of rage. Heby and Iupia looked up. The buzz of loud conversations quieted briefly and the crowd shifted to give Huy a glimpse of his nephew, Amunhotep-Huy, sitting astride another boy, his knees imprisoning the other's arms while he rained punches down on the unprotected face. Quickly passing his cup to Thothhotep, Huy got up and took the few steps to where blood had begun to stream from the other boy's nose. He was trying to free himself, wriggling and kicking. Both of them were screaming at each other. Heby came up and, grasping his son roughly under the arms, hauled him to his feet and shook him. The other boy rolled over and then stood, lifting his dusty kilt and holding it to his nose. "You're a liar!" he mumbled fiercely through the stained linen. "A liar and a cheat! I hope—" He would have said more, but his mother had run up and was leading him away.

"I'm so sorry, Heby," she said over her shoulder. "He will be punished as soon as we get him home. Your pardon for his lack of good manners."

Heby had grabbed his son by one ear and was urging him towards the house. Huy followed with an inward sigh. As they passed Iupia, who had risen from her stool and was eyeing them with a look of distress, Heby touched her briefly. Then he, Huy, and the boy halted just beyond the entrance to the house. The little hall was cool and empty of all save Heby's steward, who saw them enter, bowed discreetly to Huy, and disappeared along the narrow passage towards the rear.

"He had no right to call me a liar!" Huy's nephew burst out at once. "He's always picking on me at school, Father! He hates me and I hate him!" Huy stared down at the flushed and angry face that so closely resembled Heby's own, with its wide brown eyes, square, cleft chin, and broad forehead.

Heby relinquished his grip. "I don't care what your excuse is, Amunhotep-Huy," he said severely. "How dare you scrap in the middle of my guests on this important occasion! Look at you! Your kilt is filthy, your youth lock has come undone, and where is your other sandal? Go up to your room and stay there until I can decide on a suitable punishment. No evening meal for you, either."

"You're always punishing me for everything!" Amunhotep-Huy said hotly. "Just like Overseer Prahotep! It's not fair!" Huy could see no remorse or apology in the furious features. Amunhotep-Huy flung away from them and marched to the foot of the stairs. Both men watched the stiff, affronted spine ascend out of sight.

Heby blew out his cheeks. "I wanted to keep him at home for the next two months. It's Payni now, and the school will close for the Inundation before the end of Mesore. But perhaps it would be better to send him back to Iunu. He doesn't like Iupia. He's rude to her."

"He's rude to everyone," Huy reminded him. "He misses his mother, Sapet, of course, but since when has grief been an excuse for discourtesy? He's eight years old, Heby. He should know better."

"He does know better, he just doesn't care. Where does this constant disrespect come from? It's almost insolence, Huy. Prahotep can't seem to do anything with him. I wish Harmose hadn't retired. From what you've told me of your own schooldays at the temple of Ra, Harmose ruled the pupils kindly but firmly. Prahotep has no control over my son. I think that the only reason High Priest Ramose allows the boy to stay at school is because of you. We both pay the expenses, but it's you who are a legend there. Ramose is loath to expel him. Whipping him does no good—it only makes him angrier." His shoulders slumped. "I must get back to my guests. Truthfully, Huy, I wish they'd get onto their litters and go home."

Both men left the hall, Heby to take Iupia's hand and mingle with the crowd and Huy to lower himself again beside his scribe. She had been talking to Anhur, who bowed to him as he approached. Seeing them together, he wondered for the hundredth time why they did not marry. Thothhotep was already thirty-three. Anhur had no idea how old he himself was, but thought he might be somewhere in his middle forties. They had formed a strong attachment not long after Thothhotep had come to work for Huy. Anhur, who had been with Huy when Huy had tested the skinny girl's skill in Hut-herib's marketplace, and who had been dispatched the following day to escort her to the estate, had adopted a protective attitude towards her that Huy found rather poignant. The waiflike near-child and the bluff, outspoken soldier had slowly bonded to one another, and Huy was glad to see it. Neither showed any inclination to leave his service, and he in turn had come to rely on both of them for different reasons. His security under Anhur's capable guards was never in question, and Thothhotep had blossomed into an excellent scribe. She could not take Ishat's place entirely, Huy thought as he sank onto the grass and Thothhotep gave him back his wine. But her presence in his house had gone a long way towards alleviating the loneliness that had descended on him when he had returned from Ishat's marriage to a miserably empty estate.

"Heby sent him to his room," he commented to their questioning faces. "He's earned yet another beating."

"Your brother should let me give him to the army," Anhur said heavily. "He could begin by learning to keep a captain's weapons clean in exchange for his food and shelter. Many poor peasants begin their careers in this way. You know, Huy, he reminds me of that young cur I had to protect you from all those years ago at the temple of Khmun, the one you said attacked you and knocked you into Ra's canal lake."

Huy nodded. "You mean Sennefer. What makes a child a Setian one, Anhur? What faulty spell or incomplete magic shield at birth allows Set, with all his turbulence and chaos, to enter a baby?"

His captain shrugged. "How would I know? I was named after a minor war god and I became a soldier. I don't regret it. My sisters still love me." He grinned.

"But my nephew carries two powerful names, that of the King himself and mine. There's no use denying that my name has heka. These names should mean the growth of intelligence and confidence in Amunhotep-Huy, not spite and self-pity and ire."

"Who can say what the King's character is really like, though?" Thothhotep put in. "The One may be angry, even spiteful sometimes, under the mantle of Ma'at and his godhead. Only his courtiers are able to judge."

Huy drained his wine. *I feel sorry for Heby. The peace of his household is disturbed every time the boy comes home from school. Father and Uncle Ker dote on him, of course, and that does him no good at all. Mother and Hapzefa do their best to teach him restraint, but they're both well into their fifties and easily tired. My barge should be returning soon from taking them home, then I and my servants can leave.*

A short time later, one of his sailors found him, and gladly he sought out Heby and Iupia and said his goodbyes. "Hut-herib is only a two-day sail from us here in Mennofer," Iupia reminded him as he kissed her soft cheek. "Come and visit us before the Inundation."

"I'll try, but before the flood there'll be reaping and threshing on my arouras, and Seshemnefer grumbles if I don't spend a little time watching him direct the peasants. I'm expecting word on the latest incense caravan as well. Pharaoh's Overseer of Trade always lets me know the weight and value of my share."

Heby made a face. "Those are just excuses. You're getting old, Huy, when you'd rather lie on your couch and pant the summer away than sit in my garden and play sennet." He eyed his brother critically. "Although I'd swear you look ten years younger than you really are. What's your secret? An addiction to the mandrake root?"

Huy smiled at him while a vision of the Rekhet formed in his mind, her seamed cheeks framed in wisps of grey hair, a comb in her hand. Once, when he had visited her in her modest mud-brick city house, she had untied his braid and combed oil containing crushed mandrake through his hair. Its odour had made him feel both sleepy and alert, and later he had been accused by Anuket of having been with a woman because he smelled of the plant all considered an aphrodisiac. Henenu had asked him why he wore his hair so long, already knowing the answer. He had assured her that it was both to hide the scar Sennefer's throwing stick had made and so that he might not appear to be a priest with a shaven skull, or a Seer either. She had told him bluntly that it was also a symbol of his virginity. He had been angry often in those days, unable to reconcile himself to the unwanted celibacy the god had thrust upon him, unwilling to explore the equally unwanted gift of Seeing with which he was burdened. She had delivered a stinging lecture, he remembered.

Dear Henenu. Dear Rekhet. She had been dead for five years. Her funeral had been the largest Iunu had ever seen. Everyone she had exorcised, advised, or fashioned amulets of protection for seemed to have journeyed to bid her farewell and share the burial feast. Huy still missed her. She had willed her estate on the lake at Ta-she to him, several miles' journey into the desert west of Mennofer. There was a large, comfortable house right on the water, and several arouras of incredibly fertile land regularly produced an abundance of grapes, sycamore, and common figs, tiny brown pears, as well as many medicinal herbs and roots she had doubtless needed for those who consulted her; in addition, there was a veritable forest of acacia and castor bushes, even a few olive trees. The lake was full of fish, its verges alive with birds. It was a haven for the wealthy. Succeeding kings had kept a palace there, at Mi-wer, where there was a thriving harem. But the lake was also home to the fertility gods Sobek and Herishef. Their temples and surrounding inns were always busy with female petitioners and pilgrims.

Huy had visited his new holding, and although the house and gardens were entirely private, he found the lake itself noisy as craft of every size and description enjoyed the constant breezes. Besides, he did not want to spend much time close to the King, who moved his court to Mi-wer for most of the summer months of Shemu. Long ago he had stopped worrying at Amunhotep's silence. In spite of the success of Huy and Amunnefer's poppy crops, Huy's clay silos full of grain and flax, his income from the incense caravans, the King continued to provide a regular supply of gold—a sign, Huy believed, that he was still in His Majesty's good graces. Huy turned over the care of the estate on the lake and its servants to Seshemnefer, and trusted him to keep it running with his usual efficiency.

"Huy? Why are you smiling vacantly at the sky? I asked you whether or not you'll stop at Iunu to see the Governor and Ishat."

Huy came to himself. "I'm sorry, Heby. I don't think so. I've been away from my duties for long enough. The needy will be lining up at the gate and my desk will be littered with scrolls."

They embraced. "Take care of our parents," Heby reminded him. "My work keeps me in Mennofer. It has been wonderful to have them here."

"I always do," Huy responded, mildly irritated. Itu was still content to govern her own little domain of house and garden, and Hapu, though Huy had provided him with a peasant to take over his share of the work in Ker's perfume fields, still insisted on planting, weeding, and harvesting the fragrant blooms alongside the rest of Ker's servants. His joints were stiff and often ached. His spine was now permanently bowed. But Huy knew that if his father gave up his labour, he would soon die. Huy understood and forgave Hapu his stubborn pride, even though it sometimes exasperated him.

Anhur touched his shoulder. "The litters are here, Master."

"Very well." He turned towards Heby's gate with relief, Thothhotep beside him. Heby's house lay in the maze of similarly anonymous dwellings in the northern suburbs of the city, not far from the temple of the goddess Neith. Farther south, the famous and ancient White Walls sheltered the original town and citadel in a forest of green palms and sycamores. The city had long since grown beyond and around it, encompassing the Fine District of Pharaoh, with its huge palace, harem, and carefully tended gardens running down to the river, several other temples with their canals leading to the water—including the temple of Ptah, where Heby plied his trade—a barracks and arsenal, the chaotic naval docks of Peru-nefer, and then the southern suburbs. Nothing but narrow streets and mud-brick walls could be seen from Heby's gate.

Huy and Thothhotep got onto their separate litters. Anhur and his guards took their stations around them. Behind them, Merenra was ordering the string of servants carrying their chests.

It will be wonderful to be home, Huy thought as he twitched the curtains closed against the dust and his bearers set off towards the northern watersteps and Huy's barge. *I wonder how long it will be before Merira insists on providing Heby with a house more suitable for the daughter of the Assistant Treasurer to the King? Heby is entirely happy where he is. I cannot tell what passes through Iupia's mind when she leans over the gate and looks up and down the crowded lane that passes for a thoroughfare. I refused to See for her, and fortunately Heby had no interest in being told his future. I find it very hard to bear any such knowledge when it relates to those I love. I certainly don't want to See for my recalcitrant nephew. Can there be anything but trouble ahead for a boy who is disobedient, cheeky, and unwilling to learn?*

The late afternoon had become hot and windless. Huy dozed.

With the summer wind blowing strongly out of the north and the river's current flowing sluggishly towards the Delta, it was a full two days before Huy's barge nudged gently against his watersteps and the ramp was run out. Leaving Thothhotep and the servants to unload the baggage, he took Anhur and a soldier and approached his gate. The small crowd of Hut-herib's citizens clustered under the shade of the trees rose to reverence him, and Kar, his gate guard, came forward. "They've been waiting for a long time, Master," he told Huy, jerking an elbow at the gathering, now silent with expectation. "Merenra sent them away, but many of them wandered back. Some of them are quite ill. Do you wish me to close the gate against them once the unloading is complete?"

Huy looked them over carefully. Long ago he and Ishat had decided to allow no more than ten petitioners a day, and indeed not every day, into the garden where he would perform the Seeing and she would sit cross-legged beside him, taking down his words. He had been away from home for almost two weeks, and perhaps thirty people were huddled together, their eyes on him anxiously. As always, he felt a mixture of pity and annoyance while he scanned their faces, but as he recognized three of them, unease threaded itself through his chest. *Always a few who return, begging for the healing of a close relative who has contracted a disease or suffered an accident much like the one I Saw and for which the god prescribed. Sometimes it's worse. Sometimes the vision of a future danger, though avoided by the supplicant, has subsequently fallen on another. It happened with Nasha and Nefer-Mut. The god warned Nasha to stay away from the Street of the Basket Sellers. Nasha was obedient, but it was Nefer-Mut, her mother, who was inadvertently trampled by a donkey and laden cart on that very street. Why?* he asked himself for the thousandth time as the cloud of disquiet hardened to apprehension. *It is as though the illnesses and accidents, the future events I See, have been foreordained regardless of what is accomplished through me, and if the petitioner avoids them, they must become the fate of another. It hasn't happened often, but enough to occasionally trouble my nights. I have prayed about this. I have discussed it with Methen, to no avail.*

"Let them in," he told Kar heavily. "They can sit on the grass by the rear entrance and wait until Thothhotep is ready to assist me." He swung away, walking through the gate and along the sun-dappled path overshadowed by the luxuriant growth of the willows Anab had planted years before. Running beside them was the orderly march of date palms, now fully mature, and beyond them the narrow canal that brought water to the garden beds which Anhur and his men had dug in those first magical months when he and Ishat were exploring their new domain with all the delight of children. Huy caught brief glimpses of glittering wavelets stirred by the breeze. Ahead, Merenra was emerging between the modest pillars of the front entrance. He stood waiting impassively, looking every inch the perfect chief steward in the folds of his ankle-length sheath, the yellow ribbon tied around his naked skull fluttering against the links of the plain gold chain around his neck.

Huy turned to Anhur. "Organize the people according to need, and keep them together—don't let them wander about." He answered Merenra's obeisance with a nod. "Find Tetiankh and tell him to prepare a dose of poppy. He can do it before he unpacks my belongings. Thothhotep won't need to be summoned. She'll have seen the gaggle of supplicants straggling through the gate."

"Very well, Master. While we were away, a small shipment of carob pods arrived from Shinar. Khnit will hold them until you tell me whether you want them ground for drinking or kept to be added to food. Seshemnefer has sent word that the harvest has begun on your arouras. A scroll bearing the royal seal was delivered by a herald yesterday."

Huy's eyebrows rose in shock. "A scroll? For me?" he said stupidly. "I've had no direct word from the King in over ten years! What does he want?"

The steward permitted himself a small smile. "I expect you yourself will discover that," he observed drily. "The herald commanded me to tell you that the King is not in haste, but neither will he wait too long for your reply."

"What does that mean?" Huy snapped, his heart sinking. He was more than content to remain well out of the One's direct stare, to be, in effect, comfortably forgotten by the god on the Horus Throne. Amunhotep feared him, that much he knew. The scroll must contain something of extreme importance. "It will have to wait until I've dealt with the townspeople and slept away my fatigue," he finished, worry making him uncharacteristically short with Merenra. "Tell Tetiankh to hurry up with my drug."

Amunmose was approaching, a stool under his arm and a grin on his face. "Welcome home, Master. I'm glad you're back. Khnit hasn't bothered to give us hot food since you left. I trust the marriage festivities were enjoyable?" Huy hardly heard him, and grunted a reply. Undaunted, Amunmose set the stool down within the shade of the rear portico. "Beer will be ready for you when you've dealt with them," he said, waving an arm at the throng on the grass. He went back into the house.

Huy sank onto the stool and waited, his mind already revolving feverishly around the roll of papyrus that must even now be lying on his desk. Presently Tetiankh came hurrying, the small ceramic cup containing the poppy infusion already held out to Huy. Huy drank quickly. Long ago he had ceased to grimace at its bitterness, and he had given up any concern regarding his now total dependence on the opium garnered from his and Amunnefer's own fields. He had found that, if he took a dose before the Seeings, the headaches he always suffered afterwards lost most of their violence, leaving him more exhausted than in pain. The fact that he could no longer sleep without an added draft, and needed one upon waking, caused him some concern, but his overall health remained excellent, and the face he regarded in the copper mirror every morning as Tetiankh applied his kohl remained clear-eyed and unlined. Nor was there any grey in his thick hair. He still wore it long, stubbornly refusing any hint that such an eccentricity was unsuitable for a man of his station. The poppy did not interfere with the visions. If anything, it enhanced them, bringing a clarity to the voice of Anubis and a crisp edge to the colours and contours of what he Saw. Now, as he set the tiny cup down by his sandalled foot, Thothhotep settled herself on his other side, placing her palette across her thighs and murmuring the prayer to Thoth before uncapping her ink. Huy beckoned the first petitioner to him.

Full dark had fallen before Kar ushered the last person through the gate that gave onto the rough path leading to the town. Huy left the stool and stretched, reaching for the beer Amunmose had brought and downing it thirstily. His head echoed the beat of his heart.

"Ask Khnit to make me a carob drink please, Amunmose," Thothhotep said, sliding the lid of her palette closed and gathering up the pile of scrolls. "Master, I'm tired. May I leave the copying until tomorrow?"

"Of course. Are you hungry? Amunmose, tell Khnit to heat us some food!" he called after the man disappearing into the dimness of the dusky garden. "The night is very warm," he commented as they made their way into the house. "Too warm for the month of Payni. Shall we sleep on the roof? Iny has surely unpacked for you by now. Go and tell her to make up a bed for you by one of the wind catchers." He knew that he had begun to babble. The poppy and the Seeings had made him feel dizzy and weightless, so that he needed to balance himself against the wall of the short passage.

Thothhotep shot him a keen glance over her shoulder. "What's wrong, Huy? Something is on your mind."

She only called him by his name if she was concerned for him, Huy knew. He wanted to refuse to acknowledge the scroll sitting in the darkness of his office, to deny its existence until the morning, but he did not think he would be able to sleep until the King's need had been voiced in his scribe's soft tones. He blew out his breath. "A message from the King arrived yesterday," he told her. "I suppose we ought to read it while we wait for the meal."

They had been about to pass the doorway of the office. She halted, her hand on the lintel, her features, in the light of the two small torches flaring in the passage, full of surprise. She said nothing, only waited for his decision, and after a moment he reluctantly called for a lamp and preceded her into the room. Almost immediately a house servant appeared, set an oil lamp on the desk, bowed, and withdrew. The flame in the pretty bulbous alabaster cup leapt and then steadied to a pleasant glow. Huy and Thothhotep stared at one another in its comforting yellow glimmer, their attention fixed on the thin cylinder of papyrus. Finally, he went around the desk and lowered himself into his chair, feeling the night wind that wafted through the growth beyond the window stir against his naked shoulders. "Read it," he ordered.

At once she picked it up, examined the seal with its royal insignia of the sedge and the bee, and cracked it apart. Unrolling the scroll, she scanned it quickly then read it aloud.

"'To the Great Seer Huy son of Hapu, greetings. Upon leaving Mi-wer for a temporary stay in my palace at Mennofer, I require your presence there on a matter of great importance. I shall expect your compliance as soon as possible. Dictated to my Chief Scribe Seti-en on the fifteenth day of the month Payni, in the twenty-third year of my Appearing.' Seti-en adds his titles." Thothhotep let the scroll roll up and began to tap it against her chin, her eyes huge in the diffused light. "A matter of great importance, Master. Do you know what His Majesty might mean?"

"No." Huy stirred, worry making him restless. "As far as I know from Ramose's letters, there's no sickness in the divine family. The Horus-in-the-Nest Prince Amunhotep is well. The King's second son, Thothmes, and his wife the Princess Neferatiri produced the baby Amunemhat, and Thothmes and Second Wife Mutemwia produced another Amunhotep. Thothmes is only seventeen. Neferatiri is sixteen. Mutemwia is comparatively ancient at nineteen." He forced a laugh. "Yet none of them have expressed a need for me. I did See for the King a long time ago, as you know. I also saw for the Noble Heqareshu, Prince Thothmes' Nurse. Since then, apart from the odd Governor or two, the nobility has left me alone." He rubbed his eyes with the heels of his hands and, placing his elbows on the desk, rested his cheeks in his palms. "If the One left Mi-wer on the fifteenth of this month and the herald with this scroll left at the same time, the King would have arrived at Mennofer on the seventeenth. The herald, having to take the desert track to Iunu and then a boat to Hut-herib, came here yesterday, the eighteenth. I suppose we should go back to Mennofer at once, but in spite of the urgency of the summons I need a day or two at home to prepare myself for whatever the King might say. This distresses me, Thothhotep. I'm not sure why."

"Do you want to dictate an answer?"

"No. We'll just have Tetiankh and Iny repack a few things and leave early on the twenty-first." He let his forearms drop onto the polished surface of the desk. "Let us eat quickly, and then I must sleep. I'm very tired." *I wanted to savour being home*, he thought as they walked to the reception hall, where dishes steamed and Amunmose waited to serve them. *I wanted to go and watch the harvest continuing on my land, perhaps even winnow a little myself. I wanted to relish the wait for word of the latest incense caravan.* His appetite had left him, but he forced himself to eat, knowing that he needed the nourishment. In spite of the panoply of stars blazing above him as he lay on the roof, and a welcome quiet after the noise of Heby's street, he did not fall asleep for a long time.

Tetiankh did not question Huy's order to pack for a return to Mennofer. He asked how long the visit would be. Huy had no answer. *I should stay with Heby and Iupia, but I don't want to,* Huy thought dismally as he sat staring moodily at the brilliant shaft of morning light falling through the one clerestory window in his office and forming an irregular square on the tiled floor. *Young Amunhotep-Huy is a disruptive influence at the best of times, and I shrink from having to help Heby deal with him when I am preoccupied.*

Inns are usually rooms above beer houses, noisy and cramped. I suppose we can sleep aboard the barge. It's warm enough to spend the night on the deck. Or nights. Irritably, he shouted for Amunmose and, when his under steward's lively face appeared in the doorway, told him to make sure Tetiankh included cushions and blankets among the possessions that would be hauled aboard the vessel. *I wish I could talk to Henenu about this,* his thoughts ran on. *She would calm these irrational fears of mine, give me confidence to face His Majesty. Are you not a Great Seer? she would say,* the cowrie shells festooning her hair clicking together as she leaned towards me. *Is your name not known in every Egyptian household? Are you not a lesser lord of time? How can you be afraid?* He smiled grimly into the quiet room. *I miss you, Rekhet, and I can be afraid because everything in me, ka, heart, khu-spirit, is shouting a warning. My life has been too regular, too predictable, for many years. Once more Atum requires a change, and I am not ready.*

He lingered on his estate for another day, out of an uncharacteristic pride determined to show his power by keeping Amunhotep waiting but also in a deep reluctance to discover what the King desired of him. He even considered sending excuses south—I have fallen ill, my mother is sick, my barge has been holed—but finally he recognized his cowardice. In the cool of the following dawn, he stepped unwillingly onto the boat's ramp, Thothhotep behind him, and gave the order to cast off.

Leaning on the deck rail and watching the riverbank slide by, it seemed to him that the water was at a level considerably lower than it had been a scant three days before, giving off a rank odour of slimed reeds and mud that underpinned the tributary's usual scent of lush green growth even in the weeks before the Inundation. *It's my own inner disturbance that I smell,* he thought. Behind him, Tetiankh was attaching the awning to the wall of the cabin, stepping around Thothhotep, who was already ensconced on cushions, sipping water from the cup Iny had handed her and contentedly watching the sky, where a falcon swooped above them. This time Huy's rowers were at work, fighting the slow current. The sound of his captain calling the beat was soothing. The journey to Mennofer would be a few hours longer than usual.

They put in at sunset, and the tired rowers left the barge to sit or lie on the grass of the bank while Khnit and her assistants lit a fire and prepared an evening meal of fried fish and cabbage stew. Huy and Thothhotep waited together in silence for the food to be brought. Huy's abstracted mood seemed to have infected his scribe. He knew that she loved being on the river as much as Ishat had. Her enjoyment was less exuberant than Ishat's had been, gentler but no less deep; her observations of the scenery floating past were made calmly, but her language was rich. So far she had said little, in spite of the clouds of dust hanging over the groups of reapers plying their sickles while the golden crops collapsed before them, and the steady stream of other craft heading to nearby Iunu or the cities far to the south.

After they had eaten in a wordless companionship, she summoned Iny and disappeared, the body servant laden with natron, cloths, and oils. Later, returning clean-faced, her short hair slicked back with oil, she bade Huy a solemn good night and lay down at the foot of the cabin. Iny covered her and, bowing to Huy, retreated to the sailors' fires beginning to twinkle in the deepening dusk. Huy himself was too restless to sleep. Taking Anhur, he wandered along the tributary's path. They were very close to the fork of the Delta where the river branched into several arms. Iunu itself sat almost upon that spot. Huy, pacing beside the comforting bulk of his soldier, remembered his despairing walk along this same rutted road on his way north from Iunu to an unknown fate in his hometown. The memory did not soothe him.

In the late afternoon of the following day, having passed Iunu in the morning, they went by the northern mouth of the drainage canal that ran behind Mennofer, and the northern suburbs of the city began. The watersteps of the nobles broke the line of palms and other trees overhanging the river path at regular intervals. The houses lying beyond them were seldom glimpsed. Huy knew that behind the meticulously tended lawns and gardens, with their sheltering mud-brick walls, lay a maze of narrow streets and tiny row houses, markets, beer houses, and simple shrines. Behind this teeming hive lay the Ankh-tawy district, stretching in a wide arc to the southern canal—a place of respectable artisans who cultivated a few cramped arouras to augment their rations of bread, beer, onions, and garlic received from the overseers who directed their work in the place of the dead across the canal and out onto the desert.

East of the Ankh-tawy lay the heart of Mennofer, first the temples of past kings, then the District of Ptah, with its mighty temple and sculpture-lined avenues leading north to the famous White Walls, the ancient Citadel, and the temple of Neith, goddess sister to Osiris; and south to another small canal, the South District, and the temple of Hathor of the Sycamore. Then the south suburbs began, mirroring those of the north. A short way farther east, running all the way from the Citadel south to where the avenue from the temple of Ptah became the canal, a high wall protected the Fine District of Pharaoh, with its palace, harem, and gardens. South of this wall, hard up against it, the buildings of the arsenal and the homes of the sailors and soldiers stationed in the holy city, crowded against the great Peru-nefer dockyards and piers and the Amun shrine.

Between the Fine District of Pharaoh and the river lay the centre of Mennofer, busy and wealthy with commerce, and the wide watersteps where dozens of craft of every description jostled against each other. Two canals ran through it. The southern canal ran straight to the temple of Ptah, but the northern waterway, heavily guarded all along its length, led directly to the palace itself; and it was close to this canal that Huy's captain found a narrow berth and the helmsman expertly jockeyed the barge into it. Even before the ramp was run out, a phalanx of soldiers, their short kilts sporting the blue and white of royalty, had gathered above the watersteps. Their captain stepped forward and bowed. "This way is restricted," he called to Huy, who was facing him on the deck. "If you have business with the ministers of the Horus Throne, state it now. Otherwise you must move south to the public watersteps."

"I am the Seer Huy son of Hapu," Huy called back. "The One has summoned me."

He was surprised when the man nodded rather than sending away for confirmation. "His Majesty is temporarily in residence, Great Seer. My orders are to have you, and you alone, escorted to the palace when you arrive. Food and drink can be provided for your entourage if you so wish."

"I go nowhere without my scribe and the captain of my guard," Huy protested, indicating a painted and perfumed Thothhotep hovering at his elbow.

Even before he had finished speaking, the other was shaking his head. "The command is absolute," he said tersely. "You are to present yourself alone. You will be poled along the canal and met at the concourse."

Huy hesitated, one thought in his mind. What if the sense of foreboding that had dogged him ever since Thothhotep read him the scroll was a warning that Amunhotep wished to harm him? Perhaps even have him quietly killed? *But that's ridiculous*, he told himself. *You've done nothing to incur the King's displeasure, and besides, you are too well known throughout the country to suddenly vanish*. Nevertheless, visions of his bloated body being pulled from the river, or bloodied with stab wounds and found out on the desert, half eaten by jackals, or even headless and unidentified in some city ditch, flashed across his inner eye.

"Master, you need to decide, and really there is no decision to be made," Thothhotep murmured, handing him the scroll. "This is a direct summons."

For answer, Huy stepped onto the ramp. "Make sure that my people are given whatever sustenance they require," he said brusquely to the soldier, very aware of Anhur glowering in disapproval at his back. Reaching the end of the ramp, he took the few steps to one of the waiting skiffs and got into it. At once the waiting sailor bowed to him and, lifting his pole, shoved off. The skiff began to drift towards the towering wall, with its shadowed mouth into which the canal seemed to disappear. Huy sat tensely on the cushion provided. He had never felt more vulnerable.

Soon the little boat reached the wall and slid under it, coming to a bumpy halt before a long stone concourse that ran away to a series of pillars fronting the imposing palace which had been the northern centre of power in Egypt for many hentis. Blue and white flags rippled from tall poles set in the hands of massive stone figures seated to either side of the building's entrance. Double doors of beaten copper had been folded back, the golden brown metal blindingly reflecting the westering sun, whose strength was still white-hot. Guards stood ranged along the length of the palace, impassively watching the few well-dressed people who were hurrying across the concourse. Most were accompanied by servants holding linen sunshades over their heads. Huy got out of the skiff and, feeling the hot stone burn beneath his sandals, began to walk forward. It seemed to take him a long time to reach the blessed shadow cast by the building, but at last he stepped from heat to coolness and came to a halt.

At once one of the guards approached him, a man in a short blue and white kilt, his broad chest hidden under a leather jerkin, a sheathed sword hanging from his sturdy belt. A plain white linen helmet edged in blue framed a brown face out of which two dark eyes scanned Huy shrewdly. Huy, staring back with the vague certainty that he had met this soldier before, noted the golden Supreme Commander's arm bands gripping the well-muscled upper arms, and scoured his mind for a name.

The man smiled slightly and bowed. "Great Seer, you are expected, although His Majesty did not know how long it would be before you were free to answer his summons. Perhaps you do not remember me. I was little more than a lad when I accompanied His Majesty to your town, before he marched into Rethennu. At that time I was Commander-in-Chief of His Majesty's ground forces. Now I have the honour of controlling the navy as well."

Huy's brow cleared. "Wesersatet! Of course! The last time I saw you, you were clad in a cloth-of-gold kilt and decked in jaspers!"

"And you were anxious and a little afraid of us painted and perfumed courtiers. Believe me, your presence aboard *Kha-em-Ma'at* had us agog with curiosity about you under our nonchalance!"

"*Kha-em-Ma'at*," Huy repeated. "'Living in Truth.' The name of the royal barge. I had forgotten that, but not how I saw a great victory for the King in Rethennu. It was a long time ago, Commander."

Wesersatet gestured to one of the guards. "Tell a servant to fetch Maani-nekhtef at once. Tell him that the Great Seer is waiting." The man passed beyond the entrance just far enough to speak to someone hovering inside. Wesersatet turned back to Huy. "Please take the stool. The Chief Herald will be here presently and will take you to the Throne Room. I believe that His Majesty has risen from the sleep and is consulting his ministers there. Shall I summon Men? Are you hungry or thirsty?"

Men, Huy thought swiftly. *The chief steward. He gave me my first taste of the carob drink, and a dose of poppy so strong that I could hardly walk out of the King's presence in the cabin without stumbling.* A wave of desire for the drug washed over him. Grimly, he pushed it away.

He had been perching on the stool for no more than a few moments when a man emerged from the gloom of the palace doorway, bowed, and addressed him briskly. "I am Chief Herald Maani-nekhtef. I will announce you to His Majesty. Have you titles to be called, Great Seer?"

Huy rose, his heart thudding. "No. And please, Maani-nekhtef, announce me as Huy, son of Hapu of Hut-herib."

"Very well. Follow me."

The reception hall was vast. Huy heard the echo of his tread strike the lofty walls and mingle with the measured voices of the servants and soldiers whose presence was lost in that great expanse of marching pillars and smooth, tiled floor. Huy imagined it crowded with hundreds of lavishly clad, jewelled guests gathered to fete a foreign ambassador, perhaps, their conversations all but extinguishing the music of drum, lute, and finger cymbals, the perfume from the wax cones on their wigged heads or massaged into their gleaming bodies mingling with the fragrance of the thousands of blooms scattered about.

Coming to himself, he realized that he and his guide had crossed the hall and were now pacing along a series of wide corridors flanked by more guards standing between ebony totems that represented the gods and symbols of every sepat in Egypt. Their serene faces gazed unseeingly at him as he passed. He tried to spot the one for his sepat, the Am-khent, but the Chief Herald strode ahead and Huy hurried to catch up to him, suddenly bewildered by the sheer size of this holy place. Large doors opened off the passages at regular intervals, giving Huy a glimpse across dainty inlaid chairs and intricately carved little tables towards a view of gardens full of shrubs and riotous with healthy blooms, although it was the season of Shemu, when his uncle Ker's perfume fields would be showing no more than a dense collection of drooping stems and parched leaves, the crop of flowers plucked and crushed for steeping long since. One passage ran between what were plainly the offices of various ministers, their walls pocked with niches for scrolls, their desks large and simple, each with a small flax mat beside it for a scribe, their lamps purely functional in design. Huy saw no indication of a woman's touch, and decided that the harem quarters lay somewhere else in the complex. Perhaps foreign dignitaries were lodged in this wing of the palace, close to the ministers with whom they probably had to deal.

Suddenly they came to the end of a passage, the attending soldier opened the door, and Huy found himself blinking in strong sunlight and surrounded by lawn and a forest through which a path ran. Other buildings, their whitewashed walls bright with paintings, loomed to right and left. Each had its contingent of guards clustered about the doors. The herald had begun to slow, and directly ahead Huy saw a relatively modest structure. The soldier there was already opening the door.

"Within are the Throne Room and several private retiring rooms for His Majesty and the royal family," Maani-nekhtef told Huy. "His Majesty gives formal audiences here, although today he has been hearing the preliminary reports on projected yields of grain. I believe that it has been a fruitful year, and of course we must now pray for a good flood." Politely, he held up a hand. Huy gave him the scroll he had been clutching, then stood on the threshold. He could still see Maani-nekhtef's back as the herald took a few steps into the room, bowed, waited for some signal Huy could not see, then intoned, "Huy, son of Hapu of Hut-herib, requests admittance into the presence of the One. What is Your Majesty's pleasure regarding this desire?"

There was a spoken response in tones Huy recognized. They returned him uncomfortably to the momentous day when he had Seen for the King, when Thothmes' attraction to Ishat had intensified, when, unknown to him, his life was about to be forever changed. He could not make out the King's words, but the herald took the few steps back to him and indicated that he should enter. "Perform your obeisances and then wait," he said. "The King will attend to you as soon as he may. It has been a pleasure to serve you, Son of Hapu." He bowed, turned on his heel, and walked away with the unhurried grace and speed acquired by every herald.

Very well, Huy thought, crossing the door's lintel and moving into relative dimness. *I hope I can remember how to reverence Amunhotep.*

The room was large, but its proportions were manageable, somehow scaled on a more human level than the awesome magnificence of the reception hall. Nevertheless, it was splendid enough, with its deep blue lapis-tiled floor in which flecks of pyrite glittered, its pale blue ceiling where Nut, the sky goddess who swallowed the sun every evening and gave birth to him every dawn, arched her body in protection over the dais at the farther end. A crowd of people had fallen silent as Huy appeared. He felt their inquisitive stares as he bent, knelt, and then prostrated himself full length, but all his attention was fixed on the occupant of the Horus Throne set in the centre of the dais. There was a pause, then the voice he knew bade him rise. He did so, bowing from the waist with arms outstretched, as Chief Steward Men had told him to do all those years ago, and standing with eyes downcast.

He had thought that the dais was empty of all but the King, but when the same voice gave him permission to look up, he saw the throne surrounded. He knew Kenamun immediately. The King's closest friend, son of his wet nurse, was taking up almost the same position Huy remembered from the cabin on *Kha-em-Ma'at*, behind Amunhotep and with one hand resting on the rear edge of the throne. Sitting at the King's left hand on a stool, a young man with Amunhotep's unmistakable features was watching Huy warily, his hand joined to that of a very pretty and equally young woman in a wig of many oiled black ringlets falling to her narrow waist. A coronet of gold and green faience flowers circled her brow. Green moonstone and gold scarab earrings swung lightly against her long neck, and above the high swell of her white-clad breasts a many-stranded pectoral bearing more moonstone scarabs rested on her pale, flawless skin. To the King's right, a man was standing awkwardly. Older than the young man on Amunhotep's left, he was nevertheless much younger, Huy surmised quickly, than Huy himself. He too bore a marked resemblance to the King. On the floor before the dais, a series of men were ranged—ministers, favoured servants and courtiers, perhaps one or two High Priests, as well as the usual spread of palace guards. Huy's eyes slid over them and up to the King himself.

Meeting his look, Amunhotep smiled broadly. "Welcome, Great Seer. It has been many years since you and I faced one another." He made it sound as though they might be equals, and a murmur went up from the listening throng. "You were a clumsy stripling with the power of Atum in your fingers then," the King went on. "Today you have become a handsome man, and they tell me that the authority of the god still pours through you." He beckoned Huy closer. "In spite of the peasant stock from which you came, you have intelligence also, and so has your brother. We know that Heby is highly respected by the High

Priest of Ptah. We were sorry to hear of the death of his wife Sapet, but our Assistant Treasurer Merira is proud that Heby has chosen his daughter Iupia to succeed the ill-fated Sapet." His heavily kohled glance went to a man at the edge of the crowd, and Merira stepped forward and bowed, smiling at Huy.

"Indeed, Majesty, it is Iupia's good fortune, and mine," he said.

Amunhotep's level gaze returned to Huy. "You also have lost someone you love, although she has not died," he remarked. "Ishat has proved a worthy wife to my Governor Thothmes, and a valued ornament at court when he comes to make his annual report on the state of my Heq-at sepat. Do you still miss her, Huy?"

What is all this about? Huy wondered. *Is the King reminding me that in his divine omnipotence he knows everything that passes in Egypt? And why is he paying me and Heby such compliments?*

"Thothmes has been my dear friend ever since we were at school together, Majesty," he answered carefully. "Ishat is very happy with him. I see them often. Iunu is not far from my home."

"You did not answer the question, but it's of no matter. Thothhotep is an adequate scribe?"

"More than adequate," Huy hastened to say. "She is exemplary in every way."

"Good." Amunhotep signalled. "Men, bring a stool for the Seer." Another murmur went up from the listening people, and this time the sound was full of a surprised incredulity. Only foreigners equal in station to the King were allowed to sit in his presence, and that only because they were equal in temporal power. Of course, the King was without peer in his divinity.

The stool was produced. The chief steward smiled at Huy and gave him a swift greeting before melting away. Self-consciously, Huy sat, awkwardly aware of the honour being done to him, and embarrassed by it. Folding one tense hand into the other, he laid them against his thigh. A moment of silence fraught with expectancy fell. No rustle of starched linen or click of gem against gem came to Huy's ears. Even the breaths of those beside and behind him seemed stilled. The eyes of the King, his sons, the favoured ones on the dais, were fixed steadily on Huy, and he knew that the next words Amunhotep spoke would reveal the purpose of his, Huy's, presence here. Dread filled him with its familiar metallic taste, stiffening his limbs and cramping in his bowels. He still had no presentiment of what was to come, what mysterious crime he might have unknowingly committed. Since hearing the contents of the scroll now being held by His Majesty's Scribe, he had been sure that no royal gift was awaiting him here in the palace at Mennofer.

10

"THIS IS MY SON Prince Thothmes," Amunhotep said, indicating the young man on his right. "He has had a dream of great prophetic power that requires a most careful interpretation. The High Priests of Ptah, Neith, and Hathor of the Sycamore have all rendered a conclusion. The Purified of each temple have also spoken. But Thothmes has begged me to invite an opinion from Egypt's greatest Seer, for surely a perfect understanding of this matter will come from the creator-god through his chosen vessel. Atum's words to my son will flow from your mouth, Son of Hapu."

Huy felt himself go cold, so cold that he needed to clench his teeth together to prevent them from chattering. He forced his gaze to remain locked on the King's face. *How old is he now?* he wondered idiotically. *Forty-three? Forty-four? He has not changed much since his Appearing. He was in his early twenties when he made war so confidently in Rethennu because Atum had told me of his victories. His colour is too high, though. The veins stand out on his neck and his brow beneath the rim of the uraeus. Something is wrong here. I sense it, like the wind that sometimes blows in from the desert and brings a pestilence with it. I read it in his eyes. He knows what he wants from me, and it is not something benign.*

"Majesty, I am not one of the Purified," he managed to say, hearing the strain in his own tones. "I am not an interpreter of dreams or prophecies. Atum heals and tells the future through me. I was not chosen for any other work."

The royal forefinger began to tap against the arm of the gilded throne. "Have you been asked to unravel the meaning of dreams before? Have you ever given Atum the opportunity to do so through you?"

"No, Majesty."

"Then how do you know that the gift does not lie dormant in you, waiting for a moment such as this to be released?" Amunhotep leaned out over the gold-shot kilt hiding his muscular thighs. "Is it not true that visions of our future often come to us in dreams?"

"So the Purified say."

"Then what the Prince asks of you is very little different from the usual exercise of your ability." He sat back.

Another pregnant silence fell, and this time Huy was fully aware of the quick breaths around him, as though the courtiers and ministers had just completed some sort of strange race. *I'm trapped,* he told himself frantically. *I cannot argue against his point, though I know that somewhere it is flawed. I can't think of the right words to get me out of this magnificent room and back to the safety of my barge. Amunhotep will have his way—but why? Why does he need an interpretation from me? Because my pronouncements are respected as truth throughout the country and thus I give validation to ... to what? Anubis, whisper to me! Tell me what to do!* He waited, but the grating voice of the god did not come. In the end he sighed inwardly.

"I am Your Majesty's servant," he said. "Your will is the will of Amun. I will hear this dream."

The King's black eyebrows drew together in a swift frown and his grip tightened on both arms of the throne. *I've offended him,* Huy thought in dismay. *But how?*

At a muttered word from his father, Prince Thothmes kissed the hand of the girl beside him, let it go, and rose. He was taller than he had looked when seated, leaner than Amunhotep, his muscles lying long and close to his bones. Now he resembled his brother, the older man on the King's left. Huy knew he ought to get off the stool and reverence the Prince, but he also knew that his knees would tremble.

"I thank you, Great Seer, for your august attention in this matter," Thothmes said. His voice was surprisingly deep and rich for such a young man. "I value your interpretation of my dream above all the priests I have consulted. Know, then, that I was out hunting in the desert west of the mighty tombs of my ancestors. I was alone with my horse and chariot. I often leave my guards and servants by the pool of Pedjet-she, just beyond the canal, so that they may enjoy the shade of the sycamores there while I hunt lions and gazelles by myself. It is what I prefer." He paused, and Huy, thoroughly mystified, had the time to wonder why he was being told such inconsequential details before the Prince continued. "At midday I became tired and thirsty. Leading my horse into the shadow of the great head that juts out of the sand, he that we call Harmachis-Khepera-Ra-Temu, I drank from my water skin, lay down on my cloak, and fell asleep." He paused again, his arms at his side, his glance going to the spangled ceiling, and all at once it seemed to Huy that he was like a schoolboy using a brief respite to remember what next to recite.

"I dreamed," Thothmes continued, "and in my dream the stone mouth of the god opened, and his eyes became alive, and he spoke to me. 'Free my limbs from their prison of sand, O Prince,' he said, 'so that I may once again be worshipped, and in return I will set you upon the Horus Throne and you will rule over the Red Land and the Black Land. Egypt will be yours.' I was troubled when I awoke. I stood gazing upon the beautiful face of

Ra-Harmachis and imagined his limbs held tightly in the grip of the sand where no one suspected that the god was more than his head. Then I got into my chariot and hurried to tell my father what had transpired, but not before I commanded Tjanuni, my father's Overseer of Works, to gather a force of labourers and go out to begin digging around the god. And behold!" There was a third pause, this one, Huy was certain, for effect. "Already the supine body is emerging from the sand, still stained and damp, but drying quickly in the heat! Ra-Harmachis is taking the form of a lion, Great Seer! The Aten, the blessed rays of Ra's light, strike the earth to become lions, and this sphinx-god is the greatest lion of them all!" He regained his seat, a flush spreading over his eager features. "So, Seer of Egypt, do you believe that my dream spoke true? That the Horus Throne will be mine? Consider, and then speak!"

He and his father smiled briefly at one another, then their attention returned to Huy. He hardly noticed. His concentration had turned inward. *Where have I heard that before?* he thought furiously, desperately. *The rays of Ra are the Aten, and the Aten strikes the earth and becomes the sacred lion. Oh, of course! Ramose, my old mentor, High Priest of Ra, told me many things pertaining to spiritual truths, and that was one of them. So the monumental head rearing out of the desert between this city and the three wonders of our ancient history, always regarded as a god, is indeed a god. Of the sun. Of Ra. Of the Aten.* Relief flooded Huy. *There's nothing to fear here,* he told himself. *The Prince is obviously well educated and intelligent. He guesses, probably without being aware of the information, that the head is connected to a buried body. He sleeps, and a dream does the rest. As for his ascension to godhead himself, he is Amunhotep's second son. The Hawk-in-the-Nest is his older brother, named after his father. If I could See for him, I would expect to tell him that his death will be an early one. Thus Prince Thothmes would in time inherit the throne.*

Yet it was all too neat, too clean. Thothmes had been reciting a lesson, Huy was sure of it. The King looked smugly triumphant. Prince Amunhotep ... Huy placed his hands over his face, fingers splayed, and his elbows on his knees, in a deliberately studied gesture to give the impression that this was how he pondered the deeply mysterious ways of the gods. But he was studying the heir. Prince Amunhotep's face held no expression. His cosmetician had obviously tried to hide the dark circles under His Highness's eyes, but their shadow remained. His skin was sallow. He was staring at the far wall above the heads of the enthralled crowd. *The Prince is troubled,* Huy thought in surprise. *No, more than troubled. This young man is either very distressed or trying to control a fear of some sort. I am missing something here, a piece of vital knowledge. What does Prince Amunhotep have to fear?*

The answer came to him immediately, as though at last he had asked the right question. *Not what,* the voice of Anubis whispered in Huy's mind. *Whom. Whom does the Nestling fear?* Huy waited. Had the god spoken, or was his own ka asking the question? And answering it. In a gush of sweat, Huy knew the source of the Prince's fear: the King and Thothmes. This was no dream. This was a clever concoction between a favourite son and an unscrupulous father. No wonder Thothmes' story sounded like a schoolroom recitation. Were they planning to murder Prince Amunhotep, the first-born, the heir to the Horus Throne? But why? What possible advantage could be gained by such a ploy? Prince Amunhotep was not physically maimed. He had not spoken, but his face did not display the unfocused vagueness of the interiorly impaired. He appeared to be a healthy, entirely acceptable heir. Perhaps he was a Setian, like Huy's nephew, the rages and even the cruelty full-blown. Perhaps he had no desire to be Pharaoh, and had bequeathed the honour to his brother. But then, why the story of a dream? Why the involvement of the sun-god buried in the desert?

Huy ground his teeth under the cover of his palms. *My duty is clear. I must stand up and tell the King and Prince Thothmes that although it is likely that the god came to the Prince in a dream and requested that his body be freed from the sand, the promise that followed is not to be counted on. Only the death of the legitimate Hawk-in-the-Nest would ensure Thothmes' elevation. Such a sadness might occur in the future, but for now the Prince must make sure that the work out on the desert is fully completed, and put the rest of the dream aside.*

But the King himself heard and approved the whole vision, Huy realized. *Summoning me, surrounding me with witnesses to whatever I might say, trapping me into listening, exchanging a smile with the Prince as he regained his seat—Amunhotep is happy with this ... this construct.* Huy almost groaned aloud. Had the King and his second son conspired together to fabricate the dream? Had the King sent someone out onto the desert to dig a little, a very little, around the god, to make sure that there was indeed a holy body buried under the sand? But why, why, why?

It doesn't matter why, the stern voice of his conscience interposed. *You must tell Prince Thothmes not to trust the dream, that in all probability it is a deception inflicted upon him by the Khatyu, the devils that inhabit the fiery noontime and attack those who are foolish enough to fall asleep without a protecting amulet.*

But no—better to agree with everything, an insidious voice whispered, drowning the cries of protest from Huy's conscience. *Let Egypt see the form emerging from the desert as proof of the love of the gods towards the royal family, and presume, along with everyone else, that poor Prince Amunhotep will not live long enough to inherit anything but a sumptuous tomb. Besides, if you speak against this thing, you speak against His Majesty. He can do you harm, Son of Hapu. You are rich, but how secure would you and your household be if the King took back the arouras he gave you, took back the incense concession, maybe even decreed that your share in the poppy fields must go to someone else? He has total power to pervert Ma'at in this way.*

As if his growing anguish had opened a door, Huy heard his own voice speaking to the King in the words of Atum, as he had done so many years before: "Tell my son Amunhotep the things I shall show you, and give him this warning. He must not depart from the balance of Ma'at I have established. Already he is tempted to do so." *Was this the temptation, Atum?* Huy begged the god silently. *The desire to pervert Ma'at by passing over the heir in favour of his brother? I told them that I am no dream-reader. If I touched Thothmes, would I See a lie or the truth? I must protect those who depend on me—the members of my household, the ill, those anxious about their future. I carry them all on my shoulders. Surely I cannot be expected to contradict the One himself! I do not understand,* Huy shouted dumbly, all at once flooded by the need for a mouthful of poppy. *But you know the dream is false,* the calm voice said. *You must speak the truth and take the consequences. Atum expects such courage from his Twice Born. Do it, Huy, and be at peace.*

Taking his hands away from his face, Huy came shakily to his feet. All three men, King and both princes, were watching him, but Prince Amunhotep's expression was now one of sadness. *It doesn't matter what I say,* Huy decided as he opened his mouth. *The King is omnipotent. He will do as he wishes in spite of Ma'at.*

"This dream is of such simplicity that I need not even ask to touch the Prince's fingers," he said as firmly as he could. Once more a glance passed between father and son, and before its significance could choke off his words, Huy continued. "Part of it has been revealed as a genuine message from the god. His body is even now being released from the sand. I interpret the rest of the vision thus. At some time in the future the Horus Throne will go without fail to Prince Thothmes. Ra-Harmachis has spoken through his son. That is all." He executed a clumsy bow and almost fell back down onto the stool. *Not now!* he shouted to the clamour of rebellion beginning inside him. *I could do nothing else! I did the wise thing! I have preserved myself, my people, perhaps even Heby and Iupia, from any retribution!* At that moment he realized that he did not like the King, had not liked him even when standing in awe before him as a very young man. *Get me out of here!* he begged whatever god or spirit might be hovering nearby. *I need to breathe clean air!*

The King was smiling. "Treasurer Sobekhotep," he said, holding out his ring-laden hand, "give me the pouch." A small leather bag was passed to him. He beckoned Huy closer. "This is for your wisdom, and also for the expenses of your journey to Mennofer," he told Huy. "Go home to Hut-herib. We thank you for your service today."

Yes, my service, Huy thought dully as his knees buckled into the correct position of reverence. *Anubis, what has happened here? To me? To Egypt?* Fleetingly, out of the corner of his eye, he saw the stricken expression on Prince Amunhotep's face, then Pharaoh was dismissing him and he began to back down the room towards the door.

The King was yawning. "You are all dismissed," he called, and rose, and as Huy gained the open air, he saw everyone in the room go down on their faces like so many sheaves of harvested wheat.

He stood just beyond the threshold for a few moments, taking deep breaths of the hot, sweet air, his eyes closed against the sudden brightness of the afternoon sun. The hue of the light told him that sunset was still some time away. He was amazed. It seemed to him that he had been crouched on that damnable stool for hentis. He turned to the guard at his elbow. "Please lead me back to the main entrance of the palace," he said. The man nodded and set off, and Huy followed gladly.

They had not gone far when they came to a place where one passage crossed another. Huy's guide strode forward without looking to right or left, but before he reached the continuation of the corridor, a herald in royal livery stepped out of the right-hand way and held up an arm. The guard halted. The herald bowed to Huy. "Great Seer, your presence is required in the royal apartments," he said. "Please come with me." And to the guard, "You are dismissed."

What now? Huy thought resignedly as he followed the herald. *Has the King decided that he wants me to See for him again after all these years? Doesn't he know that if I do so I will discover the subterfuge he and Prince Thothmes concocted? Or is one of the queens ill?* Reaction from the tension of the last hour was beginning to set in, and all Huy wanted to do was lie down in the latticed dimness of his cabin and go to sleep.

He had expected the passage to go on forever, but before long it ended at a sturdy cedar door. The herald pushed it open, and Huy found himself still in the garden surrounding the building that held the Throne Room. A corner of its roof could just be glimpsed away to the right, between the trees. Ahead was a wide two-storeyed edifice, its frontage riotous with paintings of blue water teeming with fish on which several gilded barges floated. Each held the seated image of one of the gods: Ptah with his lapis helmet, Hathor, whose long hair was adorned with her two cow's horns rising out of a golden circlet, and Amun the Great Cackler, wispy white goose feathers on his head seeming to quiver in a breeze that the artist had hinted at with expertise. Rays ending in golden ankhs, the symbols of life, spread downward from his hands to the figure wearing the holy uraeus kneeling before him.

Huy had never seen such a thing before, but he had little time to be mystified. Just beyond the door, the herald paused, glancing this way and that. It was the time of the afternoon sleep, and the green lawns were empty. Huy suspected that the man was making sure they would not be seen before he set off again. The suggestion was not reassuring. Coming up to the two pillars fronting the building, the herald quickly passed between them and through the doorway. Huy followed.

"Be pleased to wait here, Master," the herald said, and bowing his way past Huy, he went out. Huy doubtfully inspected his surroundings. He was in a very short hallway. Several closed doors led off from it on either side, and ahead there was an imposing double door. Into each panel a likeness of Horus had been carved, his claws resting on the stylized stool that was the hieroglyph for wealth, his hawk's head crowned with a sun-disc. Huy realized that he was about to enter the domain of Prince Amunhotep, the Hawk-in-the-Nest. At least he thought so, and hoped he was not going to find himself face to face with Prince Thothmes, that glib storyteller, instead.

He had barely drawn two breaths when one side of the double doors opened and a man appeared, bowed to him, and beckoned him forward. Huy could smell his perfume, a distinctive combination of myrrh and lotus oil, blowing towards him on the gentle draft coming through from the space behind and stirring the folds of the ankle-length white and blue sheath. "I am Pa-shed, Chief Steward to His Highness Prince Amunhotep," he said as Huy came up to him. "The Prince greatly desires to speak with you on a matter of urgency. He humbly asks that you keep your audience with him a secret."

So he was indeed to meet Prince Amunhotep, and since the Prince had a matter of urgency on his mind, it was likely that he did not require a Seeing. Huy, tired and on edge, allowed himself a moment of cautious relief. "I shall of course respect His Highness's request," he answered.

Pa-shed inclined his shaved head, his kohled eyes meeting Huy's own, seeking an honest confirmation, Huy thought, with a good steward's shrewd assessment of both words and demeanour. He bowed again, an invitation to pass by him. Huy did so.

He found himself in a large, airy room with a window that might have looked out over the garden if the view had not been almost completely obscured by an exuberant tangle of leafy growth that gave everything in the space a restful green hue and allowed the random flow of cool air. The window faced north, as far as Huy could surmise. The constant summer wind from the Delta and the Great Green would be very pleasant here. A red and yellow reed mat covered most of the floor, and on it a variety of chairs and small tables were scattered about, together with cushions and several stands holding creamy alabaster lamps of intricate design. The walls, painted with representations of vine-hung pillars, were pierced by two closed doors. *One must lead to the Prince's bedchamber and one to his office,* Huy quickly guessed in the moment when he took in his surroundings. *This is a reception room.*

Of course, Huy immediately recognized the man turning from the window. He had shed his linen headdress and his jewellery and was wearing a pair of plain reed sandals and a pale blue knee-length kilt. Huy made his obeisance deeply from the waist, arms outstretched, head lowered, wondering why the Prince had chosen to wear the colour of mourning, blue unrelieved by any other shade. He straightened. Behind him, two servants had entered soundlessly and were placing two flagons and several dishes on one of the tables. Pa-shed had retired to the wall, where he stood with arms folded, waiting for an instruction. There was no sign of the Prince's scribe. *So this is indeed going to be a matter of the utmost confidentiality,* Huy thought, *so private that not even a scribe may hear it.* More intrigued now than apprehensive, he looked into the face that resembled the King's so closely. *Those eyes hold a greater intelligence, though,* Huy decided, *and the mouth is less sensual.*

The Prince did not smile at Huy's inspection. "Pa-shed, close the door and stand outside it in the passage," he said. He had a light voice, the tones measured, the accent refined. "I wish to see no one, unless Mutemwia seeks me. The Seer and I can serve ourselves. Has the food and drink been tasted?" Pa-shed nodded. Once the door had closed quietly, Amunhotep indicated the laden table. "You have come from a difficult audience," he said quietly. "You must eat and drink. I believe that we have the choice of two wines, white grape and a very sustaining date brew into which juniper berries for bodily strength have been crushed. I'm told that you are partial to bak pods. Eat as many as you like, and the rest will be sent to your barge. Shat cakes, figs in honey, fresh peaches, grapes, currants, a few small brown pears."

He was looking over the contents of the silver platters with an interest Huy sensed was feigned. Surprised, he realized that the Prince was hesitant to give voice to the reason why he, Huy, was there.

"How wonderful the harvest months are!" Amunhotep went on. "Please help yourself, Huy, and pour a cup of grape wine for me." He retired to one of the chairs, sat, crossed his legs, and watched as Huy poured grape wine for him and date wine for himself, and set a couple of cakes on a smaller plate. Bowing, he handed the Prince his wine and gulped thirstily at his own. He was waved to a chair. Amunhotep's eyes remained steadily on him as he refilled his cup. Then he balanced it on one knee, clasping it in both hands, and waited.

The tangled leaves outside the window stirred fitfully, their shadow mimicking the movement against the opposite wall. Voices wafted in on the breeze, the words indistinguishable.

Huy ate a shat cake, drank more wine, and waited. At last the Prince sighed and set his cup on the table beside him. Leaning forward, he clasped his hands. "You were a student at Iunu, weren't you?" he said unexpectedly.

Huy's eyebrows shot up. "Yes, Highness, I was there under High Priest Ramose, who has since retired to his estate on the river, and Overseer Harmose, who has also retired."

"You were happy there, weren't you." It was a statement, not a question. "Our present Governor of the Heq-at sepat, Thothmes, became your lifelong friend. I know him well. He is honest, generous, an exemplary husband to your other great friend, Ishat. A man to be trusted although he prays to the Osiris-one Thothmes the Third as his totem instead of to Ra, whose temple sits at Iunu."

A brief smile lit the solemn, rather sad, face. Huy wondered just where all this was leading. Amunhotep was repeating almost everything the King had said a short while ago.

"When I learned that my father had summoned you, and why, I summoned Governor Thothmes. I wanted to know as much about you as I could. I would have talked to the nobles who have consulted you over the years, but I did not want to draw attention to myself. Thothmes told me that you are courageous and truthful. Tell me, Seer Huy, where was your courage today?"

Startled, Huy grabbed at his cup before it could tumble to the floor. He wanted to stall, to pretend he did not know what the Prince meant, but those dark eyes held his with a sober command that precluded a lie.

"It failed me, as Your Highness knows," he croaked. He cleared his throat of what felt like a stone of guilt. "I sensed strongly that your brother's dream was false. I saw in my mind the consequences to myself, my family, if I told the truth."

"Yet if you had told the truth, Egypt would have begun to doubt my brother's word. Your own word carries more weight

than you know. Did you not wonder why you were not asked to
See for Prince Thothmes?"

"He wanted a dream interpreted. A Seeing would not have
provided that."

"No, but it would have revealed his duplicity and perhaps
shown you whether or not the plan he has hatched with the King
my father will come to fruition. You disappoint me, Seer. You are
not as brave as your loyal friend assured me."

"What can I say?" Huy blurted miserably. "Is there any way in
which I can put this right?"

"No, of course not. The damage has been done."

"Highness, I'm sorry, but your father and brother have fabricated
a story that appears to me to have no real purpose, unless ..."
He could not complete his sentence by forcing out the next terrible words.

The Prince's eyebrows rose, but as Huy remained silent,
Amunhotep's gaze became speculative. Sitting back again, he
crossed his long legs, drank a little wine, licked his hennaed lips,
pursed them, trying to decide, Huy thought, what to say to him.
All at once he didn't want to know what was about to come from
that orange mouth. He wanted to flee to his barge, hurry home
to the peace and predictability of life on his small estate, and go
on healing and scrying for the humble citizens of Hut-herib.

"You live far from the intrigues of court life," the Prince began
at last, and Huy's heart sank. He was going to hear things of
which he did not want to be aware, things that would destroy
whatever innocence he, at thirty-eight years old, had been able
to retain from his strange childhood. Amunhotep would give
voice to the thought he had not dared to express. "Like most
Egyptians, you reverence the divinity of your King and believe
that he rules the country effortlessly through intelligent and
honest ministers, lives in the truth of Ma'at, and is possessed of a

total omniscience," Amunhotep continued. "Is that not why every statue of a pharaoh is carved with very large ears? Does not Pharaoh hear of all that passes in his land? Like every ruler, my father relies on the reports of his governors, his two viziers, his overseers of the armed forces, taxation, building projects, everything concerning an Egypt he loves. And make no mistake, Huy, he loves this country. But the reports from the High Priests of Amun he does not like." Suddenly his face contorted, an expression of deep grief, before it was hidden by his wine cup. When he set the vessel back on the table, his features had become smooth again. "Let me try to put this as simply as possible. My father is a healthy and very vigorous man. He is interested more in the *energies* of a god than the *essence*. He does not like being considered the Incarnation of Amun here on earth. The High Priest of Amun annoys him. He left Weset, Amun's city and the seat of power in Upper Egypt, almost as soon as he had inherited the throne, and returned here, to Mennofer. His father Osiris Thothmes Glorified was content to live and rule from the great palace at Weset, but my father, as indeed my brother and myself, was raised in the north, where Ra of Iunu reigns, and the shrines of many of his hypostases litter the towns and cities of the Delta and Lower Egypt. Here it is known that Ra is far older than Amun, a universal god from the beginning, while Amun remained a local totem until my blessed ancestors raised him to prominence in return for his divine aid against the Setiu occupiers of Egypt hentis ago. Mennofer and its palace and its god are older than Weset, its palace, or Amun. The priests of Amun take pride in the fact that the kings are the successive incarnations of their god. They receive greater tribute, Amun's temple and shrines are exempt from taxes, the High Priest of Amun takes precedence over every other High Priest during religious festivals. My father and my brother no longer worship

Amun. They go to the shrine of the Aten here in Mennofer."
He held out his cup and Huy, feeling rather dazed, refilled it.
Amunhotep drank rapidly.

"But, Highness, the Aten is between Amun and the earth.
The rays of Amun are the Aten, and when they reach the earth
they become lions, holy sphinxes carved throughout Egypt."

Amunhotep shook his head. "That makes no sense to my
father. The Aten is light, rays of light, and light comes from Ra,
not Amun. The King and the Prince my brother have repudiated
Amun altogether. They are embarking on a great sacrilege, Huy.
Do you understand? Oh, yes, I think you do. My spies saw my
brother's servants go out in the night and begin to dig around
the head of Ra-Harmachis to make sure the god did
indeed have a buried body before Thothmes announced his
dream. Ra-Harmachis is a manifestation of the rays of the Aten
emanating from Amun and becoming a lion, yet my brother
would have Ra as the god of his so-called dream. He could not
have done so without the collusion of the High Priest of Ra and
his underlings, who must smell a new power coming their way.
I am the Crown Prince!" His voice rose. "I am the Hawk-in-the-
Nest, eldest son of a King! I believe that my destiny is to be the
Incarnation of Amun on earth, validated in my claim by
the priests of Amun. I have refused to agree to the intrusion of
the Aten to change this, even as the rays of Amun falling to the
ground! Sphinxes are sacred to Amun! They do not belong to
Ra! Amun is the essence, the Aten his energies! Ma'at is about
to be perverted!"

He left the chair and began to pace agitatedly about the room,
and, watching him, Huy realized that the light around him had
become tinged with a soft pink glow. Evening was coming.

"Amun and Pharaoh must remain the two most powerful
forces in the kingdom," the Prince said more calmly. His arms

were folded tightly against his naked chest, his head down, and Huy felt a wave of pity for him, this youth of—what? Nineteen or twenty? He looked vulnerable, and isolated.

"The King is about to commit a heresy," Huy ventured, remembering yet again the warning Atum had given to Pharaoh, who had perhaps even then been turning over in his mind his dissatisfaction with the south and everything in it, his loyalties moving ever closer to the deities of the north. *Ramose, High Priest of Ra and my mentor while I was at school, would never agree to this.* But Ramose no longer ruled Ra's domain. Huy did not know whom the King had appointed in his stead. *The Ished Tree*, he thought. *The Book. Neither of them under Ramose's care anymore.*

"The second part of the dream," he said. "Highness, surely they won't dare ... I ..."

Amunhotep stood still. "You know why I prayed that you would oppose my brother or at least cast some doubt upon his lie," he said without looking at Huy. "You suspected it. I have reason to believe that my father will have me murdered so that Thothmes can take the throne after him and continue to worship the Aten even above the essence of either Ra or Amun. I tried to have you brought to me before you faced my father," Amunhotep went on wryly, "but Father made sure that you were taken directly from your barge to the Throne Room. Will you See for me, Huy? My future is dark before me. I don't know what to do. Look." He pointed at a tiny vial on another table. "Pa-shed has prepared poppy for you. Please, Great Seer. Let Atum have pity on me and show me the way that I must go!" He flung himself down in the chair facing Huy and leaned forward tensely, offering one ring-clad hand with a disarming humility. "I have ordered that my food be tasted," he continued hoarsely. "I have doubled the guard on my apartment and take soldiers with me wherever I go. Yet I cannot sleep, and my days are spent looking over my shoulder, tensing for the arrow that might come, although I know that Father will not be so foolish as to have me murdered in such an obvious way." The extended fingers curled into a clench. "There are substances that kill with a drop on the skin. A pillow in the hands of an accomplished assassin is no longer an instrument of ease. Worst of all, I can confide in no one, not even the Queen my mother, whom I love. She would go immediately to the King and bluster on my behalf, or perhaps tell me that it's all nonsense and I should spend more time in hunting and less in thinking." He smiled ruefully. "I have tested my imag-ination. My father and my brother move apart and stop talking when I approach. My brother watches me out of the shadows. Father barely speaks to me at all."

"Did the High Priest of Ra invent your brother's dream?"

"No. I think it was concocted by my father and eagerly sanctioned by the priests of all the sun temples and shrines who wish to see Amun return to the status of a local totem and his priests deprived of their riches and pre-eminence. But Ma'at has decreed that the King should be the Incarnation of Amun, not Ra. My father and Thothmes will upset the balance of Ma'at, and I am afraid for Egypt as well as for myself."

Huy forced down the voices of self-censure within him and gently took the Prince's hand, laying it on his own palm and placing his other hand over it. "Highness, I may See terrible things, perhaps even your death," he said in a last attempt to run from the consequence of a responsibility he had refused to shoulder. "Do you truly want this?" The Prince nodded. The fingers lying limply against Huy's were cold. "Then please close your eyes." Huy closed his own. *Will Atum even acknowledge me now? I have failed in my loyalty to him and to Egypt. Will he take the gift of Seeing away from me?*

"A vain hope, Seer, possessor of the secrets of the Book of Thoth." The voice, so close to Huy's ear that he fancied he could feel warm breath on his temple, did not belong to Anubis. Turning with an exclamation of shock, he found himself staring into a familiar face of matchless, serene beauty. Kohled dark eyes regarded him steadily. The perfect red-hennaed mouth under an aquiline nose was parted slightly, solemnly. Gleaming black hair fell to either side of the long neck and was held to the high forehead by a thin golden band. At its rear, a white feather stirred in a breeze Huy could not feel, but he knew whence that little wind came. It soughed and gusted through the grim shadows of the Judgment Hall, filling the vastness with a sense of rootless desolation. Huy slipped to his knees and, putting his face to the floor, stretched out his arms in homage, yet he was aware of Prince Amunhotep's hand still lightly imprisoned in both of his own. "Ma'at," he said huskily, and nothing more. His throat had closed of its own volition.

"So you remember me now, Son of Hapu?" the goddess continued softly. "Where was your memory before the Horus Throne? Why did it not occur to you, Son of Perfidy, Son of Cowardice, that those you purport to hold so dear, your family, your servants, are dear to Atum also? That he would have rewarded your faithfulness to the truth you saw beneath the lies by securing your safety and theirs? And what of the lie to yourself? For I know that these meant less to you in that moment of trial than the paltry trappings of success that surround you. The Huy who lived in poverty with Ishat would not have been so craven. You have wounded me, and I am already wounded by the King who has forgotten the warning Atum gave him through your mouth so long ago. Your obligation was to remind him, to shout the words of prophecy into the ears of all gathered in that lofty room, to fill Egypt with a truth that would have saved her."

Huy, his face pressed against the cool tiling of the Prince's reception hall, felt something warm and liquid strike the back of his head and ooze across his cheek to pool beside his nose. All at once he smelled the hot metal tang of freshly spilled blood. With a grunt, he jerked himself upward. Ma'at was bleeding through the pale fingers with which she was clutching the transparent linen over her heart. The thick scarlet flow had already saturated her sheath and was spattering her naked feet. In pushing himself away from the floor, Huy had placed his palms in it. Horrified, he held up both dripping hands, in supplication or defence he was not sure.

"Saved her?" he croaked in horror. "Saved Egypt? Most Holy Arbiter of the Scales, Upholder of the Divine Balance of Creation, forgive me! Tell me how I may heal you! Undo the harm that I have done!"

"It is too late." In spite of the blood continuing to flow between her fingers, the goddess's tones were calm and even. "A doom has been set in motion upon this blessed country because of you, and you will be punished, but Atum in his mercy will give you another chance in your future to avert complete disaster. He does not wish to destroy his tool. Not yet. Now, Son of Falsehood, you may see what is in store for this estimable young man. I shall not come to you again until your heart is placed on the scales of the Judgment Hall. Take care lest it prove heavier than my feather!"

Huy, overcome with shame, bent his head, intending to kiss the bloodied feet. Instead, he found himself peering at two masculine feet encased in gold-thonged sandals, though a puddle of blood remained on the floor near where his head had rested.

"Have you changed the fate of the Hawk-in-the-Nest by your cowardice, or have you merely postponed it?" a new voice growled, and with a feeling of wary relief Huy looked up into

Anubis's beady jackal's eyes. Anubis grinned, a brief lifting of the long lips to reveal two rows of sharp white teeth. "We have become partners in the mastery of Time, have we not, Son of Hapu? Or have we? Can a human partner a god? Do you ever think about that, arrogant one? Perhaps the Book of Thoth has the answer. But you seldom think about that anymore either, do you? Let us proceed."

Huy was suddenly standing in long, dry grass, sunlight sparkling on the water of a broad river where several small reed boats of a design he did not recognize were moored. A cold wind buffeted him. He was sweating lightly, and by the taste in his mouth he knew he had just taken a mouthful of beer from the clay cup he held. His feet felt strange and, looking down, he saw that he was wearing purple coverings of rough wool on them. Above them, a tasselled skirt of the same colour and texture fell from his waist, and his chest was hidden under a yellow shirt of thick linen. Gold bracelets tinkled on his arm as he reached up to touch the woollen cap on his head. He did not think his long hair curious until a reverential voice just behind him said, "A letter has come for you, Highness. The King commanded me to bring it to you at once. We have not heard from Egypt for a long time, and the King is impatient to know its contents, though of course he hid his eagerness well."

"Artatama has been kind and generous to me while managing to maintain good relations with my brother," Huy heard himself say. "Read it to me, Ka-set, and then let's get out of this chilly air."

A scribe came into view, head bent over the scroll whose seal he was examining. "There is no insignia pressed into the wax," he said. "There is only one man of any importance in Egypt who does not identify himself on his correspondence, and we have not heard from him since your exile began nearly twelve years ago." The fragments of wax crumbled away. Ka-set unrolled the papyrus. "It is indeed from the Great Seer," he remarked.

Huy felt his heartbeat quicken with anticipation. This news must be momentous. He nodded brusquely to the scribe.

"It's written in formal Egyptian hieroglyphs, not in the language of diplomacy," Ka-set told him. "Good. To read Akkadian in the palace at home is one thing, but pronouncing it in a foreign land just makes me sad."

"The news, Ka-set!" Huy tossed the dregs of his beer into the grass and at once a servant appeared, took the cup from him, and retired.

"Yes." Ka-set had begun to smile. "'To His Highness Prince Amunhotep, respectful greetings. I trust that you are well. I have not deemed it safe to write to you before, but know that your brother King Thothmes Menkheperura is now an Osiris-one and the Hawk-in-the-Nest Amunhotep will be crowned Pharaoh. You will already be aware of the early death of your brother's designated heir Amunemhat, son of the Queen and Great Wife Neferatiri. Amunhotep, son of Second Wife Mutemwia, is twelve years old. He and I are good friends, and he will make a fine King. If Your Highness wishes to return to Egypt, he may now do so. Amunhotep is sending many rich gifts to King Artatama in gratitude for his care of you and his discretion in keeping your presence in his land a secret. Life, Health, Prosperity to you, Prince. I am your obedient servant Huy son of Hapu, Seer. Written this third day of Thoth in the season Akhet by my own hand.'" Ka-set let the scroll roll up.

There was a silence between them until Huy said, "He makes it clear that I am no longer a contender for the Horus Throne and must not consider myself anything more than the new King's uncle." He sighed, his eyes on the white-capped waves some distance from where he stood. "So be it. At least my father's and brother's madness in trying to usurp Amun and put the Aten in his place has run its course, and a weakened Ma'at may find her strength again. If the Seer and this young Amunhotep are close, the Seer will make sure the cosmic and earthly balance is restored. Ka-set, let's go home."

"I heard but did not understand." The voice did not belong to the scribe, and Huy, anxious to remove the woollen slippers from his feet because suddenly the day had become very hot, bent down. The blue and white tiling of a spotless floor met his gaze. No grass, no puddle of divine blood, and his feet were shod in thin reed sandals. Disoriented, head throbbing, he straightened. The Prince had withdrawn his hands and was watching him, a question in his grave eyes. Rising, he brought the vial of poppy to Huy, who downed it at once. Its taste no longer made him grimace.

"You said, 'Ka-set, let's go home.'" Amunhotep resumed his seat. "Ka-set is the name of my scribe. Huy, what did you See? I am ready."

Huy drained the golden cup of water sitting on the table beside him. "Prince, you are to leave Egypt until your brother dies," he half whispered. He was very tired. "I became you, standing beside a mighty river. I do not know where you were. Your scribe read a letter to you from me, telling you that it was safe to return to Egypt."

"Leave Egypt?" Amunhotep frowned and sat back. "Exile had occurred to me, but where should I go? We do much trade with the islands of Keftiu and Alashia. I would not be safe in either place. Yet beyond the Great Green the tribes and petty kingdoms are barbarous, their rulers not to be trusted. Would Agum the Third of Babylon harbour me, perhaps? Or whoever is ruling the Kheta from Hattusas? I do not know."

"In my vision you mentioned a name. Artatama. Is it familiar to you, Highness?"

The Prince's brow cleared slowly as he thought. "Artatama, King of Mitanni. You have not heard of the Mitanni, Huy? They live west of one of the two rivers that divide and harbour the

Bend of Naharin between them. They produce a few things for which we trade. The Osiris-ones Thothmes the First and Thothmes the Third conquered them and they became a vassal state, ruling themselves as they see fit but paying an annual indemnity to Egypt. It is a satisfactory arrangement for them as well as for us."

Huy vaguely remembered Mitanni. Ishat had mentioned it briefly when he was admiring the jewellery Thothmes had given her.

"Is there much trade?" he asked hesitantly.

Amunhotep shook his head. "Not much so far. A few aristocratic Mitanni families have been allowed to settle in Egypt. So you saw me in exile there? How long will it be before I may return?"

"Twelve years. Your brother will indeed become King, but he will be dead in twelve years."

"Good!" It was the first time Huy had seen malice cloud the Prince's features.

Huy got up with difficulty and bowed carefully so that his heart would not speed up and increase the throbbing in his head. "Highness, if there is nothing more, I would like to leave the palace. If you need me, I am of course at your disposal. You know where my estate lies. And once again, I am so very sorry for my lack of courage today. Be assured that Atum will punish me. May the soles of your august feet be firm on your journey to this Mitanni."

Amunhotep gave him a curious look. "Thank you, Huy. You may go. Send in Pa-shed. The soldier who brought you to me will escort you to your skiff."

Huy backed politely to the door with the sense that more ought to have been said, that this parting was unfinished, but his pain was too great for him to really care. Outside the double doors, he waved the steward within, gestured to the guard, and set off behind him unsteadily. The poppy had begun to take effect.

They passed the row of ministers' offices. The rooms to right and left became larger and more luxuriously furnished. Huy recognized them as though he had first seen them hentis ago. He felt dazed, dislocated from the self who had earlier walked this passage with anxious anticipation. The guard strode on. At last, just before Huy thought they should be nearing the reception hall, his guide halted and stepped to the side, putting out a warning hand to Huy to do the same. Huy obeyed. A group of young women was coming towards them, filling the sombre space with chatter and laughter, their thin linens billowing in the drafts blowing from the open doors to either side, their painted faces full of animation. They swept past Huy without a glance. Then the guard stretched out his arms and bowed. In the moment before Huy followed suit, he saw a face he thought he recognized, haughty and lined with age, the heavily kohled eyes and downturned mouth framed by a short black wig. Fighting through the drug-induced fog, he tried to bring a name to mind as a pair of wrinkled feet shod in carnelian-studded sandals came to rest under his gaze. He lifted his head. "Greetings, Seer Huy," the man said. "I trust that you are well."

"Royal Nurse Heqareshu," Huy answered with an inner spurt of relief. "You honour me. I continue in good health." *But you do not*, he thought. *There is more than the ravages of time eating away at your ka as well as your body.*

Heqareshu smiled coldly. "That may be so, but you do not look well today," he remarked. His black-ringed eyes had not strayed from Huy's. "I remember both the pain and the poppy shadowing your features after you had Seen for me. You have been with His Majesty, I know. Were you asked to See for Prince Thothmes?"

Huy stared at him. Out of the corner of his eye he saw a young woman approaching slowly, a baby in her arms.

Heqareshu stepped closer to Huy. "Well? Were you?" he said rapidly, glancing behind him. "Or have you been with Prince Amunhotep?"

"His Highness requested a Seeing, yes," Huy replied cautiously, his stomach tightening as though the Nurse's sudden unease had communicated itself to him.

The thin, arrogant mouth pursed. "Which Prince? Tell me! I am still the Overseer of Royal Nurses. I want to know. I must know!" A hand laden with gold descended on Huy's arm. Heqareshu's breath smelled of mint.

"Prince Amunhotep," Huy said as the woman cradling the baby came up to them and halted.

"You Saw for him? Good!" she exclaimed. "He was hoping to meet you. So was I."

"This is the Princess Mutemwia," Heqareshu told Huy.

He had removed his grasp, but Huy could still feel the strength of his fingers on his skin. Going to his knees, he reverenced the Princess.

"Oh, please stand!" she ordered. "I would not have Egypt's Great Seer collapsed on the tiles before me. I'm on my way to Amunhotep's quarters now. I can tell him that at last you are more than a legend to me."

"The Princess and her brother-in-law are close friends," Heqareshu put in. He turned to Mutemwia. "Perhaps he will tell you what vision the Seer gave him."

What are you trying to convey to me so urgently? Huy wondered.

Mutemwia nodded. She was tiny and dainty, making Huy feel clumsy. Her hair, almost as long as his own, was tied back in one thick braid. Golden earrings in the likeness of Mut the vulture goddess, consort of Amun, trembled against her neck as she gestured. Her sheath was unadorned but for a belt of silver links. A small vulture of gold and lapis rested just above the swell of her little breasts, held by a thin gold chain. Her arms and hands were bare. *She knows herself,* Huy thought. *She is not suited to the masses of jewellery other women love. She is too small. Her eyes are her greatest adornment, like the huge dark eyes of gazelles, and there is something of a gazelle about her, an inner shyness or reserve beneath the dignity of royalty.*

"I expect he will. And this"—she held out the half-naked baby—"this is my son Amunhotep. He is only three weeks younger than Amunemhat, Chief Wife Neferatiri's son, also by our husband Prince Thothmes."

"Amunemhat is not as healthy as your child, Princess," Heqareshu remarked.

Mutemwia laughed. "Everyone knows that you favour my brother-in-law over my husband, and me over the Chief Wife. Thothmes thinks it's funny. He does not take offence even though he received far more slaps from you when he was little than Amunhotep did."

Huy glanced at the baby to find his black eyes fixed solemnly on Huy's own face. Suddenly a wide, toothless smile split the chubby cheeks and two fat arms flailed the air. Huy responded to the innocent delight in the movements. Reaching out, he allowed the diminutive fingers to find and curl about one of his own. At once he found himself and little Amunhotep standing in a rain of gold dust so thick that he could barely see the baby's face. He could hear him chuckling, a sound of pleasure. As the gold cascaded through a ray of sunlight, it burst into a brief, brilliant shower of glittering specks before sifting to lie against Huy's feet. The baby was soon covered in it, as though he lay under a blanket of cloth of gold. He let Huy's finger go and began to bat at the dust, making eddies that swirled and danced between them. Then the gold was gone, the baby had begun to wriggle against his mother's breast, and Heqareshu was crooking one imperious finger at the girls who had congregated farther along the passage and were watching.

"One of you useless geese go and find wet nurse Senay! The Prince is hungry!"

"I will remember you in my prayers to holy Mut, Great Seer," Mutemwia said quietly, handing the baby to Heqareshu. "And when I make my next pilgrimage to her temple within the bounds of Ipet-isut, I shall offer her a gift so that she may ease your suffering. You saw something when my son grasped your fingers, didn't you? May I know whether ..." She paused, her hands clenching and unclenching. "May I ... Will my baby grow to be healthy and strong?"

Heqareshu was already walking away. Huy felt as though he was about to collapse with the renewal of pain. He swayed. At once Mutemwia rapped out an order to the guard, who caught Huy and lowered him carefully to the tiles. "Go and fetch a litter and three more soldiers," she told the man. "I will stay here until you return." Huy had slumped against the wall and closed his eyes. The slap-slap of the guard's sandals as he went away slowly faded. Huy felt her palm pressed lightly on his forehead. "You should stay here in the palace until tomorrow," she said, and Huy realized by the nearness of her voice that she was either squatting or kneeling beside him. "My physician is very good. There are many quiet rooms where you will not be disturbed. Soldiers from Prince Amunhotep's Division of Amun patrol these corridors."

"Highness, you are very kind, but I would like to lie in the cabin of my own barge," Huy answered, hearing the uncontrollable slurring of his words. Forcing his eyes open, he saw her worried face distorted by the dance of black and white patterns belonging to the worst of his headaches. "Your son ... You need not fret about him, I think. He and I were enveloped in a storm of gold. He was laughing, playing with it. We were both so happy." He felt the nausea begin to roil in his belly and he closed both his mouth and his eyes. There was a moment of silence. He felt her rise.

"Thank you, Son of Hapu," she said. "I am glad that his destiny will be linked with yours." Huy was too wretched to be surprised at her astuteness. The knowledge merely seeped into his consciousness to be lost under the hot deluge of his agony. She did not speak again.

Later, he heard the soldiers coming along the passage, heard the litter being set down, heard her instruct the men to accompany him right to his barge, then he was lifted gently onto soft cushions. He was able to keep the sickness inside him until the bearers stepped outside. He felt the heat of the sun strike the litter's curtains. Pushing them back, he leaned out and vomited on the stone of the concourse.

II

HUY REMEMBERED LITTLE of the journey home. He lay curled up on his travelling cot inside the barge's cabin, forehead to knees, trying not to move for the stab of pain it would bring. He knew that they were sailing north with the sluggish current of a river nearing its lowest level, but the strong summer wind always blew south, forcing the sailors to reef the sail and get out the oars. The motion of the boat lulled him into periods of an uneasy sleep where the throbbing of his head pursued him, bringing with it nonsensical, fragmented dreams. He was vaguely aware of someone lifting him gently and placing a vial against his lips. He drank the poppy and slept, waking when the boards beneath him became still and the familiar voices of his sailors echoed across the dusk. They had tied up somewhere just north of Iunu, he surmised dully. Footsteps approached the cabin. He felt himself surveyed but was too tired to open his eyes. "We can't give him any more poppy," Tetiankh said. "It would kill him."

"I'd like to help you to wash him, though," Thothhotep replied. "Is there clean linen for the cot? He's drenched in sweat."

"I think so." There was a pause. Huy wanted to tell them to leave him alone but could only grunt. "If we both try to lift him, we'll cause him distress," Tetiankh went on.

Then Anhur spoke from farther away. "I'll lift him and hold him until you're done. Change the linen and wash him while he's in my arms. He needs a physician, but I suppose we'll be home before one could be sent for. We should have put in at Iunu and sent word to the Governor. He and Ishat would have taken proper care of him." The man's forthright, rough tones had been drawing closer. Huy found himself in Anhur's careful embrace. Anhur smelled of woodsmoke and security. Huy relaxed against him.

He slept through the night, aware that his dreams were becoming more coherent as both the pain and the poppy ebbed away. By the time the barge nudged his watersteps not long after dawn, he was able to walk shakily along the ramp and up the steps, and negotiate the short path to his own little entrance hall with Anhur and Tetiankh's support. "Why was this attack so bad, Huy?" Anhur wanted to know as he and the body servant lowered Huy onto his couch.

Huy looked up slowly. The residual pangs only struck him now if he moved too fast. "I gave a Seeing to Prince Amunhotep," he said, aware that he sounded as hoarse and weak as an old man. "Then I met the Princess Mutemwia on my way out of the palace. She was cuddling her son. When he grasped my fingers, a Seeing came to me without my will. Both visions were very powerful. One immediately after the other was too much. Tetiankh, bring me water and then I must sleep again. Was I holding a leather bag full of gold when the guards brought me aboard the barge?"

Tetiankh nodded. "Thothhotep took it. She will have given it to Merenra to store."

"Tell Merenra to dole it out to the next crowd of petitioners and to give the bag away also. I don't want anything more to do with it." He felt his eyelids begin to close, but it was good, it was healthy. The couch smelled of rinsing vinegar, and the voices of his lame gardener Anab and of Amunmose, his under steward, came drifting through the slats of the blind on the window. "Tell Thothhotep to be ready to take a dictation this afternoon," he murmured. "Thank you both. Water, Tetiankh." He was already half asleep by the time the man returned with the cup. He drank deeply, turned his cheek into his pillow, and let the room slide away.

He woke to darkness and a momentary disorientation, knowing that something had brought him to an abrupt consciousness and that it was night. He had slept through the whole of the day and, judging by the deep silence of the house, much of the night as well. He sat up, aware that every trace of pain had gone and his strength had been restored. Only the dryness in his mouth and a bitterness at the back of his throat caused by the poppy reminded him that he had been viciously attacked. He was reaching for the water jug and the cup that Tetiankh always left beside the couch when he heard a sound he instantly recognized as the reason why he had woken. It could have been the sudden howl of a desert wind, and for a moment Huy believed it to be so, but then he remembered that he was in the centre of Ta-Mehu, the Delta, and the desert was far away. Besides, there was an element of life, of blood, in the cry. It came again, nearer this time, rising mournfully and ending with a series of moans, and something answered it, far away.

Huy left the couch, grabbed up his kilt of the day, and tied it around his waist as he made his way cautiously to the door. Outside in the passage, there was more light. The moon, although full, was setting, its pallid rays diffusing through the wide aperture leading onto the roof. Huy had the sensation of wading through them as he came to the sill, stepped over it, and emerged beside the wind catcher that funnelled the northern breezes down into the reception room below. Walking to the roof's edge, he peered out and down. The garden was drowned in darkness. Only the tips of the palms he and Ishat had seen Seshemnefer plant were visible. As his eyes adjusted to the dimness, he could just make out the bulk of the kitchen below and to the right, and, farther along, the cells where his soldiers and lesser servants slept. To the rear, the clay dome of his small granary could be seen as a black curve against the equally dense blackness of the estate's sheltering wall.

With a suddenness that shocked him, the wail came again, surely from something hiding between the house and the wall. Huy's heart began to pound. The spirits of the dead roamed about sadly at night, those whose tombs were neglected by relatives who ought to have been bringing flowers and food to them at the Beautiful Feast of the Valley each year. Sometimes the spirits became vengeful, tormenting their kin with evil luck. But after a moment of panic, when Huy searched his mind for anyone who might haunt him and came up with no name, he realized for the second time that the sounds, though eerie, were being made by a living being of some kind.

Retracing his steps, he hurried along the passage. Tetiankh was still asleep on his pallet just beyond Huy's door. With the long practice of the well-trained servant, he came awake at once when Huy touched his shoulder. "Something strange is in the garden," Huy told him as they descended the stairs. "Go and wake Anhur, but don't shout for the guard posted at the rear wall."

The air outside was hot and stale. It was now the beginning of Epophi, the third of the four months of the season Shemu, a time when the heat became progressively more intense until well after Isis had cried and her tears had flooded the fields. Tetiankh disappeared in the direction of Anhur's cell, his kilt a receding smudge of grey in the gloom, and as he went, Huy heard a curious snuffling coming from the vegetable plots, now verdant with the spears of lettuce, leeks, and garlic, fronds of onion, fat cabbages, and the low, snaking stems of melons in which the fruit rested. That sound was even more sinister to Huy than the howls, and he halted, able now to see a glint of moonlight on the narrow irrigation channels Seshemnefer had dug, which joined the wider canal the soldiers had made from the river to water the new palms. The channels were rippling almost imperceptibly. Something had disturbed the water. *An animal is feeding amongst the vegetables,* Huy thought with a gush of relief. *But what animal can make those terrible cries and snorts?*

The answer came at once, as though he had asked the question aloud. A shape appeared, wide-shouldered, skinny-haunched, loping across the grass into the small patch of worn earth where he stood by the rear entrance. He could see it quite clearly as it squatted on the lighter ground and stared at him, its black eyes like pebbles, its pink tongue hanging over razor-sharp teeth. For several heartbeats Huy was paralyzed with fear. He wanted to turn and flee into the house, but he could not will his feet to lift. The animal had become as motionless as he, its gaze unblinking. He could hear it panting. He thought he could smell it, a rank, meaty odour wafted to his nostrils by the breeze, but there was no breeze. The air was still. At last he found his voice.

"What do you want?" he croaked. "What are you doing here? Did Imhotep send you? Did Anubis?"

Its stare did not waver at the sound of his voice, and gradually Huy became convinced that there was reproach behind those dark beads, a judgment coupled with a latent ferocity directed at him and straining to be released. *It's going to kill me.* The thought came clearly and calmly into his mind. *Atum has sent it to destroy me because of my cowardice before the King, because I have failed the god. It will leap upon me in a moment and tear at my throat with those pointed teeth, and I shall feel its stiff bristles graze my cheeks as I fall with it fastened to my flesh.*

Footsteps pounded in the darkness and then Anhur was skirting the beast and its gaze was broken. It rose and shambled away unhurriedly, and Huy found that he was trembling. "A hyena!" Anhur exclaimed. He was naked but for a loincloth, his brown, muscled body so full of vitality and reassuring health that Huy felt his perceptions return to a semblance of normality. "What is it doing so far from the desert? And how did it get into the garden? From the path by the watersteps, I expect."

"It will have made a mess of Anab's work in its hunt for mice. Anhur, it had black eyes and a pink tongue. I thought hyenas were yellow-eyed, with black tongues." *That was what I saw in the Beautiful West when I stood before the blessed Imhotep and the creature dozing beside him,* Huy told himself. *I was uneasy then. I am doubly so now, wondering what this means.* "I don't want it anywhere near me!" he burst out. "Catch it and take it away!"

Anhur glanced at him curiously. "Easier to kill it."

"No! No. Just ... get rid of it." *It must not be destroyed,* Huy knew with certainty. *If I kill it, I will not be forgiven. But why? Why?*

Tetiankh came into sight with Khnit the cook behind him, bleary-eyed and bare-footed, a sheath pulled carelessly over her head. She bowed to Huy. "Master, I'm sorry the animal got free. I thought I'd penned it securely. Perhaps Anhur would help me catch it and put it back."

Huy stared at her stupidly. "Put it back? What are you talking about, Khnit?"

"I traded for it in the market while you were away. I had no intention of letting it rouse you from your couch!"

"Traded ... What do you want a hyena for, woman?"

She looked at him as though he had lost his mind. "Why, to fatten up and then eat, of course! Hyenas themselves will eat almost anything. There's always offal to be disposed of. Their meat is strong but tasty." *You really don't know this?* her tone implied. "We don't often see them in the Delta. There was another one in the market. They like to live with their own kind. But the trader wouldn't give me a good deal for the two of them."

Huy's panic was back, sourceless this time. He struggled to beat it down. "You meant well. I'm sorry, Khnit. I won't eat hyena meat, and I don't want them anywhere near this estate."

"But, Master, perhaps for the servants—"

"No. Anhur's men can take it back to the market and sell it for you if you like. Now go back to bed." She sniffed, bowed, and stalked off. Huy turned to Anhur. "Do you know anything about hyenas?"

It was Amunmose who answered. He had come up behind the little group, a sheet clutched around his waist. "I do, Master. We see them often on the outskirts of Khmun, and my mother has a delicious recipe for their meat. They are mysterious creatures. They can change their sex from male to female and back again whenever they want to. They live in packs, and talk to each other with many different sounds. In the wild they hunt at night, and together they can even bring down a leopard, or so it's said. Pharaoh has a leopard in his zoo, a gift from some southern tribal chief."

"How do you know this?" Huy was becoming more and more repelled. Amunmose grinned. Huy realized that he could make out his under steward's pert features, and the darkness around him was less dense. Ra was about to be born out of the vagina of Nut.

"I love gossip," Amunmose said promptly. "I listen to everyone who comes here and encourage people to tell me their news and stories. They say that hyenas have a queen, not a king, and that they belong to Set and that lions hate them."

Lions hate them. Those words, spoken so lightly by his servant, sank slowly into Huy's consciousness and beyond, as though they carried with them a subtle poison that began to infect not only his ka but his blood and the marrow of his bones. *When the rays of the sun strike the earth, they become lions,* he thought. *Ra, Aten, Amun. Light, light, light. And hyenas are in Set's domain, a place of darkness and chaos.* He looked up. A greyness was filling the garden, bringing with it the brief cool breeze that preceded the dawn. Suddenly cold, Huy shivered.

"Anhur, detail a couple of men and catch the thing," he ordered. "Don't let it escape them. They can take it to the market at once. And take heed, all of you: I never want to see a hyena in my garden again. Tetiankh, heat water for me in the bathhouse. And you, my gossiping steward, go and tell Khnit that I want something hot this morning. Soup, perhaps."

They scattered, but Anhur looked back. "It's only a filthy animal, Huy. Don't let it upset you."

I am no longer upset, Huy thought as he re-entered the drowsy half-light of the house. *What I feel is deeper and colder and more threatening than mere alarm. I see the beast with the yellow eyes as I stood before Imhotep in the Beautiful West while my body lay lifeless in the House of the Dead. I see it watching me calmly, tamely, an aura of tranquility surrounding it, and yet I sensed something in its gaze, didn't I? I was twelve years old. I had no name for it then, but I can name it now. Pity. The beast was staring at me with pity in those golden eyes. Lion, hyena. The sun and the darkness. Atum, what does all this mean for me? What is it that I really fear? Was the compassion in its eyes for my future state, as though the animal itself had the power of Seeing and was looking at what I was to become?*

Entering his room, he removed the kilt, dropped it on the floor, and sat naked on the edge of his couch. His flaccid penis, resting loosely against his thigh, mocked him. *Useless appendage,* he thought savagely. *I should cut you off and offer you to Atum of my own free will. "See!" I shall say. "Here is what's left of my manhood. You took its essence without my consent when I was a boy. I throw the rest down before you, now that I am a man."*

The need to talk to Ishat rose up in him all at once. She would discuss the hyena and its meaning. She would understand his fear and confusion. So would Thothmes. Huy saw them frequently, often stopping in at Iunu on his way home from visiting Heby at Mennofer. Their rambling house was full of the noise and laughter of their three children, who called him Uncle Huy and hugged him with delight when he appeared. Thothmes was strict with them. They were not allowed to ask if Huy had brought them presents or sweetmeats. They must bow to him both as an adult and as Egypt's Great Seer at least once when they were with him. Thothmes had named his eldest offspring Huy, and the astrologers had happily approved his choice. The boy was nine, attending the temple school at Iunu as both Huy and Thothmes had done. Intelligent as his mother and as agile and small as his father, he considered himself too old now to fling himself on Huy, and was proud simply to sit with him and talk.

Nakht, named after his grandfather, was eight. He also attended the temple school, a quiet child who enjoyed his own company. Sahura, a girl, much to Ishat's joy, was six. Thothmes had hired a tutor for her so that she could learn at home. It was a highly unorthodox thing to do. Girls were taught to run households and care for their families. Noble daughters could write their names and a few simple sentences, and often became astute business-women. But Ishat, remembering her own early ignorance, was ambitious for Sahura. The tutor was instructed to follow the curriculum set down for the boys at school in the temple. In spite of the necessary strictures imposed on Thothmes' household due to the public nature of his position, his estate was a happy place, full of laughter. Huy, having been subjected to his nephew's scowls and tantrums in Heby's house at Mennofer, would arrive at Thothmes' gate with relief.

There was seldom a chance to speak to Ishat at length, however. Her household bustled with servants, feasts for dignitaries both important and minor, and the raising of her brood. Sometimes Huy and Thothmes were able to sit peacefully together in the evenings outside, and talk while dusk settled around them and the lights from the newly lit lamps inside the house ribboned thin and insubstantial, to be lost in the shrubbery crowding the walls. Huy's need for Ishat had moderated in the years since her marriage. He had become content to see her happy with her husband and fulfilled by her children.

Besides, Thothhotep had proved to be an able scribe. Already she and he had formed memories, but she had not lived the years of childhood together, of poverty, of the early experiences he and Ishat had shared that bind one to another. He was fond of Thothhotep, and she of him. There was much about him and his gift that she understood, but she could never have Ishat's intuition and insight when it came to his soul. Ishat had been in love with him all her life, a fact that used to fill him with guilt because he could not reciprocate. That guilt had died when she chose to wed his best friend. But now, waiting for Tetiankh to summon him to the bathhouse, his stomach empty, his mind full of confusion and a nagging certainty that he was missing something vitally important to do with the two hyenas—the one inhabiting the Beautiful West and the one even now being snared in his garden—he missed her desperately. He could write to her, he supposed, and she would reply, but without the language of eyes and body, the freedom to interpret every nuance of voice, the exchange would be unsatisfactory. Hearing Tetiankh's tread in the passage, he rose, sighed, and went out.

After he had been bathed and dressed and had eaten, he sat behind the desk in his office and dictated to Thothhotep everything he could remember about the Seeings he had received for both Prince Amunhotep and the Princess's baby. "Seal the scrolls," he told her when she set down her brush and was massaging her fingers. "Then put them in a box by themselves and seal it shut also. You understand these visions, don't you, Thothhotep?"

"I think so, Master." She reached up and set her palette on the desk, then stood, laying the papyrus coils beside it. "It's a terrible matter, the prospect of a forced exile for the Prince who should be our Hawk-in-the-Nest. The One has never officially declared an heir. Now we know why." She tucked her short hair behind her ear, a gesture indicating either thoughtfulness or annoyance, Huy knew. "As for the little Prince and the gold, all it seems to mean so far is that he will be very rich and attract those things which bring security and ease with them. I will pray to Horus for Prince Amunhotep's safe return to Egypt, as your vision promises."

Huy laughed and she glanced at him, startled. "If you feel the need to pray for that event, you can't have much faith in my visions!" he said. "Well, dear scribe, I suppose we must attend to the townsfolk who are waiting for their own visions and healings. Tetiankh will have prepared my drug for me. I would like one more day to recover, but they have been camping outside the gate since we left for the palace. Seal the scrolls first and put them in a niche until you can find a box. Ask Anab for one. At least there are no letters to be dealt with."

When Kar, the gate guard, had ushered the last petitioner out of the gate, the household settled down for the afternoon sleep. Later, when Huy woke and went downstairs, Merenra told him that the hyena had been traded for a sack of chickpeas. "The soldiers were clever," he added. "Seshemnefer did not grow them for you last year, Master. He turned over that portion of your arouras and planted broad beans, with a small corner devoted to henna."

"Henna?"

Merenra permitted himself a brief smile. "I have not brought details such as this to your attention. There is never a need to do so. Seshemnefer has your permission to keep a certain portion of the profits from the arouras for himself and his wife. Khnit persuaded him to plant henna. The flowers are very sweetly scented, but as you must know from the work your uncle does, the dried leaves mixed with sarson oil make dye for the hair and the skin. The seeds give their own oil. Seshemnefer sells both oils in the lull between the harvest and the sowings of the New Year. Do you wish to alter your arrangement with Seshemnefer?"

"No," Huy replied thoughtfully, "but Khnit seems to be an astute businesswoman as well as a fine cook. Watch her, Merenra. Perhaps in the future we should employ a new cook and make use of Khnit in some other way."

He ate a quiet evening meal with Thothhotep and Anhur, walked a little by the murky and sullen depths of a river still sinking, sat on his roof to watch the huge orange moon rise and shrink to a silver ball, and went to his couch feeling tired but oddly serene. The hyena was gone. He had discharged the duties his gift demanded for yet another day. His household was orderly. Those he loved were healthy. He promised himself a visit to his parents on the following day. His head was not paining him. He fell quickly asleep.

Once more he opened his eyes onto darkness, immediately tensing for the wail of the hyena. It did not come. Words were pouring into his mind instead, not through his ears but rising from that place within himself that had lain dormant for many years. The Book of Thoth was demanding his attention. When Imhotep had asked him if he would read it, he had not considered the consequences, one of which was that on reading the words of those precious and holy scrolls they would become embedded in his ka and in his consciousness. Like a rock entrenched in the bed of a river, they lay quiet while the water of Huy's everyday life flowed over them, but they rose to the surface of his awareness in complete totality whenever he chose to turn his attention to them. He had not done so for a long time. The ultimate meaning of the forty-two rolls of papyrus continued to elude him, so that in the end he had ceased to worry at them and had left them in the place where they had been so strongly implanted.

Now they thundered through his head, the phrases majestic, ponderous, each syllable as clear and sweet as the sound of a single note played upon a flute by a master musician. Huy left the couch and stood still for a moment, fully awake and alert, aware that he was able to make his own thoughts over the undercurrent of the chanting voice. For the first time, he wondered whose voice it was. His own? Was it the voice of Atum himself? But he had heard Atum speak. The pitch of this voice was slightly higher than that of the mighty god, though just as melodious, and fraught with authority. It certainly did not belong to Anubis, whose jackal tones were throaty and harsh. Nor did it belong to the goddess Ma'at; Huy had heard her speak also. Was he hearing the voice of Thoth, who had written down the words at Atum's command?

The answer was not really important. He was powerless to stop the flood pouring through him like the water of the rising river streaming over the cataracts. *Why now?* he asked, but he knew. He knew. He had failed the creator. He had betrayed his gift. It did not matter that he himself had often hated and resented it since it had been thrust upon him. It was a grave responsibility, which he had done his best to carry regardless of his feelings. But he had failed the test of the King's displeasure. He had put the fear of losing all he had before the will of Atum and his own uniqueness and, worse, he had already begun to reason away the guilt that had descended on him.

He was suddenly sure that the hyena had slunk back into his garden, that the vile beast was sitting on the worn patch of earth close to the rear of the house, staring up at the roof with its hateful black eyes. Leaving his room, glancing to the left where Tetiankh was snoring on his pallet, he turned towards the window to the roof and was soon walking to the lip and peering down. The long recitation moved with him, the cadences singing in his blood, behind his eyes, shivering under his skin. The moon was still high, the sharpness of its outline beginning to soften as it started its slow wane, and the garden was flooded with its strange unlight. Huy's eyes searched every corner and saw nothing. The water in the irrigation ditches lay smoothly silver.

"What is it that you fear, Son of Hapu?" Huy felt the jackal's moist breath on his cheek, as he had known he would. "Is it fur and teeth? Bristles and panting tongues? Is it the cruel heart of the desert in an animal's cry? You do well to be afraid, Great Seer, oh yes. Atum the Neb-er-djer, Lord to the Limit, will punish you for your spinelessness before Amunhotep and his thieving son, but his discipline will be felt as the prick of a thorn beside the thrust of a dagger to your heart if you fail to understand the thing that ought to fill you with terror. Ungrateful child!" The god's voice became a deep-throated growl. "He has opened his hands in generosity towards you and yet the Book lies idle in your marrow. Hear it and understand! Search it and understand! Lion and darkness, lion and darkness, lion and darkness!" The words ended on a howl so like that of the hyena that Huy jerked away from the brink of the roof with a shriek.

"I have tried to understand!" he shouted. "Help me, Anubis!" But he no longer felt the presence of the god. *You have not tried hard enough*, his own thought whispered to him. *The task is hard and tiring. You fill your days with scrying and healing and tell yourself that those things are enough. You hurry from your duties to warm yourself with those you love. You shamefully neglect your study of the Book. You are thirty-eight years old. It has been twenty-six years since Sennefer sent you tumbling into Ra's entrance lake, since you agreed to read the Book, since you sat under the Ished Tree and unrolled the first scroll for the first time. Lion and darkness. Ra and Set. Amun and Set. What is the thing that ought to fill me with terror? The Book and Atum and the hyena. They are connected, all three, but it is only the hyena that fills me with an irrational fear. Irrational? Perhaps not. Lion and hyena. What does the hyena represent for me?*

Abruptly, the current of words ceased. Huy felt sweat break out along his spine. *I have asked the right question, and the answer must lie within the mysteries of the Book.* Hurrying back along the passage to his room, he snatched up a cushion, regained the roof, and, flinging down the cushion in his favourite place by the wind catcher, lowered himself onto it, drew up his knees, wrapped his arms around them, and closed his eyes. *I must decipher the meaning of the hyena*, he told himself. *It is in the Book, that much is clear. Very well. I shall set aside one hour every night to call up the Book, remind myself of what I do know, bring my intellect to bear upon it. I tried to do so as a boy, but the task was too great for me. I must succeed as a man. I must avert the consequence of failure.*

The Book is set out in five stages. The first stage, contained in the scrolls kept at the temple of Ra in Iunu, is concerned with Atum's will and his nature. I remember being in despair after I read them. They deal with Atum regarding himself. "How to describe the indescribable? How to show the unshowable? How to express the unutterable? How to seize the ungraspable instant?" *For me the question was, how may anyone ever divine the nature of Atum the creator? In the first stage Atum wills change. He enters the Duat. I had believed that there was only one Duat, a place full of demons through which the dead had to pass to reach the Beautiful West, but the Book described Atum as entering the Second Duat. "Hail Atum, he who comes before himself! You culminate in this your name of 'Hill.' You become in this your name ..."*

A chance remark by Mesta, Huy's chariot instructor, had given Huy the answer. The Second Duat was the place of Metamorphosis, where Atum chose to become "Hill," the mound, the source of all creation latent within him. The first birthing was that of magic, heka, first as a component of the god himself, unrealized outside himself, and then as the force of light. "Let us call Spirit pure energy—but it is known to us only through light. Let us call God consciousness—but it is known to us only through complementation. Let us call Light first—but known only through darkness ..."

Here Huy stopped the flow of the Book. Something in the inflection of the anonymous voice reciting the words made him want to repeat them. *"Let us call Light first—but known only through darkness." The lion and the darkness. Only by knowing darkness can we recognize Light. Knowing darkness ... Am I to embrace the hyena, try to fathom its nature, and thus know—what? Myself? A part of myself?* Suddenly his heart constricted and he could not breathe. *Yes!* he shouted silently. *Yes! Only by the hyena in me can I fully know, recognize, fathom, whatever, the true nature of Atum as Light, as Ra-Atum. Then what part of me is the hyena?*

Quickly he reviewed the components that made up a human being: the physical body, the shadow, the ka, the ba, the heart, the khu-spirit, the name. He spoke them quietly aloud, but his mind did not halt and stumble over any one of them. His heart gave a lurch and settled down again to its usual strong rhythm. He allowed the words to continue, but something of his excitement had been muted. *Of course, it won't be that easy,* he told himself, *but I won't forget that line from the Book. I will worry it like a dog with a bone until it gives up its meaning to me. After Atum conceived magic, he predicted an end before a beginning.* "All that will be created will return to the Nun. Myself alone, I persist, unknown, invisible to all ..."

The second stage was recorded on a thin scroll at the temple of Thoth at Khmun. Huy had been in a state of uneasiness from the time he stood before the double doors to the temple's inner court. Thoth's home was alive with heka, with a powerful, solemn magic. Thoth seemed to be watching him critically, waiting for him to commit some small act of blasphemy in order to punish him. To make matters worse, he had found the scroll entirely incomprehensible. "I am One that transforms into Two. I am Two that transforms into Four, I am Four that transforms into Eight. After this I am One." The god's cryptic words had eventually been explained. On becoming Light, Atum cast a shadow. Within the shadow, chaos reigned until Atum calmed it by ordering it into the four pairs of the Ocdoad, the male hypostases symbolized by frogs, the females by snakes. Water, Endless Space, Darkness, and What-Is-Hidden. But this was still only an inception, a potentiality making the conception of the eternal world possible.

Huy returned to his school at Iunu and to the reading of the third stage, when inception became conception. Now the gods, the Ennead, could begin to exist as Ra-Atum the Creator, Shu the Air, Tefnut the Light, Geb the Earth, Nut the Sky, and Osiris, Isis, Set, and Nephthys. *Atum says,* "You are Eight who have made from your seed a germ, and you have instilled this seed in the Lotus, thus giving birth to Ra by pouring seminal fluid. You have deposited in the Nun, condensed into a single form, and your inheritor takes his radiant birth under the aspect of a child." *This has enabled Atum to change yet again, to become Ra-Atum, with the full power to create whatever he wishes. He says:*

"*I am he who made heaven and earth, formed the mountains, and
Created what is above.*

I am he who made the water and Created the celestial waves.

I am he who made the bull for the cow.

I am he who made the sky and the mysteries of the two horizons ...

*I am he who opens his eyes, thus the light comes forth. I am he who
closes his eyes, thus*

Comes forth obscurity ...

I am he who made the hours, thus the days were born ...

I am he who made the living fire ...

I am Khepri in the morning, Ra at his noontide, Atum in the evening."

Any triad represented divine truths, and any doubling
represented the fleeting reality of created matter. This Huy
had learned when discussing both the Ocdoad and the Ennead
with High Priest Ramose. The concepts were not difficult to
grasp. Nor was the creation of Osiris, son of Nut, the goddess
representing the sky, and Geb, the god signifying the earth.
Osiris symbolized the cycle of birth and rebirth, and Ra-Atum
delegated authority to him when the world was created.

O Osiris! The Inundation is coming; abundance rushes in.
   The flood season is coming,
Arising from the torrent issuing from Osiris. O King, may
   Heaven give birth to thee as Orion. You are born in your
   months like the moon.
Ra supports himself on you at the Horizon.
You appear at the New Moon.

Huy was forced to return to Khmun to read the fourth stage,
the creation of time and of the material world. Everything about
Thoth's temple had made him feel as though he were walking on
eggshells, and once again he had fled the precincts as soon as he

could. He had read of the task Atum had set for Osiris—to organize and civilize the land of Egypt—and how Osiris had left the country's care and governing to his sister Isis and had journeyed south so that he could teach to the savage people of those regions agriculture, the laws of Ma'at, and the correct ways in which to worship the divine powers.

But when Osiris returned to Egypt, his brother Set ambushed him, enclosed him in a coffin, and flung him into one of the tributaries snaking through the Delta. The ocean had taken the coffin and deposited it on a beach in Rethennu, where a huge tree grew up around it. Isis, meanwhile, having been told by Shu, god of the air, where Osiris lay, went to look for him and, finding him, brought the coffin back to Egypt and hid it. But Set found it, cut Osiris's body into fourteen pieces, and scattered them throughout the country. Isis and Nephthys, her sister, went searching for each piece, and buried it where they found it. But they could not find the penis of Osiris, and so Osiris became a god of the dead.

Huy was aware of the cycle of mystery plays associated with the life, death, and resurrection of Osiris. There was the Feast of the Great Manifestation of Osiris on the twenty-second day of the month of Thoth. There was the Opening of the Tomb of Osiris on the twenty-first day of Khoiak, the Preparation of the Sacrificial Altar in the Tomb of Osiris on the twenty-third, the Exhibition of the Corpse of Sokar, Osiris's name as Lord of the Dead, in the Midst of the Sacrifice on the twenty-fourth, not to mention the Feast of the Mourning Goddesses on the twenty-fifth. "It is all to do with the permanence of life, its continuation by a change of state after death," Ramose, Ra's High Priest, had told Huy when he complained that he saw no connection between the birth of the world and Osiris's tale. "Everything, including Osiris, was created to pass from seed to shoot to maturity to death and then, having sown a new seed, to transfiguration. Make of it what you will, Huy. It is Atum's way of telling us in what manner he conceived of our creation and the creation of everything living."

Huy had been glad to turn to the fifth and last set of scrolls. He had expected a great flood of understanding as he read the last words dictated by Atum to Thoth, but he was left with anger, disappointment, and a curious sense of loss. Thoth had prefaced each of Atum's pronouncements with a list of some of his, Thoth's, twenty-two titles. Huy had become used to finding them at the beginning of each scroll and, as usual, they were there. The last one said, "I Thoth, guide of heaven, earth, and the First Duat, am now the Bridge of Atum." This was bad enough, but Atum's final pronouncement, the one that should have united all the other forty-one scrolls, was utterly nonsensical. In part it said,

> ... You will go around the entire Two Skies. You will circumambulate the Two Banks.
> You will become one with the perishable stars. You will become a ba.
> You will journey to the Land of the West. You will inhabit the Fields of Yaru in peace until Turnface carries you away.
> Free course is given to you by Horus. You flash as the lone star ...

And so on, for a few more incomprehensible lines. Atum had already made it clear that the end curved back to the beginning, but reciting the whole Book out loud again had not brought clarification. Besides, the ba was simply the spirit that animated the flesh. Freed at death, it stayed close to the body in the form of a bird with the features of the deceased.

So, of course, part of a person would become a ba. The akh, or khu-spirit, the eternal light in everyone that frees itself at death and is transfigured, was not mentioned at all. Nor was the ka, that portion dealing with one's appetites—physical, moral, and spiritual—the Setian part of a human being, where the akh is personified in Horus. Huy learned these things from his teachers, the temple priests, and even from Thothmes, during one of their late night discussions, when they lay in their cell in the dark after the lamp had been extinguished and talked until they became drowsy.

Huy, alone at night on his rooftop, came to the end of the Book with the same sense of frustration he had felt all those years ago when he had let the last scroll roll up and had sat on under the Ished Tree, allowing every one of the forty-two portions to flow past his inner vision in the hope that understanding would burst upon him at last. He had left the sacred Tree not knowing whether to be angry or relieved, a depression settling on him as he made his way to return the box with its precious contents to the High Priest.

But now he had an added reason to decipher the ultimate meaning of the Book. He must deflect the fate that would be his if he failed. Random snatches flitted through his mind.

That which I illuminated in my heart was the plan of the universe which presented itself to me. I made every creature when I was alone. I planned in my heart, I created other metamorphoses. Very many were the transformations of Khepri ...

It is I who spat out Shu, I who expectorated Tefnut. I had come into being as one god and behold, there were three ...

Nun said to Atum, "Breathe in thy daughter Ma'at. Bring her to thy nose in order that thy heart may live, that she be not removed from thee, that thy daughter Ma'at be with thy son Shu whose name is Life …"

Unity and multiplicity, Huy thought. Versa and vice versa. Why does it seem to me now that my anger, my frustration all those years ago, stemmed from an unconscious suspicion that the last scroll is unfinished? That Thoth's final declaration, that he has written the Book as Atum has instructed him, sounds like a justification for its incompleteness? Physically exhausted but mentally alert, Huy sat up. Not so, he tried to contradict himself. There has never been the slightest whisper that the Book exists as anything but the forty-two scrolls that reside in Ra's temple and live in my head. But what if the forty-second scroll was supposed to be longer, hold more? Or what if Thoth was commanded to deliberately omit something so vital that it might change the beliefs of every pious Egyptian? "Oh, don't be ridiculous," he said aloud. "You're allowing fantasy to provide an excuse for your own inability to fathom a meaning from the Book."

And what of Imhotep? his mind persisted. He read, he understood, he became a holy and revered man and then a god. Did he read what I have read, and did he see words that have since disappeared? Next time I visit Thothmes and Ishat at Iunu, I must go to the House of Life, to the archives, and acquaint myself with the details of the Mighty Seer's life.

Wearily, Huy scrambled to his feet, picked up the cushion, and re-entered the house. He had no idea how long he had been sitting on the roof, communing with the Book. He needed to sleep now that his mind had been scoured. I'm right, he told himself as he lowered himself onto his couch with a groan of pure pleasure at its cool softness. My akh, my ka, and my ba all tell me so. The last scroll waits for me to finish it as it waited for Imhotep. On that conviction he fell asleep.

12

HE SPENT THE FOLLOWING DAY with his parents, noting with a pang of concern how his father, Hapu, tried to hide the pain in his limbs when getting up from his mat on the floor after the simple evening meal. Huy knew better than to nag him. The peasant whom Huy had procured for him was a cheerful, energetic man with an appetite as large as his girth. "Your father will not stay out of the perfume fields, Master," he told Huy in private. "I have no authority to command him. All I can do is make sure that your uncle Ker assigns the heavier tasks to me. Hapu often works in the compound, simmering the flowers and handling the filtering, but he says that the powerful odours of the blooms give him a headache and he sneaks back to tend the plants. He's happiest weeding out the wild flax and the dock leaves." The wide shoulders lifted in a gesture of impotence. "He comes home with his back bent and your mother scolds him, but even she can do nothing with him."

It is as though Father is punishing himself for something, Huy mused as Hapzefa set lentil soup and barley bread before him, and Hapu, opposite, lifted his beer mug and smiled at Huy over its rim. *Is he just being obstinate or is he, like me, no stranger to the guilt that often underpins every other emotion?* Hapu's muscles stood out like ropes on his arms, his legs, his torso, unsoftened by the layer of fat that had smoothed the contours of his younger body.

Huy's mother, Itu, had thickened around the waist. Streaks of grey threaded through her black hair and her face was becoming lined, but Huy thought that aging suited her. She had always been beautiful, but now she carried with her an aura of dignified fulfillment Huy liked very much. She still used the lily perfume whose gentle aroma could return him to the days of his childhood, and her embraces were as strong and warm as ever. Hapzefa, Ishat's mother, never seemed to change. Her tongue was perhaps sharper, her movements less direct, but she still treated Huy with the mixture of affection and censure that had enfolded him since his birth. Ishat had showered her with gifts, provided her with a better house, a couple of cows of her own, and had offered to send a new servant for Hapu's household so that Hapzefa could retire, but like Hapu himself she knew no other life but that of caring for the household and did not want to change.

Huy both loved and disliked the unvarying atmosphere of his childhood home, fraught with both happy and fearful memories as it was. His younger self haunted the garden, waiting for Ishat to emerge from the orchard to play or argue with him. Stepping into the room that had been his and then Heby's, he again saw Ishat come slipping through his window, one bare brown leg pushing at the reed slats of the hanging while he lay on the cot with a wounded skull, virtually a prisoner as he waited for the Rekhet to come and exorcise the demon most people, including his father, believed had taken possession of his body. Hapu had refused to be anywhere near him. Only his mother and Ishat loved him enough to ease his terror, Itu from a stout conviction that no demon existed in him and Ishat because she was more interested in the ghoulish sight of the gash on his head, and because she was lonely without him. Huy had no desire to relive those days.

He was using some of the King's gold to have a small tomb prepared for his parents in the low cliffs to the west, between the Delta and the country of Tjehanu. The simple events of their lives would be painted on its walls, but Huy had no intention of including anything to do with his own death, his waking after five days in the House of the Dead here at Hut-herib, or his exorcism. His successes and Heby's also would be recorded and added to until the time Hapu and Itu became Osiris-ones, but no hint of anything uncommon would be depicted.

Usually his visits were pleasant, the conversations warm and light, when everyone was careful not to allude to the past. But occasionally the past hung about the house and garden like smoke, making Huy desperate to escape back to his own home.

True to his word, Huy visited his arouras west of the town, in the Andjet sepat, and stood with Seshemnefer to watch the peasants wield their sickles, the emmer, barley, and flax falling before them in a steady rhythm. The huge reed baskets were filling with broad beans, figs, dates, onions, lentils, and other vegetables used in large quantities. Seshemnefer, whose assistant was in charge of the arouras the Rekhet had willed to Huy, told Huy that the yield of olives had been surprisingly heavy at Ta-she and the grapes had ripened with no sign of rust. "Surely the gods smile upon you again, Master, as they do every year," Seshemnefer remarked, "and therefore on me also as the Overseer of your fields. I have personally harvested a goodly quantity of henna leaves. They are already steeping in the sarson oil and will make a rich orange dye for my noble customers. Is Anab caring well for the estate garden?"

Huy smiled. "He shares your magic touch, and the soil responds to his attention. Seshemnefer, if you can leave the harvesting here to your assistant, I want you to go south to Weset this year and supervise the slitting of the poppy pods with Amunnefer's Overseer. I want to know the quality of the drug from your own mouth. Also make sure that the correct amount is delivered to the King's Overseer of Physicians. He'll be hanging about, waiting to transport the poppy back north to Mennofer. The last thing I want to do at this time is antagonize His Majesty."

The man nodded. "Very well. I would like to take my wife with me if you can spare her, Master. Khnit would love Weset."

Huy considered. It was true that Khnit had been working steadily for a long time. Even though she now had two servants under her, it was no easy matter to feed everyone resident on the estate. "Amunmose will grumble, but he can be my cook for a while. Thank you, Seshemnefer. You make my fields very profitable."

Every season of Shemu, the reports from his overseers were the same: bountiful, healthy crops of all kinds, free of disease. Even the quality of the poppy yield was approaching the potency of the dark brown Keftian juice. The same could be said of the unfailing riches the incense caravans brought home to Egypt almost every year. *It is indeed true that the gods have favoured me*, Huy reflected as he walked to where his litter and the bearers waited under the palms at the edge of the field.

In the last week of Epophi two letters arrived, one from the palace and one from Amunnefer. Seshemnefer had returned with satisfactory reports after discharging his duties at Weset and so Huy, staring down at Amunnefer's scroll sealed with Amun's two feathers, could not imagine what message lay inside. He had summoned Thothhotep when Merenra handed him the letters. Now he passed them both to her across his desk. His office, though not cool, was at least dim, due to the shrubbery crowding the low window. "Read me Amunnefer's first," he said, dreading to discover what new demand the King might be making of him.

Obediently, she broke the seal and scanned the contents, then she smiled, glancing at Huy, before her eyes dropped to the script and she began to speak. "'To my friend and partner the Great Seer Huy, greetings. You will of course already know that our venture together will once more bring us much profit, but I am not writing to you today, the fifteenth day of Epophi, in my own hand, to discuss the poppy. On the twenty-second day of last month, Payni, in the evening, I arrived at my house expecting to find it empty of my wife Anuket, who for many years has preferred the company of others to my own. I was surprised to find her waiting for me in the reception hall, painted and dressed as though for a feast. When I asked her if I had forgotten the visit of some dignitary who must be feted, she replied that the only dignitary present was I. Since you Saw for her all those years ago, she has struggled against the lure of wine with little success, but on that day of Payni she declared that she had woken to find herself entirely freed from the need for it, and that she would not be leaving the bounds of the estate unless there were social obligations to fulfill. For several days I waited to see her resolve weaken, but a month has passed and, true to her word, she drinks only juices and water. Her health is improving. If she leaves the house, it is with me or her steward and guards. Both of us have begun to wonder if perhaps through her efforts she has at last been able to avert the fate you Saw waiting for her, and which she eventually related to me. We are cautiously beginning to believe that the change in her is enduring. We rejoice, and I am sure that you, as one of her oldest friends, will be glad also.'" Thothhotep allowed the scroll to roll up. "He signs it 'Governor of the Uas sepat, Amunnefer. Life, Health, and Prosperity to you and all who live beneath your sunshade.' Shall I open the other letter?"

Huy gazed at her but did not see her. He was not aware that he was gripping both thighs. *The twenty-second day of Payni,* his mind repeated. *The twenty-second … That was the day when I stood before the King and his sons and betrayed Ma'at, and suddenly, on that very day, for no reason at all, Anuket is able to take a final step away from the terrible fate I Saw for her. Atum has done this. The discipline Anubis promised is upon me. My vision for Anuket will be proved false, as false as my craven words of appeasement to the King and Prince Thothmes—but will it fall on someone else? Someone I love?*

One of his hands was lifted. He looked down to see Thothhotep kneeling beside his chair, her features disfigured with concern. "Huy, what is it? You've gone pale. I remember transcribing the Seeing you gave for the Governor's wife. That was more than fifteen years ago. But this is good news, is it not? Huy!"

She had begun to shake his fingers. Laying his other hand over hers, he stilled the movement. "I have not told you what transpired when the King summoned me," he said, the need to unburden himself overcoming any reticence he might feel. "You keep your counsel and mine, Thothhotep. You've proved as much. Bring a stool, and then I will try to explain to you why this letter fills me with horror."

She went to the corner, dragged out the stool, and sat down facing him. She did not pick up her palette from the desk where she had placed it. Quickly, Huy spoke of Prince Thothmes' fictitious dream, the response he himself should have made, and the response he did make. He spoke of the two hyenas, the one beside Imhotep and the one that stared him down in his garden. He described as best he could the flooding of his consciousness with the Book and Anubis's warnings.

Her eyes did not leave his face until he fell silent. Then she folded her arms and her head went down. After a long time she said, "There will be two consequences, yes? One will be a punishment for failing both Atum, who gave you your gift, and Ma'at, whose feather represents cosmic and earthly justice, truth and integrity held in balance by the King in his person and by every Egyptian who strives to live in her. The other will overtake you if you do not decipher the meaning the hyena has for you. I must confess that I cannot wrap my thoughts around the connection between the lion, the darkness, and you. Have I understood you so far, Master?"

He nodded. In using his title once more, she was placing herself back in the position of the trusted inferior in case the confidence he had just shared with her might have embarrassed him. He was grateful for her sensitivity.

"You are not a god," she went on, "and surely Atum cannot expect you to be the perfection that he is. You experienced a moment of weakness. What of it? We all fall short of what is required of us sometimes."

But my weakness before the King has the power to resonate throughout Egypt, dear Thothhotep, he answered her silently. *That is why I shall be chastised.* On impulse, because he had wished Ishat to be sitting there instead of Thothhotep and regretted the desire, he ran his hand down the cap of her glossy hair and rested it against the bare nape of her neck.

He was rewarded with a brilliant smile. "Atum created us and placed us in this glorious land," she said. "Does that not indicate a love for us? For your childhood friend, the Lady Anuket? Perhaps Atum has chosen to avert her dire fate."

She sits at my feet day after day, recording my visions for those who seek healing or reassurance, he thought, removing his hand. *But still she does not understand.*

"Perhaps," he said. "Read me the other letter and then I'll reply to Governor Amunnefer."

At once, she left the stool, picked the scroll up from the desk, and cracked the seal bearing the royal stamp of the sedge and the bee. "It's not from His Majesty," she said. "Princess Mutemwia writes to you. She dictates the usual greetings, then she says, 'The sight of you holding my little son was most pleasing to me, and I continued on to the apartments of my dear friend with a light heart. It was to be the last time she and I shared wine together. She is travelling, and is not sure when she will be returning to Mennofer. When next you have cause to visit this city, I shall be privileged to receive you. Dictated this eighteenth day of the month Payni, year twenty-three of the King.'"

"So Prince Amunhotep has gone." Huy left his chair and came around the desk. "The Princess obviously did not even want her scribe to know why she was really writing to me. I wonder if the King will bother to discover where he went. Probably not. He knows that Amunhotep would never plot with foreigners to take the Horus Throne by force. So before too long we will find ourselves ruled by another unscrupulous liar." He began to search through the niches of scrolls set into the walls of the room.

"Before how long?"

"I don't know. Prince Amunhotep will be in exile for twelve years, therefore Prince Thothmes will not sit on the throne into his old age. The King himself does not look well. His veins visibly pulse and his colour is florid. We may soon have to endure a period of mourning. Ah, here it is." He unrolled the papyrus on the desk, holding it open with both hands. Ishat's bold script leapt to his eye and for a moment he was engulfed in a wave of hunger for the past. Thothhotep had come up beside him and was leaning forward over his arm. "This is the vision I had when the Noble Heqareshu came for a Seeing," he explained. "It was just before I hired you. I gave him only a part of what I Saw. The rest I dictated to Ishat and stored away. I did not understand it, but I do now." Grimly, he read of the wounded hawk that had hovered over the baby Thothmes, and how he had put out an arm so that it might perch on him. It had struggled to balance itself on his wrist, but when he had turned his face towards it, it had sunk its beak into his lip and disappeared. *I bled in that vision,* Huy remembered. *Atum was trying to tell me something about my own future, to warn me. I have done great harm to Prince Amunhotep, the rightful Hawk-in-the-Nest. That's why the Horus of my Seeing attacked my mouth.*

Huy let the scroll roll up and replaced it in its niche. *If I had interpreted the vision correctly, if I had been on guard for such a moment, would the future of Egypt have been different? Does Anubis show me what is to come or only what might be? Am I a prophet or a sage? Will Anuket carve a new fate for herself?* Shocked, Huy realized that he did not want a slim and healthy Anuket. He wanted her drunk and abused and lying filthy and naked in an alley. He wanted her punished for all the pain she had caused him. *Even now,* he thought with sick comprehension. *Even now, when so many years have gone by, I have not really forgiven her, although I no longer love her.*

"Pick up your palette, Thothhotep," he said harshly. "I must dictate a congratulatory letter at once to Governor Amunnefer, and one to the Princess also, thanking her and asking her to keep me acquainted with events in Mennofer. Then I must visit Methen."

He found Khenti-kheti's priest in his two-roomed cell just off the god's small forecourt. Methen was eating his evening meal. He rose and embraced Huy. "How wonderful to see you!" he exclaimed. "Have you eaten? Come and sit beside me and give me your news. I hear that you were summoned to the palace last month. I meant to pay you a visit, but both of us have had little time to spare for leisure."

His food steamed on the small table. Huy pulled the only other chair close to it and sat watching fondly as Methen spooned up the vegetable stew. They had been friends ever since Methen had found Huy naked and half insane outside Hut-herib's House of the Dead and carried him home to his stunned parents. Methen had brought him poppy for his pain and an unwavering affection that Huy returned. The priest had petitioned for the exorcism that freed Huy from the doubt that he was possessed, and together with High Priest Ramose and Henenu the Rekhet he had become a valued mentor. Now Henenu was dead and Ramose had retired from the temple at Iunu to his estates near Pe in the Sap-meh sepat of the northern Delta. Huy had not seen him or received a letter from him for a long time. Huy had been twelve when Methen had rescued him, and Methen in his late twenties. He had seemed very old to Huy. Now he was in his mid-fifties. Lines fanned out across his temples and faint grooves marked the edges of his mouth, but even in repose his expression remained warmly benevolent.

Huy recounted his shameful audience at the palace while Methen briskly scoured his bowl with a piece of bread, sat back, and sipped at his beer. He offered no advice and Huy did not ask for any. Huy went on to speak of the hyena, and again Methen remained silent, one of the reasons why Huy valued him so highly. Huy finished by telling Methen about Anuket's surprising change, and here Methen smiled.

"Has it occurred to you that Atum has at last decided to save her out of his regard for you? That he has more sympathy for the agonies of your youth than you imagine? Your love for her died when you saw her at Ishat's marriage feast. Can a god regret something he has caused, even though he will not alter the consequences of his decision? Does he wonder, as you used to do, what would have happened to Anuket, to you, if you had been allowed to retain your sexual potency and she had chosen to run away with you? She has been unhappy with Amunnefer, but she has obviously decided not to punish him, and herself, anymore. I think your fears of Atum's retribution may be unfounded."

"Perhaps so," Huy said. "All I can do is wait as my own future unfolds. Methen, I keep remembering what the Rekhet said to me once when I visited her at her house in Iunu. I was deeply troubled because of my enforced virginity. I still believed that I could shed it and retain my gift, or, better still, shed it and thus rid myself of the gift. She had calmed me and was braiding my hair. 'Some great work waits for you in a future I cannot see,' she said. 'Something vital to Egypt. Your courage must not fail, for if it does, then Egypt will go down into chaos.' What if the 'great work' was openly condemning the King and Prince Thothmes for their deceit, and in losing my courage to do so I have condemned Egypt to the chaos of which she spoke?"

"Is that what you believe? What you fear?"

"Yes. No! I don't know. I cling to the prospect of the second chance Anubis granted me."

"Then stop worrying about it. The moment of weakness has receded into the past. It can't be retrieved and corrected. You think too much of yourself, dear Huy, if you suppose that you are above human error."

Huy managed a laugh. "Your ability to comfort me hasn't changed since you picked me up outside the House of the Dead. Actually, Methen, I came to you today for information."

Methen's eyebrows rose. He grinned. "And here I was thinking so much of myself that I supposed you had been missing me!"

"Of course I missed you." Huy pulled Methen's cup towards him, swallowed a mouthful of the beer, and pushed it back. "You come to my house less often than you used to."

"I know. I'm sorry. I assume that as long as you don't need me, you need not see me."

"That's just stupid!" They smiled at one another. "Anyway, I want you to tell me about Imhotep."

Methen blinked. "All right. But why?"

Huy sighed and crossed his arms, leaning them on the surface of the table. He was suddenly aware that the shaft of light flooding into the room through the open door had acquired the colour of copper. The sun was approaching the western horizon, where Nut's mouth was waiting to swallow it.

"The Book has woken in me, Methen. I turn my attention to the flow of the words when I am alone in the night, before I sleep. I'm becoming convinced that it is incomplete." He had been afraid of a burst of laughter from the priest, an assumption that he was joking. He had kept his eyes on the empty soup bowl as he spoke so that he might not see his friend's face, but after some moments of silence he glanced up. Methen's own eyes had narrowed. His expression had sharpened.

"That is the last thing I expected to hear you say," Methen finally responded. "What makes you think so?"

Huy unfolded his arms and laid his hands palms up on the table. "At the end of the recitation, Thoth says that he has written the Book as Atum has instructed him. He sounds almost … almost petulant. Apologetic. And the end of the Book is very abrupt. It's not even a summing-up. Atum, through Thoth, says that the end curves back to the beginning, but it doesn't seem to. The break is somehow … jagged." His fingers curled loosely in on themselves.

Methen shook his head. "How many years has the Book been a part of you, Huy? Twenty-five, twenty-six years? And this suspicion only strikes you now?"

"I've allowed the pleasures and concerns of my life to drive the Book deep into my akh. The King and the hyena have shocked me into the realization of a task undone. I am able to be more objective now, to not only listen to the words but look at them with the eyes of my mind as they glide by. The rest of the fifth and last stage is either unwritten or lies somewhere other than the temples of Ra at Iunu and Thoth at Khmun."

The doorway darkened. Methen's servant came in, a lighted taper in his hand. Quickly he touched it to the wicks of the two clay lamps, one on the table and one in the second room beside Methen's narrow cot, blew it out, and bowed to both men. "Greetings, Great Seer." He smiled. "I trust you are well? And your household?"

By the time he and Huy had exchanged courtesies, the faint odour of warm, unscented oil filled the air. The man collected his master's dishes and quietly left. Methen was staring thoughtfully at Huy, his lips pursed.

"That's why you want to know about Imhotep," he said. "He was reading the Book when you stood before him in the Beautiful West. You think that he read it during his early years, just as you did, but that he read it in its entirety, or realized that a part of it was missing and found that part."

"Yes. What can you tell me, Methen?"

"His statues and monuments fill Egypt. According to their inscriptions, he was the Chief Architect to the Osiris-King Djoser in the dawn of history, and he designed the first of the mighty tombs that crowd the City of the Dead on the plateau outside Mennofer. The King valued him so highly that Imhotep was allowed to have his name carved on one of the King's likenesses— a unique honour."

"I know that he is worshipped as a healer as well as a Seer."

"He wrote a book of wisdom that has since been lost." Methen passed a hand over his shaven skull, disturbing the play of light and shadow Huy had been watching shift across his friend's face as he spoke. "That's really all. Of course, you're aware that he served as High Priest at the temple of Ra at Iunu."

Huy jerked forward. "No, I didn't know! He read the Book, Methen! Would there be more about him in the House of Life at Iunu?"

Methen shrugged. "Perhaps, but I doubt it. If the archives had held more information, you may be sure that your teachers would have insisted that you learn it. Iunu is very proud to be the city where the great Imhotep served the god."

"Somehow he was able to absorb the Book in its entirety," Huy insisted. "How else was he able to become so famous as a healer and a Seer that he's regarded as a god himself? Next time I visit Thothmes and Ishat, I'll visit the House of Life as well."

"Huy, are you sure about this? Sure that you're not just using it as an excuse to avoid the hard work the study of the Book demands?"

Only you can speak to me like that, Huy thought with a rush of respect. *You have earned the right, and I listen to you. Already I have become so renowned that no one dares to question me.*

"No, I'm not sure," he confessed. "I have a strong intuition, though. As for the Book, I disembowel it like a worker in the House of the Dead and I put it together again, and still it will not form the coherent wholeness of a meaning. However, I persist." He got up and Methen rose with him. The sun had set, and the shreds of light creeping through the doorway were a delicate pink fading rapidly to grey. The two men embraced. "I love you, Methen," Huy said. "Come soon and eat with me and sit in my garden."

"If I do, it will have to be before the month of Thoth when there are so many gods' days to observe! Next month I make my annual visit to my parents. I'll try to come to you at the end of Mesore."

They said their goodbyes. Methen retreated into his cell and, in the gathering dimness, Huy crossed the little outer court of Khenti-kheti's shrine, empty of worshippers at that hour. His litter-bearers were clustered just beyond the wall of the shrine, playing knucklebones in the dust. Anhur was pacing. He greeted Huy with ill-concealed relief, snapped at the bearers as they scrambled up, and Huy was carried home.

For the next few days, Huy found it difficult to settle calmly to his tasks. He did his duty by those who came to him for aid almost without reflection, presuming that Anubis would guide his visions and remedies as the god had always done. Sleep came to him late and hard. As he lay on his couch and the Book unwound through his consciousness, he became increasingly convinced that its final portion was missing. The knowledge made him anxious to be gone, to begin a search for it in the House of Life at Iunu, to seek out every likeness of Imhotep and read the archaic inscriptions on them in the hope of stumbling across some clue that would lead him on to the solution he sought. He was already taking the poppy three times a day and admitted to himself that he had developed an addiction to it, but he bade Tetiankh strengthen his evening's dose, hoping that under its influence he might enjoy a full night's rest. The drug stupefied him so that he lay prone and naked in the hot darkness of his room, his muscles lax and unresponsive, while the stanzas of the Book continued to whisper behind his closed eyes. He needed a concerted effort of the will to stop it so that his mind was free to wander and then to sleep, but the stronger poppy seemed to sap his inner coherence. In the end he told his body servant to return him to his regular nightly dose.

When there had been a lull in the number of petitioners clustering outside his gate, and no letters waited for his attention, he decided to go south. The harvest was almost over, and Egypt had begun to sink into the stagnant timelessness of high summer. Humans and animals panted in the shade. Cracks began to appear in fields already denuded of their crops, and the peasants unlucky enough to be still reaping sweated and cursed the god who seemed to be expelled each dawn from the sky goddess Nut with malicious speed, and who poured an uncharacteristic venom upon their skin until the moment when he reluctantly slid into her mouth. Dust hung everywhere, often eddying in the scorching air to coat the drooping palms and sycamores and sift behind teeth and eyelids. The irrigation canals were empty. The river itself was at its lowest level, its northward current barely perceptible. Much of the Delta remained green, the soil fed by the trickles of many tributaries. Iunu was situated at its southern tip, where it began to fan out. Although the land to either side of the river still held to a semblance of fertility, it took Huy's exhausted crew an extra day to reach the city.

Thothmes' estate lay just to the north of Iunu's wide water-steps. All were relieved when the captain gave the order to tack west and the Governor's own set of steps came into view. Anhur hailed the guards on the bank, two sailors hurried to secure the mooring rope, and the ramp was run out. Huy sent Tetiankh on ahead to warn the house that he had arrived. Apart from his body servant, only Anhur and Thothhotep, with her servant Iny, had accompanied him. All were hot and thirsty.

Huy had barely stepped across the threshold of the reception hall when Thothmes came hurrying towards him, a distress bordering on panic filling his face. He was unpainted and unshod. The odour of incense clung to his clothes as he grasped Huy's shoulders. Instinctively, Huy jerked back. "I sent a runner for you yesterday," Thothmes said. "You must have passed him on the way. What are you doing here? Did the gods impel you to come? Never mind. The physician says she is dying, but if you See for her, Atum will make her well again."

Huy wrenched himself free of his friend's frenetic grip. For one dizzying moment he was young again, walking thankfully towards the cell they shared at the temple school after he had spent time in Thoth's temple at Khmun, and Thothmes was racing towards him with the terrible news of Nefer-Mut's accident. "You must save her! You must!" Thothmes had begged, but his mother had died. Huy had stood with her in the Judgment Hall and watched her enter the Paradise of Osiris. "There is no Duat for you," Anubis had told her. "The Son of Hapu has saved you from that ordeal." Huy had never been able to understand how or why.

"Make sense, Thothmes!" he barked now, out of his own mounting dread. "Sahura. Is it Sahura? What has happened?"

Thothmes gave him a blank look. Then the frenzy went out of his eyes. "Not Sahura—it's Ishat," he rasped. "She was coming home late from the Naming Day feast of one of her friends. She was slightly drunk and the bearers and two guards were tired. They were taking a shortcut through the Street of the Beer Houses. It was a stupid thing to do!" His voice had begun to rise and he struggled visibly to control it. "Intef should have known better!"

His fingers had curled around one of Huy's long braids and he was pulling Huy deeper into the house, like a child with a special surprise to show, but his features were distorted by fear.

"A group of foreigners came out of one of the beer houses. They seemed very drunk, but when they attacked the litter, their actions were full of purpose. It was dark. My captain, Intef, could not understand their language. They barred the way. The bearers tried to go around them. Ishat started to shout at them. They set upon my men. The bearers were unarmed. One of the guards was badly injured. Ishat fell out of the litter and began to run, but some of them pursued her. The rest were beating the bearers to the ground. Ishat was caught. They tore off her sheath, Huy. They broke three of her fingers taking off her rings, and beat her about the face when she tried to stop them taking her earrings. She was screaming and struggling. They had her down. They were going to ... to ... But there were soldiers from Iunu's garrison drinking in one of the other houses, and they heard her and rushed into the street and saved her. The foreigners ran away into the darkness. Not one of them was caught, Huy, not one! These things do not happen in Egypt, where Ma'at is revered! The soldiers wrapped her in a cloak and put her in the litter and brought her home. The bearers are injured, but they'll recover. Ishat ... Ishat had bruises all over her body and an eye swollen shut and some of her hair pulled out. She was in great pain. The physician set her fingers and gave Iput a salve for her bruises and put her to sleep with a large dose of poppy, but then she didn't wake up! She can't wake up, Huy! The physician said that there must be some invisible injury inside her head. He can do nothing—but you can. Atum can, can't he?"

Huy had listened to Thothmes' almost hysterical recital with a mounting horror mingled with alarm, scarcely aware of their progress through the reception hall, along a wide passage, and through the tall double doors leading to the women's quarters, where Ishat had made a retreat for herself away from the demands of her position as a Governor's wife. *This is the future I Saw for Anuket,* Huy thought, the words erupting in his mind and flooding him with panic. *Anuket has triumphed over her fate. She is free of it, but instead Atum has visited it upon her sister-in-law Ishat, her kin, as though, once shaped, it must be fulfilled at any cost.* His limbs trembled and he was forced to steady himself against the wall. *I Saw for Ishat years ago in the hovel we shared,* his feverish thoughts ran on, *and in the vision she was painted and bejewelled, but Anubis gave me no more than that. Has Anuket's deliverance meant a doom for my dear friend? A doom that Atum transferred to her so that my vision for Anuket did not mark the god as a liar?* Real terror sliced through him as he stumbled after Thothmes.

The children and the servants filled her small reception room. When they saw Huy, they surged towards him. Thothmes let go of his hair. Sahura and Nakht flung themselves sobbing at Huy. The boy Huy, his namesake, had started towards him but then hung back, biting his lip, his eyes huge with the tears he was trying to suppress. Huy untangled himself and beckoned him.

"I want you to take Nakht and Sahura into the garden," he said. "Anhur will go with you. He has many fine stories to tell. Put them on mats under the trees and give them a little wine," he ordered the servants. "If they can fall asleep, so much the better." At once Anhur scooped up the two younger children and went out. Huy squatted and, placing his hands on the older boy's cheeks, kissed him on his hot forehead, almost moved to tears himself by the child's likeness to Ishat. "You must be brave," he said, "but not so brave that you dam up your fears until you cannot cry. Whatever happens, tonight you and I will share the cabin of my barge. We haven't seen each other for a long time, have we? I want to hear all your news." The relief on his namesake's face was reward enough for Huy's effort to pause and deal with the boy's defencelessness when all he really wanted to do was hurry to Ishat's couch.

"I've had no strength to give them," Thothmes said when they were alone. "I cannot lose Ishat, Huy!"

"Come with me and prepare your palette," Huy said to Thothhotep, who was standing just behind him.

Thothmes turned and led them through another doorway and partway along a passage with several doors opening off it. Huy had been here many times. He followed Thothmes into Ishat's bedchamber.

The shaft of sunlight falling from the clerestory window high up in the wall was murky with the smoke of frankincense. Its scent gave Huy the impression that he was entering a holy place. Frankincense was extremely expensive and usually reserved for temple use. The priest wielding the long shaft of the censer had been chanting softly. Now he fell silent, bowed to Huy, and left the room. The physician rose from his stool by the couch. He also bowed.

"I have set the fingers with linen stiffened in resin, Master," he said in answer to Huy's raised eyebrows. "I have applied a mixture of honey, castor oil, and myrrh to her cuts and bruises. I applied these remedies when the Lady Ishat was first brought home. She was shaken but alert. I gave her a small dose of poppy for her pain, and shortly thereafter she fell asleep. Three days have passed, and she will not wake."

Huy rounded on Thothmes. "Three days? She's been unconscious for three days and you send for me only now, Thothmes?"

"We kept expecting her to wake up," Thothmes replied miserably. "Her injuries, apart from the broken fingers, were not serious. You love her too. There seemed no point in asking you to come, and the next time you visited us she would tell you all about it, once it was over."

"It is my belief that a vehedu has entered the Lady Ishat through the metu of her ears or nostrils, and lodged in her head," the physician broke in. "I cannot locate it, let alone dispel it. The Governor hoped that prayers might dislodge it, but to no avail."

Huy stared at him while the information reeled slowly through his mind. The vehedu were the unseen carriers of pain and of the illnesses of internal inflammations and fevers. They could enter through any bodily orifice and travel through the metu, the channels inside the body responsible for the movement of essentials—air, blood, mucus, semen, nourishment, the proper passage of urine and feces. It was entirely possible that Ishat had fallen victim to some unknown vehedu passed to her from the filthy foreigners who attacked her.

The physician bowed again and moved towards the door. "Now that you are here, Great Seer, neither I nor the priest is needed. With your permission, Governor, I shall go to my quarters until I am summoned." Thothmes nodded once in his direction. The door closed behind him.

Unwillingly, now full of a strange reluctance, Huy approached the couch. Ishat was lying on her back under a clean white sheet, her hands loose across her chest, three of the fingers of her right hand encased in stiff, slightly yellowed linen. Both forearms were heavily bruised and cut where she had tried to defend herself. Her head, resting on the spotless pillow, looked curiously malformed because of the narrow patch of red scalp showing just above her ear, where her hair had been torn out, and the black swelling of her eye on the same side. Huy wondered whether the physician had tied a piece of raw beef against her eye, and decided that the remedy was so commonplace there could be no doubt. The other eye was fully closed. Huy looked for any movement of the eyeball, but her whole face, unnaturally pale and oddly lax, was still. *She looks dead already*, Huy thought with a stab of fear as he took the stool the physician had vacated and carefully lifted her undamaged hand, placing it between both of his own. A soft movement behind him reminded him that both Thothmes and Thothhotep were present. Huy had forgotten they were there. He closed his eyes. *Now, Anubis, Atum has deigned to prescribe for and heal much lesser folk than Ishat through me. You know how much I love her. Tell me what to do.*

"Atum's gaze roams elsewhere, Great Seer," the familiar voice of the jackal god answered the thought at once. "There are more pressing affairs to be dealt with in Egypt than the fate of one peasant woman, no matter how important she might be to you—the seed of heresy within the bosom of the King, for instance. Atum seeks a man who will root out this danger to his beloved daughter Ma'at. He had believed," Anubis went on conversationally, "that he had found such a one long ago, but he was sadly mistaken."

"Do not mock me," Huy begged. "I have admitted my guilt before the Great He-She. I am culpable. I deserve to be punished—but not this way, Anubis! Not at the expense of an innocent life! What ails Ishat? Tell me!"

"You are very free with your commands, arrogant human." The words had become a hiss of moist animal breath that Huy felt against his ear. Out of the corner of his eye he caught a glimpse of a white kilt, a black, tightly muscled calf, a long black foot encased in golden sandals studded with blue lapis. "Atum is not concerned with this female's guilt or innocence, only with her use as a discipline for you," the god went on. "He gave her to you once to ease the years of your poverty. He removed her when you no longer needed her. She is his tool."

"And so am I!" Huy shouted. "He has taken me, body and ka and akh and ba, he has used me times without number, as is his right! If I have betrayed a flaw, was it not created in my mother's womb, with Atum's full knowledge?"

"And what a flaw," Anubis purred. "Atum must now pass his rod over Egypt's future and conjure another for this, the land he loves above all others, because of you. Don't you know that your audience before the King was the most vital moment of your life, and that every god watched it with bated breath? You have condemned Amunhotep and, yes, his son Thothmes to the judgment, and Ma'at will not be lenient."

"Then leave me alone," Huy whispered. "If Atum has decreed that Ishat is to die, just go away."

"You deserve her death!" Anubis snarled.

Suddenly Huy found himself on his feet and facing the god's angry black eyes. The long furred nose almost touched his own. With a jolt of horror, Huy realized that the room had lengthened and widened. Dull ochre light illuminated the fetid air. The rank smell of death filled his nostrils. Motionless forms on plain slabs filled the sombre space. *I have been here before,* he knew with terror. *This is a House of the Dead.* He did not want to look behind him, but in spite of himself he found his body turning, his gaze dropping to the figure at his rear. Ishat lay naked, the marks left by her attackers clear on flesh that seemed pathetic and so very frail. Even as he stared down at her, one lifeless arm slid from the panel on which her corpse was lying and brushed against his hip. There was a flurry of movement as two men came close.

"The Governor's wife," one of them said. "What a pity! She was well loved throughout the sepat. The Great Seer could do nothing for her, although he tried. Well, we must begin her Beautification." He leaned over her, the obsidian disembowelling knife poised, and Huy stumbled away with a cry.

"Have pity, Atum! Pity for Thothmes and her children, if not for me!"

"Did you have pity for the wounds of Ma'at?" Anubis growled. He was leaning towards Huy, his eyes narrowed and now yellow in their nest of fur. As he spoke, Huy could see past his slick fangs and long tongue to the dark maw of his throat. *He could devour me if he wished*, Huy thought. *One word from Atum and he could gulp down the forces of my life and leave me nothing but a body and a name. Yet he is kind, this divine jackal. He leads the dead into the Judgment Hall, to Ma'at and her feather and the scales. He wishes Sobek, eater of souls under the scales, to go hungry.*

"No, I did not," Huy replied with resignation. "I cared only for my own preservation, Anubis, something I bitterly regret. I accept the consequence."

For answer the god swung round and, sweeping his staff carelessly over Ishat's carcass, drew his lips back over his teeth in a disdainful smile. Instantly, Huy was back in Ishat's bedchamber, her hand in his, the scent of frankincense strong in his nostrils.

"She merely sleeps," Anubis said. "Atum has decreed that now she may wake. He accepts your sad little spasm of humility. Have you learned your lesson, Seer?"

Huy opened his mouth to agree and felt Ishat's fingers withdraw. Startled, he looked up. Her one good eye was open.

"Huy, what are you doing here?" she said, her voice thin but clear. "Gods, my hand hurts! So does breathing. And my eye!" She gingerly touched the swelling. "Did I take a fall?"

Thothmes ran to the couch and bent to kiss her. "You remember nothing, Ishat? Coming home through the Street of the Beer Houses? The foreigners who attacked you?"

She frowned and tried to sit up, then winced. "Ouch! I'm bruised, aren't I, my dearest? I remember coming home late and bidding Intef and the bearers a good night. I was tired, but I went to the nursery to make sure the children were all right, then I came here to my own quarters so as not to wake you."

Thothmes and Huy exchanged glances. *Atum has done all this,* Huy knew with certainty. *Were the foreigners inhuman, a host of Khatyu sent to chastise me by injuring Ishat? The attackers were not caught. They melted away into the night. They will never be caught, Ishat will recover completely and in perfect ignorance of the events that overtook her, and I have been horrendously warned to never again betray the creator.* Thothmes was gripping Ishat's hand and stroking her face, talking to her quietly.

Huy got to his feet. "I'll dictate later," he said to Thothhotep. "The vision was for me alone, and I must never forget it." He touched Thothmes on the shoulder. "I have an errand to run in the House of Life," he told him, "but I'll return for the evening meal. I promised to spend time with young Huy on my barge. Ishat, you are indomitable. You will heal quickly."

She smiled up at him faintly. "I'm appalled at what Thothmes has told me. Thank you, darling Huy, for the Seeing."

"I did nothing," he replied. "Make a sacrifice to Atum when you are well enough."

"I shall. Send me the children as you go. I want to see them."

Huy started for the door, Thothhotep behind him. *I did nothing,* he repeated soundlessly as he gained the passage. *I have no pain of my own because the canal that flows between god and petitioner is dry this time. No divine force streamed through me. My discipline is complete.*

The heat outside struck him forcibly and he began to sweat. He could see Anhur with the children clustered around him in the shade of a tree. "Your mother will be well!" he called to them as they saw him and scrambled up. "Go and see her! Anhur, get me the litter and bearers from the barge. And beer! Thothhotep, you had better come with me and take note of whatever I find at the temple." *I'm not even tired,* his thoughts ran on as he and his scribe waited above the watersteps. *I feel light and slightly dislocated from everything around me. The burden of my guilt has gone.*

He and Thothhotep drank thirstily before they got into the litter and the bearers set off along the river path. They rode in a familiar and companionable silence. The curtains remained open and gusts of hot air fluttered Thothhotep's linen against Huy's naked leg. "I don't tell you often enough how fond I am of you," he said to her abruptly. "You are efficient and intelligent and an essential member of the estate. Are you happy, Thothhotep? Do I allow you to go home to Nekheb often enough? Do you miss your sisters?"

She glanced across at him in surprise, plucked eyebrows lifting, dark eyes warm in their encircling kohl. She was wearing a pair of earrings he did not recognize, the centre of each a disc of moonstone held by petals of green faience. He supposed that Anhur had given them to her. She never wore rings; she had said that they interfered with the practice of her work. But often her thin upper arms were gripped by plain spiral bracelets engraved with her name. *She has remained too scrawny,* Huy thought with loving humour as she opened her mouth to reply. *When she came to us, Ishat was horrified at her physical state and we both tried to fatten her, but to little avail. She insists on keeping her hair short, an unflattering look for a very slender woman, but on her it is attractive. I must remember to give her more faience pins for it on her next Naming Day in Khoiak.*

"I write to them every month, Master," she said. "They're married now. I always send something for the public scribe who reads the letters as well. I'm very happy in your employ. My parents are in good health and do not need me. I lack for nothing, and if I may be permitted to say so, I admire you and I am proud to serve you." Her gaze strayed to Anhur, who had one hand on the roof of the litter and was pacing beside it.

You and Anhur should sign a marriage contract, he thought to himself. *Why don't you? I must ask Anhur when I think of it next.* For answer he patted her knee and fell to watching the brown, brittle stalks of parched river growth glide by.

Huy did not want the High Priest of Ra's House to know that he was within the holy precinct. He had no idea who had succeeded Ramose, his old guide and mentor, but he strongly suspected a complicity between this High Priest and the King's plans for his son Prince Thothmes. Leaving his bearers on the watered grass under the trees to either side of the god's domain, he, Thothhotep, and Anhur crossed the stone apron between the small lake where craft coming up Ra's entrance canal could moor and the pylon that signalled the outer court of the temple itself. Before reaching the pylon, Huy veered to the right. The House of Life lay within the shelter of the temple's surrounding wall, between the row of storerooms giving onto the outer court and the sheltering main wall itself. Huy had sometimes been sent there by one of his teachers to fetch a scroll needed for class study. He was familiar with the cool, musty rooms whose walls were closely and neatly pocked with niches, themselves crowded with rolls of papyrus. The sleepy guard on the door recognized him and waved him on, and just inside the doorway the archivist rose from his stool and came bustling forward.

"I am addressing the Great Seer, am I not?" he said, bowing. "I am Tehuti, Overseer of this House of Life. How may I serve you?"

Huy returned his bow. "I'm seeking the life and works of the mighty Imhotep. Having been a pupil here, I know that he was a High Priest of Ra."

Tehuti looked at him curiously. "Very little has survived from those far-off days. Papyrus will last a very long time if it is cared for properly, but stone makes a better surface on which to inscribe the events of the past." He tapped his chin. "We do have copies of most of the inscriptions on Imhotep's monuments, and I believe we also have a few, a very few, accounts of his deeds." He bent and swept up one of the small baskets on the floor near him. "If your scribe will accompany me," and here he looked doubtfully at Anhur, "I will collect what there is." He set off with Thothhotep at his heels.

"You can join the bearers outside if you like," Huy said to Anhur. "I may be here some time. I doubt if the archivist has any designs on ending my life."

Anhur did not respond to Huy's gentle teasing. "Huy, do you remember the old keeper of the House of Life at Thoth's temple in Khmun?" he asked. "You spent a lot of time with him. I liked him."

"Khanun. That was his name. I promised to send him a letter as soon as I had solved the riddle of the Book of Thoth. I wonder if he's still alive?" *Half of the Book is here somewhere, in one of these rooms,* his thoughts ran on silently. *I can feel it, holding its secrets to itself and yet reaching out to me. How familiar this place smells! I might be a student again, waiting to hurry back to the schoolroom carefully clutching some boring work of wisdom or advice with which to torment the class.* He smiled ruefully to himself and settled down to wait.

But the archivist knew his charge well. Presently he came striding back. Thothhotep was carrying the basket, now containing perhaps ten scrolls. "There are tables over here," Tehuti gestured. "Unless I can be of more assistance, I shall leave you to your reading. May Thoth guide your heart and your thoughts." Then he was gone.

Thothhotep carried the basket to one of the tables. Huy took the chair behind it. Anhur sank onto the floor, yawned, and put his back against the wall.

"Shall I read for you, Master?" Thothhotep asked.

Huy considered, wondering how much of the papyrus contained information couched in an Egyptian dialect so ancient that she would not be able to decipher it. "No," he decided. "I'll read, and dictate the facts I want to take home. Prepare your palette."

In the end, the information Huy found was disappointingly scant. Apart from designing the main temple to Hathor at Iunet in the south, Imhotep had been Vizier and Overseer of Works to the Osiris-King Djoser. In that capacity he had drawn up the plans for the Divine One's tomb, a pyramid of steps, and had supervised its construction. He was a devotee of Thoth and had been buried in the City of the Dead on the plateau across the river from Iunu with many beautified ibis birds and baboons, the creatures sacred to the god of wisdom and writing. He was an accomplished physician and was purported to have written a book of medicine, since lost. Apparently he had also written a book of spells, a few scrolls of which had survived as copies. Huy unrolled them eagerly. "These works are to be chanted aloud," he read. "The very quality of the sounds and the intonation of the sacred words contains within itself the force of the things said." There followed several incantations to be used for a variety of purposes. Huy laid those scrolls aside. Imhotep's sparse biography went on to say that he had written a wisdom text and that he had great skill in reading the ancient scrolls housed in the temple of Thoth at Khmun, where it was the habit of the scribes employed there to throw a little water on the ground in memory of their patron before they began to take dictation.

There was nothing else. All was much as Methen had related. Huy returned the scrolls to the basket for the archivist to put away, but he was not disappointed. Imhotep had studied the ancient works stored at Khmun. He had also been a High Priest of Ra. That he had read and pondered the Book of Thoth was almost a certainty. Could he have penned the commentary that had been included with each portion of the Book, the explanations of Atum's mystifying thoughts and actions that Huy had found helpful when he himself was attempting to understand them? Could the great man have resisted such a challenge? Huy did not think so. Nor did he believe that Imhotep would have dismissed the suspicion that the Book's final stage was either incomplete or missing. *He sought it,* Huy told himself with excitement as he bade Anhur find the archivist. *He sought, but did he find? And finding, did he recognize something so strange, perhaps even dangerous, that he chose to leave it where it was? What, then, should I do? Wait for Atum to lead me to it, or pursue it on my own? I have no idea where to begin, therefore I'll go home, continue to heal and scry, and hope that enlightenment may find me.*

The archivist had arrived and was bowing, his eyes going briefly to the basket to assure himself, Huy thought with a smile, that none of the scrolls had been damaged. "Is there nothing else pertaining to Osiris Imhotep stored here?" Huy wanted to know.

The man shook his head. "Nothing, Master. It's rumoured that Imhotep was also a High Priest of Ptah at some time in his illustrious life, but as far as I can ascertain, no written record of such an appointment exists."

Huy was tempted to ask if he might see the Book of Thoth and the commentary. He had a confused idea that simply by looking at the commentary's script, Imhotep would give him direction. But his good sense prevailed and, thanking the archivist, he and his companions left the temple precincts, Huy afraid that he would be recognized and delayed.

"Are we going home, then?" Anhur inquired as they approached the litter.

"No," Huy replied. "I want to eat with Thothmes and then spend the evening with little Huy, and in the morning we'll take the barge south to Mennofer. I need to talk to Heby."

He dictated what he had learned to Thothhotep before re-entering Thothmes' house, shared a cheerful meal with Thothmes and Ishat in her bedchamber, where she was sitting up and nursing her maimed hand while her husband did his best to feed her, and took young Huy into the cabin of his barge, listening carefully and with affection to the boy's unselfconscious conversation before sending him off to his couch.

He was still on his cot the following morning when his vessel turned obediently against the small, sullen tug of the current and the sail was unfurled to catch the strong north wind. No oars were necessary, and by the time the moon had reached its zenith the next night, they were tying up at Mennofer's communal watersteps.

13

HUY ATE HIS MORNING MEAL before ordering out the litter. By the time Heby's gate guard waved him through the high brick wall separating the house from the noisy maelstrom outside, a thin film of dust had insinuated itself onto his skin and settled on the litter's cushions, even though the curtains had been closed. Thothhotep fluffed at her hair and shook out the folds of her sheath before following him across the patchy grass and drooping trees to the welcome shade of the three little pillars fronting the house's entrance. A servant rose from his stool in the shade and welcomed Huy with a smile. "My Master is at work in the temple and will return at noon," he told Huy, "but my Mistress and your nephew are within. Let me tell them you are here."

It was not long before Iupia came hurrying from the dimness to greet him. Huy bowed to her as the daughter of a noble, then she embraced him warmly. "Heby will be so pleased to see you," she exclaimed as she ushered them inside and sent a servant scurrying for beer and honey cakes. "So will Amunhotep-Huy. He didn't go to school today. He has a cough. My father's physician has prescribed licorice and ground cumin seeds in honey for him, so I expect him to be better in a few days. How very hot it is! We all sleep on the roof. Heby has taken to watching for the rising of the

Sopdet star, but of course it's a little too soon. All of us long for the Inundation." She was shepherding them through the cramped entrance hall and into the reception room, where the only light came from two clerestory windows.

Huy, passing through one of the shafts of light, felt its heat fire his shoulder before he sank onto a chair and into the blessed coolness provided by the thick walls. *Heby's first wife, Sapet, was such a quiet young woman,* he thought as Iupia prattled on. *Iupia shows her breeding by her conversation. Raised in a home where other aristocrats were regularly entertained, she has learned to leave no awkward silences and to speak while saying nothing. Nevertheless, she has no arrogance, and she loves Heby for his many fine qualities. How odd that my disagreeable nephew should display none of the sensitivity of his dead mother or the grace of his father.*

The servant entered carrying a tray that he proceeded soundlessly to unload, placing the cakes on the table beside Iupia and pouring the beer. "Please go and tell my son that his uncle is here," Iupia ordered, and Huy's heart sank. "We're trying to decide whether or not to hire a tutor for him." Iupia offered the cakes. Thothhotep had settled herself cross-legged on the floor, the correct place for an inferior, her palette ready beside her. "He does very poorly at the temple school, but he simply must have an education. Heby thinks he needs a more stringent routine and a tighter control imposed on his behaviour, and naturally I can say nothing because I'm only his stepmother. Well, his disposition might improve with a brother to amuse. He'll be nine when my baby is born."

Huy had been listening with half an ear, but now he got up and took her hand, kissing her on both cheeks. "Iupia! That's wonderful news! Heby must be very happy!"

She laughed. "The birthing stool will claim me sometime towards the beginning of Athyr, only three months away. You did not notice, did you?" Standing, she pulled the front of her yellow sheath tight over her belly. Huy saw a slight bulge. "This child will be my first, therefore his presence is not very obvious."

"*His* presence?" Huy teased her. "You will have a boy?"

"But of course. The Purified of Ptah have predicted it. Heby consulted them."

"Do you want me to See for you, Iupia?"

She considered, her head on one side, kohled eyes raised. Huy thought that she was as beautiful in her way as Sapet had been, with the coronet of yellow faience flowers cutting across her fore-head and her golden scarab earrings half lost in the thick braids of her wig. There was an animation to her that had been absent in the delicate Sapet, a vitality that was not sexual but that had the power to attract.

"No, I don't think so," she replied. "I enjoy the surprises each day brings, even those deemed unlucky for me by my father's astrologer. Ah! Here's your nephew! Amunhotep-Huy, do rever-ence to your uncle."

The boy did look mildly ill. His complexion was pasty. As he came up to Huy and bowed, Huy could smell the cumin on his breath. "I'm sorry that you're not well, Amunhotep-Huy," Huy said kindly.

The boy grimaced. "My throat hurts when I cough, that's all. There is vehedu in the city's constant dust. Don't take that plate away, and bring me a cup!" he snapped at the servant, who had reappeared. The man sketched a bow and retreated. "Iupia, can I have the last cake?" She nodded. He scooped it up, flung himself into the chair next to Huy, and began to eat. "Father might have me taught at home, Uncle Huy," he said between mouthfuls. "I'd prefer that. The boys at school don't like me. Nor do the teachers."

Huy did not know what to say. He watched the cleft chin, a mark of stubbornness, move up and down as the boy chewed.

Iupia's own hennaed mouth was pursed. He was saved from the necessity of saying anything by Heby's arrival together with the servant, who set a fresh dish of cakes on the table, emptied the jug of beer into Amunhotep-Huy's cup, and took it away to be refilled. Coming to his feet, Huy hugged his grinning brother. Heby smelled of sweat, dust, and ink. He was barefoot, carrying his grimy sandals in one hand. "This is wonderful!" he breathed, then he sneezed. "Iupia has told you our news? Good! And you, my son, is your cough better today? And do you remember that a child should stand when an adult enters a room?"

Amunhotep-Huy slid off the chair with a scowl. "I am not much better, Father. May I sit again now?"

Heby sighed and waved him down. "I need some time in the bathhouse, and clean clothes. Will you stay for the night, Huy? What has brought you here? Are Hapu and Itu well?"

Huy nodded with a mild pang of guilt. He loved Heby and enjoyed Iupia's often amusing talk, but he disliked his nephew more each time he was forced to spend time in his sullen company, and so visited less than he should. "They remain in good health," he said. "I'd like to stay, but I'll sleep on the barge so that I can start for home early tomorrow. May I join you in the bathhouse?"

Heby's property was larger at the rear than in the front, and his bathhouse well appointed. Together, he and Huy stood on the bathing slabs to be scrubbed and, later, lay side by side in the shade just outside, to be oiled and massaged. Huy told his brother what had happened to Ishat. "Her wounds are not serious," he finished. "Mostly cuts and bruises, and of course it will take some months for her hair to grow back." He hesitated. Heby was lying on his stomach, his chin resting on his arms, his expression full of the question Huy knew he would not ask. "Yes, I scryed for her," he went on, "but what I Saw had everything to do with me, Heby."

Under his brother's even gaze, he unburdened himself of everything. Heby, like Methen, was a good listener. Before the full story was told, the bath servants had picked up the pots of fragrant oils and withdrawn. The men sat side by side, their brown nakedness gleaming. Huy's unbound hair now fell almost to his waist. Heby had also kept his hair, but cut level with his chin. Anyone watching them would have recognized the kinship between them, two handsome brothers with strong features and lean bodies at the height of a vigorous maturity. The watcher, however, would have been unable to decide who was the younger. Heads turned to one another, elegant hands gesticulating as they talked, they seemed to embody the health and intelligence of Egypt's finest sons.

Heby shook his head. "Imhotep may have been a High Priest of Ra," he was saying, "and he definitely served Ptah as a priest, but our archives hold no other information about him at all. Several books of spells attributed to him are here, but they're copies of the originals at Iunu." He stood and stretched. "I think it entirely possible that he knew the Book as thoroughly as you do, and if it is incomplete, that he found the rest of it. How else could he still be venerated as a great magician and Seer? If his reputation rested solely on his facility in designing tombs and monuments, he would now be nothing more than a name with which to torture students. You don't choose to become a Seer, Huy; the gods choose for you, as you are well aware! Come to my room and borrow one of my kilts while yours is being washed."

"If I were you," he continued as Huy followed him into the house, "I'd assume that Atum assigns no task to his creatures that they cannot ultimately perform. Imhotep helped to shape the Egypt of yesterday. It's your destiny to shape this age using the same gifts and tools Imhotep had." He was climbing the stairs as he spoke, with Huy behind him, his voice slightly muffled. "All you have to do is go home, keep doing the will of the god, and let the future unfold around you."

They had reached Heby's bedchamber. Huy, watching him riffle through the contents of one of his tiring chests, felt a wave of relief. *My own conclusion has been confirmed. I must stop peering ahead and learn to value the present, even though fully half the petitioners who find their way into my garden come to learn what the future holds for them. My future, like that of Imhotep before me, is already set. May I compare myself to him? Perhaps. After all, it was Imhotep who greeted me in the Beautiful West and offered me a chance to decipher the Book of Thoth. Did Imhotep ever fail his god?*

"Here, tie this around you." Heby tossed him a white kilt. "You needn't bother with anything else, we have no guests tonight. Prahotep!" After a few moments his steward entered, and seeing Huy, he smiled and bowed to him. "Huy's grubby kilt is in the bathhouse. Have it washed. And set another table, will you?" Prahotep left. Heby yawned. "I expect that Iupia is already on her couch. Take the guest room for the afternoon sleep, Huy. Prahotep can find a mattress for Thothhotep, and Anhur doesn't mind snoring under a tree. The Chief Priest and I spent the whole morning tallying the harvests from Ptah's various holdings. I love my work, but sometimes it can be very boring."

Huy's sleep was dreamless and he woke to the sense of peace and security he always felt in Heby's house. It was as though Heby was the older brother, Huy often reflected, protecting him and offering practical, down-to-earth advice when necessary. Heby was not in the least awed by Huy's unique gift. He respected it, loved and tolerated Huy as his blood kin, and treated him without a hint of adulation.

Huy's own kilt and cleaned sandals had been left just inside the door. Putting them on, he went downstairs.

By the time he folded himself behind his little table, with Thothhotep and Anhur seated behind him and Heby, Iupia, and his nephew close by, he was hungry. The sunset was always lingering at this time of the year, and although the hour was late, the reception room held pinkish shafts of light in which tiny dust motes hung suspended. There was no evening breeze to give an illusion of coolness. Although she kept up a stream of lively talk, Iupia only picked at her food, but both Huy and Heby ate heartily. Amunhotep-Huy stayed mercifully silent, coughing occasionally and clearing his dishes but offering no contribution to the general conversation. He gave no argument when Heby bade him good night and sent him to his room with a nursery servant. He merely bowed to the company and retreated.

Iupia sighed. "He's so unhappy. We simply don't know what to do with him, do we, Heby?"

"The Division of Ptah has permanent barracks here, just to the west of the Peru-nefer docks." Heby was not looking at his wife, his gaze resolutely fixed on something just above Huy's head. "It's almost never at full strength. The soldiers take turns to go on leave, patrol the borders, conduct training manoeuvres out beyond the City of the Dead to the west. Iupia's father, Merira, knows almost everyone at court through his position as Assistant Treasurer. I've been thinking of asking him to inquire of Commander Wesersatet whether there's an officer who would take Amunhotep-Huy in the afternoons when school is over, give him lessons with the bow, teach him to wrestle. A soldier's discipline might be good for him."

"He's only eight!" Iupia protested. "He's too young, Heby. He could get hurt." Her response had been immediate, and Huy realized that this was an old argument between the two of them, its formula rigidly set.

"Well, perhaps with a genuine scrape or two his whining over imaginary injuries would stop. How old were you when you began military training at school, Huy?"

Huy was saved from answering by Anhur, who had stirred and cleared his throat. "I know Wesersatet well, Master," he interposed. "Before Huy petitioned for my transfer into his employ, I was assigned to guard the King under the Supreme Commander. He was just a Commander of the Army then. He's a good man. He'd find someone suitable for your son."

Heby reached for his wife's stiff fingers. "We've tried everything else but a tutor, Iupia," he said softly. "He's so disruptive that the temple school is most reluctant to take him back. Huy wanted to See for him, but I refused. I was afraid of what would be in store for such a … a …"

"A Setian one?" Iupia looked to be on the verge of tears. "I did not give birth to him, Heby, but I ache for him all the same."

"You spoil him. Your guilt gives him whatever he wants." Heby turned to Anhur. "I shall speak to my father-in-law and I'd be grateful if you would approach the Supreme Commander on my behalf. Somewhere there's an answer for Amunhotep-Huy. What do you think?" His gaze had gone to Huy.

"I think it's a good solution," Huy agreed. "I'm sorry, Iupia."

She shrugged. "Will he still love us?" Her question had no answer, and after a moment she left her cushion, took a formal leave of Huy, who would be gone at dawn, and left the hall with her body servant trailing after her.

"The boy would have destroyed my gentle Sapet by now," Heby said grimly. "For all her distress, Iupia is stronger. I worry about her because of her state." He got up. "I'm sorry, Huy, but I must go to her. Anhur, send me a reply from Wesersatet as soon as possible. Do you want the lamps lit?" Prahotep and the servants were waiting, and Huy realized that at last full darkness had fallen.

"No. We'll go back to the barge at once." He stood and embraced Heby. "Thank you for your advice. You're such a comfort to me, Heby. Write to me about my nephew and Iupia's health and your own well-being. I don't expect to be tying up at Mennofer again for some time."

The street was more crowded but less noisy than it had been when Huy arrived at Heby's house. The citizens of Mennofer strolled aimlessly, enjoying the coolness the night had brought, and Huy left the curtains of the litter open as he and Thothhotep, with Anhur beside them, were carried back to the watersteps, which were even more crowded than the dusty streets. People sat chatting in groups, milled about above the steps to finger the cheap wares displayed by the stall keepers, and stood to watch a trio of dancers who were dipping and twirling to the high-pitched music of a lone flute. Craft were jostling against each other at the moorings, their sailors sitting drinking beer on the steps or dozing splayed out on the still-warm stone.

"Tell the captain to round up my rowers and get the barge out of this mess," Huy told Anhur as the litter was lowered. "He can tie up somewhere out of sound of the city. Thothhotep, you can sleep on the floor of the cabin if you like. Tell Iny to drag your pallet inside. And tell Tetiankh I want poppy as soon as he can prepare it." He had done without the dose he habitually took in the middle of the day. He was perfectly aware that his mounting irritation, the itchiness of his skin, his slight nausea, had their source in his craving. Crossing the ramp past his two guards, he went into the cabin. He had begun to sweat. Tetiankh had changed the linen on his travelling cot while he had been gone, and a lamp sent out an inviting glow from the small collapsible table. The air in the small space was still hot. Tetiankh bowed his way in, closed the door behind him, and proffered the vial. Huy downed the contents at once. *He had it ready for me*, he thought as the drug began to soothe him and the servant began to take off his clothes. *He has become so efficient that most of the time I am unaware of his presence.*

"The water for your washing is not hot, Master," Tetiankh apologized. "I could find no space close enough to the barge to light a fire and heat it. I think that the whole city lives on the watersteps at night now that Mesore has ended."

Today is the fifth of Thoth, Huy thought. *A new year has begun.*

"I don't care to be washed tonight," he said aloud. "Bring me water to drink. That's all I'll need until the morning." He drowsed, vaguely aware of Thothhotep settling herself on her pallet just inside the doorway, and by the time the barge had shaken itself free of its cramped mooring and was turning its prow to the north, he was asleep.

Mindful of his new resolution, he did his best to concentrate his mind on the present. In the weeks that followed, he diagnosed, prescribed, and scryed for the people who continued to cluster hopefully outside his gate. At the end of the month a letter arrived from Amunnefer, who reported a bountiful crop of poppy from his and Huy's fields and a continued improvement in Anuket's health and behaviour. The news was an invitation to dip into his memories, but true to his resolve, he denied the whispers. Nor did he allow himself to ponder the worrisome contrast between what he had seen when he took Anuket's hand, her unexpected decision to amend her behaviour, and Ishat's brush with violence. He knew that the answers were beyond him. Seshemnefer arrived at the estate in person to proudly list the weight and amount of the harvests from Huy's arouras. At the same time Merenra made an accounting of the latest gift of gold from the palace. For years it had arrived punctually in spite of Huy's growing wealth from his own holdings, but now Huy listened to the news of its arrival with a sense of shame. *It has become a bribe, a payment for my collusion,* he thought as his steward bowed himself out of the office. *I should send a request to the King to direct it elsewhere, but then he would fear that I was about to change my pronouncement regarding the Prince Thothmes' so-called dream.*

Anhur had wasted no time in approaching Wesersatet regarding Huy's nephew, and the Commander had cheerfully arranged for Amunhotep-Huy to be taken under the wing of one of his officers. A short letter from Heby let Huy know that a tutor had been engaged to fill the boy's mornings, and in the afternoons he was escorted to the army's barracks. "The tutor will be a drain upon my modest resources," Heby had written, "and I will not approach Iupia's father for assistance, seeing that Amunhotep-Huy is not her son. I know that, if I need to, I may ask you for help without shame, but I will not do so unless it becomes entirely necessary." *There's that word again,* Huy thought, his eyes leaving Heby's neat professional hieratic script for a moment. *Shame.* Pushing the reflection away, he continued to read:

> Amunhotep-Huy goes to the barracks after the sleep. Soldiers can be rough and crude, as you know, and Iupia and I were concerned that the boy might learn unaccept-able language and behaviour, but he is in the care of a fine man who conducts his lessons in wrestling, target practice, and the care and maintenance of weapons well away from the army's main billets. Amunhotep-Huy comes home bruised and filthy, but so far his complaints have been surprisingly few. Even his academic work is improving. Iupia continues in good health. I have included a bag of Mennofer's famous pistachio nuts for you to enjoy. I love

you. Your brother Heby, Chief Scribe in the temple of Ptah, by my own hand, this tenth day of the month of Thoth, year twenty-four of the King.

Huy laid the scroll on his desk with a word to Thothhotep, sitting cross-legged at his feet, to file it away in the niche reserved for family correspondence.

The river had begun to rise. Far away in the south, Isis was crying, and with her tears came an intensifying heat and an annoying eruption of fly and mosquito life. The month of Thoth also brought five gods' feast days when no one worked and the celebrations of gratitude and relief at the prospect of yet another year of bounty continued. The flood of those seeking healing or counsel from Huy always dwindled to a trickle as the whole of Egypt gave itself over to the rites of worship. So he was surprised and alarmed to find a scroll without an identifying imprint waiting for him when he returned from his duty to Khenti-kheti's shrine and a short visit with Methen. Thothhotep had been waiting for him in his office. She handed it to him.

"It was delivered by a man dressed in the coarse linen of a peasant," she told him, "but his hands were soft and his body obviously shaved and oiled. His accent was refined. Kar would not let him through the gate and Merenra has of course joined his family to celebrate the Uaga Feast, so I was sent for. The man knew who I was. He was very polite but refused to give me his name. 'You and your master will see me again,' he said. 'It is better that I remain anonymous to you both. No reply is expected to this message. Long life and health to you and the Great Seer.' He went away along the river path."

Instead of going to the floor with her palette, she continued to stand while a frowning Huy turned the papyrus cylinder over and over. He had been thirsty by the time he alighted from his litter

in the shade of the house's entrance pillars, but now he ignored
the twin flagons of water and beer Ankhesenpepi had left for him
on the desk.

"It may be from Prince Amunhotep in Mitanni," she added.

Huy was about to rebuke her for the obvious curiosity in the
words. Instead, he cracked the seal and went to perch on the
edge of the desk. "Take the stool, Thothhotep," he said. "It's too
hot to stand." He unrolled the scroll as she obeyed. The characters that met his eye were uneven, some large, some awkwardly
tiny. The lines of hieratic sloped down then up. The spelling was
poor. Glancing to the end of the letter, he exclaimed in astonishment. "It is from the Princess Mutemwia, by her own hand!
No wonder it resembles the scrawls of a young schoolboy.
How many women apart from you and Ishat do you know who
can even read, let alone write! I am impressed." He began to
read aloud.

To the Great Seer Huy, greetings. I believe that you will
want to be made aware of the things of which I write. If
not, I beseech you to at least keep your own counsel.
Firstly, my friend is well and enjoying her visit in foreign
lands. Secondly, the god Harmachis-Khepera-Ra-Temu has
now been completely freed of his prison of sand. His
Majesty has begun to build a temple dedicated to the god.
He has set up a stela to honour the mighty Osiris-Kings
Khufu and Khafra, whose bodies rest in their tombs behind
the god. On the stela he has caused to be inscribed a peculiar likeness of a disc adorned with half of the royal uraeus,
the cobra Lady of Flame of Lower Egypt. The vulture Lady
of Dread of the south of Egypt is not there. The disc has
arms ending in small hands holding ankhs. Thus this disc
is bestowing life as "lord of what the Aten encircles." I pray

daily to Amun for your protection. My son does well. I will not forget how you and he reached out for one another. Princess Mutemwia by her very own hand, this fourteenth day of the month of Thoth, year twenty-four of the King.

Huy's thirst had suddenly returned. Letting the scroll roll closed, he poured water for himself and Thothhotep, passed her a cup, and drank in large gulps.

For a long time both of them were silent. The room filled with the sound of the leaves beyond the window aperture rustling together as they were stirred by the breeze. An unintelligible blend of voices and the rattle of cutlery against metal drifting from the reception hall meant that the noon meal was about to be served. At last Thothhotep spoke. "The things the Princess says, the nameless servant who delivered the letter, the fact that she penned it herself—all of it points to secrecy, doesn't it, Master?"

"Yes." In spite of the water, Huy was still thirsty. "Do you understand why, Thothhotep?"

"About the friend in foreign lands I do. Prince Amunhotep has settled into his exile and is safe. As for the rest, I'm not sure."

Huy regarded her thoughtfully. "When I first met you in the marketplace, you were proud and spoke your mind without fear," he said with seeming irrelevancy. "Since then you have become more cautious, more circumspect. You accomplish your tasks with efficiency, but the outspokenness, the pride, are they still there, Thothhotep? Are you perhaps a little afraid of me, even after all these years in my employ? There is sometimes an awkwardness between us where, because of your position, there should be complete harmony. You know all my affairs. I am vulnerable before you, and never more so than today, with the contents of this letter waiting to be explained to you. I need you to understand it all.

But you must either tell me what walls you off from me or make it clear that you want to proceed no further than scribing for my businesses and for the petitioners who dog my days."

She had listened to him with an increasing agitation, her hands gripping each other, her features falling into an expression of deep distress. Jumping up from the stool, she began to pace, the empty cup clutched against her small white-clad breasts, until he had finished speaking. Then she halted in front of him. "A good scribe is self-effacing," she burst out at once. "He takes the dictation. He remembers the contents of his master's correspondence and must be ready to bring it to mind when asked to do so. He must copy and file. He must be tactful and sometimes invisible. All these things I have tried to be! And I have succeeded. But I am fully aware that I can never be to you what the Lady Ishat was. Friend, counsellor, confidante—these are far outside the limits of a scribe's responsibilities. I did not want to be compared to her and found wanting! I did not want your private thoughts of me to be scornful. I do not want ... do not need ..." She faltered and her gaze dropped. "I do not want you to ever see me as Ishat's poor imitation."

Huy did not move. "That is the twisted pride preventing me from indeed seeing you as confidante and friend," he said heavily. "That is the wall. I want more from you than a scribe's diligence, Thothhotep. You've known from the start that this is no ordinary household. You are an intelligent woman. I desperately need that intelligence, all of it, at my disposal, even if sometimes it clashes with my own." He slid off the desk. "Sometimes you must walk behind me. So did Ishat. But at other times I want you next to me, I need to be able to unburden myself to you, I want to trust you to expand the concept you hold of your responsibilities to me. Would you like to tell me what you know about the contents of the Princess's letter? Think hard about it before you say yes, for if you do, our relationship will change."

"You are asking me to be one of your counsellors," she said slowly, "but you are also asking me if I will take the risk of sharing knowledge with you that might become dangerous in the future." Now she faced him squarely. "I have almost forgotten what danger is like. It has been many years since I washed my one sheath in the river every evening and put it on every morning so that I could sit in some marketplace and hope for a commission. But the peril you speak of has little to do with physical hazard. I saw your distress when you returned from your audience with the King." She placed the cup on the desk with careful deliberation and folded her arms. "I asked you nothing. If you had wanted me to know what had happened, you would have told me. As your scribe, it was not my place to pry." She smiled faintly. "And you are fortunate in your servants, Master. They do not gossip. When Anhur and I talk together, we do not discuss the state of your mind or heart."

"I have never paused to compare your competency with Ishat's," Huy replied. "Your strengths are different. I did not try to engage another Ishat when I tested you in the marketplace. I was simply looking for a good scribe who could adapt to the moods and routines of this house. Now I need more from you, so I will ask you again: shall I keep this matter to myself?"

"No." Gathering up the folds of her sheath, she regained the stool. "I keep the secrets of your visions. You must know by now that I am trustworthy. What is happening to the King?"

Huy considered her for a moment. Her body had relaxed and she met his eyes calmly. Her question had been shrewd. Quickly he told her of Amunhotep's growing preference for the god of the sun in his various aspects, his open dislike for Amun's priests, the warning Atum gave him through Huy himself a long time ago. He spoke honestly of his own great failure.

"I fear that the King is preparing to announce Prince Thothmes as his official heir, but that is only a small portion of what he can do," he finished. "He can declare Ra as Egypt's pre-eminent deity. He can impoverish Ipet-isut by deciding to tax Amun's temple there. He can dismiss Amun's priests in favour of his own choices. The temple to Ra as the god of the horizon personified in the great stone lion, the stela glorifying the Aten—these things are only the beginning."

"He will increasingly give preference to the Delta, to Ta-Mehu? You believe that such a policy will eventually divide Egypt?"

Huy nodded. "Ma'at will become unbalanced. The Princess Mutemwia, as a wife of Thothmes and a great friend of his elder brother, is already very afraid. She herself has no influence. Her son Prince Amunhotep is not in direct line for the Horus Throne any more than Pharaoh's second son Thothmes is. But Mutemwia obviously remembers the great storm of gold dust I Saw enveloping Amunhotep and me when I encountered her by accident in the palace and the little Prince's fingers closed around my own. I think she believes that the Seeing has much to do with her child's future inheritance. Thothmes' son Amunemhat by his Chief Wife Neferatiri is still a baby, but if Thothmes inherits the Horus Throne, Amunemhat will be the Hawk-in-the-Nest. Mutemwia's child will then be too close to godhead for comfort. The threat of his elimination becomes all too real."

"And Prince Thothmes will make sure that Amunemhat is raised to venerate Ra over every other god. He will also seek to keep the rightful heir out of Egypt. Or have him assassinated," Thothhotep added. She was about to speak again but hesitated. Huy prompted her gently. "It seems to me that the Princess Mutemwia is making you her accomplice," she went on hurriedly, the colour of embarrassment flooding her cheeks. "She intends to keep you secretly informed on these matters, hoping that you may be able to avert disaster, or at least divert it in some way, with your gift." She spread her hands. "How, I cannot imagine. Am I right, Master?"

The weight of her words, the outward expression of his own thoughts, settled around Huy's heart. "I am afraid so," he agreed. "Her trust is a great compliment, but it is also a great threat. There's no need to send her any reply to this letter." He touched it briefly. "All we can do is wait for matters at court to unfold. You do realize that if the King or Prince Thothmes discovers her correspondence to me and they are indeed plotting murder, she might very well be interrogated. I can imagine the questions now. 'Highness, His Majesty and your husband Prince Thothmes are concerned for you. Are you ill, that you must write to the Seer so frequently?' Or worse: 'Highness, the King suspects the Seer of distrusting the holy dream sent to your husband by the god buried in the desert. I am instructed to read his letters to you so that the King may confound any blasphemy against the god or your husband they may contain.' Either one of them, King or Prince, could ruin me." He laughed without humour. "That prospect filled me with terror when I stood before Amunhotep. It made me weak. Now I face the same outcome because the Princess Mutemwia has decided to make me her accomplice. I wonder if Atum and Anubis are smiling." Bending, he smoothed down Thothhotep's cap of shining hair in a rush of protectiveness. "We understand one another now, don't we, Thothhotep?" he said quietly.

Taking his hand, she kissed it respectfully and stood. "We do," she answered. "I am grateful to be in your employ, Great Seer, but I am more thankful to be in your confidence."

"Good! Then come on the river with me this evening. Its level is still low, but the water birds will be finding many juicy morsels in the mud. I like to watch them when I can. Anhur will of course accompany us."

"Master, it is not necessary—"

Huy cut her off. "My reliance on Anhur may increase as the weeks pass," he said brusquely. "As the captain of my bodyguard, I should perhaps tell him a little of what we have discussed today. He goes wherever I go, Thothhotep. It has nothing to do with you!" His grin took the sting out of his words.

She grimaced. "I have fallen into the habit of apologetic self-effacement and you are right, Master, it does not suit me, and I am sorry for it." She picked up the Princess's scroll. "I think I should keep this and any future correspondence from Mutemwia away from the office. The bottom of my tiring chest will do admirably."

Huy did not protest. "You and Anhur should sign a marriage contract," he said as she was walking to the door. "I would be generous if you did, and besides, that way I would have no fear of losing either of you!"

"Anhur has told me that he will never leave you," she answered without turning around. "As for me, it would be very hard to train another scribe to take my place, and besides, the work here is always interesting!"

That's the Thothhotep I encountered in Hut-herib's ramshackle marketplace, he thought, the enforced grin fading from his face. *I believe I am right to trust her now, and perhaps Anhur also, although his solution to every problem is always a practical one. This is one danger I must not share with either Thothmes or Ishat. Thothmes is incapable of dissembling. His duties take him to the palace too often, and the King is not a fool. And although Ishat would understand everything and keep her counsel from her husband, it would be unfair of me to ask her to do so. This is something Thothhotep and I will face together. We have made a promising beginning today. I feel less alone.* He continued to stand leaning against his desk and frowning into the hot dimness of the room.

After the last meal of the day, Huy ordered out his boat and he, Anhur, and Thothhotep spent the long hours of sunset drifting slowly north on the current. The helmsman had little to do but keep the vessel away from the exposed shoals and sandbanks that would soon disappear under the flood water. Crested egrets and white ibis, their feathers tinged pink by the last slanting rays of soft light, stalked through the mud on slender legs half hidden by thick mats of reeds that stirred stiffly as the boat's sluggish wake reached them. Often Huy noticed field flowers or a carefully woven wreath that had been cast into the river as an offering to Hapi and had floated towards the Great Green only to be snared by the straggling growth invading the edge of the water. Fleetingly he was reminded of all the times when he had stood with Thothmes, Anuket, and the rest of Nakht's family, one of the bouquets Anuket had so carefully crafted in his arms, the aroma of the blooms filling his nostrils as he waited to toss them into Hapi's domain. *I must not confide in Heby anymore either*, his thoughts ran on, still occupied with the time spent in his office with his scribe. *Those I love must be able to truthfully deny any knowledge of the letters if necessary. How much should I tell Anhur? Will I need to be guarded more closely? Should I begin to have Merenra or Tetiankh taste my food and drink? Would Amunhotep dare to murder a Seer? I wish you were still alive, Henenu, with your clicking cowrie shells and your wand and your brisk, cogent advice. I wear the amulets you made for me on my fingers and the sa you crafted for my protection around my neck, but will these things blunt the blade of a dagger or render a poison as harmless as milk? Did Mutemwia consider the danger to me and mine when she chose to make me her collaborator?* Deliberately he turned his face to the dying sun, now spreading a pool of blood between the trunks of the trees on the western shore as Nut began to swallow it.

"So beautiful," Thothhotep breathed beside him.

Anhur stirred. "Beautiful, yes, but we should get the rowers seated and start back upriver soon. The helmsman can't navigate in the dark at this time of the year," he remarked.

Huy gave the command. The oars were run out and ponderously the barge began to swing towards the south. By the time the sailors brought it bumping gently against Huy's watersteps, dusk had fallen. The ramp was run out. Huy was the first to disembark. Climbing the steps, he had passed through his open gate, greeting Kar as he went, and had started along the short path to the house when a furtive movement low down in the bushes to his right brought him to a halt. *No, no,* he thought frantically, his heart suddenly pounding. *It can't be!* The other two had come up behind him.

"What is it, Huy?" Anhur growled. "What's wrong?"

Wordlessly, Huy pointed. A hyena had emerged from the gathering shadows. Seeing the group, it paused in the ugly half-crouch Huy had begun to loathe, and it seemed to be staring directly at him. "I told you to get rid of it!" Huy croaked. "It's come back, Anhur! I thought that your men sold it in the market!"

"They did," Anhur replied easily. "I expect it escaped and remembered the good feeding here, especially now, with mice trying to get into the granaries. I'll fetch a guard or two and we'll kill it this time."

"No." Huy found that he was trembling. "Trap it and have it taken well out into the desert this time. Its death here on the estate would be a very bad omen for me." He could have sworn that at the sound of his voice the creature's ears had pricked higher, as though it were listening.

Anhur took a step, and at his movement the beast started for the gate at a shambling pace. Kar had already closed it, but the hyena became fluid, flowing under it and disappearing even as one of the guards stationed just beyond the gate aimed a kick at its indistinct shape.

Anhur glanced at Huy quizzically. "You really hate them, don't you? I can have the garden scoured for them every evening if you like." His tone was offhand.

Huy shook his head. "It's a warning and a reminder to me," he said. His voice was still unsteady. "I think I'll be seeing it often in the future." He felt both pairs of eyes on him as he resumed his pace and, reaching the house, he bade them an abrupt good night and left them.

14

IN THE FOLLOWING MONTH of Paophi, on the ninth, Huy celebrated his thirty-ninth Naming Day. The river had continued to rise, and with it the annual irritation of flies and mosquitoes, their presence adding a further annoyance to the increasing heat. As usual during the Inundation, Huy dealt with an increase of fevers that required him and Thothhotep to spend much time venturing into Hut-herib itself. The river road would remain accessible only for perhaps another month, and Huy, hot, tired, and in constant pain, eagerly awaited its flooding. But it was the pleading of distraught parents begging him to return their drowned children to life that most distressed him. Every year it was the same. Youngsters who had played safely and happily in the shallows were caught unawares by water that had become deeper. Few of them could swim. Huy, entering the small, dark homes of the town's ordinary citizens to be faced with pallid corpses and weeping women whose eyes filled with hope when they saw him, was forced to explain that he was unable to raise the dead. Often he could feel the unspoken accusation: "The gods gave your life back to you, Son of Hapu. Why are you so favoured when my little one's breath has fled?" To that he had no answer. In spite of the truth the whole town knew by now, there were always those who believed that the fate of their children must be different.

Iupia gave birth to a lusty boy on the first day of the month of Athyr, the last day of the festival of Hapi. The river was reaching for its highest point, the flood was ample, and the fierce heat had begun to abate. "He is to be called Ramose," Heby had written in a letter that took longer than usual to arrive at Huy's estate as it had to be carried along the edge of the vast, placid lake which Egypt had become.

> Iupia is very well and so is the baby. Amunhotep-Huy ignores him, but this does not worry us. Your older nephew has thrown himself completely into his training with Irem, the officer in charge of him, and if he becomes rude or disobedient, all I have to do to compel his obedience is threaten to withdraw him from the barracks and make him study with his tutor in the afternoons as well as the mornings. There are rumours abroad that our Governor might appoint me Mayor of Mennofer, a position that must of course be approved by the King. I don't know why or how my name appeared as a replacement for Nebamun, who has been sent south to Weset as Overseer of the Desert. The position would mean that I would have to relinquish my post as Chief Scribe for Ptah, but our circumstances would improve. I pray to Ptah and try not to daydream too much!

"Heby is well known among the priests and administrators of the temples in Mennofer," Huy had mused to Thothhotep as she walked to one of the niches in the wall of the office and laid the scroll with all the others from Huy's brother. "But outside that august community, he is anonymous. Few are even aware that he's my kin, and the thought of our parents having any influence with the Governor of Mennofer's sepat is just ridiculous. Nor is Heby ambitious enough to petition for the post of Mayor himself. He's never asked me to speak on his behalf for any preferment."

"Perhaps Iupia's father as Assistant Treasurer to the King is so pleased with his new grandson that he wants more recognition for his daughter's husband," Thothhotep ventured, coming back to the desk and picking up her palette. "Will you dictate a reply to Heby at once, Huy?" She was smiling at him. In the last few months Huy had seen the pride and confidence that had impressed him at their first encounter begin to return, and he had rejoiced at their increasing closeness, but now he was frowning into the distance, oblivious to her expression.

"I don't think that this is Merira's work," he replied slowly. "He has never pushed Heby to seek advancement. Nor has he ever seemed ashamed of Iupia's choice for a husband."

"The King, then?"

Huy laughed grimly. "I doubt it. Amunhotep has no interest in my family and he has already rewarded me with gold for my public confirmation of Prince Thothmes' so-called dream. No, dear scribe, I see the Princess Mutemwia's hand in this. She is deliberately befriending me and has now begun to groom my brother for a future that so far only she can imagine. How many scrolls have we received from her in the last three months?"

"Four. According to her, the King and Prince Thothmes have begun to make regular offerings to the god Ra-Harmachis now that his body is free of all sand, and a wall has been erected around him to prevent further subsidence. The stela is finished and has been set up. Work on the temple continues. Her little son thrives. The Prince in Mitanni is well."

"But His Majesty is not. Didn't the Princess mention that Amunhotep has been suffering from shortness of breath and occasional weakness in his limbs?" They stared at one another for a moment. "A change is coming." Huy spoke into the cool peace of the room. "I can feel it sometimes as an inner flutter." He blew out his lips. "Meanwhile, I shall dictate to Heby and tell him that I'll be with him for his Naming Day on the twenty-first of Mekhir, almost three months from now. By then all the crops will be in the ground and beginning to sprout. It should be a pleasant jaunt. I must take a gift for baby Ramose." *Mutemwia has not asked me for a Seeing on her own behalf,* Huy thought as the words to his brother rolled off his tongue. *For one so young, she brings a formidable intellect to bear on the invisible current of desires, ambitions, and machinations flowing through the King's court, and arrives at her own conclusions regarding them. She is confident enough in her deductions to use them as a basis for her own plans, and it is clear that those plans include me. Am I to be a playing piece or a partner?*

Absently, he signed the curled papyrus Thothhotep was holding up to him and left her to arrange for its delivery while he began to wander around his garden. The flood was still high but had begun imperceptibly to recede. The canal feeding life to his glistening soil was full, and soon the dike holding the water it contained would be rebuilt. Anab and his assistant were busy seeding the flowers and vegetables that would make a small paradise of his holdings, their bent brown backs happily exposed to a kind sun. Word had come from Amunnefer regarding his plans for the poppy fields once the river had regained its banks. A new incense caravan had left Egypt the week previously. Seshemnefer's report on the house and land Huy had inherited from the Rekhet was more than satisfactory. *All is well,* Huy told himself as he rounded the rear of his two conical silos and started back towards the house. *Even Anuket is holding her own. Then why am I so restless?*

Athyr ended and Khoiak began, then Tybi. As usual, Thothhotep was careful to observe every god's day during the month of Tybi, and Huy, out of the worrisome sense of something impending, took to accompanying her to Hut-herib's shrines and temples so that his mind might be temporarily occupied. Petitioners were beginning to congregate outside his walls as the river path, muddy and slippery, became visible once more. Obedient to his gift, he dealt with them dutifully, the ensuing headaches either mild or debilitating, depending on the length and clarity of his visions. He gladly entertained Methen. He visited his parents, and on the nineteenth of Mekhir he ushered them aboard his barge for the journey south to Mennofer to mark Heby's twenty-eighth Naming Day, on the twenty-first. His new nephew, Ramose, was thriving, and both Heby and Iupia were in fine health. Two months later, Heby was declared the Mayor of Mennofer and his letters to Huy became long missives dictated to his new scribe, Nanai, regarding the challenges and intricacies of the position. Huy sent congratulations.

The season of Shemu began with the month of Pakhons. The sun became gradually less kind as the crops attained their full height and began to turn from a lush green to the first tinges of beige. Thothhotep went home to Nekheb to visit her family, her absence adding to the ongoing feeling of vague uneasiness that had dogged Huy now through the four months of Peret and into Shemu. Mutemwia's letters seemed to mirror his own mood. They were polite, short, and contained no new information. It seemed that Egypt was continuing to enjoy the state of peaceful changelessness every citizen valued.

Huy moved routinely through the days, and at night, after taking his poppy, he allowed the Book of Thoth to unroll through his mind while he lay on the roof under a blaze of summer stars. The harvest began. The air became full of dust motes as the labourers threshed and winnowed the grain. In the orchards, the fruit hung heavy on the laden boughs, ready to drop into waiting baskets. The grapes were trodden, the rich purple or golden liquid pouring into the jars full of promise. The perfume distilleries exuded such a heavy aroma that passersby could not bear it and drew their linen over their noses. Thothhotep returned from the south exhausted but happy, retiring to her quarters at once so that Iny could cut her hair and begin to repair the damage done to her hands and feet by the harsh, dry southern climate. "I ran about barefoot and unpainted the whole time I was there," she told an amused Huy. "It would have been pointless to take Iny with me. My cousin, the one who wanted me to marry him, has finally married one of my sisters after all this time. They seem well suited to one another. My parents liked the gifts I took for them. I did enjoy myself, Huy, but I'm glad to be home again. Is there anything needing my attention? If not, I would like to see Anhur."

I used to find these months appealing, even though they are hot, Huy thought as he watched her stride away. *There's a sense of the eternal about them in spite of the activities of the harvest. The days are long, the twilight lingers, time seems to be removed from our awareness. But this year the timelessness is simply bringing my internal agitation to the fore. It is as though I itch without any source for the inflammation. I will welcome the Inundation in spite of the new round of fevers and dead children it will bring. Anything is preferable to this feeling of imminence.*

The letter from Princess Mutemwia arrived on the same morning as the annual supply of poppy and a report for Huy from Amunnefer. It was the fifteenth day of Thoth. The New Year had begun. Merenra delivered both scrolls to Huy as he had finished his morning meal and was making his way to the office. The fog shredded apart in his mind. Asking the steward to find Thothhotep, Huy entered his office and dropped into the chair behind the desk, sitting tensely with his hands flat on the table's surface, both scrolls before him. "Something from Mutemwia," he said to her as she came in. "Read it to me, Thothhotep."

Stepping briskly forward, she quickly cracked the scroll open. "Her Highness's skill has improved somewhat," she remarked as she scanned the contents. "Oh, Huy!" She mastered herself immediately, her features falling into the properly noncommittal expression.

Huy found his shoulders hunching in anticipation. "Read!" he snapped.

She no longer reacted to his sharper tones. She nodded. "'To the Great Seer Huy, greetings. Know that my father-in-law is very ill and is not expected to live. He refuses to send for you. If I am unable to write to you again regarding this matter, then Mayor Heby your brother will doubtless keep you informed. As always, I desire no answer. Written by my own hand this third day of Thoth in the year twenty-five of the King.'" Thothhotep looked up. "She no longer signs her name, but of course I recognize her hand."

"I thought that he looked unwell when I last answered his summons," Huy commented. "Naturally he will not send for me. Even on his deathbed he does not dare to have his subterfuge exposed. Well, let him die!"

"Will you have the news carried to Prince Amunhotep in Mitanni?"

"No." Huy got up. "The Princess will do that. And in another ten years her husband will also be dead, if my Seeing for the Prince spoke true. Take a dictation to Heby. I'll tell him that I've heard a rumour regarding the King's health, and ask him to send me reports on the progress of whatever's wrong with him." *Why do I feel so vindictive towards Amunhotep?* he asked himself as Thothhotep sank to the mat beside the desk and opened the drawer of her palette. *Is it because I still take his gold, or because he and his younger son were the cause of my failure before Atum? I wonder if Thothmes will continue to supply my household once he takes the throne. But of course he will see it as buying my ongoing*

silence, and I must accept it as an implicit guarantee to him that I will
keep my mouth closed.

Thothhotep was busily smoothing her piece of papyrus, a
brush between her teeth. "How old is Prince Thothmes now?"
Huy asked her.

Taking the brush, she began to mix her ink. "I'm not sure.
About eighteen, I think."

Huy sat on the edge of the desk and folded his arms. "And he
will imagine a long reign, but ten years is all that the gods intend
to give him," he remarked with an inner pang of pure spite that he
knew he should be directing at himself. "Poor Thothmes! Begin,
Thothhotep. 'To the illustrious Mayor of Mennofer, greetings …'"

BUT ANOTHER YEAR was to pass before Pharaoh finally expired.
The letters Huy continued to receive from both Heby and the
Princess during this time often guardedly referred to
Amunhotep's remarkable hold on life, *as if,* Huy mused grimly, *he*
is afraid to let go and face the ordinary fate that I believe awaits him.
No Holy Barque to receive him—only the dim draftiness of the
Judgment Hall and the accusing eyes of a maimed and weakened
Ma'at. Huy shied away from the responsibility of his own part in
the King's probable fate. That sense of imminence, of something
rolling inexorably towards him, deepened as the year progressed,
its advance smothering everything but the continuous unrest
deep within him and the sonorous words of the Book of Thoth.

The harvest ended. The New Year had begun, but the Inundation
was late. Egypt seethed with distress. Men spoke darkly of the
inevitability of famine. But at last Isis began to cry and the usual
gods' feasts were celebrated with a relieved near-hysteria. Huy stood
apart from the countrywide rejoicing. His Naming Day in the
following month, Paophi, came and went with a visit and gifts from
his parents, and it took all of Huy's control to feign a cheerfulness he

was far from feeling. Athyr, and his new nephew Ramose's Naming Day, seemed to plod by like some huge, ponderous beast slowed by its own sheer size. Khoiak, Tybi, Mekhir—the months were all the same to Huy, who waited, a fly caught in a web that hung outside the sane and regular passage of days, and he knew that struggling to free himself would be useless. His crops grew and matured, and the harvest began.

Phamenoth and Pharmuthi crept by. Once again during Pakhons, Thothhotep made her annual journey south to visit her family, and Huy took to spending his nights supine on the roof of his house, staring up at the stars, hands clasped behind his head, as he waited. Waited for what? He did not know. The stars wheeled above him. Three more times the moon waxed and waned, and then once more it was the month of Thoth. The Sopdet star rose. Thothhotep, brown and healthy, came home. The Inundation began, and at last Huy's long vigil, his wait for something indefinable, ended. The invisible web imprisoning him fluttered. Huy almost physically felt it loosen its hold, and he took the first deep breath of freedom he had been able to draw for a whole year.

Amunhotep died on the twenty-ninth day of Thoth. Isis had dutifully cried and the river had begun to swell. Heby wrote to tell Huy that Amunhotep had at first taken to his couch with complaints of a headache as well as the pains in his limbs, but had subsequently and suddenly lost the use of his right arm and leg and could not speak. Mutemwia's letter was more formal. "The King died last night and is being Beautified for his seat with the other blessed Osiris-ones in the Sacred Barque," she had dictated, for the letter's script was exquisitely neat and the spelling faultless. "The court and the country will mourn him until the middle of Khoiak, when his body will be laid in his tomb. I and my son Amunhotep intend to visit you at the end of

Paophi, as I require a Seeing. Long Life and Prosperity to you,
Seer. Dictated to Scribe of the Harem Nefer-ka-Ra by Her
Highness Princess Mutemwia, the thirtieth day of Thoth, year
twenty-five of the King."

"That's the end of next month," Thothhotep said with some
agitation. "Do we have enough room for a royal entourage,
Master? And the river will still be rising. Why would she brave
the current?"

*The end of Paophi. I shall be forty-one years old on the ninth.
Forty-one. Where are my grey hairs, Atum? Why does my belly not
sag? Where are the lines that should be appearing on my face? Your
patience is a terrible thing, Great Neb-er-djer. I feel it infusing me,
holding me up, steady and relentless. What will happen to me when
I have at last fulfilled your task for me? Will you plunge me into an
instant old age?* He shivered.

"Merenra is perfectly capable of organizing the household for a
royal visit," he answered her absently. "The Princess is not coming
for a Seeing, Thothhotep. She is not in the least concerned with
her own fate, and if her health was poor she would have sent for
me. All her hopes and fears go towards little Amunhotep, her son,
and whatever she has to say to me is not for the ears of palace
servants or the courtiers constantly passing by her doors. Until she
arrives, we must get about our ordinary business. This scroll need
not be hidden." *She has begun to deliberately forge a bond between
herself and me,* his thoughts ran on as he stood immobile in his
office while Thothhotep filed away the Princess's scroll. *Her son is
how old now? Three? She is coming so that he may begin to recognize
me as ... what? An uncle? An authority? What do you want of me,
Mutemwia of the soft gazelle's eyes and gentle manner?*

There was no Naming Day celebration for him that year. His
forty-first birthday passed in the gloom of an Egypt grieving for
its dead god. Even the peasants, who cared very little what

person sat on the Horus Throne and who had nothing to do while all building projects halted until after the King's funeral, sat about and commiserated with one another. Huy and Thothhotep, fly whisks in hand, made their annual treks into Hut-herib with the curtains of their litter closed against the swarms of hungry mosquitoes. On the days when he did not heal or scry, Huy often found himself standing outside his gate on the edge of the flood, watching his watersteps gradually become submerged. There was little river traffic. Flotsam drifted by, dead tree branches, the occasional bloated body of a drowned cow or goat, sometimes a carelessly tethered raft or skiff. Almost the whole month of Paophi was taken up with festivals of thanksgiving to Hapi, god of the river, and even they were subdued.

He was not a great pharaoh, Huy mused as his feet took him unchecked along his path and through the gate. *He triumphed against the rebellious eastern chiefs early in his reign. He started a small temple at Ipet-isut that was never finished. He repaired a few others, particularly in the far south, between the First and Second Cataracts. He will be remembered for his physical prowess and little else. I wonder if Kenamun, his foster brother and best friend, will now try to wriggle as close to Thothmes as he was to the father? I need not care. Thothmes will never allow me to See for him for the same reason that the King did not summon me when paralysis struck him. All I have to do is endure the nine years Atum predicted for Thothmes' reign. Then Ma'at can be restored in all her purity.*

Punctually at noon on the last day of the month, a series of barges all flying the royal colours of blue and white were skilfully eased out of the north-flowing current with a proficiency Huy wholeheartedly admired, and sailors splashed into the water to rope them to the poles at the foot of Huy's watersteps. Ramps were run out and carefully positioned so that no aristocratic feet would become wet.

Huy, Thothhotep, and the household staff were waiting halfway along the path, having been warned at sunrise that Her Highness's vessel, tied up a little to the south of the town, would arrive within hours. Anhur and his soldiers, clean and polished from their sandals to the oiled leather caps on their heads, were ranged to either side. "I'm very nervous," Thothhotep whispered to Huy as the first members of Mutemwia's staff paraded onto the ramps.

"You look better than acceptable," he whispered back. "You are quite lovely today. You will probably be dealing with any problems the Princess's scribe may have while he's here. Just remember that this is your domain, dear sister, and you are his equal."

She turned a well-painted face to him in surprise and pleasure. "Huy! You have never called me your dear sister before!"

"Hush!" he responded sharply. "The herald is approaching."

The man wore a short white kilt trimmed in blue, a white linen helmet also edged in blue, and rings on every finger of his hennaed hands. He stopped a few paces from the pair. Behind him straggled a small crowd of similarly clad and hennaed men.

"Her Highness the Princess Mutemwia is pleased to grace this house," he called. "Do her reverence." Huy, glancing over the company, could not see her, but he, Thothhotep, and the few members of his staff bent deeply together, arms outstretched. *Next time we meet, she will be a Queen,* Huy thought fleetingly, his eyes on the ground. He straightened and she was there at the end of the ramp, smiling at him, one hand enfolding the fist of a sturdy little boy, who was looking about him with a fearless interest. She and he stepped from the ramp onto the path, followed by two men Huy recognized but was unable, in the stress of the moment, to name, a man with a palette under his arm, and a young woman he had never seen before.

The herald moved to one side. To Huy's utter amazement, Mutemwia relinquished her grasp of her son, laid both hands on

Huy's shoulders, and, raising herself on the tips of her toes, kissed him on both cheeks. She smelled deliciously of a perfume combined, Huy thought, of lotus, narcissus, and henna, with an undertone of spices doubtless imbuing the oil that provided a base for the flower essences.

Mutemwia laughed. "It is satke oil. I saw your nostrils dilate, Great Seer, and I do not forget that you were raised beside the fields of Egypt's most famous perfume maker. Your uncle, is he not? Nefer-ka-Ra, Pa-shed, Tekait, do homage to our Great Seer. You also, Amunhotep." The child executed a graceful and obviously well-rehearsed bow.

Huy bowed back then squatted, looking directly into the child's dark, kohl-ringed eyes. "I like the ornament on your youth lock, Highness," he said. "I too used to wear a frog at the end of my own lock, and I still do when I have my hair braided."

"I love frogs," Amunhotep responded. "I love snakes too, and lizards. The Princess my mother shrieks every time she sees lizards on the walls of my apartments, but I command Heqarneheh to leave them alone and bring flies for them to eat."

"There are many lizards among the palm trees along my canal, and a house snake that comes to drink milk every morning outside the rear entrance," Huy told him.

The young Prince nodded sagely. "A house snake is very good luck." He glanced up at Mutemwia. "Mother, I'm thirsty. I would like a drink of milk myself, please."

At once the man Mutemwia had introduced as Pa-shed stepped forward. "We have met before, Great Seer. I am Prince Amunhotep's chief steward, but until he returns from exile I serve the Princess. Is there fresh milk in the house?"

Huy stood and crooked a finger at Merenra. "I remember you now," he replied. "My steward Merenra will see to the royal needs with your assistance."

At the child's request, a young man had detached himself from the onlooking group and came up smiling. "I am Heqarneheh, nurse of the Prince Thothmes' son Amunhotep," he explained to Huy as Amunhotep pulled himself from his mother's grasp and attached himself to Heqarneheh's linen. "I believe that you are acquainted with my father, Heqareshu, who is now retired. Let's find you some milk, my little princeling." Together with Merenra and Pa-shed, the pair set off along the path.

"Nefer-ka-Ra, go with the Seer's scribe. She will see to your needs," Mutemwia ordered. "Now I would like to see my quarters and then break my fast. It's noon, and I'm hungry!"

"Highness, my steward has prepared our guest room for you," Huy told her as they moved towards the inviting dimness of the house entrance. "It is the only accommodation I'm able to offer you, but if it is not suitable, please choose any other place in the house."

"It will be perfectly adequate." Mutemwia gestured to the girl behind her. "Tekait, have my chests brought in and unpack them at once." Standing inside Huy's pretty but small reception room, she studied it with curiosity. "Your estate is quite modest," she said in surprise. "I had imagined Egypt's Seer to be living in much grander circumstances. Is this what the King gave you and the Lady Ishat in gratitude for the details of his successful campaign?" Her tone had become dismissive. *Like me, she harbours an aversion to our dead Pharaoh,* Huy thought. *I wonder what she feels towards her husband, Prince Thothmes, soon to be crowned King?*

"The gratitude was mine and Ishat's," he hastened to assure her. "Moving here from the town was like entering the Paradise of Osiris. We were very happy within these walls." She nodded once but did not comment further. "A meal has been prepared for you, if you will choose a place," Huy went on, indicating the scattering of cushions set behind his little inlaid tables. Ankhesenpepi, now in charge of two other house cleaners, had spent the previous day scouring every inch of Huy's domain. The black and white tiles gleamed. Even the blue-painted, star-dotted ceiling had been wiped. A small bouquet of wildflowers—tiny white mayweed blossoms, yellow wild poppies, sun-coloured crown daisies, and blue lupines and cornflowers—rested on each table. "I would like to have included persea for their fragrance," Huy said as Mutemwia sank gracefully onto the cushions she had selected and waved Huy down beside her, "but the flowers have gone and the persea fruit is ripening instead. I—"

Mutemwia leaned across and touched Huy's knee. "You are flustered and anxious, having me here. I am flattered, but it is I who should be nervous in the presence of Egypt's treasure. Now, may we eat? Heqarneheh will bring Amunhotep as soon as the boy has drunk his milk."

Amunmose was waiting in a state of obvious agitation for Huy's signal. As he brought the tray of food forward, Huy prayed that he would not fall over his feet. Beyond him, Anhur and his soldiers, together with the sparse contingent Mutemwia had travelled with, filed into the hall and took up their stations around the walls. Anhur was standing beside one of the men Huy had vaguely recognized.

"But of course!" he blurted suddenly. "It is Wesersatet, the Supreme Commander of All His Majesty's Forces! He and Anhur will have much to talk about."

Mutemwia took a sip of the shedeh-wine she had chosen and dabbled a stick of celery in the garlic oil. "My husband insisted that he command the soldiers travelling with me," she said. "I was pleased. I like Wesersatet. Not only is he talented in the many areas of his responsibility and devoted to all the members of the royal family, but he maintains an agreeable non-partiality. He found Captain Irem as a military trainer for your older nephew, did he not?"

Huy put down his cup. "Highness, is there anything about my family that you do not know?"

Her gaze narrowed, those limpid brown eyes with their blue-and-gold-dusted lids and sweeping black kohl twinkling at him. Her orange mouth quirked. "No," she answered promptly. "Is that grilled ox liver I can smell? How wonderful!"

At that moment the Prince and his nurse appeared. Amunhotep wriggled down beside his mother while Heqarneheh filled his plate and stood by watchfully as he began to eat. The child's manners were already faultless. He did not talk with food in his mouth, struggled with his spoon rather than using his fingers in a desperate attempt to capture whatever morsel he wanted to taste, and when fingers were called for, he swirled them afterwards in the scented water of his finger bowl and dried them slowly on his linen napkin. But when his meal was over, he deluged the others with a stream of questions and information, most of it directed at Huy: Why are you a Seer? Do you have a wife? Why not? Where are your children? Have you got dogs for me to play with? May I paint outside on your walls after the sleep? Why is your hair so long? I am learning to swim. I can write my own name and some other words too. Wesersatet made me a bow. I shot a cat by mistake but I didn't hurt it. My grandfather has gone to be with Osiris and my father will soon be the King.

Huy answered the questions as best he could, and when he spoke, the boy fell silent, listening to him with solemn attention. Then all at once he yawned and Mutemwia told Heqarneheh to put him on the cot in her bedchamber. When the nurse and his charge had gone, Mutemwia smiled ruefully. "He wants to know everything, and I have instructed his tutor Menkhoper to make sure that all his questions are answered as truthfully as possible. He sleeps in my quarters, not with the other children in the harem."

You have complete faith in my vision for your husband's brother, Huy thought. *You are already grooming your son to take the Horus Throne when his father dies. Then what of Amunemhat, the son of Thothmes' Chief Wife Neferatiri? He was mentioned in the Seeing that sent Prince Amunhotep into exile. He is only a few weeks older than Mutemwia's boy. Will he indeed die?*

A young woman was walking across the gleaming floor with a determined expression on her face. Mutemwia put her head close to Huy's. "Here comes my body servant Tekait to remind me that it's time I went to my couch. She was aptly named after an ancient fire goddess. She burns with zeal for my welfare, but occasionally her flames roar too loudly and I must sternly dampen them." Mutemwia rose to meet the girl. "You must sleep also, Huy," she said in parting. "After the evening meal there are matters I wish to discuss with you."

Huy came to his feet but found himself bowing to her retreating back. The swirl of air she left was redolent with her perfume. At once two soldiers detached themselves from their station by the wall and followed her. Wesersatet had already left in the little Prince's wake. Anhur ambled over to Huy.

"I'd like to find Thothhotep and make sure she and the Royal Scribe have found something to eat," he said. "It's all a bit intimidating, isn't it? The Princess seems gracious as well as beautiful. You won't need me for a while, will you, Huy?"

Huy dismissed him, all at once tired. He had begun to sweat lightly. His legs were trembling and the meal he had eaten had begun to churn in his stomach. Resignedly, he recognized his need for poppy. Making his way to his room, he saw that Tetiankh had left a vial beside his couch. Huy drank it down quickly, shed his sandals and kilt, and, tossing his pillows on the floor, set his ebony headrest in their place. Lying down, he closed his eyes, feeling his upper spine crack as his neck relaxed against the cool wood. *How is it that she knows so much about me and Heby, and probably Uncle Ker and my parents also? Do I have a spy, even a benign one, in my household? Perhaps Methen is in correspondence with her. Did Pharaoh have me closely watched also? And what about his son, our new King? I must talk to Merenra. A steward knows everything that goes on under his charge. But he's one of the servants provided by Hut-herib's Mayor so long ago. All those people are in their middle age: Merenra, Tetiankh, Seshemnefer, Khnit, as well as the servants I chose myself. Seshemnefer is away caring for my arouras most of the time, but what of Tetiankh? Will the Princess tell me the truth honestly if I dare to ask her?* The house had gone quiet, and even the birds nesting in Huy's trees had fallen silent under the afternoon's heat. His stomach settled, his limbs no longer trembling, Huy slept.

The evening's feast was a cheerful affair. Mutemwia's staff was co-operating easily with Huy's, *a sign,* Huy mused, listening to the babble all around him as he sipped his beer, *that the Princess has trained them kindly and well. I wonder if Prince Thothmes has any idea how extraordinary his secondary wife is.* Apart from a few soldiers guarding the entrance doors and the passage to the rear garden, everyone was dining together. Anhur had the leg of a roasted goose in his hand and was gesticulating with it to Wesersatet, who had his chin cupped in his palm and his elbow on his littered table and was listening with a smile. Thothhotep and Nefer-ka-Ra both had their palettes out, and Mutemwia's scribe was showing Thothhotep something he had written on the clay plate he had scoured with a piece of linen. The one herald in the Princess's entourage, obviously, due to his hennaed hands, a noble, seemed to have brought his own body servant with him.

The man was bending to hear something the herald was saying. Huy looked in vain for the man who had delivered each scroll that had arrived from Mutemwia over the last months, and was not surprised at his absence. *She'll keep him secret,* his thoughts ran on under a gust of laughter from Anhur. *She spins a web using men like him to catch information like flies. I am beginning to admire her very much.* She was talking with her son, stroking his shaved skull, straightening his youth lock, her features full of a sober attentiveness while the child prattled on. His nurse sat cross-legged nearby.

I like this, Huy told himself. *The hall full of happy noise, the mingled aromas of good food and many different perfumes in the air. Ishat would have loved it too. But of course, such feasts must have become commonplace to her by now.* He thrust away the pang of sadness. Ishat was healthy and content, and if she walked in memories sometimes, as he did, it was surely without the grief that had dogged her. She was aging, as she had wanted to do. He remembered how she had described her fear of him, the aura of stale timelessness she felt surrounding him, the prospect of being caught in that changelessness with her long love for him forever unslaked. Now her hair was tendrilled with grey. Laugh lines had formed to either side of her mouth and eyes. Nevertheless, her husband continued to adore her and at last she had achieved the peace of loving him back.

"Master Huy? Great Seer?"

Huy came to himself with a start. Heqarneheh had come up to him and was bowing several times to get his attention. "I'm sorry," Huy said. "What is it?"

"The Prince would like to go fishing. The Princess asks if you would take him out in your skiff. With a guard, of course."

Huy glanced towards Amunhotep. The child was craning back at him earnestly. He did not look tired in the least. Huy got to his feet and beckoned, and Amunhotep trotted to his side. Huy answered Heqarneheh, "I will, but given the continued rising of the river, we won't go far from the watersteps. The soldier talking to Wesersatet is my captain. Go and tell him he's needed." As Huy was speaking, he felt small fingers close around his own. "Highness, do you have a fishing rod?" he asked. The boy began to tug him towards the entrance. Heqarneheh was approaching Anhur.

"Yes, I do. Heqarneheh will fetch it for me, and I have already collected worms from your garden for the bait. I don't think that I shall be able to catch anything, though. The fish will be down deep near the bottom now that the sun has gone and they've finished feeding on flies and mosquitoes."

"Why do you want to go fishing, then, Highness?" They had reached the open doors and were passing through the pillars and out into a darkness softened by pallid moonlight. Huy heard Anhur's step behind them, and with a quick bow Heqarneheh hurried past.

"I mostly want to sit in a boat and enjoy being on the water here where it's quiet," Amunhotep responded promptly. "When I go fishing at home, I have to go in a litter through the city from the palace to the river and then wait while Wesersatet or another commander orders the people off the river road and then puts me in one of the royal skiffs and then makes sure that no other boats are too close to me. Or I have to go through the barracks to the Peru-nefer docks. It's a great nuisance. Look how easy this is!"

They were almost at the watersteps, where Heqarneheh was crossing the ramp from the royal barge, a miniature rod and a clay pot in his hands. Amunhotep reached for them. Huy bent down and picked him up, carried him through the water under which half the steps were submerged, set him gently in the skiff, and clambered in after him. Anhur followed. Heqarneheh settled himself on the sand by the gate. Grasping the pole, Huy pushed them away from the bank.

"Don't hit the current," Anhur warned. Even on its edge there was a slight tug at the manoeuvrable little craft. Huy let it take them just past the point where torchlight ended and full night began, then he poled them back towards the bank. Amunhotep was stirring the worms in the pot with one thoughtful finger.

"Here in the shallows you just might catch something, Highness," Huy said.

Amunhotep nodded. He selected the bait he wanted, drove a hook through it while Huy held the rod, tossed it overboard, and took the rod from Huy with a sigh of satisfaction. "This is fun," he announced. "Is this the way the peasant boys fish, Master?"

"Not unless their fathers are fishermen," Huy told him. "Most peasant boys cannot afford to trade for hooks. They wade into the river and try to net the fish."

Amunhotep was silent for a moment, obviously digesting this information. "When I am King, I shall make a decree that every boy must be given fish hooks," he decided. "By then I shall be forbidden to fish or eat fish, because the King may not offend Hapi. So I must fish every day and eat fish every day while I can. I like doing both."

"So you will be King one day?" Huy asked cautiously.

Amunhotep shot him a quick look. "Yes. My mother the Princess tells me that I will. I'm not supposed to talk about it to anyone because she is only my father's Second Wife and inferior to Princess Neferatiri and everyone thinks that Neferatiri's son will be the Hawk-in-the-Nest. But he won't. Not ever."

"But Highness, you are talking about it to me," Huy pointed out. *And to Anhur,* he thought privately.

"I'm allowed to tell you anything, Great Seer," the boy tossed off impatiently. "My mother says that you already know I'll be

King. She says that now my uncle has gone away, you are to be my new uncle. If I like you, of course." He wiggled the rod up and down. "I think I like you. I'm not sure yet." Huy sensed rather than saw Anhur's eyebrows go up. "My mother also says that sometimes you may tell me things I don't want to hear and I must listen to you carefully and not get angry. Menkhoper and Heqarneheh do the same thing, but I still like them, so don't worry." He made a face, a thoroughly childlike grimace that unexpectedly tugged at Huy's heart. "I wish they'd play the games I want to play sometimes, though. The other children in the palace are rather stupid and boring." His attention returned to the fluid darkness of the water. "I'm not going to catch anything tonight, am I? Never mind. I can sit here and listen to the owls and the animals snuffling about in the grass by the bank. I go to the King's zoo, but it's not the same."

Huy waited for more, but the Prince seemed to have run out of breath. Gradually, all three of them succumbed to the warm tranquility of the night. Amunhotep began to hum a lullaby Huy remembered Hapzefa singing to him when he was no older than this self-assured little creature. Huy wanted to put an arm around him.

Huy expected him to grow tired and bored long before he did, and it was Anhur who yawned as Amunhotep at last drew in his line, pulled off the worm, and tossed it into the water. "That was lovely," he said, "but I'm a bit sleepy now. Let Hapi keep his fish. Don't carry me up the watersteps, Master. I want to wade."

Once Anhur had tethered the skiff securely to a pole, Huy lifted Amunhotep and set him down thigh-deep on one of the drowned steps. Seeing them come, Heqarneheh had scrambled up and was waiting. Amunhotep plunged his hands into the water, rubbed them over his face, and crawled onto dry land.

Bidding Huy and Anhur a polite good night, he took his nurse's hand and together they disappeared along the path. Anhur let out a long breath.

"Gods, Huy, just what was all that about? Clearly we both need to keep our mouths closed if we want to stay out of trouble, and equally clearly the Princess has some plan that includes you. I hope it doesn't also include infanticide."

"No." They had begun to walk towards the house. "I believe that Prince Amunemhat, Neferatiri's son, will die before he can succeed his father. It's all very secret, Anhur. Only Thothhotep and I and now you know what's in the future for Mutemwia's princeling."

"Well, it doesn't concern me in the least, I thank all the gods. All I really have to worry about is how long *you're* going to live." He bowed briefly. "Sleep well. I'll make a round of the guards on duty in the house before I fall onto my cot." Huy watched him stride away, his brisk, open personality evident in his straight carriage and confident step.

Mutemwia had wanted to speak with him after the feast. Huy imagined that by now she would have gone to her couch, and so he was surprised to see lamplight oozing out from under the door to his office. Wesersatet was standing guard in the passage outside. He saluted Huy as Huy approached. "Her Highness is waiting for you," Wesersatet said. "She knew that the Prince would be on the river for a long time. She and Nefer-ka-Ra have been playing Dogs and Jackals in the meantime." He smiled. "You need not be apologetic. Neither she nor her son goes to the couch early, and both of them find it difficult to get up in the morning!"

Huy returned his smile. "Thank you, Wesersatet." He turned and knocked, and, hearing Mutemwia's voice tell him to enter, he did so.

She was sitting in his chair and leaning over a game board on the desk. She had obviously been prepared for bed. Her face was free of paint and gleamed with the nightly application of honey most women favoured as an antidote to premature wrinkles. Her hair had been braided and hung down her back unadorned. Thin reed sandals lay by the chair where she had shed them to tuck her feet under the voluminous white sleeping robe draping her. She looked to be about twelve years old. The scribe sitting opposite her rose at once, bowed to her and then to Huy, and, gathering up the pieces of the game, backed to the door and left, closing it behind him. Huy bowed in his turn and approached her.

"So," she said. "Did my son enjoy himself? I presume he caught nothing. Please sit, Huy."

"It was too late for the fish, Highness. Sunset would have been better." Huy sank a trifle wearily into the chair the scribe had vacated. It had been a long and stressful day.

"Tomorrow Wesersatet and Heqarneheh can take him out at dusk, providing the flood doesn't become much stronger. Going fishing from the palace requires so much preparation that much of the time he can't be bothered, and he refuses to catch the fish in any of the royal ponds—he says it's too easy." She sat back, her heels still hooked over the edge of the chair in which she was sitting, her body enveloped in the gossamer tent of her sleeping robe. "And what do you make of my young Prince, Huy? Do you think him intelligent? Well behaved? Is his speech coherent and sensible?"

Huy studied her carefully. *She may look like a girl, with her face washed and her lobes free of jewellery, but she watches me with astute eyes. How old is she now? Twenty-two this year? Where did she obtain her education?*

"Highness, such questions are not for any commoner to answer," he said aloud. "Who may judge a Prince apart from his family and perhaps his noble peers?"

"Nevertheless, I ask them of you and I require an honest assessment of Amunhotep."

Huy spread out his hands. "Highness, I cannot answer them after so short an acquaintance with him!"

"Then give me your impressions. I intend to stay here for six more days so that you and he may become used to one another."

"To what end?" he dared to ask. "The Prince told me this evening that I am to take the place of his absent uncle—if he likes me, that is!" A small smile came and went on Mutemwia's face. "Surely you have carefully chosen the men and women who have charge of his well-being and schooling, and he will become as closely attached to them as our Osiris-King was to Kenamun, the son of his nurse. There is no favoured place for me in little Amunhotep's life."

She folded her arms across her bent knees and, resting her chin on them, stared at him pensively for a long time. The house had fallen into a deep silence, apart from an occasional sputter from the lamp. The reflection of its flame flickered dully on the surface of the desk through its thin alabaster cup, and all at once Huy was reminded of words he had read when he unrolled the commentary on the second part of the Book of Thoth at Thoth's temple at Khmun. "Yet the Light cast a shadow, grim and terrible, which, passing downwards, became like restless water, chaotically casting forth spume like smoke." It referred to the moment when Atum willed himself to become pure energy in the form of light, and thus cast a shadow. Huy, utterly bewildered, had argued to the High Priest Mentuhotep that as nothing had existed yet apart from Atum, the Light, how could he cast a shadow? Mentuhotep had told him that light would indeed cast a shadow without an object standing in its way. No one knew how, but if a piece of new white linen was held very close to a flame and stretched so that there were no folds in it, a faint, causeless shadow could be seen.

Now Huy, watching the soft, diffused glow of the lamp so close to him, felt a mild disquiet brush him and vanish.

At last the Princess stirred, sat forward, and placed her feet on the floor. "Answer my question," she said. The authority in her tone was unmistakable.

Huy took a long breath. "Very well, Highness, since you insist. I have known the Prince very briefly so far. His self-assurance is obvious, as is his physical resemblance to you and to his royal father. His intelligence is not yet so clear, but from his conversation I deduce a quick mind, ripe for further development. His character seems to be a blend of independence and a child's desire for acceptance and affection. It is impossible for me to make any further assessment for now."

"For now." Her gaze narrowed. "If I send him and his nurse to you for a time each Inundation, will you watch over him, take him with you when you venture out, play games with him, keep him safe?"

Huy was completely taken aback. He had not expected this. "Why?" he managed, although the reason was beginning to take shape in his mind.

She slapped both henna-stained palms on the table, an indication of her annoyance. "Are you being deliberately obtuse, Great Seer?" She bent forward. "Ever since my little one reached out and grasped your fingers, I have pondered the vision that came to you with his touch. I have also pondered the Seeing you bestowed on my brother-in-law. I have combined the words of the letter he received from you in Mitanni during that vision with the storm of gold in the centre of which you saw my baby. I shall soon be called Majesty, though I walk behind Chief Wife Neferatiri. Yet according to the will of Atum, made known through you, my husband will have a mere nine years on the Horus Throne and my son Amunhotep will mount it instead of

Neferatiri's offspring." Reaching across the table, she tapped the back of his hand with one long forefinger. "He will need you then," she went on quietly. "He will be only twelve years old. I will be Regent, governing until he achieves his majority at sixteen. I will need you also. Egypt's Great Seer will stand beside the throne as Amunhotep's adviser, his confidant, the one who will convey to him the will of Atum. With you in the palace there will be no unrest among my husband's sons by his lesser wives and concubines. Until then I want him to get to know you, trust you, even love you, and I want you to love him also. Give me your thoughts on all this." A childlike anxiety now filled her features, returning her, in Huy's eyes, to the appearance of an insecure young girl, an impression totally at variance with her words.

Huy was appalled. *Is this what was in your mind, Ramose, High Priest of Ra, Henenu, Rekhet and mentor, even you, Methen, when all of you spoke of my destiny? Am I to rule the being who will rule Egypt?*

His hands slid off the table and covered each other in his lap. "Highness, I am sometimes forced to wonder if my visions of the future show me what *may* be, not what *will* be," he said, his voice uneven, his mind full of Anuket and what had happened to Ishat instead. Instead? "In my vision for Prince Amunhotep, I saw the place of his exile, I saw a letter arriving for him from me in which I explain to him that he may return to Egypt but not as King, because your son has already been declared ruler. Amunemhat, Neferatiri's boy, will have died by then. But Highness, your brother-in-law is the Osiris-one's rightful heir. His father transgressed Ma'at when he proclaimed your husband as the Hawk-in-the-Nest. Now your husband will be crowned King after the period of mourning for his father is over. But when he dies, his brother deserves to come home to take his place. What if some action, some decision of yours or Neferatiri's or even of Thothmes' himself, changes the future? Negates what I saw? What if little Amunemhat survives? You are presuming a great deal." *What cause am I arguing for?* he asked himself as he felt tension stiffen his shoulders and fold his fingers in on themselves. *Why do I feel such panic?*

"I have absolutely no intention of transgressing Ma'at and earning myself an unfavourable Weighing by having Amunemhat murdered," Mutemwia hissed. "Are you suggesting such a dreadful thing? But mark this, Huy. Atum has spoken through you. My son will reign, not his uncle—of this I am determined. Much as I love the Prince, his years in Mitanni will not have fitted him for godhood. My son will fully restore Ma'at and the worship of Amun as Egypt's pre-eminent deity. This I can promise you, and I believe that if you chose to take my son's hand in yours, you would See a return to such harmony in his future!"

Huy could sit still no longer. Rising to his feet on legs gone weak, he bowed for her forgiveness in standing without her permission. "Highness, you have not heard me," he managed. "Sometimes my visions of their future become … twisted in the lives of those for whom I See. This happens often enough for me to doubt the validity of what Atum sends. Or rather, I fail to see how the future fate of some may be warped into the fate of a member of their kin. What if Prince Amunhotep comes back from exile and demands his rightful place?"

"I heard you," she answered calmly. "I know my friend. He will come back wanting nothing more than a peaceful life on his estates. He will not forget the strain and fear under which he lived before he left."

Huy's throat went dry. "Will he fear you, Highness?"

"I swear on the life of my precious baby that he will never have reason to fear me. Or him. You will see to that if you take up the burden I wish to lay upon you." Once more her regard became critical. Her eyes travelled his face. He watched her note the tension apparent in his chest before her gaze returned to his mouth. His breath had become shallow. "You are sweating, Huy," she said kindly. "The time for your evening poppy is long past. You have become entirely reliant upon the drug, have you not?"

Who spies for you in my household? he thought, close to despair. *Whom have you suborned since you and I met in the passages of the palace? Must I scatter my staff and hire strangers?*

She waved one graceful hand dismissively. "No, I have no spy here on your estate. The Mayor of Hut-herib, Mery-neith, sent me a scroll containing everything pertaining to you and your family he had gleaned from his taxation records and his work among the townspeople. The High Priest of Ra, Ramose, now retired, answered my request for a report on you in glowing terms. Governor Thothmes and his lovely wife Ishat visited me in my quarters at my request, and I myself, yesterday, met with your good friend the priest Methen. I am no pretty harem acquisition, Huy," she said scornfully. "I administer my own estates, I make sure I know exactly what passes among the King's many women, I watch and listen at every royal audience. No one spoke ill of you. Yet, on examining their words, written or spoken, I deduced much that they did not say. Your failure to speak out regarding my husband's so-called dream I knew about from my Prince now in exile. The probability of your sexual wounding at Atum's will—Ishat hinted at this during our conversation when she remarked that you suffered from all the strictures imposed by the gods on Egypt's Seers through the ages. She would not elaborate, but her polite stubbornness gave me my answer. The sense of responsibility you display towards the townspeople and peasants of this sepat is evidence of your compassion and discipline. Your growing dependency on the opium poppy is unfortunately inevitable, given the pain Atum inflicts on you."

She swung to her feet and, coming around the table in a swirl of thin linen and a rush of perfume, cradled his face in her hands. The gesture, so smooth and unexpected, nearly unmanned him. "Will you be able to control it?" she said gently. "You must control it, Huy, if you are to guide my son through his destiny as the Incarnation of Amun. I have seen the dissolution of those nobles whose greed for the poppy now rules their lives. They have become prisoners of the drug." For a moment those warm palms lingered on his face, then she removed them and folded her arms. "This is Egypt," she continued with seeming irrelevance. "As a Princess my power to command you is limited, therefore I merely beseech you. Will you receive my son into your home once a year for a month or so? You have much to teach him."

Your mind is made up, he thought, looking into those huge, limpid eyes, *and you have a will of iron. Your husband is no match for you. You have utterly ignored my argument regarding his unfortunate brother, and you expect me to do the same. Well, I see no harm in acceding to your first request. I am beginning to like the boy, and he will be good company for me.*

"May I take him into the town with me as Thothhotep and I go about our business?" he wanted to know, his words an obvious capitulation.

Mutemwia smiled widely. "Certainly, providing you use your judgment as to what he may or may not see. It is good for a ruler to observe the lives of his subjects. So, this matter is settled?"

"Yes."

"Then I shall bid you a good night." She began to move towards the door, then stopped and turned. "Your scribe. She has a diverse history. I presume that she has read every scroll I have sent you so far, and it is too late to ask you this, but do you trust her?"

Huy nodded. "Implicitly, Highness."

"Good." Then she was gone. Huy heard her address Wesersatet briefly, and by the time he himself reached the passage beyond, it was empty.

Making his way upstairs to his bedchamber, stepping over Tetiankh, who was deeply asleep, he walked to his couch and stood for a long time looking down on the vial of poppy his body servant had left on the table. He wanted it desperately, wanted the glow it spread through his body, the slight dislocation from reality it provided for his mind, the vivid colours with which it imbued his dreams, but in the end he left it where it was, pulling off his kilt and loincloth and crawling beneath his sheet as he allowed the words of the Book of Thoth to begin their unreeling behind his weariness.

It took him a long time to fall asleep. Quite apart from his body's uncomfortable demand for the drug, the intense exchange between himself and the Princess needed dissection. Had he in fact been betrayed by those he knew and respected, or had they seen the Princess's interest in him as an avenue for his advancement and had thus been eager to oblige her? The latter was far more likely. And what of her refusal to hear any argument for the exiled Prince's reinstatement if Atum chose to alter the vision he, Huy, had seen, and to heal Ma'at's wounds through the correct elevation of the elder son? *Am I to keep that possibility before Mutemwia's eyes, feed it into her ears, so that she sees it as at least an equal possibility to the crowning of her son?* That prospect made his belly suddenly shrink and returned him to full consciousness. Resignedly, he sat up, reached for the vial, and took the opium in one gulp. *Atum, help me to resist the desire to have my dosage increased,* he prayed as he lay down again. *No matter what events occur in the unfolding of my own future, save me from succumbing totally to this blessed seduction.*

He fell asleep at once.

15

PHARAOH AMUNHOTEP THE SECOND'S funeral took place in the middle of the month of Khoiak, when the river had reached its highest flood level and there was a lull between the Feast of Hathor and the Feast of Sacrifice. Princess Mutemwia, little Amunhotep, and their entourage had remained with Huy for a further six days. During that time the Prince had gradually wriggled out from under the constraints of blood and protocol, and spent his time running half naked about the house and garden, eating whenever he wanted to, and fishing every sunset. Sometimes he left the watersteps with Wesersatet and his nurse, but more often he began to prefer the company of Huy and Anhur. Something about Anhur's terse comments and the comforting solidity of his body drew the boy to him physically, as though, in demanding to sit on Anhur's knee or having Anhur's arms circle him as the captain of the guard showed him a better way to hold his rod, he was finding a security he had lacked. Huy recognized the need under Amunhotep's cheerful prattle. It touched him, and a genuine fondness for the Prince grew in him. Mutemwia seemed content to allow her son the freedoms that life in the palace precluded. *As long as he is guarded, she obviously sees no reason to interfere with his happiness, and besides,* Huy often thought, *she wants him to look forward to being here every year. He must come to regard my household as one of his own.* The memories of his days in Nakht's house flowed through his mind. He had been older than Amunhotep was now when his association with Thothmes' family began, but the way in which he had been slowly integrated into their daily lives was the same.

It was true that neither mother nor son was able to retire until almost everyone else had taken to their couches, cots, or mattresses. Huy wondered if it was because the palace was a busy, noisy place and these two needed peace and silence or if there was a certain safety in knowing that those who continually surrounded them were unconscious. Wandering about his domain after darkness had fallen, Huy often encountered the Princess, always scrubbed and in her sleeping robe, walking alone under the palm trees beside the small canal that fed his garden or sitting with her back against a sycamore trunk, barely visible but for the grey blur of her voluminous linen. At first he imagined her driven by unrest, but she would call to him and he would approach to be welcomed with a smile and an invitation to keep her company. They spoke of many things during those night hours. Mutemwia questioned him closely about his childhood and his schooldays at Iunu, and particularly about the terrible day when Sennefer had aimed a throwing stick at him and changed his life forever. Huy remained aware of the gulf of blood and station between them in spite of her informality with him, and was careful never to overstep that invisible channel. Huy could tell that she was weighing his words, judging his suitability as a future adviser for her son, yet the knowledge ceased to make him tense. She was delightful to be with, a woman of intelligence and spirit, and they were becoming as friendly as it was possible for a commoner and a royal Princess to be.

Sometimes Huy entered his room to find young Amunhotep already there, perched on his couch and talking to Tetiankh as the servant trimmed the lamp or laid out his master's clothing

for the morning. The child never looked tired. Healthily brown
and clear-eyed, he would greet Huy with a grin and often a hug,
and once Huy was under his sheet, would lie beside him and
demand a story. Huy groped among the history lessons he had
endured and found tales of the mighty deeds of kingly ancestors,
but he was seldom able to finish them without interruption.
Amunhotep was full of questions. Why were the vile Setiu
allowed to rule Egypt? When they had been driven out, why did
King Ahmose stay in Weset, far from the proper palace at
Mennofer? Why were the men of Kush always rebelling? And
where, he asked once with relish, did Huy think the penis of
Osiris might be? Isis had found all the pieces of him that Set had
scattered except that. It could be buried anywhere. Even
perhaps deep under the soil in Huy's garden? Why didn't Isis
spend more time looking for it after she had found the rest of the
god's body? Didn't he need it anymore?

Huy was less secure talking about the gods than he was in
describing the Osiris-King Thothmes the First's many battles.
Osiris-King Thothmes the Third had spent seventeen years
campaigning in the east and had secured many vassal states for
Egypt. The boy was happiest hearing about the exploits of this
great-grandfather after whom his own father was named. Then
the questions became statements: "My father could do that if he
wanted to." "My father has a bigger army than that." "My father
is much richer than that." With a pity that was fast becoming a
genuine affection, Huy realized that Amunhotep rarely saw his
father, perhaps had never even spoken to him. He was, after all,
only the son of a Second Wife. She would soon be a Queen but
would not be entitled to wear a Queen's crown. That honour
belonged to Neferatiri, Thothmes' Chief Wife. Huy was usually
relieved when Heqarneheh arrived to carry the drowsy little body
to his cot in his mother's room and he himself could relax.

Children are absorbing and amusing, but tiring also, Huy often decided before he slept, *and this royal child is no exception.*

As always during the Inundation, Huy was called to the town to deal with the customary rash of fevers, and on the nights when he returned home aching and exhausted, Mutemwia forbade Amunhotep to bother him. Amunhotep had begged to be allowed to go into Hut-herib with Huy and Thothhotep, but his mother had refused. "You are still too young," she had said. "Later, when you are seven or eight, you may ask the Seer very politely if you may accompany him." Amunhotep had stared at her, obviously deciding whether to sulk, whine, or acquiesce grudgingly. Acquiescence had won out, and Huy was free to swallow his poppy and lie in the blessed dimness of his bedchamber alone.

Then it was the middle of Athyr, and like a flock of graceful birds the members of the Princess's staff lifted their heads, fluffed their bright feathers, and rose from the house to settle noisily on the barges. Mutemwia stood at the foot of the ramp with Amunhotep, who was almost unrecognizable in his silver bordered kilt, gilded leather sandals, and kohled eyes. A small protecting Eye of Horus in gold and black onyx hung from a slender chain around his neck, and a tiny golden ankh earring glinted in the sunlight as he looked up at Huy. "I am to come back to your estate next year if the gods will it," he said. "Actually, I hope they want me to come sooner. I have enjoyed living like a commoner, and the fish here are very tasty." He tugged at Huy's hand until Huy bent low. "You are my new uncle," he whispered. "I like you very much. If you and Anhur will move to Mennofer, I will order new apartments built for you in the palace gardens. Will you come?"

Huy glanced up at Mutemwia. She nodded. "There are many poor people who need me here, Highness," he said, "and you must grow and study hard and obey those who have authority over you. But the time will come when you will send for me, and then I will see you in Mennofer."

Huy saw a flash of purely adult speculation flit across the child's strong features. "When I am King," Amunhotep whispered again, his mouth barely moving. Then, in an abrupt and entirely youthful change of mood, his arms went around Anhur's naked leg. "If my father goes to war, don't go with him," he said loudly.

Mutemwia reached for his arm and gently pulled him away. "I shall continue to write to you, Seer," she told him. "I thank you for your hospitality."

Huy bowed. "I look forward to reading your letters," he replied. "May the soles of your feet be firm, Highness."

At once Wesersatet and her guard moved forward; turning, she preceded them along the ramp and onto the deck. The ramp was run in. Huy could see the helmsman begin to manipulate the giant steering oar as her barge and then the others backed slowly away from the watersteps.

"The flood is still rising and there's a current," Thothhotep remarked. "She puts great faith in her sailors."

"You may be sure that her husband provided her with his best," Huy said, his eyes on the little fleet now forming a string of vessels on the distorted and murky surface of what had been the river. "I wonder what went through his mind when she requested them for a visit to me. Did he fear a Seeing? But she will be clever, Thothhotep. She will either convince him that no Seeing was ultimately necessary or she will concoct an innocuous vision to tell him about. I have not known such a resolute woman since—"

"Since Ishat," his scribe put in. He swung to her, but she was smiling. "The Princess is indeed remarkable. It's a pity that she's not Chief Wife."

Huy sighed. "She doesn't need to be. She has complete faith in my vision. She sees her future in far more powerful terms than as a secondary wife. She believes that she will be Regent in Egypt."

"And you?" The voice was Anhur's. "What do you believe, Huy?"

The barges had disappeared. Huy turned his back on the turgid water. "I believe that Atum wills the vindication of Ma'at," he said heavily. "Further than that I will not go." Neither of his companions commented. For a while the three of them loitered on the path to the house while Anhur's soldiers, their duty as an honour guard over, strode briskly past. Huy was aware that a pall had settled over him. "The house will seem empty for a while. I will miss the Prince's laughter and the sight of the Princess wafting through my passages at night with her sleeping robe afloat."

"There are no letters for you in the office," Thothhotep said regretfully, "and we do not go into Hut-herib today. What will you do, Master?"

"Escape from all the cleaning and refurbishing going on in the house, and sit in the shade of the garden," he replied gloomily. "I suppose you and Anhur will amuse each other." For answer they bowed, linked arms, and strolled away, their heads together. *Years ago I was trapped by a King's generous gratitude*, he thought, squinting after them, *and that generosity made me weak in the presence of his son. Now I am facing yet another cage, the bars forged of a growing affection and a sense of new obligation instead of gold. If my vision for our absent Prince spoke true. If Thothmes has a mere nine years to reign. I find myself desperately wishing that it lied, that for once I was a mouse in Anubis's mocking claws, that the Prince is busy raising an army in Mitanni to wrest the throne from his usurping brother and I will be left to continue the work of the god among my own kind.* He recognized that these thoughts arose from a temporary sense of aimlessness now that his guests had gone, but he could not rid himself of them, and in the end he took a cushion out onto his roof and lay down in the shadow of one of the wind catchers. He did not sleep.

At the beginning of Tybi, Thothmes was crowned, becoming King Thothmes the Fourth. His Horus name, Ka-nakht-tut-Khau, meant Mighty Bull in His Risings Like the Form of the Sun. Other titles included Perfect of Diadems, Enduring of Kingship Like Atum, and Powerful of the Scimitar Who Subdues the Nine Bows, the traditional enemies of Egypt. The throne name he took was Menkheperura, "Everlasting are the Manifestations of Ra," a detail that Huy, listening to Thothhotep read to him the account of the ceremony Ishat had written, did not miss. "The Aten is one of the manifestations of Ra," he said when Thothhotep had finished. "There is no mention of Amun anywhere in his titles, and of course his name only means Son of Thoth. I wonder what changes we shall see in the administration."

He had not been invited to the crowning ceremony and was not sorry. Mutemwia had sent him a hurried letter to tell him that Thothmes, busy and distracted with the endless matters of precedence and protocol a coronation demanded, had simply welcomed her back and asked no questions. All Egypt's governors, mayors, and other officials had crowded into the temple to see the Double Crown set on Thothmes' twenty-year-old head. Heby was among them, and in the second week of Tybi, Huy received a scroll from him.

Our new King is very handsome, and bore himself with dignity throughout the ceremony. Great Royal Wife and Queen Neferatiri positively glittered in the golden vulture crown, and even her little son Amunemhat was weighed down with a golden Horus for his youth lock, golden Horus earring dangling past his collarbone, golden necklaces hung with lapis ankhs and likenesses of Heh, god of eternity, almost obscuring his chest—gold everywhere! The feast afterwards went on all night, with dancers and magicians and fire-eaters entertaining us. Long before the King left the dais, Iupia and I were tired and ready to start for home, but of course we could not leave until His Majesty did. Iupia fell asleep on her cushions. All the same, it was a magnificent occasion and I feel privileged to have been invited.

Rumours are flying among my staff that there will be conscription, that the King will mount a military expedition into Rethennu. Is it necessary? I don't know. The east seems to have remained quiet since his father's memorable foray, which you Saw for him in such detail, but of course Egypt's spies in that region will be sending the palace more accurate information than I have. Your nephew, Amunhotep-Huy, is beside himself with anticipation. According to him, the soldiers stationed in the barracks here in Mennofer have been engaged in much drilling and mock battles lately, and Officer Irem, his trainer, is sure that the King will go to war. Amunhotep-Huy has already begun to beg me to let him march with Irem, but as he is still only eleven I cannot allow it. How many ancestor-kings have NOT found it necessary to discipline Rethennu? Very few. So, dear brother, you may find yet another royal hand extended to you for a Seeing as Thothmes passes Hut-herib before striking east. Egypt has eight battle months when the flood recedes and the Black Land becomes dry. We can only wait and see what happens.

Iupia and I are in good health and so is baby Ramose, thank the gods. He is a quiet baby, toddling about quite contentedly by himself. His vocabulary is already much larger than Amunhotep-Huy's was at his age. But do come and see for yourself. It has been too long since you and I have embraced. How are Hapu and Itu? You seldom write to me and do not tell me how our parents are.

"It's true," Huy admitted to Thothhotep as she placed Heby's thick scroll on the table and poured herself water from the jug at Huy's elbow. "I'm reluctant to leave the estate. I don't dictate letters to Heby, yet I love him very much. I send Merenra to my parents with little gifts so that I don't have to go to them myself. It's as though I'll attract the King's attention if I stir from here."

Thothhotep did not laugh. Slaking her thirst, she replaced the cup on the desk and pulled a stool near to Huy. "The King has already turned his attention to you, Master, if only briefly," she reminded him as she sank onto the stool. "He must have instructed Royal Treasurer Sobekhotep to continue the grant of gold that his father began. Merenra told me yesterday that the regular amount due at the start of the spring months had arrived."

Huy did not know whether to feel glad or threatened by the news. "Will he go to war, I wonder? All the signs point to a rapid advance on Rethennu. Will he take the army further? Is Prince Amunhotep safe from him in Mitanni? Or does Thothmes feel so secure now that the Double Crown is on his head that he will leave his older brother alone?" Bemused, he ran a hand through his unbound hair. Heby's letter had arrived very early in the day and as yet Huy had not been to the bathhouse.

"The question you really want answered is, will the King require a Seeing from you as he passes the town?" Thothhotep pointed out. "He doubtless remembers his father's victories that you foretold. But he won't stop here and send for you, will he?"

Huy met his scribe's steady gaze. "No, he won't. He will never offer me his hand. He's afraid that if he does, I'll know the truth of his dream for certain. He might send one of his generals, though, or even Wesersatet. Would that be safe for him?" Thothhotep did not respond. Her hand went to her palette, and Huy shook his head. "No, I won't dictate an answer to Heby today. Seshemnefer arrived last night. He wants to discuss with me what crops to sow on the arouras at Ta-she and those I own west of Hut-herib, and Anab is already nagging me about our garden here." He got up.

"Huy, why don't you go with Seshemnefer when he returns to Ta-she?" Thothhotep said. "The Rekhet left you a beautiful house on the edge of the lake, and the surroundings will be bursting with fresh green growth. You need a rest."

"Perhaps I do," Huy admitted, "but I have no desire to be anywhere near the palace at Mi-wer, to be accessible to the nobles and officials stationed there, even if Thothmes does go east." He placed both palms flat on the surface of the desk and leaned over them. "I want the next nine years to pass quickly," he said harshly. "I want to bury myself here until our new King dies. I feel the pain of Ma'at's wounding, Thothhotep. I have seen it. Let Thothmes stand in the Judgment Hall like every ordinary citizen so that whoever inherits the Horus Throne will begin to heal her! I suppose that I am speaking treason," he went on more quietly. "So be it. File Heby's letter. I'm going to the bathhouse with Tetiankh."

By the second week of Tybi, the flood water had drained into the soil and back into the confines of the river's banks. The peasants could be seen standing in the naked, silt-clogged fields. The maze of canals used to feed water to the coming crops had been sealed against any outflow as over the coming months the level of the river would gradually begin to drop. Rumours of a projected military campaign were at last confirmed. His Majesty would take his troops east at the beginning of the following month, Mekhir. But by then Huy no longer cared whether or not Thothmes went to war. On the twenty-eighth day of Tybi a letter from Amunnefer arrived. Huy, enjoying the cool breeze, was in the garden talking to Anab over baskets of bedding plants when Thothhotep brought him the scroll. Seeing Amunnefer's seal impression in the wax, Huy handed it back to her. "It will be his estimates for the cost of tending the poppy arouras this year," he said. "Make a note of them yourself, Thothhotep, and file them. You can give me the amount of gold later."

She had taken the scroll and gone away and Huy had dismissed it from his mind, but almost immediately Amunmose came hurrying over the grass, his expression solemn. "Master, you are needed in the office," he told Huy. "Thothhotep asks that you join her at once." An intimation of what was to come brushed Huy, the merest feather touch of dread. He wanted to go on standing in the sunlight with his kilt moving gently against his thighs and the fresh green smell of the new plants over which Anab was bending in his nostrils. Amunmose was walking back to the house, and after a moment Huy followed him reluctantly. *It will not be about disease in the opium or trouble among the peasants,* he knew instinctively. *This is something much worse.*

Thothhotep was standing in the middle of the office floor with the scroll in both hands, a stricken look on her face. *You have broken the discipline of a good scribe, Thothhotep,* Huy thought as he rounded the doorway. *You have shown your master a reaction to the contents of a letter before being asked to give one.* He halted, too tense to go to his chair. "Read it to me," he said.

She swallowed. "Master, I—"

"Read it!"

She fumbled to unroll the scroll, her throat working again, her tongue moving briefly over dry lips. "There is no greeting," she began, her voice uneven. She cleared her throat, shot him an agonized glance, and went on:

Know, then, that my wife and your old friend, Anuket, is dead. On the second day of Tybi she became restless, refusing to eat and calling for wine. I did not worry over her request. For a long time she had taken no wine at all, and when I saw her gradually return to full health I did not forbid her a cup of shedeh during feasts on our estate or when visiting friends. She herself never asked for more. But on that day of Tybi she shut herself up in her apartments and would let no one enter. I was forced to leave her in the evening to attend to affairs in my administrative office adjoining the old palace. When I returned, she had gone, taking with her only a cloak. She had refused an escort from my household guard. I began to search for her in the company of my soldiers, and just before dawn I found her. I cannot tell you of her state except to say that she was lying naked in the shadows of the Street of the Beer Houses and she was dead. Her body even now lies in the House of the Dead here in Weset. My soldiers and the police of Weset have scoured the city for any hint of her attackers, but apart from a beer-house owner who remembers a woman of aristocratic speech drinking alone in a corner of his establishment, we are empty-handed. Nebamun, the King's Overseer of the Desert west of the city, is searching there, but I sense that neither he nor Weset's police will find anything or anyone. Something happened within Anuket, something terrible. Was this the culmination of what you foresaw in her future, Huy? She will be placed in my tomb in the second week of Pharmuthi. Until then, I have closed the doors of my house to everyone, and this is the final letter I will write. I have already written to Anuket's brother and sister at Iunu. By my own hand, the fourth day of Tybi, year one of the King, Amunnefer, Governor.

"It takes about three weeks to travel the miles between Weset and the Delta, sailing against the current," Thothhotep said lamely as the scroll rolled closed in her hand with a polite rustle. "The period of mourning—"

"Leave me." Thothhotep laid the scroll on the desk without looking at him and quietly went out. *The period of mourning has already run for twenty-six days. In another forty-four days it will be over, and Anuket will be entombed during Pharmuthi, the twelfth day of Pharmuthi if my calculations are correct. If I'm to attend the funeral, I ought to leave here during the first week of the month before. That's next month, Mekhir, and Mekhir begins in three days, so I should warn Merenra to prepare for a long journey and then a week at least in Weset with Amunnefer. It would be a good idea to travel south in a flotilla with Thothmes and Ishat and Nasha. After all, Iunu is on the way ...* A sudden pain brought him to his senses and, looking down, he saw that he was holding an earring smeared with blood. His necklet on which hung the sa amulet the Rekhet had made for him lay on the floor at his feet, together with the thin hoop of bracelet he had been wearing. His ear was throbbing. Stupidly, in a daze, he fingered his lobe and his hand came away wet. *I must have torn off my earring without unscrewing it,* he thought, watching it fall to lie on the small pile of his other jewellery. *What a foolish thing to do!* Nevertheless, he had already pulled his braid forward automatically and was tugging at the frog ornament holding it tied. His eyes followed its swift descent to the floor with mild interest.

Then all at once reality deluged him. Anuket was dead. Anuket was murdered. Strange men, wild men, had ... had done what? Dragged her from the beer house and raped and beaten her? Stabbed her? Flung her from one to the other and then strangled her? "Amunnefer did not say," he said loudly, "but surely these were base creatures living without Ma'at. They will be found eventually and the King will give her justice." *No, they will not be found,* something inside him whispered back. *Anuket could not escape the fate her name demanded, the fate Anubis showed me, the fate she herself could not have imagined that day long ago in her father's herb room when she told me that her name meant "to embrace."* She had been sitting cross-legged on the floor surrounded by a clutter of leaves, twigs, and flowers, in the act of twisting the stems of two white water lilies together, as he entered. The room had been redolent, as always, with the aromas of thyme, mint, dill, spices, and flowers, odours that always brought her tiny face to mind when they assailed his nostrils. On that day she had settled a wreath of yellow daisies around his neck and he had suddenly, irrevocably, fallen in love with her. She had been named after an ancient water goddess who embraced the fields with the Inundation, a minor deity but a symbol of chastity, of purity. Over the long passage of the hentis she had slowly become a goddess of lust and obscenity. "No totem of Anuket stands in my bedroom!" her namesake had told Huy vehemently. "I shall try to embrace all that is good. I have never felt lust, but if I ever do, I shall not allow it to engulf me. Even if I feel it!"

Huy, now standing swaying in his office, unaware that he had begun to dig his fingers into his hair, could hear her voice, could see that dainty oval face with its wide brows drawn together in a frown of seriousness, the graceful, vulnerable hands stilled on the wet and quivering petals of the waxen lilies. He had kissed the top of her head, he remembered, had put his mouth against the black, sweet-smelling sheen of her hair, lost to all else but the throb of desire within him. "You felt it in the end, and you forgot how you told me that you would never let it engulf you," he went on aloud to the niches full of scrolls, the tangled shadows of shrubbery on the tiled floor, his distorted reflection on the polished surface of the desk. "You lived your name, Anuket. Anuket!"

The memories were pouring into his mind with all the force of a desert wind, and he let them come. Running into the passage, he stumbled for the stairs, his unbound hair streaming down his naked back. Briefly he was aware of his body servant's shocked expression as he fled towards his bedchamber. "Bring me poppy, a lot of poppy," he croaked as Tetiankh backed against the painted wall of the upper passage. "Keep everyone away from me for the rest of the day, Tetiankh—and hurry up! I refuse to suffer this pain!" Falling into his room, he saw his long censer lying beside Khenti-kheti's shrine. A few fragrant ashes remained in its bowl. Knocking them out onto one trembling palm, he knelt, ground them into his scalp, and began to weep, not for the licentious, wine-soaked woman he had encountered at Thothmes' wedding but for the lovely child who had made him her youthful prisoner, both of them briefly fresh and innocent before the slow tide of maturity with its subtle corruption flowed in to taint their hearts.

He knew, as he drank the poppy a worried Tetiankh had brought, that he was being cowardly, and he did not care. Lying on his couch, he let the blessed opium blunt his grief and then cocoon it. He slept while the household filled with the news the scroll had brought, the word spreading quickly and dying as his loyal servants heard and then closed their mouths. It was still dark when he woke to the sound of gentle breathing, and, sitting up, he saw Tetiankh on his pallet inside the door instead of outside it. *He is concerned for me,* Huy thought as he lay down again. *I suppose that in the morning I must endure the mute expressions of sympathy on the faces of all I meet, and for their kindness I will be grateful. I must dictate a letter to Thothmes and Nasha, and to Amunnefer. He loved Anuket very much, but will there be a tiny portion of relief mingled with his tears of loss? And you, Ishat. In spite of your happiness with Thothmes, will you allow yourself a moment of purely feminine spite at her shameful end?* Searching himself, Huy found a bed of resigned acceptance under the spate of memories. *She tried to avert the fate her name decreed,* his thoughts ran on. *It was a valiant effort, but it failed. Or did it?*

Suddenly alert, he sat up again, settling his pillow at his back and pulling the sheet up over his waist. The attempt was not her own, he knew with the clarity of certainty. *O Atum, how merciless you are in the pursuit of your mysterious will! My punishment for standing mute before the King was the attack on Ishat, but you did more, did you not, implacable one? For a brief time you took Anuket's destiny and laid it on Ishat. You did not care about Amunnefer's hope as he saw his wife become sober. You disregarded Thothmes' anguish when he believed that Ishat would die. All that mattered to you was my humiliation, the conviction that my visions had become false. I failed you, and you retaliated with the callousness of a cruel and selfish taskmaster. Did Anuket have a choice when she woke on the morning of the second of Tybi and felt again the craving she supposed she had conquered? Do the visions, once told, remove the freedom of choice from the petitioner, fix unchangeably a fate that might have been subject to the will of those who extend their hands to me if their future had remained unknown? Is that how you steer Egypt, by using the visions you send me to force the unfolding of this country's fate? Yet I had a choice when I sat on that accursed stool with the courtiers watching me like vultures, and I made the wrong one. Your anger was great and your judgment swift, Holy One. In agreeing to help his mother nurture young Prince Amunhotep towards ultimate godhead, did I make the right decision and thus Anuket's true destiny was returned to her?*

All at once Huy realized that he had finally been able to give shape to the puzzle that had occasionally dogged him since the earliest days of his gift, namely, why was it that a handful of those for whom he had Seen, or healed by Anubis's prescriptions, returned later with relatives suffering a similar malady, of either body or event? "Because I foresaw the future of the wrong person," he said aloud, forgetting that Tetiankh was asleep in the room. The servant sighed. Huy heard the soft movement of his sheet as he turned over. *Then why did I not See the original petitioner's correct future?* Huy's thoughts ground on.

There was something wrong with his reasoning, he knew, something that should be obvious, perhaps even familiar, but the flaw in his argument eluded him. The soporific effect of the poppy had worn off, leaving him aching for a lost love, for the comfort of Ishat's presence, withdrawn from him years ago, for the cheerfully ignorant child he had been before Sennefer's throwing stick and the permanent scar it had caused, now hidden by his hair. His sadness grew, encompassing Thothmes, Nasha, and Amunnefer, all of them in mourning as he was, but he found that he could not cry anymore for Anuket. She had been Atum's gaming piece. Would the weighing of her heart against Ma'at's feather in the Judgment Hall be favourable because of it? Huy wanted more poppy, but he fought the hunger, not because the Princess Mutemwia had cautioned him but because, now that the first agony of loss had passed, he would not insult the memories any further. He would honour the young Anuket he had known best. Pain came with that resolve. Lying down, he stared into the dimness above him while the remainder of the night wore away.

In the morning, he dictated a letter of condolence to Amunnefer and a more informal missive to Thothmes and Nasha:

I have been reliving our youth together. Neither aging nor death can erase those magical years. The child in me will always be gliding through the marshes on hot summer afternoons while you, Thothmes, try without success to bring down a duck, and you, Nasha, loll indolently on your cushions with a mug of beer in your hand and tease both of us while the guard yawns and the reeds around the skiff rattle gently against each other. Somewhere deep inside me I still stand on Nakht's raft in the torchlight while the guests drink and chatter and Anuket weaves between them in bare feet, her slender body swaying to the rhythm of Nakht's musicians, a garland to place around my neck in her outstretched hands. I am sending gold with this letter, a contribution towards the endowment of the tomb Amunnefer will doubtless share with her when it is time for the weighing of his heart. I shall not travel to Weset for her funeral, Thothmes. Forgive me. The rumours of war have been confirmed, and in the event that the King should wish to consult me before marching east, I should remain here. If he does not summon me on his own behalf, he may do so for Wesersatet or one of the generals. I love you both very much. Come to see me when you return to Iunu. Kiss Ishat for me.

Huy stopped pacing and looked down at Thothhotep. "Finish with the usual dating and I will sign it. Do you think I'm wrong to stay home, Thothhotep?"

She glanced up at him, brush in hand, a smudge of ink across her nose. "You have your own reasons for not making the journey to Weset," she retorted. "I must confess, I'm surprised, though. The Lady Anuket was one of your oldest friends." Her head went down again over the papyrus uncurled across the palette on her thighs.

I cannot speak of how I could not bear to see Anuket's bandaged body standing in its coffin beside the tomb's entrance, Huy thought, going to his chair. *To imagine the mourners wailing in their blue sheaths is dismal enough, and the funerary priest, the Kher-heb, approaching her corpse holding the Ur-hekau, the rod used as part of the ceremony to reopen Anuket's mouth and eyes. Those beautiful eyes,* Huy remembered with a pang, *and that mouth full of an ingenuous invitation. No. If my mind would present her to me as she was when I last saw her, with the pouches of dissipation under her eyes, her slim lines blurred by too much flesh, an ill-fitting wig on her bald head, I could endure the ritual that will leave her in the darkness of dank rock. But that image is ephemeral, that image has no substance beside the girl I worshipped.*

Thothhotep was holding up a loaded brush and the scroll for him to sign. With a gust of breath, he wrote his name and title—Huy, Seer—and handed the scroll back to her. There was no need to tell her what to do with it. Anhur would hire a reliable herald in the marketplace or delegate one of his soldiers to take the road the short way south to Iunu. *It's almost time to hire a permanent herald or even two,* Huy thought as Thothhotep left the floor, gave him a quick bow, and went away. *Doubtless the Princess will resume her correspondence to me, and almost every day there are letters delivered that require an answer. Perhaps Merenra can see to it.* He knew he ought to get up, go into the passage, resume the customary activities of the day, but he sat on, gazing unseeingly at his ringed hands resting on the table, the office an oasis of silence around him.

The King did not consult Huy, nor did any of his commanders. He and his army filed past Hut-herib on the east bank of
the river—to the delight of the town's citizens, who lined the
west bank to watch the cavalcade go by—and then struck
out towards Rethennu. Huy was relieved. Two weeks later, a
letter arrived from Heby. "I allowed Officer Irem to escort
Amunhotep-Huy into the tents of the officers while the army
was briefly bivouacked here," Heby had dictated to Nanai,
his scribe.

He had pestered me for the privilege until I gave in.
However, I cautioned Irem not to let him mingle with the
common soldiers. Amunhotep-Huy is becoming quite an
expert on Egypt's military history and his work in other
areas of his study has improved beyond all my hope. His
behaviour has also improved. His lessons with Officer Irem
are suspended until the King returns, as Irem, a Captain of
Fifty, has marched east. One word of interest, Huy. Your old
enemy Sennefer has apparently been in the army for a long
time and is now commanding the Division of Set, an
appointment I find entirely suitable, Set being the god of
chaos and stirring up trouble when he feels like it.
Amunhotep-Huy met Sennefer and a few of the other
generals and can easily recite their names, ranks, and char-
acteristics. Of course, your nephew did not recognize
Sennefer as your attacker. Huy, I am very sorry to hear of
the death of your friend. Iupia and I went to Iunu to
offer the Governor and Ishat our regrets in person, but they
and the Lady Nasha had already sailed for Weset.

Huy suppressed the moment of guilt. *I am not strong enough*, he
thought as Thothhotep walked across the office floor and slid

Heby's scroll into the niche holding the pile of his previous correspondence. *Thothmes will understand.*

"Master, do you wish me to make a note of Governor Sennefer's position as Commander of the Division of Set for your future reference?" Thothhotep inquired.

Her use of Sennefer's administrative title gave Huy a jolt. *Why, of course he's a Governor now. Governor of the small Nart-Pehu sepat, a little southeast of Ta-she. How did he end up as a military commander, seeing that my inadvertent vision for him when I met him again at the temple school in Khmun was of his death in battle? He sneered at my peasant roots and bullied me unmercifully in and out of class at Iunu. His personality is perfectly suited to life as a soldier. Perhaps he convinced himself that my gift is false, that I am a proficient liar, so that he could enter the army. Or perhaps the Osiris-King Thothmes the Third decreed officer status for him as a compensation for removing his right to carry the throwing stick, the hunting weapon only the nobility may use, after his attack on me. When did his father die? I don't know. But when he did, Sennefer would have been forced to take up his father's governorship. Now our new ruler goes to war and needs all his commanders. Sennefer will die, I know it. Does he? Does he remember the day I grasped his arm and saw him slumped across a chariot's rail, gasping out his life?*

"Master?" Thothhotep said, and Huy came to himself.

"No, don't bother," he replied. "It would be a waste of good papyrus."

SIX MONTHS LATER, when Epophi, the first of the two harvest months, was over, the King came marching triumphantly home. Again he bypassed Hut-herib without visiting Huy, who knew nothing about Thothmes' campaign, and indeed could not have cared less. A letter arrived from the Princess, now Queen, Mutemwia. Huy welcomed it.

He had marked the day of Anuket's funeral three months previously in Pharmuthi by offering on Khenti-kheti's altar one of the precious gifts she had given him. On his fourteenth Naming Day she had gently removed the one earring he had owned and replaced it with one made of red jasper and pale yellow-green moonstone teardrops held in golden claws. "The jasper is for the redness of your blood, warm and healthy with youth," she had told him, "and the moonstone is for your gift. The moon belongs to Thoth." He had worn it on special occasions, but when he had left Iunu he had wrapped it in linen and put it in one of the compartments of the cedar box his uncle Ker had given him years before. Now he laid it carefully at the feet of the benignly smiling wolf-god with a prayer for Anuket's ka, embraced Methen, and hurried back to his estate.

For his fifteenth Naming Day, Anuket had given him a pair of calfskin gloves to protect his hands while driving a chariot, and once she had bathed and dressed a cat's scratch and insisted that he accept an ointment in a delicate little blue faience bottle. These things had also ended up in the cedar box, where they remained, for Huy could not bear to take them out and handle them after he fled the temple school. There was no need to preserve them now. The remains of the ointment had dried and crusted inside the bottle. Huy told Tetiankh to clean it out and then use it for kohl powder. Although he had become proficient at handling a chariot, he had not driven one since returning to Hut-herib. Still, he gave the gloves to his under steward Amunmose with instructions to oil and store them against a day when they might be of some use. These actions served to relegate the ache of his memories to the night hours when he woke and could not sleep again. Otherwise he could think of her without distress.

The Queen's letter was full of news. "I shall send my son to you at the beginning of Paophi, with a gift for your forty-second Naming Day on the ninth," she wrote in her own unsteady hand.

He is looking forward to seeing you and Anhur. He and his staff have been living in the palace at Mi-wer. I sent him there because of a terrible fever that has been taking its toll of the children here at Mennofer's palace. His half-brothers by Thothmes' other women, Akheperura and Siamun, are dead, along with many others. Such fevers are common during the Inundation, as you know, but they seldom last into Peret. This one is unusually vicious. You are to keep Amunhotep with you until then, so that he may remain healthy under your care.

Here Thothhotep's carefully modulated voice ceased. She glanced across at Huy, who was sitting on the edge of his desk.

"Yes, it's an overwhelming responsibility," Huy answered her unspoken comment. "I wonder if she will tell her husband where his princeling has gone. I don't think so. I knew nothing of the deaths in the harem at Mennofer. Did you?"

Thothhotep shook her head. "The Queen does not mention the names of any of the children of the nobles. Did more than the seed of Pharaoh die? Surely so! I suppose that only the royal offspring are of any interest to her. I shall continue reading. 'The Good God has commissioned the striking of a scarab to commemorate his victories in the east.'" Thothhotep was frowning and peering at the scroll in an effort to interpret Mutemwia's scrawl. "'It will read thus: *The Chiefs of Naharin bearing their revenue see Menkheperura proceeding from his house. They hear his voice like the son of Nut, his bow being in his hand like the son of Shu's successors. When he goes into battle, Aten being before him, he destroys the mountain countries, trampling the desert countries, treading to Naharin and to Karoy to ensure that the inhabitants of foreign countries are subjects to the rule of the Aten forever.* He has also ordered the twelve enemy tribes of Egypt listed on his new chariot, six from the east and six from the south. As for Mitanni, when the King reached Naharin, Artatama sent envoys to him bearing much purple gold and thus he did not enter Mitanni. Your old enemy Governor Sennefer was killed in a skirmish with tribesmen in Zahi as the army was progressing towards Naharin. *By my own hand Mutemwia, Queen and Second Wife, the tenth day of Mesore, year one of the King.'"*

"Write to Her Majesty welcoming the little Prince and his retainers," Huy said, sliding off the desk. "This house is fast becoming too small. Tell Anhur to have his men gather bricks and construct quarters for the servants who will arrive. It will have to be somewhere against the rear wall—that's all the open ground I have left. Talk to Merenra about mats and furnishings." He grinned ruefully. "I am quite sure that our shrewd Queen knows how wealthy I am, down to the last uten of weight. She will not see me impoverished by her requests, but neither will she provide more gold than she deems necessary. She has created an excellent network of spies, Thothhotep. I wonder if Thothmes has any notion of how closely she watches his affairs."

"And yours, Huy?" Thothhotep said. "Are you not concerned at how intimately she examines every detail of your life?"

Huy considered the question. "No, I'm not," he replied finally. "Her ambition for her son and her vigilance over the course of her husband's growing heresy are coupled with great intelligence, and a tolerance unusual in one so exalted."

"You have named it at last," Thothhotep said. "*Heresy.* It is just as well that Thothmes will live no longer than the few years the gods have ordained for him."

Their eyes met in the tacit acknowledgment that their mutual complicity was now absolute. Huy nodded, turned, and left the room.

16

THE RIVER WAS STILL RISING and the Delta air hot and humid when Prince Amunhotep and his crowd of servants disembarked from four barges on the third day of Paophi. Anhur's soldiers had only just finished the mud-brick building they had hurriedly erected during the few weeks between the arrival of Mutemwia's letter and the appearance of her son, and the not unpleasant odour of whitewash lingered over the estate. Anhur himself stood beside Huy and Thothhotep on the path, his men forming a guard along its edge and the rest of Huy's staff clustering behind their master. Huy did not recognize the first official who came gliding from the ramp and along the path to halt in front of him. He was not a dwarf, but he was the shortest man Huy had ever seen, the beringed hands held out as he made his obeisance as small as a woman's. Not until his blue-ribboned head went down did Huy see that he was slightly hunchbacked, his left shoulder higher than his right. The deformity obviously did not affect his bearing; he had walked from the deck of the royal barge and up to Huy with studied grace.

"I am Nubti, the Prince's Household Steward," he said. His voice was also a surprise: it was a masculine rumble even deeper than Anhur's. "I realize that so many people taking up their residence here will be an inconvenience for you, Great Seer. Therefore the Queen Mutemwia has commanded me and the rest of the Prince's servants to put ourselves entirely at your disposal." He waved back at the men now clustered on the bank of the water, their waiting gaze on him. "We are all in subjection to your will and the direction of your own steward. The lesser servants may of course sleep on the barges. The nights are still very warm."

Huy returned his bow, introducing Merenra, Thothhotep, Anhur, and his few other staff members. "Merenra, you and Nubti can begin sorting out accommodations at once," he ordered his steward. "The Prince will of course occupy the guest room, and you must erect tents on the roof for Royal Nurse Heqarneheh and anyone else who needs to be close to him. Now, where is my charge?"

Without turning, Nubti raised a hand and clicked his fingers. At once the crowd parted and Amunhotep came walking through with his nurse Heqarneheh behind him. *He's grown,* Huy thought, smiling, watching the child's face light up in response. *He's put on an inch or two, and his features are slightly more defined. I wonder how long it will be before he kicks off those gilded sandals and drops the jewel-bordered kilt in Heqarneheh's lap.* Huy and his companions bowed low, arms extended in worship.

The Prince's hennaed feet came together under Huy's gaze. "Stand upright, Great Seer, new uncle, all the rest of you," the childish voice commanded firmly, and Huy straightened to look down into a pair of kohled, sparkling eyes. "I have longed to see you again, and at last here I am! My mother the Queen has warned me to be obedient to you alone, so I hope you won't have made up a lot of rules for me to follow, and I still have to do my lessons every morning." He made a face. "Common children are allowed to enjoy their freedom during the Inundation, but not me! Oh no! My tutor Menkhoper is back there somewhere"—he waved a nonchalant arm in the direction of the group still waiting by the ramps—"and apparently you are to make sure that I study. Is the house snake still living in the garden? When can we go fishing? Anhur, will you teach me to shoot with a bow? I brought the one Wesersatet made for me." His shoulders rose and his hennaed fists clenched in a gesture of pure glee. "Oh, I am so excited to be here!"

"Your Highness's mastery over his vocabulary has grown," Anhur said drily.

Amunhotep nodded. "I talk too much and don't listen enough," he replied without the slightest sign of contrition. "So says my body servant. Great Seer, Anhur, I will embrace you now." Huy bent and Amunhotep's arms went around his neck. A soft mouth was pressed against his cheek. Releasing Huy, the Prince threw himself at Anhur, jumping until Anhur lifted him. "You may carry me inside the house," Amunhotep said, "and give me beer and sweetmeats."

"You may have milk and bread with honey," Heqarneheh contradicted him. As they moved towards the entrance, Huy looked back. Nubti and Merenra were dispersing the crowd, and Amunmose was hurrying after Huy together with an older man wearing a plain kilt, unlike many of the Prince's entourage. *I must impress on Merenra the need for a quiet house for at least a couple of hours in the afternoons,* Huy thought as the coolness of the reception hall enveloped him. *Especially if Thothhotep and I have been working among the petitioners all morning. This promises to be an interesting few months.*

The afternoon was chaotic as the guests found their quarters and collected and unpacked their belongings. Huy retreated to his office, answering his steward's harried questions from time to time and speaking briefly with the Prince's tutor, Menkhoper. It was decided that Amunhotep's morning lessons should be held in the coolness of the office as soon as Huy and Thothhotep had dealt with their own correspondence. "As well as tutoring His Highness in the academic disciplines, I am also the Chief Scribe in the House of the Royal Children," Menkhoper explained to Huy. "Any letters from the House will be delivered to me. My Mistress, Queen and Royal Wife Mutemwia, has ordered me to show you the contents of every scroll that arrives." He looked at Huy with a frank interest. "She puts great faith in you, noble one, and expects you to be actively involved in the Prince's education while he is here. The captain of your household guards is to begin lessons in wrestling and archery, and she requests that you foster a respect for architecture in my young charge. Of course, there are few monuments in this vicinity," he added, "and at the palace Amunhotep has tutors in stonemasonry, shipbuilding, and the like, but my Mistress seems to feel that your perspective on these things will benefit her son. She asks for regular and private reports from you regarding his progress and his behaviour while he is here. She also insists that none of us interfere in any way with your work of Seeing, but that Amunhotep is on no account to accompany you on those occasions. He may be taken into the marketplace of the town if well guarded, however. My Mistress wishes him to observe the life of the commoners." His tone was supercilious. "I do not ask why."

"Then all he has to do is observe me," Huy retorted, amused. "I am a Hut-herib peasant."

"Even so." Menkhoper was unperturbed. "But forgive me, Great Seer, you are hardly a typical example of Egyptian peasantry. Part of my task in educating this most precious boy is to teach him that in this country every man is equal under Ma'at and before the judges except the King, and then it is only his divinity that sets him apart. Perhaps my Mistress desires that truth more forcefully impressed on him than mere words could do." He spread out his hands. "My responsibility is great, yet the Prince is a joy to instruct. He is intelligent and intuitive."

It was on the tip of Huy's tongue to ask this rather likeable man if Mutemwia had confided in him her long-ranging plan for her son, or if Amunhotep himself had mentioned it, but caution closed his mouth. After stowing two sacks of pieces of broken clay at the foot of the shelves together with a small mat, and filling several niches with scrolls, brushes, and pots of ink powder, he bowed and went away, leaving Huy to listen to the ebb and flow of new life in his house. Feeling slightly lost, he did not venture into the passage until Amunmose summoned him to the reception hall for the evening meal. Blue and white liveried servants mingling with his own hurried to and fro, adroitly dodging the many small tables that filled the modest space as they lit the lamps, placed cushions on the gleaming black-and-white-tiled floor, and began to unseal the wine jars. Nubti and Merenra were watching the bustle critically.

Amunmose, who had followed him, wiped the sweat from his chest with the hem of his long under steward's gown. "Gods, Huy, is it going to be like this every night?" he breathed. "I haven't had a moment to myself all day! Khnit says she needs more help in the kitchens."

"Tell Steward Nubti to assign some of his household servants to assist her," Huy replied. "Don't worry, Amunmose, a routine will soon be established and you'll be able to go back to guzzling my beer every afternoon in the shade by the palms. You must admit that all this has brought the house alive."

"I liked it half dead," Amunmose muttered, and plunged into the throng.

Amunhotep and Heqarneheh entered together. The boy hurried to where Huy and Anhur had risen from behind their tables to reverence him. He had been washed and was wearing an unadorned kilt, plain reed sandals, and a simple gold hoop through the lobe of one ear. Waving them down, he wriggled between them and at once a servant brought him a table. "Heqarneheh made me wear sandals," he announced. "It's rude to be unshod while eating, he says. Well, I knew that, but it was worth a try. I was too excited to sleep this afternoon, but I'm not tired. May we go on the river tonight, Anhur? We don't have to fish, just enjoy the water, you, me, and Uncle Huy. Are we having cucumbers? My royal mother smears cucumber on her face to feed her skin, she says, but I like it to feed my belly. Is it too late in the season for nehet figs?" He was examining the contents of the dishes presented to him on a tray. "Oh, give me a bit of everything!" he said to the servant. "Hurry up so that everyone else can be served."

His thigh was warm against Huy's. He smelled of rosemary steeped in olive oil. One thin black tendril of hair had worked loose from the clasp holding the braid of his youth lock and was wisping against the shallow dip below the diminutive ridge of his collarbone. In spite of the boy's self-confident prattle, Huy found himself moved by the vulnerability those few strands seemed to betray, the touching defencelessness of the young frame. He wanted to tuck the wayward tress back into the braid and put a protective arm across the fragile shoulders.

"I'm so glad you're here, Highness," he said.

Amunhotep turned to him with a dazzling smile. "So am I!" he said fervently. "I've brought you a gift for your Naming Day on the ninth of this month, and after we've been to the shrine of your totem to give thanks for your continued preservation, I'll give it to you. I know you'll really like it!"

After the meal, the diners scattered. The season was Akhet, when the dawn came early and the sunset late, and the sky was still rosy soft with the last of the light when Anhur lifted Amunhotep into the skiff. Huy clambered aboard and poled the vessel away from the watersteps. Amunhotep took a deep breath. "There are no city odours here," he said. "Only the faint scent of smoke from the kitchen and a whiff of everything damp from the flood. Egypt is the most wonderful place in the world, isn't it? Our fate is very kind, to place us here. Tell me a story about my ancestors, Anhur, as you did when I stayed last year."

So Anhur began a long and involved tale of the military exploits of the Osiris-King Thothmes the First, five generations earlier, his deep, comforting voice making Huy nod with the need for sleep while the sound of the river was an almost imperceptible tremor and the night darkened around him.

Heqarneheh and the Prince's body servant were waiting for him by the gate as Anhur guided the skiff to a bump against a tethering pole, and it was Huy who swung the child into his arms, waded up the watersteps, and set him on his feet before his guardians. After he bade Huy and Anhur a formal good night, Amunhotep's hand found his nurse's and the three of them vanished towards the house.

"If I have to do this every night, I'm soon going to run out of stories," Anhur remarked as he and Huy fell into step together. "You must have plenty, Huy, from your time at school in Iunu."

"I do, but I think that he needs to hear the reassuring quality of your voice more than the exploits of the ancients. You do realize that the Queen has placed the responsibility for raising him entirely in our hands during the Inundation months?"

"Of course I do!" Anhur replied sourly. "And Amun help us if we put a foot wrong! Will you go into the town with Thothhotep and work tomorrow, Master?"

Huy laughed. "Yes, I must, but don't worry, our Prince will be busy at his lessons and won't be allowed near you! Sleep well, old friend." They parted, Anhur towards his cell and Huy turning into the rear passage of the house. *Am I allowed to think of him as the child I never had?* Huy wondered in a rush of affection for Amunhotep. *Is he a compensation for the impotence that ensures my ultimate loneliness? Atum, may I freely love this royal child although my love could very well supplant the devotion that rightfully belongs to his father the King?* As if in answer, he heard, faintly and from far away, the shriek of a hyena followed by its sinister bark of laughter. The sound did not disturb him. *So you remain nearby,* he spoke to it silently as he began to mount the stairs. *You keep your peculiar vigil, but tonight your cry is not meant to terrify me. At the god's command you laugh at me, but the echo of your amusement holds no judgment. Therefore I will allow myself this surprising happiness.*

It occurred to him as Tetiankh was handing him his nightly dose of poppy that this new and unexpected relationship with the Prince might very well be the chance Anubis had spoken of when he had told Huy he would be allowed an opportunity to put right the wrong he had done in not censuring the Osiris-King and his son Thothmes, now King over Egypt. Had Atum amended his intention for his beloved country to accommodate Huy's moment of fallibility by circumventing a future where Thothmes' brother, the rightful heir, sat on the throne, in favour of an alternate fate, with Mutemwia's son as the Divine One instead? *If so, then I am resting in the centre of Atum's will,* Huy thought, closing his eyes as he heard Tetiankh pull the door shut behind him. *I have been given the chance to earn his forgiveness.*

Sometime in the night, Huy came drowsily awake to find Amunhotep climbing onto the couch beside him. "I miss the Queen my mother," the boy whispered, breathing sweet, warm air against Huy's cheek. "She always makes me feel safe in the night, as you did the last time I slept beside you, Uncle Huy. She says the prayers of protection over me, but tonight Heqarneheh forgot. Heka is a gift from Atum to ward off the blows of fate. So says Menkhoper. You have strong heka. Everyone says so. May I stay with you until Ra is reborn and the demons retreat?"

For answer, Huy lifted an arm and Amunhotep snuggled into his body. Almost at once Huy felt the Prince's muscles loosen in sleep. He himself soon drifted into unconsciousness. He dreamed that he was sitting in a tree high above the grey expanse of the Inundation, and even in his sleep he knew its meaning: he might expect the destruction of all his woes.

The house soon settled into the regular rhythm of life that Huy had predicted to his under steward. The Prince rose late in spite of all his nurse's attempts to lure him from his couch, and by the time he had eaten his morning meal, visited the bathhouse, and been hurriedly kohled and dressed in little more than a loincloth and sandals, Huy and Thothhotep had dealt with the correspondence, Thothhotep had taken away Huy's answers to be copied, and Menkhoper was preparing the office for Amunhotep's morning lessons. Huy was present when he was not doing the healing and scrying work of the god among the townspeople. He had reluctantly ordered Anhur to go into the marketplace and make it known that until the middle of Tybi, when the water would be rapidly receding, he would receive no petitioners on the estate. "It's too great a risk to the Prince's security, having strangers congregating in the garden," he had told Anhur. "Besides, no matter how tight-lipped we are, the news of his presence here must already be spreading, and many people will be curious to see him. It's a nuisance for me and for Thothhotep and particularly for the litter-bearers, but it can't be helped."

Huy soon found that he did not need to remonstrate with Menkhoper over any aspect of the morning's lessons. The man was a good teacher, often turning the knowledge he was trying to impart into an enthralling or light-hearted story. He was also firm with his aristocratic pupil without becoming harsh. Amunhotep obviously respected him, as much for his ability to control a child who was fully able to try craftiness and subtle deception to get his own way as for his enlightened method of teaching. The second meal of the day was now eaten in the early afternoon, after which the household retired for the sleep. Huy had been forced to insist that the Prince remain quietly in his own room during this time, and had set a guard on the door to prevent Amunhotep from slipping free and roaming about by himself, for the boy never needed to rest. He played sennet or Dogs and Jackals with his long-suffering body servant, or practised his letters on the pieces of broken clay Menkhoper gave him. After the sleep he was placed in Anhur's care, and gleefully disappeared with his friend to practise with his little bow or to learn the first simple wrestling holds in which every noble Egyptian boy delighted. Huy was more than grateful to Anhur for this respite. Often he himself returned home from Hut-herib sick and exhausted, and needed a couple of hours and a dose of poppy in the dimness of his shuttered bedchamber to recover.

During the remaining hours before the evening meal, Huy unrolled the ground plans of various temples and monuments on his desk and, with Amunhotep sitting on a high stool beside him, explained how deep the foundation for a pillar of a certain height and weight had to be dug, why commemorative stelae were hewn out of granite instead of the prettier limestone, what tools the masons used, and what considerations an architect had to take into account when designing for the gods. If the Prince's interest flagged, Huy would produce sketches of Egypt's huge trading vessels and speak of their voyages and their cargo through the Great Green to Alashia and Keftiu and Arzawa in the north. He had requested the blueprints from the Mayor of Hut-herib, from Heby in Mennofer, and from Thothmes at Iunu. The drawings of the ships he had done himself at school. Amunhotep was full of questions, retaining almost everything he was told, and Huy delighted in his company. Every week he dictated a letter to Mutemwia describing her son's progress and the state of his health and general well-being. Letters came from her to Amunhotep, and Menkhoper made the boy read them aloud, a task he attempted with much frowning, squinting, and lip biting.

On the ninth of Paophi, Huy's Naming Day, he and Amunhotep, with Heqarneheh and a suitable number of guards, skirted the flood and entered Hut-herib so that Huy could thank the totem of his town for yet another year of life. He was now forty-two and entirely aware that he appeared ten years younger. His belly remained tight and flat, his legs well muscled, his hair (still obstinately worn long) thick and black. There was no suspicion of a sag in his arms or pouches of flesh on his back above the belt of his kilt. His gift to Khenti-kheti this year was a pouch of gold dust and the crops of barley and flax reaped the previous season from his arouras west of the town and stored safely in the domes of his clay silos. He embraced Methen, introduced the Prince, who received the priest's obeisance with dignity, and recited the prayers of thanksgiving with more than his usual attention. He was healthy, handsome, and rich, and standing beside him was the sturdy little scion of royalty he had already come to love. On this day the Book of Thoth seemed like an ephemeral mirage flickering far back in his mind. So did his dependence on the drug that now poured gold into the chests Merenra hovered over protectively. He was standing within the will of Atum, he told himself, and that was a triumph.

After taking his leave of Methen, he and his entourage made their way to his parents' house. He had debated with himself whether or not to have the Prince returned to the estate before he attended the modest feast his mother, Itu, and Hapzefa, Ishat's mother, were preparing for him, but Amunhotep had protested loudly at the prospect of being left behind. "I am supposed to be experiencing the lives of the peasants," he had pointed out. "This is a good way to begin, Uncle Huy—a whole afternoon with the most fortunate citizens who cared for you after Sennefer attacked you! Incidentally, isn't it wonderful that he is now dead and probably gobbled up by Sebek for what he did? I bet his heart weighed much too heavily on the scales!"

Looking into the sparkling eyes of this miniature demon of vengeance, Huy stifled the urge to smile. *When you are older, I will tell you of those sad days in my father's house, and of why I understand Sennefer's misery, but you are too young to understand any of it now.*

"Very well, we will go on to my parents' after our visit to Khenti-kheti's shrine," he had said. "But Highness, you must promise not to leave the boundaries of the garden. The fields and canals that lie close to the house are still flooding. They are dangerous."

His mother ran to embrace him as he approached the house. Enveloping her in his arms, inhaling the lily perfume she had worn ever since he could remember, noticing the lightness and frailty of her, he felt his chest constrict with love and pity. Behind her, Hapzefa came hobbling, aided by a walking stick. "Another Naming Day, and you've hardly changed since I chased you naked around the pond!" she called, her voice now the only robust part of her.

Huy had long since built a small mud-brick house by the hedge dividing the garden from his uncle Ker's orchard and settled a gardener and a house servant in it. His mother did only those chores she chose to perform, and spent most of her days gossiping with Hapzefa, who had become too lame to do much work, and reminiscing with her husband, Hapu. Huy's father had eventually been forced to leave Ker's perfume fields to the care of younger men. He could no longer stand upright, the knuckles of his hands were so swollen and painful that often he was unable to feed himself, and a weakness in his legs had relegated him to the chair Huy had provided for him. After a lifetime spent in lowering himself to the floor for food or prayer or to entertain, Hapu's pride suffered. He would not thank Huy for increasingly taking care of his modest household, but he had expressed his gratitude, albeit grudgingly, to Heby, and Heby had told Huy. Huy's pity went to Itu, who had been beautiful and kind and gentle, and whose sweet nature still shone through the ravages of aging.

"And you still send shivers of apprehension down my spine, Hapzefa!" he called back, releasing Itu and hurrying to plant a kiss on the servant's lined cheek. "Mother, Hapzefa, I have brought the King's son Prince Amunhotep to meet you. In deference to your age and out of respect for your undoubted wisdom, he does not require you to perform any obeisance."

Taken aback, they stared at the boy walking towards them. Itu did bow. "Welcome to this house, Highness," she said as he came to a halt and stared up into her face. "We are most honoured by your presence."

"Yes, you are, and I am honoured to meet the mother of Egypt's Great Seer," he replied with aplomb. "I want to meet his father now."

Hapu was rising from his chair in the reception room of the house as Huy and the Prince, followed by the women, crowded into the cramped space. Bent over, he appeared to be bowing, but Huy knew that he could stand in no other way. "I wish you great fortune on your Naming Day, my son," he said to Huy. "Now, who is this handsome young man?" Huy realized that his father had heard nothing of the greetings outside. He introduced Amunhotep, and boy and man gazed appraisingly at one another for a moment before Amunhotep's eyes slid to the one hand steadying Hapu on the arm of the chair.

"You may sit," he offered, and Huy could have sworn that he was overcome with a brief shyness as Hapu eased himself down. "As the father of the Twice Born, you are surely beloved and protected by all the gods," Amunhotep went on. "You must be very devout, to have been given the seed which created him. I shouldn't be surprised if you are allowed to just walk through the Judgment Hall without having your heart weighed when the time comes for your Beautification."

Hapu's eyebrows shot up. A smile touched his lips. "Your Highness is most polite," he replied, "but I must confess that my work in the fields left me little energy or time for much devotion apart from the evening prayers to Khenti-kheti, and even then they were sometimes forgotten." His glance went to Huy. "The heka surrounding Huy has nothing to do with me or my lack of piety. It comes directly from Atum."

"I'm not very devout myself," Amunhotep said. "There are many things I'd rather do than pray. I rely on the heka surrounding the King my father to keep me safe and healthy, and he, of course, gets his magic from Amun." He shrugged. "Lately there has been much worshipping of the Aten in the King my father's harem and in the palace. That god has become fashionable since the King my father returned from the east victorious. I get bored when my tutors try to teach me about the gods. It's all very confusing." He and Hapu nodded gravely at one another. Amunhotep turned to a hovering Itu. "Mother of Uncle Huy, is there ... He said that on his Naming Day there would be ... Is it noon yet, do you think?"

Itu had been frowning. Now her brow cleared. "Highness, if you will sit, Hapzefa and I will bring Huy's Naming Day feast. It must indeed be nearly noon." She and Hapzefa backed out of the room.

Amunhotep sank onto a cushion facing Hapu across the faded beige of the old flaxen mat that had covered the dirt floor for as long as Huy could remember. Huy lowered himself beside him. There was an awkward silence until Amunhotep said, "You have laboured in the perfume fields all your life, Father of Huy. I am most interested in the production of perfume because the King my father's Treasurer, Sobekhotep, has told me that its sale to foreign countries brings much wealth to Egypt. What sort of perfume do the foreigners like best?"

Huy, marvelling at the child's civility, saw no reason to join the conversation that ensued. His father, after a hesitant reply, began to speak of the flowers he had tended with a knowledge and affection Huy had not suspected. He was still extolling the virtues of lotus essence over lily when his wife and Hapzefa brought in the meal and set it on the floor.

There were bowls of a spicy pork stew, a steaming lentil soup made fragrant with cumin and coriander, a salad of oiled chickpeas flecked by pieces of mild green onion and garlic, and pale yellow butter to spread on fresh bread. There was shedeh-wine, and dark barley beer for Hapu. Hapzefa brought out a plate of the honey cakes Huy had loved as a child. Everything was offered to Amunhotep first, and after a moment, when he looked about for the servant who would put the food into his clay dish, he happily applied his spoon himself. Huy watched him unobtrusively, anxious lest he might choke, but the Prince ate slowly and politely, emptied his mouth before speaking, and complimented the women on their cooking skill. Huy gave him a little watered shedeh to drink, the taste of last year's pomegranates bittersweet on his own tongue.

At last the plates were scoured and talk faltered. Huy looked at the Prince and nodded. Amunhotep rose. "It's time for the afternoon sleep," he said. "I and Huy must go now. Thank you, father and mother of Huy, for your hospitality." He smiled at them all as Itu and Hapzefa struggled to their feet and bowed, and Hapu inclined his head. Huy kissed them.

"Do you need anything, Father?" he asked Hapu, knowing that his father would deny any lack. Hapu shook his head. Huy felt Amunhotep's hand creep into his own and together they went out into the fierce early afternoon sunlight, both blinking after the dimness of the house. Anhur and the guards fell in behind them. The litter-bearers emerged from the shade of the orchard where they had been dozing. *Ishat used to come creeping into the garden through that gap in the acacia hedge,* Huy thought as he waited for the Prince to settle himself among the cushions. *The air here is full of her, and I am here also, she and I perpetually young, perpetually linked to each other although we are now living out our several destinies apart. I am not comfortable here. The power of the past to unman me is too strong.*

"Uncle Huy, what was that meat?" Amunhotep asked as the litter was lifted.

Huy closed the curtain beside himself and leaned over the boy to draw it across on the other side. "It was pork. Pig's flesh, Highness," Huy replied in surprise. "You haven't eaten it before?"

"No, of course not. It's the food of the poor, and servants. I didn't like it much." He yawned widely. "The shedeh was good, though. It's made me sleepy." He turned a troubled face to Huy. "Your parents are very old and infirm, Uncle Huy. Life must be hard for them now in that tiny, dark house, but it must have been even worse when you and your brother the Mayor of Mennofer were little. How could anyone exist in such a small place?"

"That house is large compared to the dwellings of most of Hut-herib's citizens," Huy answered carefully. "My family are peasants, but because my uncle Ker was fortunate enough to be granted land by your great-grandfather the Osiris-King Thothmes the Third, my father was given work that enabled him to build our house. Ker was a clever and adventurous young man who loved flowers and became apprenticed to a perfume maker here in the Delta. When the man died suddenly, Ker applied to the King for the fields that of course had gone khato, and the King deeded them to him in exchange for a share of the profits as well as the usual taxes. Ker hired my father. Most peasants do not live as well as my family does."

Amunhotep was quiet for so long that Huy thought he had gone to sleep. It was hot and close in the confines of the litter. The rhythmic sway of the bearers was soporific. But at last the boy sighed and stirred. "You lived with your servant Ishat in the centre of Hut-herib, where there is noise and filth all the time, didn't you? My mother the Queen told me so. Hut-herib is very smelly and ugly. I shall be glad to return to your estate. Do the peasants have enough to eat, Uncle Huy?"

"Yes, they do, Highness," Huy assured him. "Egypt abounds in vegetables and crops of every kind, and as long as Isis cries, no one goes hungry. There are fish in the river, and pigeons and hares to eat. You need not worry."

"I am not worried," Amunhotep said loftily. "I would expect Amun to bless all of us who live under the rule of Ma'at, but some more than others, of course. Your scribe is very pretty, isn't she? She loves Anhur. Does she sleep with him, do you know? My father the King sleeps with many women. When I am in my quarters in the harem, they fawn upon me and all they ever talk about among themselves is who will go to my father's bed next and how to make themselves more attractive. The concubines, I mean. I get very tired of them."

Huy was becoming used to the seemingly illogical leaps in the Prince's conversations. He fought his thick-headedness and did his best to concentrate on what was being said. "So your mother allows you to mingle with the concubines, Highness?"

Amunhotep favoured Huy with his broadest grin. "Well, no, not really," he confessed. "But they come to the door of my apartments

with gifts for the guards, and they whisper and giggle and sometimes persuade the men to let them in. Sobekhotep appoints the guards because his title is Guardian of the Prince as a Child as well as being Overseer of the Treasury, but my mother the Queen threatened to have him dismissed if he did not discipline them. The women still try to get in. They think that I talk with my father the King every day, but I don't." The grin had disappeared. Huy did not miss the note of longing in the words.

"Have you no friends in the palace, Highness?" he inquired.

Amunhotep nodded and rolled his eyes. "I sometimes play with Minhotep and Ptahemhet and Paser. They're the sons of my father's officials who are closest to my own age, and we study together under Menkhoper and the other teachers. I like them well enough. I like my half-sister Petepihu better. She's the daughter of Yaret, another of my father's wives. She's older than me. She'll take me out into the palace gardens and tell me the names of all the birds. We play sennet together. But my mother the Queen doesn't really like me living in my harem apartments, and sends me there only if people in the main palace are getting sick. Uncle Huy, may I give you your Naming Day present this evening? I've waited a very long time for you to see it."

The gift was a heavy collar made up of six rows of alternating dark orange carnelian and blue faience glass tiles held together by thin strings of gold and separated at regular intervals by golden frogs and lizards. Huy, seated cross-legged before the remains of the evening meal, speechlessly lifted the piece from its linen bed on his lap and held it up, watching the lamplight glint on the exquisite workmanship of the figures.

The Prince leaned close. "I ordered the jeweller to put frogs on it for you because you like frogs, and lizards on it for me because I like lizards. Or mostly for me," he corrected himself. "Lizards are sacred to the creator-god Atum. I asked Menkhoper, who knows almost everything. Frogs are for *wehem ankh*, 'living again,' and very appropriate for you. Are you pleased? Put it on!" He was clearly proud of himself, and wriggled behind Huy so that he could close the collar's hasp while Huy held it against his chest. The sa amulet the Rekhet had made for him hung just a little lower on its chain.

"Highness, I am pleased and honoured and humbled," Huy managed. "It's a magnificent present, a treasure."

"You don't have to dine in it every night, but wear it some-times while I'm here." Amunhotep knelt up and enfolded Huy's head in his arms. "I love you very much. Can we go fishing now?"

AS THE YEARS PASSED, Huy and all the members of his household began to look forward to the months of the Inundation, when Prince Amunhotep would arrive with his retinue, settle into the guest room, and bring the estate to life. Huy, loving him, seeing the changes both physical and intellec-tual in him each year, missed him when he was gone. The letters from his mother continued to arrive, always giving Huy a vivid account of everything occurring at court, but Mutemwia herself no longer accompanied her son to the Seer's house. Huy admired her wisdom. It was certain that the King knew of his child's yearly stay near Hut-herib, and equally clear that he did not care, probably because Amunhotep was not his heir. Amunemhat, son of Chief Wife Neferatiri, held that honour, and as long as Second Wife Mutemwia was not living at Huy's estate with her little boy, she was not plotting sedition. The King's gold continued to arrive punctually at Huy's watersteps, but no word ever came from the One himself.

It was a time of prosperity and satisfaction for Huy's family also. In year five of the King, Huy's nephew Ramose turned six and was enrolled at the temple school in Mennofer, and the following year his other nephew, Amunhotep-Huy, finished his education and was appointed as a scribe at court to Tjanuni, the King's Overseer of Soldiers. Huy had no doubt that the boy would do well among the men he liked and did his best to emulate. He had wanted to enter the army itself, but Heby, his father, had protested against his desire so vehemently that Amunhotep-Huy had sulkily acquiesced to both Heby's urging and that of his military tutor Officer Irem, and had accepted the position of army scribe instead. Heby's own position as Mayor of Mennofer had given him a reputation to uphold. Only the sons of peasants volunteered to march with the infantry. The sons of nobles and highly placed administrators entered officer training, but even that route was denied to Amunhotep-Huy by his father and Irem, a man with his own ambitions, who was happy to be allied to the family of both the Mayor of Mennofer and Egypt's famous Seer and who had no wish to see the country reminded of the family's lowly origins by one of its members. Huy heard nothing from his older nephew, but Ramose began to send him letters as soon as he graduated from pieces of clay to papyrus. Huy enjoyed them. Ramose wrote increasingly ably of his life at school, his warm, unaffected words returning Huy to his own years with Thothmes at Iunu's temple school in a past long gone.

Mutemwia's scrolls spoke to Huy of a King who was governing well and who had begun to build at Ipet-isut, the great temple complex dedicated to Amun at Weset in the south. Amun had become Amun-Ra some time before, a fact Huy had lightly dismissed from his mind until the King and his father the Osiris-one Amunhotep the Second began to quarrel with Amun's priests and to openly prefer the Aten and other hypostases of Ra. Every King set out to enlarge and beautify Ipet-isut in homage to the country's most powerful god, and Thothmes was no exception, though Huy, reading between the lines of Mutemwia's perpetual scrawl, surmised that if Amun had not begun to be linked with the power of the sun, his Incarnation on earth would not have bothered to so honour him. Thothmes had a sandstone court built and decorated within the temple precinct, and also a shrine for the god's barque, the precious stone being taken from the alabaster quarries on the east bank of the river opposite Khmun. He raised an obelisk that had been commissioned but not finished by his grandfather the Osiris-one Thothmes the Third. He had new copper and turquoise mines opened in the eastern desert where Hathor, goddess of love and beauty, and patroness of the area, had a temple. He was proceeding along the path of every ruler before him, and Huy, knowing how little time the King had left to leave any stamp upon his reign, felt a fleeting pity for him. So far he had done nothing to make his people anxious or afraid. He had not anathematized Amun publicly. He had not demanded a position of superiority for the Aten. Yet Huy, remembering the man's great lie, was sure that among his courtiers and in the scant privacy of his own quarters the Aten alone received his prayers.

Carefully, Huy questioned Prince Amunhotep regarding the spread of Aten worship in the harem where the boy often stayed, but Amunhotep had no interest in the rivalries of the gods. "I carry Amun's great name," he said to Huy once, "and that is enough for me. My father hates the south anyway. He always has. You'd think he'd love it because Ra's heat burns so strongly there and his light dazzles the eyes. What are you worrying about, Uncle Huy?"

Huy quickly turned the conversation into safer avenues, jolted by his adopted nephew's perception, and tried to ignore his fears; for this was year six of the King, when the flood was high and the days were long, and the somnolence of peace and good order lay over the land.

17

THEN, IN YEAR SEVEN of the King, the Crown Prince Amunemhat died. He and Prince Amunhotep were both nine, but Amunemhat had been several weeks older than Mutemwia's son. The news did not come to Huy in a letter from the Queen; it was delivered in a scroll from Ishat. Huy immediately recognized her vigorous hand as Thothhotep broke the seal and unrolled it.

The month was Mekhir, the heat was mild, the fields were thick with green crops, and Huy and his scribe were sitting in the shade of the house's rear entrance, lazily surveying the explosion of growth in the garden. It was just past noon. On the pond, the blue water lilies were closing and the white ones beginning to open, their perfume carrying faintly to Huy on the light breeze. He often thought of Heby's first wife, the lovely and quiet Sapet, when he looked at them. Brightly hued butterflies hovered over the trembling blooms of papery red poppies, the delicate white of the narcissus, the rich blue of the cornflowers Anab was tending around the verge of Huy's pond. Cornflowers also marched in orderly rows between the swaying palms lining the irrigation ditch beside the house. Anab would soon pick their petals, crush them, and sell their juice to the dyers. *It's a pity to denude them*, Huy was thinking idly, *but I could hardly refuse the man's request to enrich himself a little more.*

At that moment Amunmose appeared behind him, handed the scroll to Thothhotep, and stood squinting into the distance. "A perfect day, Master," he commented. "Rakhaka warns you that the noon meal is ready and he doesn't want the soup to get cold. He's flitting from table to table like a hawk that can't quite catch the mouse, and glowering at me as if it's my fault that you linger out here. He needs mint for the salad." He stepped past Huy and walked briskly towards the herb patch, greeting Anab on the way.

It was then, glancing at Thothhotep, reluctant to go inside, not really caring what was in the letter, that Huy recognized Ishat's hand. Amunmose was returning, sprigs of mint in one hand. Huy could smell the fresh tang of it as the under steward approached.

"Tell Rakhaka that I don't mind cold soup," he said, his eyes on Thothhotep's hands as she unrolled the letter. "I must attend to this matter first."

Amunmose grimaced. "I'm afraid of him. He makes wonderful food, but he's so bad-tempered. I wish Khnit was still cooking for us."

"Khnit is much happier taking care of my house at Ta-she. You have more authority here on the estate than the cook, Amunmose. If Rakhaka abuses you, shout back at him."

"He doesn't shout at me, he glares," Amunmose said. "When I glare back, I just look like a sheep in pain. He has no sense of humour. He never understands my jokes."

Huy waved him away. "I wish you'd find someone else to deafen with your constant talk. Get married, Amunmose, but in the meantime, leave us!"

"Shall I read this to you, or would you like to read it for yourself?" Thothhotep asked as the under steward vanished into the dimness of the passage.

For answer Huy nodded and closed his eyes, leaning back against the wall in anticipation of hearing Ishat's words spoken aloud. She always wrote as she spoke. Huy smiled as Thothhotep began:

To my darling Huy, greetings from the utter peace of this household. Thothmes and your namesake have gone on a tour of the sepat to assess the health of crops and animals, Nakht is of course at Ptah's temple taking dictation from the High Priest, and Sahura is sleeping in her room after crying herself into hysterics over the son of one of Thothmes' friends who's not interested in marrying her. She is of course in love with him and will of course get over it. Thothmes will wait before assessing other likely candidates. Sahura isn't much like me. All she really wants, at fifteen, is her own home to run. Fifteen, Huy! And Nakht seventeen and Huy eighteen and apprenticed to his father the Governor! But why am I telling you these things about the children that you already know, old friend? Perhaps because, when I hear of the death of any child, I give thanks to the gods that mine are still healthy and strong. We saw so many little corpses when we worked together, didn't we? Well, here's another one of great importance to you. I doubt if you've heard, but if you have, forgive me for repeating the news. Our Hawk-in-the-Nest, Amunemhat, is dead. There's always fever during the Inundation, particularly in the Delta, and Thothmes tells me that the young Prince was not robust. So that leaves your little aristocrat the next in line for the Horus Throne and Mutemwia in a far more exalted position than that of Second Wife. Unless Neferatiri produces another son. I get the distinct impression that the King does not trust Mutemwia and doesn't much like his son by her. Everyone knows how she favours you and how often Prince Amunhotep boasts of his life with you each year. She's very ambitious. Do you think she might have had something to do with Amunemhat's sudden death? What is she really like? Thothmes says that she stays away from court affairs unless the King commands her presence, and then she's all smiles and gracious words. Do you like her? By my own hand this tenth day of Mekhir, year seven of the King, Ishat.

Thothhotep looked up with eyebrows raised under the fringe of her short hair. "How many of the Lady Ishat's letters have you had to destroy, Huy? This is most definitely another one." Pushing the one errant black tress back behind her ear, she tapped her knee with the scroll.

"So the heir is dead," Huy murmured, "and if my vision for the King's brother in exile spoke the truth, Amunhotep will rule." Suddenly hungry, he stood up and stretched. "Burn Ishat's scroll before we eat, Thothhotep. I won't write a reply. It's time we paid a visit to Iunu anyway." *Is Mutemwia so cold-bloodedly ambitious that she would take the enormous risk of poisoning her son's rival?* he asked himself as he followed Thothhotep's thin spine into the house. *I don't think so. Even without the vision, she is too clever and, yes, too much a servant of Ma'at to endanger the fate of her soul with murder. There's warmth in her, and shrewdness, and a firm awareness of the value of every Egyptian's life, peasant or noble. No, Mutemwia will not be able to resist a moment of exultation at this change in her son's fortunes, but she will not gloat.* He glanced up as he entered the reception room to see Rakhaka standing against the wall with an agonized look on his face.

"Thothhotep will be here shortly," he said with an inner smile, and took his place behind his table.

After the seventy days of mourning and Beautification, Prince Amunemhat was buried in the tomb his father had begun preparing for his family, and within days of the funeral Prince Amunhotep was officially declared the Hawk-in-the-Nest. Only then did Huy receive a letter from Mutemwia, dictated and couched in formal language. Huy applauded the caution that had prevented her from writing to him to tell him of the young Prince's death. A scroll also arrived from Amunhotep himself. Thothhotep fingered it curiously before breaking the seal. "I think this has been sealed twice," she said. "Look where the first wax has coloured the papyrus very faintly red and the second pressing was done a little to the left of it." She and Huy stared at one another.

"I pray that he hasn't written anything damning," Huy said. "The King has no love for me. I remind him of his perfidy. Would he dare to lie again to implicate me in some fabricated plot that would see me imprisoned? Crack it open, Thothhotep."

She did so and Huy, anxiously watching her face, saw her breathe a quick gust of relief. She read:

To the Great Seer Huy and my good friend, greetings. Know that I, Prince Amunhotep, have now been proclaimed Heir to the sacred Horus Throne by my august father King Thothmes Menkheperura Living for Ever, and as such will no longer be able to enjoy the delights of your estate. I will miss them very much, but my heart will be soothed by the presence of my father the King, who has bidden me to take up residence in the apartments of my predecessor, close to his own. I thank you for the care you have shown me. I shall write to you again. Long life and happiness to you. Dictated to the Scribe in the

House of the Royal Children Menkhoper, this twenty-eighth day of Pharmuthi, year seven of the King.

"A polite and sensible letter," Huy said. "We will miss him very much too. Obviously his father will begin to keep a sharper eye on him and of course add statecraft to his lessons. He'll be very busy. I hope Menkhoper will be allowed to go on teaching him."

"Nothing he learned here will be wasted or forgotten, Master," Thothhotep put in. "He's well past the early years when a child gulps down knowledge like good wine and is still thirsty. That wine never sours. Besides ..." She hesitated.

"Besides, his father has only three more years to live," Huy finished for her. Their eyes met. "Take a dictation in reply to this letter," Huy said after a moment of mutual silence. "I must congratulate our Prince on his ascension."

In the following year, Thothmes gathered up Amunhotep and his daughter-wife Iaret and travelled south with the Division of Ra, five thousand men, to discipline the tribesmen of southern Wawat, who were hindering the gold shipments. Every week that Amunhotep was away, Huy received a letter from him, his words excited, fretful, or descriptive, giving Huy a vivid picture of the King's foray into the wild country below the river's Second Cataract. The Prince wrote in his final scroll:

We are on our way home. I have seen many marvels. I have watched the Trogloditesi die. Every day I have ridden behind the King my father in his chariot when he inspected the soldiers, and every evening I have sat with him in his tent. He has offered wine to Amun and to Khnum, the creator-god of the First Cataract, in celebration of his triumph, and he told me that he will cause a rampant sphinx trampling down the wildmen of Wawat and Kush to be inscribed on both panels of his throne, including the words, "Horus with the powerful arm, effective in crushing all foreign countries." I have behaved with courage throughout these months and the King my father says that he is very proud of me. I have even been obedient to Iaret, who has whined about the heat and complained every day about the food. I don't like her at all and I will be glad to see the face of my mother the Queen after all this time.

After all this time, Huy repeated to himself as Thothhotep fell silent. *Another year is almost over. We wait for Isis to cry. My little Prince is now nine. Thothmes sacrificed to Amun and Khnum, but his throne will show a sphinx, symbol of the physical manifestation of the Aten. Why do I return with such anxiety to his preference for the sun over the totality of Amun? Every King takes a sun-name. Every King is entombed with funeral rites that emphasize his unique relationship with Ra.* He shook his head. *Am I trying to thrust a spear into nothing but a shadow?* The vision of a shadow returned him to thoughts of light, of the sun, and he growled at himself impatiently. "Has an accounting of my crops come yet from Seshemnefer?" he asked Thothhotep. "It's time to put aside an estimated amount for the taxes."

The first eleven months of year nine of the King passed uneventfully. Amunhotep's letters arrived spasmodically and were always short. "I am either hot and tired from my military training or eyesore and tired from poring over scrolls and tablets dealing with everything from the bases of architecture and stonemasonry to trying to learn Akkadian, the language of diplomatic correspondence," he wrote once in his own hand.

"I remember my time with you and Anhur as a series of peaceful days interspersed with nights of blissful security. I miss you both. Is Anhur well?"

Huy, sitting alone on his roof, his hair loose and ruffled by the pleasant breezes of Tybi, set the scroll down by his bare feet and sighed. No, Anhur was not well. Now in his late fifties, he suffered from shortness of breath and a loss of weight due, Huy was sure, to an infestation of worms. Huy had wanted to See for Anhur, but the man had refused the favour. "I'm approaching my old age, Huy," he had said. "Will the gods keep me young as they do for you? I don't think so. Soon I must ask to be released from your service and be put out to pasture. Most of your servants are aging. Surely you've noticed!"

But Huy had not noticed. Now he saw Tetiankh's sagging jowls, Merenra's increasing portliness, Kar's habit of cocking his ear when spoken to. The thought of retiring the bulk of his staff was almost as daunting as losing Ishat to Thothmes had been all those years before. Seshemnefer and his wife, Khnit, caring for his holdings at Ta-she—were all of them ready to leave his employ? He could support them all, no doubt. That was not what concerned him. He shrank from the ultimate necessity of hiring new staff, meeting strange faces in the passages of his home, trying to determine whom to trust. What if Thothhotep, now in her forties, decided to go with Anhur when he took his leave? In the end Huy thrust such conjectures away. The passing of time would see everything resolved.

On the fifteenth day of Mesore, the last month of the King's ninth year, Thothmes died suddenly during a feast celebrating the abundant harvest the whole country had enjoyed. According to a letter from Heby, who together with Iupia had been present, the King appeared to be choking. A flurry of agitated servants had flocked to the royal dais, obscuring Heby's view, and when they dispersed in a shocked silence, King Thothmes lay slumped across Queen Neferatiri's lap, quite dead. Huy, hearing his brother's words issuing from Thothhotep's mouth, had a moment of dislocation. They were in Huy's office, where the worst of the heat could not reach them, and somehow the dimness coupled with Thothhotep's carefully modulated voice seemed at variance with the violence of the news. Huy felt no surprise. Each day he had woken with the knowledge that the usurper, King or not, was one step closer to the Judgment Hall and Ma'at's scales, not the blessed sanctuary of the sacred barge with Egypt's great rulers. Now his vision had been realized. Thothmes was gone and the throne stood empty, waiting for the body of a young boy to grace its golden seat.

But for Huy, that death was eclipsed by two others. A month into the seventy days of mourning for the King, Huy's father died. Word came to Huy in person from his uncle Ker's steward, who told him that Hapu had been found lying in the garden, his chair toppled beside him, an empty mug by his outstretched hand. Huy told Thothhotep to send word to Heby immediately and ordered out his litter, first sending Merenra to Hut-herib's House of the Dead with gold and instructions to spare no expense in his father's Beautification. Sitting tensely in the swaying litter, he examined his inner self, and though the memories of his years as Hapu's son flowed in abundance through his mind, they brought no emotion with them. For the first twelve years of his life he had loved and respected his father, but that deep affection had soured, become tinged with a mild resentment he had never been able entirely to overcome, when Hapu had turned from him in fear before the Rekhet's exorcism had proved him free of demonic influence. Fiercely Huy tried to conjure only those early years so that he might begin to grieve honestly for the man who had sired him, but his bearers set him down outside the house where he had been born and he stepped into the clinging humidity that heralded the start of the Inundation with little more than a pang of sadness for his own mortality.

Itu rose from the floor of the tiny reception room as he entered, her lined face further disfigured by tears, the soil she had ground into her hair powdering her shoulders and clinging to her mouth. Huy took her into his arms. "The servants from the House of the Dead have already taken him away," she said, her voice muffled against his chest. "His weighing will be favourable, won't it, Huy? He cared little for the gods, but he revered the laws of Ma'at and did harm to no one!"

Only to me, Huy thought, and rejected the spasm of bitterness at once. "Of course he will be justified," he said, standing her away and cupping her hot cheeks, engulfed in a wave of love and protectiveness for her. "He laboured honestly, he cared for his family, he did not eat his heart without good cause."

"He was seldom angry," Itu agreed more calmly. "Oh, Huy, he lived in so much pain in spite of the poppy you provided for us, but he did not complain. 'I've exhausted my body in a good cause, Itu,' he used to say. 'Perfume for the King and food for my family.' What shall I do now without him?"

"You will come and live with me," Huy said quickly to stem a new outbreak of weeping. "Hapzefa can retire. Ishat will probably have a home built for her and her husband on the grounds of Thothmes' estate. Sit down and I'll find you something to drink. Have you eaten today?"

"But if I leave my house, it will fall into ruin and my garden will fill with weeds," Itu protested between sobs. "Hapu would not want that."

Huy squatted in front of her, dismayed at her gauntness, the jutting collarbones, the ropes of tendons standing out on her neck. Her hair had not been dressed. It hung in grey locks to her frail shoulders, and all at once Huy was drowning in an ocean of wistfulness, a longing for the past when she was lovely and vigorous and smelled of lilies.

"I'll send someone to live here and tend house and garden," he said.

She shook her head. "Give me someone indeed, but I intend to stay here. Now I must go to Khenti-kheti's shrine and pray for Hapu's ka. Will you take me there, Huy?"

They went into the town together in Huy's litter. Methen greeted them sombrely, joining them in the supplications for Hapu's safe journey. While he repeated the words, Huy's mind wandered. The tomb he had begun to prepare for his parents as soon as he and Ishat had moved onto the estate was finished. That was good. How many mourners should he hire? The more mourners, the greater the deference shown to the memory of the deceased and his family. Ishat would know. Huy wanted her nearby with a kind of homesickness he had not felt in years. He needed to reminisce with her, speak to her of his father in the certain knowledge that she, above everyone else, would understand the conflict within him that had never been resolved. *Whom else should I notify of Hapu's death?* he wondered. *Ker and Heruben already know. They will declare a holiday for their other field workers so that the funeral will be well attended. I must have the finished tomb opened and readied and tell Anhur to set a guard over it. Oh, Ishat, I need you now!*

Heby and his family arrived four days later. Apologetically, Huy was forced to request that his brother and sister-in-law sleep on their barge, and Ramose in a tent erected in the garden; there was no space left in the house. Amunhotep-Huy did not demur when asked to quarter with Huy's soldiers. "I would have wanted to do so anyway, Uncle," he told Huy. "I would rather throw my pallet down on the floor of your little barracks than share a tent with Ramose."

In spite of the solemnity of the occasion, the house filled with chatter and laughter as well as bouts of weeping. Hapu had led a long and useful life, something that Ishat pointed out in her letter to Huy and Heby. She wrote, "Thothmes and I will come north for the funeral. I have already made plans to care for my parents here, and will take them back to Iunu after Hapu goes to his tomb. Thus our youth sinks ever more deeply into the past, Huy darling, and our own Beautification looms nearer. As I love life and hate death, I dread being laid in the darkness of a cave hewn out of the rock far beneath the earth. How can any Egyptian bear to leave this blessed land?"

As I love life and hate death, Huy repeated silently, pressing Ishat's scroll to his cheek in the relative solitude of his office. *An ancient oath that arrows straight to the heart of everyone born and raised in a country that is the envy of every foreigner.* Beyond the door he could hear Amunhotep-Huy shouting something unintelligible and Amunmose replying politely but forcefully. Amunhotep-Huy was now twenty. He had long since left Heby's home for two rooms of his own beside his employer's house in the army barracks west of Peru-nefer in Mennofer. Tjanuni had no complaints regarding the loyalty and efficiency of his scribe, but Heby, in his letters to Huy, had described Amunhotep-Huy's harshness in his dealings with servants and the common soldiers. The young man could scarcely conceal his impatience at being dragged to Hut-herib for his grandfather's funeral. He showed Itu, his grandmother, every deference, but away from her he bullied his half-brother Ramose and kept Huy's staff in a state of watchful nervousness. *Whipping never worked with that boy*, Huy mused, reluctant to leave the sanctuary of the office for the maelstrom of family activities. *Perhaps if he'd been allowed to join the army, if he'd marched into Wawat with the Division of Ra and seen men wounded and dying, his disposition might have been changed.*

He continued to go about the town prescribing and scrying with Thothhotep as the river rose and the flood spread, fighting his private battle against the constant need to take more and more poppy, while he mourned for his father as best he could. The whole of Egypt was also in mourning for the Osiris-King, but Huy seldom thought of him. The life of the palace seemed very far away. He had received formal letters of condolence from Mutemwia and from the Prince. They told him nothing other than their sympathy, and he was content to exist within the curious hiatus of waiting while his father's disembowelled husk lay under the deft hands of the sem priests and his mother sat on the roof under a linen canopy, her thoughts turned inward while she squinted unseeingly into the bright afternoons.

Huy's Naming Day on the ninth of Paophi passed quietly, without the usual gifts and feast. Huy, critically examining his features in the polished disc of his copper mirror and then angling it downwards to reflect the rest of his body, could see no evidence of aging even though he was now fifty years old. *Atum continues to preserve me,* he thought, laying the mirror down and sitting so that Tetiankh could kohl his eyes and braid his hair. *I exist suspended in time, while all around me its passage slowly breaks down and decays everything and everyone I hold dear. Long ago Anubis told me that I would be given a chance to redeem my moment of cowardice. It is obvious to me that that moment has not yet come. How can it? My life now follows the rigid path set before me by my ability to prescribe for the sick and predict the future for the anxious. Ra is swallowed each evening and is born each dawn, and we in this household follow the habits long established by custom and daily necessity. There is a staleness to my life. I resemble a donkey that walks blindfolded round and round a grinding stone, and Atum is the master holding the goad. I know how the grain is ground. I know how it sifts into the basket. Has all the turbulence of my youth come to this?*

Three days later, he had finished his morning meal and was about to leave his couch when Iny, Thothhotep's body servant, burst into his room followed by an annoyed Tetiankh. "I apologize, Great One," he said loudly. "I could not reach your door before the girl thrust it open."

Huy gestured impatiently. "Never mind. What do you want, Iny?"

The servant managed an agitated bow. "Your mother, Master," she blurted. "Please come."

Huy's heart sank. Even as he stood and reached for yesterday's limp kilt, he knew what he would find. Following Iny along the passage with Tetiankh behind, turning into the guest room, his bare feet padding over the huge lion's pelt presented to him when he and Ishat had first occupied the estate deeded to him by the Osiris-King Amunhotep, he approached the couch. Itu's dark eyes stared up at him lifelessly, her grey hair tangled on the pillow, her lips curved in a tiny smile. Huy lifted the hand that lay on the sheet over her breast. It was quite cold.

"Fetch my brother," he ordered his body servant, then he bent, kissing the loose cheek and tenderly closing the eyes that had always spoken to him more clearly than her words. *Already you were lonely for him,* he thought as he drew up a stool. *You loved him very much and served him well. In spite of the happiness your children and grandchildren brought to you, the prospect of a life lived without the part of you that was Hapu was too much to bear. Your weighing was easy, my mother, and he was waiting for you, young and vigorous once more, under the shade of the Ished Tree. I envy you.*

Hapu and Itu were buried together at the beginning of Tybi, two days after the Feast of the Coronation of Horus. The flood had withdrawn, leaving its blanket of life-giving silt on the little fields. Where the ground had begun to dry, the peasants were at work, rhythmically tossing the new seed as they walked, their progress followed by clouds of greedy pigeons. The Delta air was heavy with the fragrance of thousands of blooms, and the palm trees had put out delicate, pale green spears. Huy was taken aback by the number of Hut-herib's citizens who attended the funeral along with the crowd of peasants, many of them as old and bent as his father had been, who had worked the perfume fields beside Hapu. Ker and Heruben, Huy's aunt and uncle, stood solemnly with the other members of the family while Methen conducted the rites and the forty blue-clad mourners Huy and Heby had hired interjected the sonorous words with cries and moans. They were not needed, Huy reflected, glancing around at the crowd gathered behind him and Heby. Many of those present were weeping, including Hapzefa, who was supported between Thothmes and Ishat, her husband behind her.

The Governor and his wife had arrived at Huy's watersteps the week before. After a hurried greeting, Ishat had gone to greet her mother, Hapzefa, and her father. Thothmes and Ishat settled into Huy's guest room. In spite of the sad occasion of their visit, Huy was overjoyed to see them. "You should have this ratty old lion skin burned," Ishat had said, staring down at it while her laden servants waited in the passage to enter and unpack her belongings and Thothmes' entourage was still unloading his chests from the barge. "I'll wager that it's full of fleas. We never liked it anyway, did we, Huy darling?" She turned and flung her arms around him, enveloping him in the perfume blend of myrrh, cassia, and henna flowers, returning Huy vividly, almost savagely, to their years together here on his estate.

"Lions hate hyenas," he blurted over the top of her head, the sweet familiarity of her embrace filling him with a sense of security.

"So they do, but I don't see any hyenas lurking, do you?" She stepped back, looking him up and down with a smile. "Gods, Huy, why don't you age? Look at me, with my greying hair and the wrinkles around my eyes in spite of the sacrifices I make to Hathor on her feast day every Khoiak and the honey and olive oil Iput massages into my skin! Let's go downstairs and have some wine and gossip a bit. Iput, you can go ahead and sort out my things."

Iput bobbed to Huy as she entered, her arms full of boxes. "It's good to be here again, Master," she said in answer to Huy's greeting.

Thothmes and Heby were deep in conversation at the foot of the stairs as Huy and Ishat descended. "A matter of administrative policy," Thothmes said apologetically as he and Huy embraced. "I'm sorry that your family has lost Hapu and Itu," he added. "I remember them fondly. Ishat wants you to herself for a while. We'll meet again this evening."

"It's a good thing that we left the children at home," Ishat remarked as she linked arms with Huy and they emerged into the afternoon sunshine. "Your house is far too small to accommodate three extra people besides Thothmes and me. Let's sit under the hedge in the shade."

"I had completely forgotten about events in the palace," Huy said, lowering himself onto the grass beside her. "I've had no letter from either the Queen or the Prince since they acknowledged my father's death."

"The Prince is now the King. I'm surprised that you weren't invited to the coronation, but of course Mutemwia knows that you're still in mourning." Ishat leaned back on one elbow and, pulling off her wig, ran impatient fingers through her hair. "All the governors were commanded to appear—not that I'd have missed the occasion for anything. It was held in the audience hall of the palace. The astrologers chose the second day of Athyr for Amunhotep's crowning—why I can't imagine, since it falls within the long and rather tedious celebrations for the Amun-Feast of Hapi, and besides, the flood is still fairly high at the start of Athyr." She squinted across at Huy and grinned. "The Prince's father had only been entombed ten days before. My belief is that Mutemwia pressed for her son's immediate legitimization before any other contender surfaced."

"The only man with a strong claim to the throne is the Prince's uncle, still living in exile," Huy replied. "I don't think that he'll consider himself capable of ruling after so many years away."

"I agree, but don't forget all the little sons of Thothmes and his concubines running about in the harem. Many of those women are entirely unscrupulous when it comes to the advancement of their children. Amunhotep is only twelve years old. He's vulnerable." She rolled onto her back and stretched out her arms luxuriously. "How good it is to be here with you! We don't see enough of each other, Huy. Our days are overfull of responsibilities. The children miss you, particularly Nakht. My quiet one. He didn't want to attend the coronation, but your namesake came with us to Mennofer. He climbed up onto the pedestal of one of the pillars in the hall so that he could watch the proceedings." She batted at a bee droning past her face to reach the yellow acacia blossoms clustered on the branches behind her. "I heard it all and saw some of it. Amun-Ra's High Priest set the hedjet and the deshret on the Prince's head while he knelt, and I must say that the white and red crowns suited him. Mutemwia stood just behind the Horus Throne, and every time Amunhotep sat, she placed a hand on his shoulder. There's no mistaking who's Regent. She was wearing a Queen's vulture headdress that made her look taller than she really is, and her sheath was sewn all over with droplets of gold. They made a striking pair, Huy, the young King with his mother, Nekhbet's golden vulture head seeming to lean over him in protection and warning, as well as the holy uraeus on his own crown. I got a good look at them as they proceeded out of the hall surrounded by all the court dignitaries. Amunhotep seemed tired and Mutemwia was pale. The feast afterwards was beyond description, but Thothmes and I left early. Young Huy stayed on. So." She cocked one eye in his direction. "Your vision for our new young King was true. Are you pleased?"

"What titles has he taken?" Huy asked tersely.

Ishat sat up. "You're worried that he'll follow in his father's footsteps and give an increasing prominence to the Aten? Let me see. There's an emphasis on his devotion to Ra, of course. Every King pays homage to that god's power." She screwed up her nose. "His given name means 'Amun is satisfied.' His throne name is Nebmaatra, 'the Lord of Truth is Ra.' His Horus name Ka-nakht kha-em-ma'at, 'Strong Bull, Appearing in Truth.' I can't remember his Two Ladies name or his Golden Horus name, not that it matters. There's no mention of the Aten."

"He has little interest in matters of religion anyway," Huy said with relief. "His mother's influence on him is strong. She knows exactly how she wants him to govern."

"You like her, don't you?"

Huy smiled. "Yes, I do. She's a complex woman."

"And a beautiful one." Ishat yawned. "I expect that she'll summon you to See for the One before long." Grabbing up her wig, she scrambled to her feet. "I'm going inside to sleep while the house is calm. If you see Thothmes, tell him not to disturb me."

Two days after the funeral, Huy's house emptied. Heby and Iupia returned to Mennofer with their sons, Thothmes and Ishat sailing south with them as far as Iunu. Huy, standing above his watersteps as the long flotilla drifted into the north-flowing current and a flurry of commands rang out, watched the forest of oars appear with a sense of both liberation and abandonment. Behind him his arouras lay deserted under the sparkle of the morning sun, and in the house, he knew, his servants would be sweeping away all evidence of occupation. *Despite the turbulence my nephew created, it has been good to wake to the sounds of feet other than my guards' or Thothhotep's padding past my door,* he thought rather dismally. *To see the faces of those I love turn towards me as I enter my reception room to share food with them. To hear their voices, raised in laughter and conversation, fill the air with warmth, their presence pervade it with perfumes and colours and the welcome touch of friendly flesh. And most of all, best of all, to have Ishat here, to know that in her presence there is no need for explanations and that one word will bring our past back to us in all its hope and intimacy. Thothhotep has not filled the void Ishat left behind. Her loyalty to me is beyond reproach, but her true affection belongs to Anhur.*

She was waiting at his elbow, Anhur beside her, and Huy turned to them with a sigh. "I shan't need either of you for the rest of the day. I'll resume my work tomorrow. Anhur, go to Merenra and tell him to make up a mixture of ground frankincense and fenugreek in honey for your breathing. I don't like the way you sound."

Anhur shrugged. "It's nothing much, Huy. It'll pass."

"No, it won't." Thothhotep grasped his brown arm. "With your permission, Master, I'll go to Merenra myself and then make sure that Anhur takes his medicine." She was about to say more, Huy could see it in her eyes, but at his nod she started briskly for the house.

"There are changes coming," Anhur said unexpectedly. "Can you feel it, Huy? And even if you can't, I know from experience that if a long period of peaceful routine is broken by a death, then two more deaths follow, and after that either chaos or at the least a new pace of life."

"Anhur, I had not believed you full of the superstitions of the ordinary soldier," Huy said in astonishment. "You are far from an ignorant man! Three deaths?"

"I know the difference between nonsense and a genuine hunch," Anhur retorted sourly. "The King was the first death, your father the second, and your mother the third. It won't be as it was before, around this place. The gods are stirring."

The gods are stirring. An absurd comment meaning nothing, Huy thought, *but ominous all the same.*

"Go and nurse your sick lungs, old friend," he said testily. "Or rather, let Thothhotep nurse them for you. Our daily round of work and leisure has been temporarily disturbed, that's all. Within a week all will be as it was."

But as he walked back along the path, his footsteps seemed suddenly loud to him, the facade of the house, with its small, brightly painted pillars, alien. He halted, senses alert. In the tangled acacia bushes to either side, the bees hummed among the blooms and fledglings set up a tuneless piping from hidden nests. Off to his right, the palm trees, long since mature, rose straight against the deep blue of the sky to branch out into crowns of spiked leaves jerking spasmodically in the breeze. To his left, the grass beneath the spreading sycamores still glistened from the morning's watering. Ahead, just visible beyond the bulk of the house itself, a corner of the garden showed Huy the rows of newly sprouted vegetable crops interspersed with a scattering of flowers, the inviting blue of Anab's cornflowers predominating. Beyond the garden, past the guards' cells and the kitchen, the two clay domes of Huy's silos huddled against the mud bricks of the rear wall. He saw his under steward straighten from among the row of feathery dill fronds, a basket full of young lettuce on his arm and a sprig of dill in one fist, and step around the lily-choked pond before moving towards the rear door and out of Huy's sight. All is as it should be, Huy told himself. All is sinking back into predictability. Then why am I seeing my surroundings as though for the first time? Anhur and his silly notions.

Yet the sense of estrangement stayed with him through the rest of the day. While his guests had been present, he had gone to his couch too late and too preoccupied to call the Book of Thoth to mind, but that night, as he lay on his couch watching the steady orange glow of his night light on the table beside him and listening to the silence in the house, the words of the Book began to echo behind his eyes. He recognized them, of course, but they formed and then fled as though they had been written in a foreign language. His mouth remained closed, but he had the distinct and confusing impression that the stanzas of the Book were spreading out the door, along the passage, rolling into every corner, filling his house, so that in the end there was no room left for him at all. He was shut out.

The month of Tybi proceeded quietly for Huy, who continued to travel the short distance between his estate and the town when needed and to deal with the petitioners allowed to gather once more on his grounds. Beyond his walls, Egypt came to life in a flurry of sowing and planting. There were few holy days to be observed. Huy woke every morning knowing exactly what would fill the time before his couch beckoned to him again. Such knowledge should have brought him contentment; instead, his sense of dislocation grew. It was as though time was holding him in a place entirely separate from those around him. When Merenra entered the office with some request or a domestic problem, Huy knew what his steward was about to say. Stepping from the rear entrance into the garden, he inhaled the aroma of frying fish before he glanced towards the open kitchen and saw Rakhaka's lean form bending to lay the fillets into the sizzling olive oil. Even while holding a petitioner's hand, waiting for his surroundings to dissolve into a mirage filled with Anubis's rough voice, he heard the god speak before his fierce animal jaws parted. Huy felt himself invisibly cocooned by the Book, wrapped in a grandeur and mystery so thickly dense that time itself could not penetrate the wall it had formed. It no longer seemed to originate in his mind. Its only source was heka, magic, and Huy knew better than to struggle against it, although he started to wonder if its force would eventually drive him insane. His servants began to look at him strangely, but he did not attempt to explain his state. Doggedly he went about the tasks Atum set for him, and he waited.

His guests had left on the fifth day of Tybi. The twenty-ninth of every month was a holiday. It marked the day when the world was created, as well as the conjunction of the sun and the moon, and Huy was called out only for the direst necessity. A contented silence always lay over the country. The populace slept or visited friends or idled away the hours on the river. There were other holidays during each month, some claimed by busy servants, some ignored, but the observance of the twenty-ninth day was strictly marked. So Huy, sitting at his desk and picking through the cold food Rakhaka had set out for him the night before, was astonished to see a Royal Herald open the door of his office and step smartly into the room. He came to his feet.

The man bowed twice. "A thousand pardons for approaching you unannounced, Great Seer. Your gate guard was nowhere to be seen, and of course your servants are enjoying their leisure today. I bring you a letter from the palace. I was instructed by His

Majesty to place it directly into your hands." His blue-trimmed white kilt and white linen helmet dazzled where he stood in the rectangle of brilliant sunlight falling from the narrow clerestory window high in the wall. His silver rings sparked briefly as he held out the scroll and then withdrew his arm. He smelled of mimosa blossoms.

Huy, his long hair unbraided, face unpainted, smothered the need to apologize for his appearance. "Thank you. My steward is unavailable, but let me bring you wine and a dish of sweetmeats."

The herald shook his head. "My barge is at your watersteps and I must be on my way. His Majesty does not require me to wait for a reply. May I be dismissed?"

Huy nodded. At once the man bowed, turned on his heel, and was gone. His sandals tapped briskly on the tiles of the passage before the sound gradually faded. It was then, standing with the scroll held gingerly in both hands, that Huy realized there had been no intimation of the man's appearance at his door; the curious disparity distancing him from the world around him had gone. He looked down at the beige cylinder with its imposing red seal. "A change is coming," Anhur had said such a short time ago. "Can't you feel it?" *I can now,* Huy thought, running his thumb over the imprint of the sedge and the bee, royal symbols of Upper and Lower Egypt, before breaking the wax. *It is here, accomplished even before I read the words that have brought it about.* Carefully he unrolled the letter, sinking back onto his chair as he did so. He read in Menkhoper's neat, clear hand:

To the Great Seer Huy of Hut-herib, greetings. Having found much favour with My Majesty and having proved your loyalty to Her Majesty the Queen my Mother, you are commanded to remove yourself and all your household to the quarters that have been prepared for you in the Fine

District of Pharaoh at Mennofer. You are appointed King's Personal Scribe and will be known henceforth as Amunhotep son of Hapu. You will no longer be permitted to exercise the gift the god Atum has bestowed on you except in the service of your King. Your esteemed brother Heby has already demonstrated his administrative ability as Mayor of Mennofer. I am advised to bestow on him the task and title of Overseer of the Cattle of Amun and Overseer of the Two Granaries of Amun in the sepats of Lower Egypt. His elder son Amunhotep-Huy is now Superior King's Scribe of Recruits and his younger, Ramose, though required to remain in Mennofer, will hold the position of Steward in the Mansion of the Aten at Iunu. A reply to this letter is not required. I expect your attendance at court by the beginning of Shemu. Dictated by His Majesty Amunhotep Nebmaatra to the Scribe in the House of the Royal Children and Tutor Menkhoper, this twenty-sixth day of Tybi in the season Peret, year one of the King.

There was a postscript added by Amunhotep himself:

Mother and I are both very excited to think that we will soon be able to see you every day. Menkhoper and my other teachers will go on with my education, but I'm relieved that you will be taking Menkhoper's place as my personal scribe. I hope you're pleased with your family's promotions. I miss you so much, Uncle Huy. I can't eat fish anymore and I have to keep my royal head always covered, which is a terrible nuisance, and I have to sit in audience every morning and listen to the reports of my ministers, who are all old and boring. Mother says that you may send a letter now to my blood relative in Mitanni, inviting him back to Egypt.

Letting the scroll roll up, Huy slowly clasped his hands together and placed them on the desk. *So this is what the god has been preparing me for,* he thought deliberately. *This will be my task, to stand behind our young King, even as his mother does, and through him chart the course Atum has planned for this, his blessed country. This is why I came back from the dead. This is why I have been taught to wield the scrying gift. Both Methen and Ra's High Priest at Iunu predicted this power for me when I was still at school. Amunhotep loves me. Mutemwia trusts me. Atum has laid the weight of these two responsibilities on my shoulders in the faith that I will not fail him. King's Personal Scribe. King's personal Seer. The fate of commoners will no longer concern me, by Mutemwia's express wish. I know the decision to bar me from all but those she chooses was hers alone. So was the resolve to appoint Ramose as steward of the Aten shrine at Iunu even though as yet he's too young to be active in that post. Thus she builds a channel along which information regarding all activity surrounding the worship of the Aten, at least in Iunu, will flow to her from a reliable messenger. How very astute she is, this woman with the body of a young girl and the intellect of a sage! I admire her wholeheartedly.*

All at once the full significance of Amunhotep's letter burst upon him, and he began to both laugh hysterically and cry, cradling himself and rocking back and forth on the chair. "Find Merenra and order him to start packing up this house," he said aloud to the empty room. "Find Thothhotep and dictate a letter to Prince Amunhotep in Mitanni. You won't have to compose it afresh, though, will you, Huy son of Hapu? No—Amunhotep son of Hapu. It's Amunhotep now. The words of that scroll already exist in the record of your vision for the Prince, given twelve years ago. You must dictate letters of congratulation to Heby and your nephews also. So much to do!"

Hearing the near-madness in his tones, he shut his mouth abruptly and rose. His legs were trembling. *How many members of my staff will want to retire?* he thought suddenly. *Who will choose to age quietly here rather than enter the maelstrom of court life? How will I find new servants I can trust?* The prospect sobered him at once. *I shall miss my life here, miss it very much. My destiny is about to be fulfilled, but all at once I am afraid. A dose of poppy will take away the fear.* He sighed and, picking up the roll of papyrus, went out.

For several days after the Royal Herald's surprising appearance at his door, he roamed the town and its environs. His litter-bearers took him to his parents' house, still empty, the small, untended terrace of soil around the pond already becoming choked with clover and dock leaves, the unwatered grass yellowing. He stood in the tiny room where he had slept as a child, where his mother had tended him after his return from the House of the Dead, where Ishat had come creeping through the window to tease him and keep him company in defiance of her mother's fear of him. Leaves from the acacia hedge had blown in to lie heaped in the corners. A spider's web hung trembling from the ceiling. *Neither Heby nor Heby's two sons will have any use for the place,* Huy reflected as he walked back out into the sunshine, *and by Atum's decree I will remain as barren as a woman with a diseased womb. I must send a message to Ker, tell him to place the family of one of his stewards here or even one of his field foremen. I can't bear to think of the walls gradually falling into decay, the pond drying up, wild animals building their own peculiar nests in what was once a clean and happy home.*

He wandered through the narrow streets of Hut-herib itself, crossing the dikes made to raise those coming and going above the level of the flood water during the Inundation, inhaling the sour odour of the mud below. He was often recognized by citizens, who bowed to him and made way respectfully for him to pass. He was hardly aware of them. Here in the marketplace he had first seen Thothhotep, sitting muffled in linen, her palette by her hip, and had taken her for a man. The memory pained him. It reminded him that he had come here to seek a replacement for Ishat, that he had been struggling against an entirely unjustified jealousy and resentment towards Thothmes for wanting to take her away, that he had shrunk from being left alone. Quickly he made his way to Khenti-kheti's shrine.

Methen was in the outer court, bending to put on his sandals before leaving the precincts, when Huy's shadow fell across him. His face broke into a smile as he straightened and threw his arms around Huy. "I've been hearing rumours," he said as together they moved the short distance towards the two rooms of his cell. "My scribe met your under steward at the market. I presume that you gave your servants permission to speak of your summons to Mennofer?"

"I did." Huy stood aside for Methen to precede him. *You are aging also, dear friend,* he thought with a pang. *You, Merenra, Anhur, even Ishat, all of you succumbing to the terrible ravages of time.* He took the stool by the table. Methen peered into the jug on its surface before taking two cups from a shelf, pouring out beer, and settling into the chair. "My under steward Amunmose loves to talk," Huy said. "I've been meandering around the town for the last couple of days, saying goodbye to the last fifty years of my life. I left this visit until the last. I didn't want to say goodbye to you."

"But why should you?" Methen looked startled. "Mennofer's only two days' sailing away. We'll certainly be back and forth."

Huy swallowed a mouthful of beer. "It's more than the physical distance." He licked his lips. "I sense that this parting from you and my estate and Hut-herib will be as sharp as the slash of a disembowelling knife in the House of the Dead."

Methen's gaze narrowed. "Your intuition comes from the god, do you think? Your destiny is about to enter a new chapter, perhaps the final one, the culmination of every test, every trial you've endured, and you're afraid?" He leaned over the table, pushing his cup aside. "Egypt is in your hands, Huy, don't you realize that? Queen Mutemwia trusts you. Amunhotep loves you. This is what Atum in his ruthless wisdom had planned for you from the time you stood before Imhotep in the Beautiful West and agreed to read the Book of Thoth! This is why the god breathed life back into your lifeless corpse all those years ago! You and the Book and the King are all linked. Your fates will converge into the one moment Atum desires."

"His ruthless wisdom," Huy repeated. "Yes, I do realize that I am being summoned to place my hand over the hand of the King on Egypt's rudder. Is it any wonder that I am clinging to the familiar?" He gave the priest a twisted smile. "I have no idea who Amunhotep's ministers are or what they do. I will have to learn, and everything will be strange." Impulsively he reached across and took Methen's hand. "Come with me," he begged. "I'll need my own priest, someone to approach the gods on my behalf, to advise me in spiritual matters, to be an incorruptible link with the past. You know everything about me. Be my guide, Methen!"

The High Priest's expression had become grave. "We are the closest of friends, Huy, but the time when you needed any advice but that of Anubis and the god is long gone. Atum is the only guide you need. I would not dare to stand between the god and you." Placing his other hand over Huy's, enfolding it in his warmth, he squeezed it and let it go. "Write to me as you used to do when you were a student at Iunu. I will always reply. Do you remember the day when you came to make an offering of some toy or other to Khenti-kheti because it was the anniversary of your Naming Day and you were about to be sent away to school?"

Huy nodded. "I told you not to fear the unknown, that you would be privileged to acquire the great gift Thoth gave to us, the ability to read and write. Forgive me if I repeat that admonition. Approach the unknown as a challenge and your position in the King's counsel as an honour. How innocent this anxiety of yours is! Now we will drink our beer and enjoy each other's company as we always have."

He's right, Huy thought as he shrugged before lifting his cup. *He's the only person to whom I could express this fear, the fear of a child, and know that he does not secretly despise me for it.*

"My litter-bearers have been trailing after me all day," he said. "I must go. Embrace me, old friend. Pray for me often."

Once more Methen's long arms went around him. "May the soles of your feet be firm, Huy son of Hapu," he said, using the ancient blessing given before a journey. "I shall expect a letter from you as soon as you are settled into your new quarters."

On the following day he made the visit to Mery-neith, the Mayor of Hut-herib, that he had been deliberately putting off. It was Mery-neith, on the instructions of the Osiris-King Amunhotep the Second, the present ruler's grandfather, who had arranged for Huy and Ishat to take over the estate. "I am giving the care of my parents' house into the hands of my uncle Ker, who will install one of his workers there," Huy told the man. "If you could make sure that the property is being kept up ..."

Mery-neith nodded vigorously. "Of course I will. I buy perfumes for my wife and daughters from your uncle, so the task will be easy. You do not wish to transfer the deed to your brother, or perhaps offer the house for sale? It does not return to the throne as khato. Your uncle gave it to your father. Now, what of your estate? It also belongs entirely to you."

"I can't let either of them go just yet," Huy admitted. "I'll keep the estate for somewhere to stay when I return home." *Why, so it has become*, he thought with surprise. *My little jewel of an estate, the dingy, dusty town, the familiar demarcations of river and tributary, the odours and sounds of this part of the Delta—all of it has truly become my home. I have taken it comfortably for granted until now, when I must leave it.*

"Thank you, Mery-neith," he finished. "I regret that we have seen so little of each other over the years."

Mery-neith bowed. "I also, Great One. May the gods preserve you in good health."

There was nothing left to do but speak politely of inconsequential matters for a while, return to the estate, and give Merenra the final command to empty the house.

He approached his steward in private, giving Merenra the choice between going with him to Mennofer or staying to take care of the house and grounds. Relief flitted across the man's face as Huy spoke. "I did not want to leave your employ, Master. If you had not given me the option of remaining here in my customary position, I would have followed you to the palace. But since you have decided to keep the estate, I will be happy to go on administrating it as always. I have enjoyed my charge since our first days together, but now my stomach often pains me and my back has weakened. I will let you know how much gold I will need to perform this lesser task. Thank you."

Huy wanted to grasp his shoulder, kiss the solemn face, tell Merenra how much he would be missed, but the man would have been offended by a show of such informality. Huy merely nodded in understanding. "Is Amunmose ready to be promoted to chief steward?" he wanted to know. "I assume I'll need to engage another under steward and probably more servants."

"Amunmose has become fully capable of more responsibility," Merenra replied. "He has learned to go about his work with his mouth closed more often than open. A stewardship within the confines of the palace will do him good. The pace of daily life there will be more brisk."

"I suppose it will." Huy dismissed him and went in search of Anab. His gardener was setting out bedding plants. He straightened slowly as Huy approached, shifting the balance from his club foot with unconscious ease.

"I know what you need to say to me, Master," he began, "You gave me a garden to tend in spite of my lameness. You have allowed me to profit from the cornflower juices. But in the palace you will have no use for me. Will you please find me another master before you go?"

"Don't be ridiculous!" Huy snapped, taken aback. "You either come with me or stay right where you are. I will not have you pottering about under someone else's thumb! Which will it be?"

Anab squinted at him cautiously. "I have heard that the King has prepared apartments for you. The Overseers of the Royal Gardens will certainly not want to be bothered with me. You will have no garden of your own anymore. May I indeed stay here? You are keeping the estate?"

"I am." Huy had not considered how insecure the news might have made his staff. Did they not trust him to look after them? "And as far as the royal gardeners are concerned, they would find themselves very fortunate if you chose to join their ranks. Move into the house with your wife and son, Anab. Merenra is staying. Kar is very old and will not want to leave his hut at my gate. I'll make sure the place remains guarded. I don't really want to part with any of you. Surely you knew that!"

Listening to Anhur's laboured breathing that evening as he, Thothhotep, and Anhur sat over their meal, watching Thothhotep's furtive, worried glances at the man she so obviously loved, made Huy decide to remove any choice from the captain of his guards. Anhur would never willingly abandon him. He had become like a father to Huy, protecting him and occasionally giving him the sharp edge of his tongue, as though Huy was still the apprehensive boy who had been his charge at Khmun. Losing Thothhotep as well was almost unthinkable, but it was up to him, Huy, to give them what they really needed. Emptying his wine cup, he beckoned to Amunmose, standing watchfully against the shadowed wall with his arms folded, a good distance away from Rakhaka. The under steward hurried forward.

"Do you need more wine opened, Master?" he inquired.

"No. No more wine. I'm pleased to tell you that Merenra has spoken highly of your competence, and therefore you are promoted to chief steward upon my move to Mennofer. You will also be my food taster. Merenra is staying here." He felt Anhur's wary gaze turn to him as Amunmose straightened then bowed lavishly several times.

"Master, I am greatly flattered!" he managed to say after a moment of speechlessness. "I did not think that Merenra would be so generous towards me! He often says—"

"I don't care what he often says," Huy cut in. "Perhaps he hates you. The work will be hard, and if there is ever poison in my food, you will die. There will be those who will try to bribe their way into my presence through you, my steward, or buy your influence with me, or even attempt to suborn your loyalty with gold or lies or threats. Do you really want to face all that?" He looked up into the man's face. The cheerful, mobile features had become grave, the eyes sober.

"I still talk too much, but I have learned to say nothing while doing so," Amunmose replied. "I am completely content, Master, and you know that you have had my loyalty since the time you remembered me and sent to Iunu for me. It has always been my privilege to serve you. Tell me, are there many beautiful women at court?"

Anhur laughed hoarsely. Rakhaka, a dim form in the deepening shadow between the lamps, cleared his throat.

"I have not forgotten you," Huy called to him quietly. "You will come with me and prepare everything I eat, Rakhaka. Is that acceptable to you?"

"Yes, Master." The answer came at once.

Huy dismissed them, and when they had gone, he sighed and turned to Thothhotep. "I want you to go and fetch your palette. I will dictate a letter to the Governor of your sepat in the south, the Nekhen. I will ask him to purchase a small house somewhere on the river close to Nekheb, or perhaps Esna, for you and Anhur. He needs the dryness and heat of the south for his lungs, Thothhotep. Both of you are dismissed from my service." His voice broke. "I will make sure that you lack for nothing. Don't say it, Anhur! Not now!" He held up a hand against the angry protests Anhur had begun to splutter. "Think about a capable officer to replace you. Thothhotep, come to my office."

He scrambled to his feet and fled the room, leaving a stunned silence behind him. Making his way the short distance to the office, he lowered himself behind the desk feeling stupefied. It was some time before Thothhotep knocked and entered. She said nothing to him, merely going to the floor on her mat, placing her palette on her crossed legs, and whispering the scribe's prayer to Thoth while she readied her ink and brushes. Then she waited, head down. "You're pleased, aren't you?" Huy asked her softly.

She nodded once. "He would have followed you into the Duat. He will be angry now, and feel betrayed, until he realizes how much it has cost you to let him go."

"You also, my slender little reed," Huy said thickly. "I shall miss you a great deal. Now take down the letter."

On the twentieth day of Mekhir, Anhur and Thothhotep left for Nekheb. The Governor of the Nekhen sepat, like all Egypt's governors, had been brisk and efficient in carrying out Huy's request. Gold and a deed had been exchanged. Anhur, his eyes wet with the tears he stubbornly refused to shed, would not make any recommendations regarding his successor to Huy. "There is no one under my command capable of such leadership," he had said. "I trust no one but myself to see to your safety, and I am no longer familiar with the officers quartered in Mennofer. The palace is guarded by men from the Division of Amun. You must make your own inquiries, Huy."

He did not apologize, and Huy did not push him for a more definite answer. He and Thothhotep had at last signed a marriage contract in Huy's presence. Huy had given them a feast and many gifts, but an atmosphere of sadness had pervaded Huy's pretty reception room in spite of musicians, a troupe of local dancers, plenty of wine, and the noise of Anhur's men and the rest of Huy's servants, guests for the occasion. Now, in his attempt to remain calm, Huy enfolded both of them in a fierce embrace and dared not speak for fear of breaking down.

"Nekheb is a very long way from Mennofer, Huy," Thothhotep said. She was openly crying. "Almost a thousand miles, and many days of travelling against the current. Don't forget us. Write to us and I promise to reply. Perhaps one day the King will send you south on some errand, and then you will stay with us."

Huy cradled her thin cheeks and kissed her, then he watched them walk along the ramp and up onto the deck of the boat he had bought for them, two of Anhur's guards following. He had wanted to send them with a blessing—"May the soles of your feet always be firm, my dear ones"—but his throat was too dry. The oars were run out, the helmsman put both hands to the tiller, and the barge began its long journey.

Huy stood woodenly on his watersteps, longing for them both already. *How shall I replace them?* he wondered dismally. *What*

*shall I do if the King has already chosen new servants for me? Shall
I establish my independence at once by respectfully but firmly refusing
to accept them? I must make every effort to keep the tone of my
relationship with Amunhotep unchanged, remember that he is royal
but try to forget the awesome power he now wields as King, love him
as ever but not allow him to engulf me. I must begin my time as his
Personal Scribe and adviser as I intend to go on. Will I still be able to
rely on Mutemwia's full support even though there are bound to be
times when we disagree on matters of policy, particularly if
Amunhotep prefers my advice to hers? Her authority as Regent will be
almost as absolute as her son's. Will its exercise change her?* Huy
knew that such questions arose from a momentary feeling of
defencelessness. They were futile and premature, and with an
effort he dismissed them from his mind.

The vessel bearing away so many of his memories was at last
lost to view. Turning, he walked slowly back towards his house.

ACKNOWLEDGMENTS

I WISH TO THANK my researcher, Bernard Ramanauskas, for his work in collating the scattered material relating to the life of the Son of Hapu. In particular I appreciate the shape and coherence he has given to the profound ideologies of the Book of Thoth.

I have gratefully quoted from *Egyptian Mysteries: New Light on Ancient Spiritual Knowledge* by Lucie Lamy, translated from the French by Deborah Lawlor, and from *The Hermetica* by Timothy Freke and Peter Gandy, published by Judy Piatkus Ltd., London.

Over **6 million** novels sold worldwide

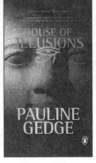